WHAT OTHERS HAVE SAID...

An unflinching indictment of lukewarm faith, a quickening call to fiery living. In Mike's story, as in life, there is no stable ground between hot and cold.

—ERIN HEALY
AUTHOR OF *THE PROMISES SHE KEEPS*

With an eerie and thrilling premise, *The Resurrection* is a riveting story that touches on the raw nerve of every person of faith—that unasked question of whether it is, ultimately, all possible, truly believable...all true. Whether the great miracle of faith still exists in a world populated by deceit. A brooding and suspenseful debut that will give you goose bumps and make you think long after you've turned the last page.

—TOSCA LEE
AUTHOR OF *DEMON: A MEMOIR*

In *The Resurrection*, Duran's prose is both lyrical and captivating, his storytelling entertaining yet thought-provoking. It was easy to forget this is his debut novel. I can't wait to see what he has in store for us next.

—MIKE DELLOSSO
AUTHOR OF *SCREAM* AND *FRANTIC*

Mike Duran masterfully blends fear, evil, hope, and redemption to paint a memorable portrait of how even the least of the servants of the Light can overcome the prevailing darkness around them. *The Resurrection* is a debut novel that promises many more are sure to follow.

—TIM GEORGE
FICTIONADDICT.COM

Like the ominous events creeping into the lives of these colorful characters, *The Resurrection* sneaks up on its readers, alternately charming and challenging assumptions until the very end. Though this is Duran's first novel, it speaks volumes about what lies ahead for this exciting new voice in Christian fiction.

—SIBELLA GIORELLO
CHRISTY AWARD–WINNING AUTHOR OF THE RALEIGH HARMON
MYSTERIES

Mike Duran's chilling debut depicts a raging battle of faith as mysterious powers of darkness war over the inhabitants of a small coastal village. With echoes of Frank Peretti's spiritual warfare and Athol Dickson's lyrical prose, *The Resurrection* is a tale that is one part ghost story, one part supernatural thriller, and one part spiritual awakening. Duran leads the reader on a metaphysical journey where dangerous forces are unexpectedly unleashed when a boy is raised from the dead.

—MERRIE DESTEFANO
AUTHOR OF *AFTERLIFE: THE RESURRECTION CHRONICLES*

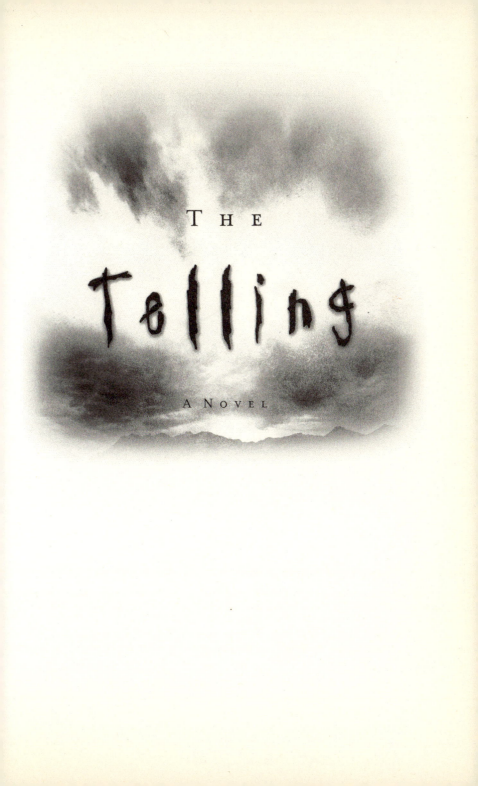

THE

Telling

A NOVEL

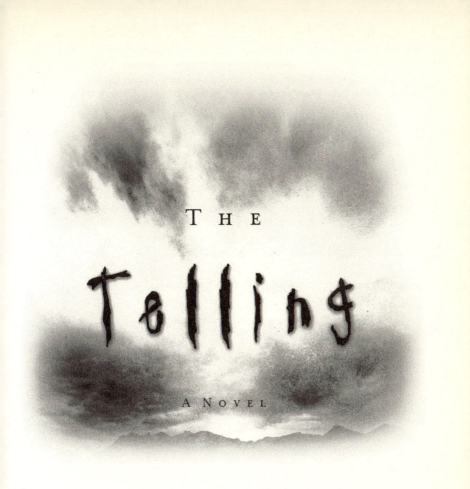

THE Telling

A Novel

MIKE DURAN

REALMS

Most CHARISMA HOUSE BOOK GROUP products are available at special quantity discounts for bulk purchase for sales promotions, premiums, fund-raising, and educational needs. For details, write Charisma House Book Group, 600 Rinehart Road, Lake Mary, Florida 32746, or telephone (407) 333-0600.

THE TELLING by Mike Duran
Published by Realms
Charisma Media/Charisma House Book Group
600 Rinehart Road
Lake Mary, Florida 32746
www.charismahouse.com

Scripture quotations are from the Holy Bible, New International Version. Copyright © 1973, 1978, 1984, International Bible Society. Used by permission.

The characters portrayed in this book are fictitious unless they are historical figures explicitly named. Otherwise, any resemblance to actual people, whether living or dead, is coincidental.

Cover design by Gearbox Studio
Design Director: Bill Johnson
Map created by Mike Duran
Author photo by Alayna Duran

Visit the author's website at www.mikeduran.com.

Library of Congress Cataloging-in-Publication Data:
Duran, Mike.
  The telling / Mike Duran.
      p. cm.
  Summary: "Zeph Walker has been blessed with an uncanny ability to sound souls--to intuit people's deepest sins and secrets. He calls it the Telling, but he has abandoned the gift to his unbelief and despair...until two detectives escort him to the county morgue, asking him to explain his own murder"-- Provided by publisher.
    ISBN 978-1-61638-694-8 (pbk.) -- ISBN 978-1-61638-861-4 (ebook) 1. Young men--Fiction. 2. Psychic ability--Fiction. I. Title.
  PS3604.U723T45 2012
  813'.6--dc23
                                                    2012002368

First edition

12 13 14 15 16 — 987654321
Printed in the United States of America

For Lisa, who saw past the scars

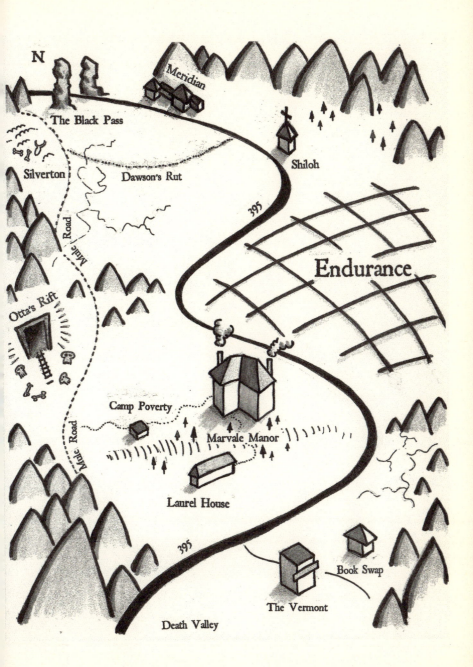

ACKNOWLEDGMENTS

I want to give special thanks to the following: the folks at Charisma House who believed in me; my critique partners Merrie Destefano, Rachel Marks, and Rebecca Miller for their honesty, camaraderie, and laughter; my mother-in-law, Betty Morris, for her encouragement and support; Melody Fredricks for helping make this a better story; Jim Hooper, the Silver Fox, for making Endurance come alive; my agent, Rachelle Gardner, for her indefatigable zeal and professional wisdom; Alton Gansky, my editor, for his keen eye and love for words; the community of commenters at deCOMPOSE who keep coming back for more; the members of North Hills Community Church who walk alongside me; Janet Keough and Kelly Van Osdel for praying for me; and my family, who blesses me beyond words.

Part One

THE MADNESS

By Their smell can some men know them near,
but of Their semblance can no man know, saving
only in the features of those They have begotten on
mankind, and of those are there many sorts...
—H. P. LOVECRAFT, *THE DUNWICH HORROR*

On approach, fits and agonies of Mind assailed the author.
Frightening displays of Workmanship most curious to the
eye, as to be found in Cathedrals of religious origin, embel-
lished the site. There rose before the ungodly gash a Bloodless
mound of Limbs and gristle, corrupt and inhuman anatomies,
such as to be henceforward believed the very Pylon of Hell.
—JOURNAL ENTRY, JOSEPH BLESSINGTON
OCTOBER 1873

Chapter 1

He used to believe everyone was born with the magic, an innate hotline to heaven. Some called it intuition, a sixth sense; others called it the voice of God. Zeph Walker called it *the Telling*. It was not something you could teach or, even worse, sell—people just had it. Of course, by the time their parents, teachers, and society got through with them, whatever connection they had with the Infinite pretty much vanished. So it was, when Zeph reached his twenty-sixth birthday, the Telling was just an echo.

That's when destiny came knocking for him.

It arrived in the form of two wind-burnt detectives packing heat and a mystery for the ages. They flashed their badges, said he was needed for questioning. Before he could object or ask for details, they loaded him into the backseat of a mud-splattered Crown Victoria and drove across town to the county morgue. The ride was barely ten minutes, just long enough for Zeph Walker to conclude that, maybe, the magic was alive and well.

"You live alone?" The driver glanced at him in the rearview mirror.

Zeph adjusted his sunglasses. "Yes, sir."

"I don't blame you." The detective looked at his partner, who smirked in response.

Zeph returned his gaze to the passing landscape.

Late summers in Endurance were as beautiful as a watercolor and as hot as the devil's kitchen. The aspens on the ridge showed gold, and the dogwoods along the creeks had already begun to thin. Yet the arid breeze rising from Death Valley served as an ever-present reminder that beauty always lives in close proximity to hell.

They came to a hard stop in front of a white plaster building. The detectives exited the car, and Zeph followed their cue. A ceramic iguana positioned under a sprawling blue sage grinned mockingly at him. Such was the landscape décor of the county coroner's building. The structure doubled as a morgue. It occupied a tiny plot of red earth, surrounded by a manicured cactus garden complete with

1

indigenous flora, bison skulls, and birdbaths. Without previous knowledge, one could easily mistake the building for a cultural center or art gallery. Yet Zeph knew that something other than pottery and Picassos awaited him inside.

The bigger of the two detectives, a vaquero with a nifty turquoise belt buckle and matching bolo tie, pulled the door open and motioned for Zeph to enter. The man had all the charm of a cage fighter.

Zeph wiped perspiration off his forehead and stepped into a small vestibule.

"This way." The cowboy clomped past, leaving the smell of sweat and cheap cologne.

They led him past an unoccupied desk into a corridor. Bland southwestern prints adorned sterile white walls. The stench of form-aldehyde and decay lingered here, and Zeph's stomach flip-flopped in response. The hallway intersected another where two lab technicians stood in whispered conversation. They straightened as the detectives approached. After a brief nod from one of the white-jacketed men, Zeph's escorts proceeded to an unmarked room.

"We got someone fer you to ID." The cowboy placed his hand on the door and studied Zeph. "You don't get sick easy, do ya?"

He swallowed. "Depends."

"Well, if you're gonna puke, don't do it on these." He pointed to a set of well-polished eel-skin boots. "Comprende?"

"No, sir. I mean—yes! Yes, sir."

The detective scowled, then pushed the door open, waiting.

Zeph's heart was doing double-time. Whose body was he about to see? What condition was it in? His mind raced with the possibilities. Maybe a friend had suffered a car accident. Although he didn't have many friends to die in one. Perhaps the Hitcher, that mythical appari-tion who stalked the highway in his childhood, had claimed another victim. More likely Zeph's old man had finally keeled over. However, he was convinced that his father had stopped living a long time ago.

Zeph drew a deep breath, took two steps into the room, perched his sunglasses on the top his head... and froze. In the center, framed under a single oval swath of light, lay a body on a autopsy table—*a body that looked strangely familiar.*

"Take a good look, Mr. Walker." The detective's boots clicked with precision on the yellowed linoleum. He circled the rolling metal cart, remaining just outside the reach of the fluorescent light. "And maybe you can help us figger this out."

Zeph remained near the door, hesitant to take another step.

"Go ahead." The second detective sauntered around the opposite side, gesturing to the body. "He ain't gonna bite."

The detectives positioned themselves on either end of the table. They watched him.

A black marble countertop, its surface dulled by a thin blanket of dust, ran the length of one wall. In front of it sat a single wooden stool. The low-hanging lamp bleached the body monochrome. Zeph had seen enough procedurals and CSI knock-offs to know this was not an autopsy room. Perhaps it was used for viewings, maybe occasional poker games. But as the detectives studied him, he was starting to wonder if this was an interrogation room. Scalpels, pincers, saws. Oh, what exotic torture devices one might assemble from a morgue! Nevertheless, this particular room appeared to have not been used in a long time. And by the fevered sparkle in their eyes, these men seemed inspired about the possibility of doing so.

Zeph glanced from one man to the other, and then he edged toward the corpse.

Its flesh appeared dull, and the closer he got, the less it actually looked like skin. Perhaps the body had been drained of blood or bleached by the desert sun. He inched closer. Sunken pockets appeared along the torso, and he found himself wondering what could have possibly happened to this person.

The head lay tilted back, its bony jaw upturned, cords of muscle taut across a gangly neck. A white sheet draped the body at the chest, and just above it a single bloodless hole about the size of a nickel notched the sternum. He crept forward, trying to distinguish the person's face. First he glimpsed nostrils, then teeth, and then...something else.

That *something else* brought Zeph to a standstill.

How could it be? *Build. Facial features. Hair color.* This person looked exactly like him. There was even a Star of David tattooed on the right arm, above the bicep—the same as Zeph's.

What were the chances, the mathematical probabilities, that one human being could look so identical to another? Especially in a town the size of Endurance.

"Is this..." Zeph's tone was detached, his eyes fixed on the body. "Is this some kinda joke?"

The detectives hunkered back into the shadows without responding.

Goose bumps rose on Zeph's forearms as the overhead vent rattled to life, sluicing cool air into the room. He took another step closer to the cadaver until his thigh nudged the table, jolting the stiff and bringing Zeph to a sudden stop. He peered at the bizarre figure.

Their similarities were unmistakable. The lanky torso and appendages. The tousled sandy hair. Thick brows over deep-set eyes. *This guy looks exactly like me!*

However, it was one feature—the most defining feature of Zeph Walker's existence—that left him teetering in disbelief: the four-inch scar that sheared the corpse's mouth.

Zeph stumbled back, lungs frozen, hand clasped over the ugly scar on his own face.

"Darnedest thing, ain't it?" The cowboy sounded humored by Zeph's astonishment. "Guy's a spittin' image of you, Mr. Walker."

Zeph slowly lowered his hand and glanced sideways at the man. "Yeah. Except I don't have a bullet hole in my chest."

The detective's grin soured, and he squinted warily at Zeph.

"Indeed you don't." The second man stepped into the light. "But the real question, young man, is why someone would want to put one there."

Chapter 2

*Z*eph had seen his share of miracles.

Once, on the circuit, he watched a traveling evangelist from Bakersfield fill seven cruets of anointing oil from a single vial. Try as he might, Zeph could not detect sleight of hand on the evangelist's part. The "miracle oil" was auctioned to raise money for an additional wing for that church, a wing that was later named rather conveniently after said evangelist. That bothered Zeph, not because he coveted a church wing with his inscription, but because he couldn't fathom using his "gift" to garner props.

Yes, Zeph Walker had seen his share of miracles. Some would even say he performed them. Nevertheless, the corpse lying before him was unlike any miracle he had ever seen.

"We're treatin' it as a homicide."

Zeph wrenched his gaze away from the bizarre look-alike and stared at the second detective. He had introduced himself as Lacroix. A. J. Lacroix. He spoke with an enunciated southern drawl, one refined by culture or intentional parody. His gestures, like his inflections, appeared deliberate, if not theatrical.

"Course, this is pending autopsy, toxicology, and whatnot. Nevertheless, our estimations surmise a small caliber round at point-blank range—execution style." Lacroix looked into the light and struck a contemplative pose. "Murder's rare in these parts, Mr. Walker, as you well know. What'd we have, Chat, three last year? And two of those was that incident downtown at the bus depot. Drifter went E. Pluribus haywire, cut up a buncha folks, took hostages, and completed his descent into madness by shooting himself with a stolen revolver. Said the worlds were being *fused* or somethin'. Either way, at this juncture we find ourselves with another murder victim—which is unacceptable for a town this size. Which brings me back to my previous question."

Lacroix leaned forward, hands spread atop the metal table, his white hair bleached under the light. "Why would someone wanna kill you, Mr. Walker?"

Zeph glanced between the men, his thoughts careening like a runaway diesel down the Black Pass. He could be out the door, down the hallway, and back into the parched, Death Valley air in seconds. The chances of this leathery old man and his booted side-kick catching him were slim. But why run? He had nothing to hide.

...unless you counted Blaise Duty, and the witch in the sanatorium, and that punk he busted up in the diner, and—

Zeph ran his fingers through his hair. "How'd you find me?"

"Were we not supposed to?" Chat glowered.

"Some newfangled science," Lacroix said. "Facial recognition technology—compares pictures with a database of stored images. Mugshots. Real high tech. And I guess your info was in the system." Lacroix cast a sidelong glance and let it linger. "Now why would a nice young man like yourself have a mugshot, hmm?"

Zeph's mouth was as dry as a salt flat.

"Look." He forced down a swallow. "That was a long time ago. I–I barely go out anymore. The Book Swap—you saw it, right? People come and exchange books. Not many, five, six customers a week maybe. Usually the same folks. But there's no one who..." Zeph glanced at the corpse. "I go fishing, but it's always alone. And the Food Warehouse. I–I go there once a month. Monday mornings, usually. But this—I mean, this is the first time in weeks I've even been off my property."

"So you *are* in hidin'," Chat quipped.

Zeph's gaze faltered. "Well, I suppose you *could* say that."

Chat straightened and nudged up the brim of his Stetson. Then he looped his thumbs behind the thick rawhide belt. "No offense, boss. But word on the street is they call you..." A slight smile creased his lips. "Zipperface."

Zeph blinked.

Zipperface. The name stirred something inside him, an emotional toxin lying just below the surface of his psyche. *Zipperface.* That's what the kids would yell after they pelted his house with pomegran-ates and ran hooting down the street. *Zipperface.* That's what High and his gang at the diner used to call him before Zeph went into exile. *Zipperface.* It's the name he'd been running from for the last eight years.

As rage and self-pity uncoiled inside him, Zeph countered the detective's jab the only way he knew how. "The last person who called me that got *his* face rearranged." Zeph winked at the detective. "No offense, boss."

Chat plucked his thumbs from the belt and glared at Zeph.

Lacroix stepped between them. "You'll forgive my partner for his impertinence. But being uncooperative in a police investigation is not wise. Not only might it incur the wrath of said police—it might hinder the circumvention of another crime. Whoever did this is still unfettered and wandering the streets of this beautiful city. And if you are the target of this gunman, Mr. Walker, for whatever reason, then there is no guarantee that the next victim will not be you."

Zeph took a step back, his combative posture wilting before them.

"That's what I thought," Lacroix said. Then he went to the counter, retrieved some blue surgical gloves, and wormed his fingers into them. "Now there is one more bit of information that may prod you toward cooperation." He returned to the corpse. "And I warn you—it is not a pretty sight. Mr. Walker." He motioned Zeph forward.

The thought of looking into that face again, going anywhere near that papery shell of a man, sent chills of nausea up his spine. Nevertheless, Zeph drew a deep breath and wobbled toward the body.

Lacroix nodded as Zeph approached, took the edge of the sheet, and gently lifted it, forming a tent over the lower half of the corpse's body. The detective stared underneath and shook his head. "I will admit, it has us flummoxed. Not only are we unable to extract fingerprints from this man—" Lacroix leveled his gaze on Zeph. "—but we are undecided as to whether or not he is a man."

Before Zeph could turn away, Lacroix pulled the sheet back. What Zeph saw knocked the wind out of him.

Instead of legs, two dry casings, much like skins shed by a large reptile or grub, lay in uneven folds atop the shiny metal. Either the lower half of this man's body had been drained and dry-cleaned or he was the world's first reptile-human hybrid.

Zeph opened his mouth, but there were no words to fill it.

"It's decomposing fast—whatever it is." Lacroix squinted in

thought. "And apparently they are unable to slow the process. The CDC fellas already done their thing—in case you're wonderin'—assured us that viruses or biological agents are not involved. Whatever is happening to this man is purely organic, a physiological anomaly of the highest order. Not contagious in any real sense... unless you count the willies as somethin' that can be contracted."

After a moment staring at the inhuman appendages, Lacroix drew the sheet back over the lower half of the corpse and let the white cloth settle.

Zeph stared blankly, shaking his head in slow incremental beats. Was there any way to explain this? Miracles were one thing, but this person—this *thing*—seemed like something of another order. The world Zeph Walker had carefully cultivated for the last eight years had been punctured; he stood helpless as his already dwindling sanity deflated.

And with it came a familiar sound rising inside him.

Lacroix removed the gloves, deposited them in the trash can, and returned his gaze to Zeph. He started to speak, stopped, and then said, "You look pale, young man. You'd better sit down." He gestured toward the stool.

However, sitting would not stop what was about to happen.

Inside Zeph Walker something was brewing, something that he hadn't felt in a long time. A murmur, beyond the range of the human ear but as tangible to him as the wonder it evoked. It was as if heaven was drawing a breath to speak. The room seemed to bristle with expectancy, the synapses of his nerve endings firing in anticipation. Was he breathing? Was his heart still pumping? It didn't matter. Zeph's world was on mute. Everything—the detectives watching him like dumb brutes, the bizarre doppelgänger that lay mocking him under the fluorescent light—all of it seemed utterly inconsequential to the words that were unfolding inside his head.

The wound festers.

His mother had called it *ruach*, the breath of God.

The land awaits.

Sometimes the words came in his sleep or in the middle of conversation.

Between them...

Yet whenever they came to him, Zeph knew they came for a reason.

Stands your darker self.

He only wished he could stop the words from ever coming again.

Zeph tapped his forehead with the heel of his hand, as if doing so would dislodge the words from his brain. Sometimes if he shouted at the top of his lungs, the prophecy would vanish. Yet no amount of shouting could erase the words he had just heard.

"What the—" Chat's eyes were the size of silver dollars.

Zeph ignored the detective's startled gaze and kept tapping his forehead, his jaw clenched, his mind battened against the magic of the Telling.

Finally the words evaporated...and the nausea came.

"Walker!" Chat stepped toward him. "You all right?"

Zeph swayed, punch-drunk by the premonition. *The wound festers.* What wound? *The land awaits.* Awaits what? *Between them stands your darker self.* He peered at the look-alike but did not have time to decipher the cryptic words. His head was spinning.

Zeph barely made it to the trash can in time to vomit. Luckily he was nowhere near the detective's shiny eel-skin boots.

Chapter 3

Waking to gray.

Something skittered behind him, and Fergus Coyne tried to turn, but his legs weren't working again. Where was he? How'd he gotten here?

Fergus tried to focus, but a veil seemed to drape his eyes.

"Ghaww!"

He managed to turn his head, but not without white heat shredding his temples. His vision cleared just enough to recognize the bone chimes dangling overhead, plinking out a discordant tune.

Then the mallet fell.

According to Pops, the shadow of an eclipse traveled at eighteen hundred miles an hour along the earth's surface. Fergus had witnessed an eclipse firsthand, the terror of that black wall racing along the loch, swallowing everything in its wake. One could not help but scream at its approach. Fergus did. Like a little girl. Of course, he was only a child then. The shadow wall had roared toward him, eating up the land as a black hole does the light. He'd learned afterward that hysteria was common during a total eclipse. And hysteria aptly described what Fergus had felt.

However, this darkness, the one now battering his brain, was something altogether different. It had a voice.

Seer, seer,

Come hither yonder hill.

It was a nursery rhyme, he thought. Dark and dreamy, the kind that summoned the kelpies and the merfolk.

Where the hollow waiteth

And the word is yet unhewed.

The unhewed word. Like a slab of granite waiting for the chisel, Fergus wielded the power to shape what was *not* into that which *is*. In the beginning was the Word. Yep, he believed that. Pops said twenty-two fundamental letters comprised the Hebrew alphabet, and with only those letters God formed the world.

10

If God could do it, why couldn't they?

His eyes were open, but Fergus could not see. The roaring night beat down on him, a cataract of silence drowning out everything else. Deafening. Churning up debris.

Plink.

She hung herself with an extension cord on the balcony, overlooking a white-capped sea.

Plink.

Bad Fergie! You drove her to it. Bad Fergie!

He tried again to wrench himself from the nightmare. Yet the lunar cone of that dark trance settled on him with deathly quietude, a curtain sheer but intractable, lowered from the scaffolds of his own mind.

The void raged, waiting for Fergus to fill it.

With words.

Grimel. Nun. Vau.

It was like a second language to him.

Daleth. Zain. Samech.

If I speak in the tongues of men and angels. *The tongues of angels.* It was a verse from the Bible. No matter—he could do both! Fergus Coyne had deciphered the tongue of angels.

As he lay cocooned in that trancelike web, listening to the darkness, someone came near, and his breathing stopped. Tall. Angular. Broad. Hands glowing like nuclear copper. Bending over to witness his torment. Who was this stranger? Perhaps he would be so kind as to put Fergus out of his misery...

That's when he heard the woman's cry—a thin, catlike mewl, intertwined with the whisper of subterranean air.

Mum?

Then Fergus Coyne could no longer bear it, and his world went black.

Chapter 4

Mystery Spots and Magic Landscapes?" Tamra Lane read the words, lowered the sticky note, and cast a skeptical gaze at her grandmother. "They actually publish these kinds of books?"

"Shh!" Annie stopped brushing her long gray hair, leaned back on the rocker, and glanced at the doorway of her apartment. "If it isn't out of print or been burned by the government—yes!"

"So that last book on angels and Armageddon wasn't enough?" The sarcasm was thick in Tamra's tone.

"No." Annie peered defensively. "Now please go shut my door."

"Okay." Tamra huffed. She laid her Vespa scooter helmet on the sofa and shrugged off her backpack next to it. As she reached the door, she glanced into the hallway. Both ways. Despite her grandmother's worries, no one was spying on them. Tamra clucked her tongue and closed the door. Now she was becoming paranoid.

A beam of morning sunlight pierced the curtains, and through them the Sierra Nevadas' snowy crags glistened. Tamra returned to the living room and held up the sticky note. "Well, I doubt there are any mystery spots around here anyway."

Annie laid a length of hair down one side of her blouse. "Maybe that's why they stay a mystery—some people just don't want to see them."

"You don't need to get snippy."

Annie looked away and began plaiting her hair.

"Look, Nams." Tamra approached her grandmother. "If it's that bad here, why don't you come stay with us?"

"We have already been through this." Annie lifted her chin in defiance.

"Yeah, and you never have a good answer."

"I'm tired of being a burden to everyone—that's my answer."

"Nams, you're—"

Annie held up her index finger and silenced Tamra. "You and

Dieter deserve more than what you got. You don't need me crowding your space. Besides, I've got work to finish here."

Before Tamra could counter, Annie closed her eyes and continued weaving her hair into two long elegant ponies.

Tamra shook her head in frustration. "Here, let me do that." She stuffed the sticky note into her jeans pocket and began to braid her grandmother's hair.

As far back as Tamra could remember, her grandmother had donned two plaited ponytails, remnants of her old-world background. As Tamra separated and then wove the silken strands, she found herself hoping that her hair would be this beautiful when she reached her grandmother's age. Seventy-two and going strong. Annie Lane worked out at the facility's gym and could probably outlast people half her age. Tamra once suggested her grandmother enter a triathlon, but athletic competition was the last thing on Annie's mind. Her stubbornness was legendary. And the way she was going, it would probably be the death of her.

Tamra finished and patted the long fine braids into place. Then she looked straight at Annie. "Are you still having problems with Eugenia? Is that what this is about?"

Annie studied her granddaughter for a moment, as if hesitant to continue. "It isn't just Genie. It's a lot of people." Then she leaned forward and whispered, "They're changing, Tam. They aren't themselves."

The conviction in Annie's eyes sent chills up Tamra's neck. Her grandmother trafficked in conspiracy theories and pseudoscientific nonsense. However, she was anything but part of the lunatic fringe. Annie's background as an English teacher was evident in her prim and proper manner. She was exact in her words, precise in her mannerisms, and unnervingly direct in her pronouncements. Annie Lane possessed the type of tenacity that was born of certainty or utter madness. And if the look in her eyes was any indication, she was dead certain about people changing at the retirement facility of Marvale Manor.

Tamra pulled away and attempted to sound unflustered. "Changing? Is that so weird? I mean, everybody changes."

Annie remained solemn. After a moment she rose from the rocking chair, crossed the room, and stood before the mirror, surveying her braids. "The other day there was a commotion down the hall. Someone yelled, and then there was a loud crash. I thought maybe the General was up to his tricks.

"It was Vera's son. He comes down from Tahoe every couple of weekends to visit. Stays with her the night. Very nice man, about twice your age. Divorced. Well, he was standing in the hallway, across from her room. White as a ghost. Apparently, he'd broke something on his way out—a vase or one of her nice figurines. But he was just standing there, staring at her, ranting that this wasn't his mother. That she was...different.

"People came out of their apartments—he was making such a commotion. And Vera..." Annie turned and peered at Tamra. "She just stood there with a little smile on her face, without saying anything. It was disturbing, to say the least."

Tamra gazed at her grandmother but could not find a reasonable rejoinder. Surely a son would not mistake his mother for another woman. And surely a mother would not allow such accusations from her son—much less in a public place.

Before Tamra could query, Annie resumed. "I guess he sent someone later, a doctor or some sort of professional. He had them check her out. But nothing came of it. Apparently, the woman living there is still...Vera West."

Tamra shifted her weight. She did not like where this was going.

"Then last night," Annie continued, "I was up, reading my Bible. I haven't been sleeping with all this going on. And I began putting the pieces together. Something big is going on—I've always believed it. And now I'm sure of it." Her voice was hushed, rapt with certitude. "It's the Madness—*the Madness of Endurance*. It's here again."

"I knew it!" Tamra wilted. "I thought you'd given up on that!" Then she put her hands on her hips. "No—there's gotta be another answer."

"Then how else do you explain Vera? And Genie? And Leland Feather down at Laurel House? And—"

"Okay!" Tamra crimped her lips. "Okay. I don't know. But it can't be some...some crazy Old West fairy tale."

Annie shook her head. "The Madness of Endurance is not a fairy tale. It's a matter of record."

"Yeah, but here and now? In the twenty-first century?"

"Why not *here and now?* Just because we have computers and the Internet and fancy telephones like yours doesn't mean there aren't *devils*. No. The devils have not gone away. We've just become blind to them."

Tamra remained obstinate, her lips pursed in skepticism. Of course there was more to life than what one could smell and touch. Twenty-five years old, growing up in the shadow of evil, Tamra could not help but believe in devils. However, at the moment, conceding the point would only enable her grandmother's paranoia.

"I couldn't sleep last night," Annie continued. "I was up, sitting right there reading my Bible." She pointed to the rocker. "It was late, after one o'clock. And I heard someone walking down the hall. Real soft, as if they were trying to be slippery. So I put my ear to the door. And then I heard someone else."

"Okay. So it's not against the law to be out after one o'clock."

"No, but around here? And with everything going on? So I decided to investigate."

"Nams! You promised you'd stop that."

"Shh!" Annie glanced at the door and lowered her voice. "I promised no such thing."

Tamra folded her arms and glared at her grandmother.

"Please. Just hear me out." Annie matched Tamra's glare, and Tamra softened. "So I waited until they passed, then I peeked out. Well, they were down the hallway—Vera and Genie—in their nightclothes. At one o'clock a.m.! They disappeared around the corner at the Back Nine, and I heard them go into the courtyard. Now, what would they be doing outside at that time of night?"

As much as she wanted a good answer, Tamra did not have one.

Annie nodded at her granddaughter's muteness. "So I slipped on my sweater and went after them. But when I got to the doors and looked out, they were gone."

"Please tell me you did not go outside."

Annie said confidently, "You can't find the truth without risking something."

"Hello? You guys had a prowler here a couple weeks ago, did you not?"

"Which made me all the more curious. Maybe there's a connection. Maybe the prowler is one of us."

Tamra threw her hands up in frustration. "You're gonna kill yourself—it's only a matter of time."

"You can't find the truth—"

"—without risking something. I heard you."

"I will admit, I was a little scared."

"You?" Tamra said sarcastically.

"I might be divinely covered, but I am not invulnerable. In any event, it was cold. The moon was bright, and the whole area was illuminated. I listened but didn't hear anything. So I began walking, following my instincts. And then, near the fountain at the upper courtyard, I saw them. Many of them."

Tamra furrowed her brow. "Other people?"

"Yes. A lot of other people. I hid behind one of the sheds, so I couldn't see everyone who was there, but I saw enough of them. Samuel J., from the north wing. And Violet and China, the evening receptionist. And Vera and Genie. Ten, twelve of them perhaps. And—this is the strange part—they were just standing in a half circle, unmoving, gazing up into the mountains. Not talking, just…staring. As if they were waiting for something to descend out of the sky and whisk them away." Annie drew out this last sentence, raising her hand like a Shakespearian actor. Then she shrugged and gazed at her granddaughter, as if waiting for an explanation.

Yet Tamra gawked. Finally she said, "That is strange."

"Isn't it? I hurried back and locked the door. I've been awake ever since."

Tamra stood for a moment dumbfounded by the tale. "Did you report it? Maybe talk to the director or somethin'?"

Annie shook her head. "That's just it—I'm not sure who I can trust anymore. What if the director is…one of them?"

Tamra huffed in frustration, but the gesture lacked sincerity. Her grandmother had no reason to lie. Exaggerate? Maybe. Annie could be charged with zealotry, maybe even fanaticism. But she was not a liar. However, the implications of this seemed preposterous. How could people be changing, becoming someone other than themselves? And was it possible for some fabled event to really be behind it?

Tamra wandered to the couch and plopped onto it.

Annie followed, pulled the rocker over, and sat facing Tamra.

"I know what you think." Annie's eyes were intense. "But this is not a case of paranoia or some old folks' disease. Something is happening here, Tam. I've been following it. I've seen the evidence of it. You've got to believe me."

Tamra bit her bottom lip.

Annie moved in closer. "I am telling you, as God is my witness, that woman living next door is not Eugenia Price. She's been...replaced. Swapped out—I don't know how else to describe it. It's happening slowly. Subtly. But if we don't do something, it will happen to all of us."

They sat in silence for a moment, Annie's ominous warning hanging in the air like a Death Valley thundercloud ready to explode.

"This is crazy." Tamra shook her head. "Okay. So what do you want me to do?"

Apparently satisfied that she'd won that round, Annie nodded. She brushed her ponytails behind her. "I need you to track down that book."

"Book? Oh yeah, *Magic Castles and*—"

"*Mystery Spots and Magic Landscapes*. Don't get smart!"

"Sorry. All right, I'll go to Spellbinder's before work."

"No. Not Spellbinder's."

"Nams, that's the main bookstore in town. If anyone's gonna have it, they will."

"Perhaps. But I want you to go somewhere else."

Tamra squinted with suspicion. "This isn't another wild goose chase, is it? Okay. Where else do you want me to go?"

"Near Carson Creek, by the rundown theater."

"That's the old part of town. There's no bookstore over there."

"A book swap is there. It's been there a long time. It's nothing more than an old cottage that sits next to a house in a residential neighborhood. Just use that fancy phone of yours, you'll see. There's a young man who runs the place. He's had it for a while now and kept it open. I need you to speak to him." Annie folded her hands on her lap and began rocking. "And don't look at me like that. His name is Zephaniah. Zephaniah Walker."

"*Zephaniah?* That's different."

"So is he."

"But if you want to talk to him, why don't we just—"

"Why don't we just do like I say?"

Tamra scratched her head. What was she getting herself into? "Okay. I'm gonna do this. But you have to promise me you'll stop sneakin' around. Promise?"

Other than sitting politely with her hands folded on her lap, Annie gave no sign of compliance.

"You are too stubborn." Tamra rose, went to the rocking chair, and hugged her grandmother tightly. "Please. Be. Careful."

"Believe me, dear. I'm in good hands."

Chapter 5

Tamra left her grandmother's apartment with her backpack slung over her shoulder, her scooter helmet dangling at her side, and her mind swirling.

Two years ago, some time after the death of her husband, Annie Lane sold her ranch and used part of the money to buy Tamra and her little brother a house of their own. It was unexpected and, in a way, unwanted. Tamra had learned to stand on her own and support herself. Taking handouts was not her style. But in this case she had no choice. Tamra learned later that her grandmother had been on the waiting list for Marvale Manor; when the spot came open, Annie pulled the trigger. Tamra had pleaded with her grandmother to forgo the retirement community and move in with them. Annie had no major physical issues; in fact, she was in remarkable shape for her age. Moving in with her granddaughter seemed both logical and the right thing to do—even though they argued often. Nevertheless, the woman remained true to her bullheadedness. She didn't want to be a burden to her grandchildren.

Besides, Annie believed God had one last assignment for her. And when it came to believing God for something, Tamra knew it was best just to stay out of her grandmother's way.

Located in the foothills of the rugged, idyllic mountain range, Marvale Manor touted itself as the most tranquil retirement setting in America. Having ventured out of California only once, Tamra had little to base such claims on. Still, she had a hard time believing that a retirement home in a small town on the northern fringes of Death Valley could earn such lofty acclaim. Besides, Marvale's tranquility was giving way to something insidious. At least, according to Annie Lane.

Tamra passed by the atrium and its well-arranged sofa settings, turned into the main hallway, and headed toward the reception desk. As she went, she studied the facility and its residents in a way she hadn't done before. Could it be that people really were changing, that something malevolent and imperceptible was happening to the residents here? Yet apart from mass hypnosis or an alien invasion, how could something like that even happen?

In one of the reading nooks, underneath a faux Victorian print in an overly gilded frame, a man with powder blue polyester pants sat with a newspaper draped over his knees. He was not wearing socks. Tamra smiled at him as she passed—an intentionally cheesy display on her part—and the old man reciprocated with a huge grin and a vigorous wave. *Well, he didn't seem that strange.* She passed one of the large floor vases adorned with a silk floral arrangement just as a middle-aged couple left a nearby apartment. They closed the door, whispered something to each other, and walked down the hall without acknowledging her. Most likely they were visiting a parent. But this early? Tamra studied them as they walked away. The woman held the man's wrist limply, without emotion. And the way they walked was almost...robotic. Their skin also looked—

Stop it! What are you doing?

Tamra shook her head. She couldn't get sucked into this. She had to remain objective. That's how paranoia poisoned people—it planted a seed and then strangled objectivity. She had seen the same thing happen to her father, though in his case it had to do with methamphetamine addiction rather than a supernatural malady. Besides, even if her grandmother was on to something, Tamra couldn't allow her own imagination to run wild.

Which is one reason Tamra headed straight for the reception desk.

The Marvale complex was originally built as a hotel. It didn't take long for the local entrepreneur who built it to realize his miscalculation. Eleven years after its completion the property was sold and converted to a retirement home. A Victorian-style façade graced the single-story structure, which consisted of four wings broken into geographical quadrants. The aerial shot of the facility posted in the lobby revealed that Marvale was shaped like a huge cross, each wing representing an arm. Of course, Annie was quick to read something divine into this. But Annie was quick to read something divine into anything. A recreational area with kitchen, dining room, and patio where the residents could play shuffleboard and enjoy the sun occupied the facility's southeastern section. Except for Ben Wilson's use of it, the Jacuzzi there went unused, although her grandmother seemed to enjoy telling stories about the retired commercial actor flirting with all the ladies from inside the steaming waters. It made Tamra wonder if Annie didn't enjoy the man's braggadocio. Bridging the rec area along the front of the facility were the lobby and several offices. Tamra approached the reception desk there.

"And how is that feisty grandmother of yours today?"

Hannah, a middle-aged wannabe fashionista with a slightly frenetic disposition, sat behind the desk chewing gum and filing her nails. She glanced over the top of a pair of black horn-rimmed glasses.

"Well…" Tamra set her helmet on the counter. "That's a good question."

"Mm-hmm." Hannah pinched her lips together and nodded emphatically. "There's a lot of that goin' around."

"Really? What do you mean?"

"Okay, lemme guess." Hannah set the file down, brushed away a lock of hair from her dazzling jet-black updo, and launched into a recitation that might as well have been a dramatic monologue. "Miss Annie doesn't seem like herself. Somethin's different about her. You ain't sure what. She's not sick or anything—no fever, no rash. She looks the same—hasn't grown horns or anything. Fact, there is nothing physically different about her in the least. She's just…*not herself.* Colder, kinda distant. Very mean. And hungry. Always hungry. Her memory's intact—by that, I mean she knows your name, your birthday, significant events, etcetera. So it ain't Alzheimer's or somethin'. But there's an emotional disconnect, as if the real Miss Annie is not there anymore. And you can't reconcile the two—she's there, but she ain't there—so you think you might be delusional. But other folks are havin' the same delusion, which throws your theory out the window. And this is why you're standing here at my desk with your biker jeans and cool purple helmet." She tapped her sparkly fingernails on Tamra's scooter helmet, signaling the completion of her spiel. Then Hannah picked up her file and continued working her immaculate cuticles.

Tamra stood momentarily stunned by the receptionist's presentation, both for its melodrama and how much it corroborated Nams's suspicions.

"Actually," Tamra cleared her throat, "my grandmother's all right. It's some of the people around her she's worried about."

"Well, she's not the only one. We've had a dozen different complaints about people."

Tamra moved closer and folded her arms atop the counter. "And, um, would China be one of them?"

Hannah stopped and peered over the top of her glasses. "Me and China never got along anyway. But to answer your question— yes. Fact, she had a meeting with Nurse Ratched yesterday and, between you and me," she leaned so close that Tamra could smell the cinnamon on her breath, "I hope they give her the boot."

Tamra took a step back to free herself from the cinnamon fog bank. "Well, what's wrong with her? I mean, what's going on? Does anybody have an idea? Ya know, how could people all of sudden just..."

Hannah shrugged. "Ya got me. But the theories are startin' to fly. Maybe it's somethin' in the water. Or the food. Maybe it's a contagion, ya know, a virus that messes with people's makeup. Maybe we're all just delusional. Who knows? Apparently it's scared folks enough that we're hiring security and finally installing cameras. The General's been harpin' on that one for years. And—oh! You'll like this—a psychologist is comin' too."

"Huh?"

"You heard me, hon. A shrink. Maybe they'll analyze the lot of us, find out the entire place is cuckoo." She tilted her head back and laughed, her bright pink gum teetering on equally pink lips.

However, Tamra could not seem to find any humor in the unfolding mystery. So she thanked Hannah, retrieved her helmet, and prepared to leave.

"And, oh," Hannah said, sliding her nail file into the drawer and rearranging paperwork on her desk. "We got a visit from a coupla detectives."

"Okay, so this is getting weird."

"Tell me about it. Guess someone down at Laurel House stumbled upon a body."

"A body? Well, it is a convalescent facility. I'm guessing folks *do* die down there."

"Yeah, but when they went to retrieve it, the corpse was missin'."

Tamra squinted. "What?"

"That's right—gone. Into thin air." Hannah snapped her fingers. "They did a bed count. Searched the premises. Nothin'. But the witness was so adamant that they started a police investigation into the matter."

Tamra was speechless for a moment. *It's the Madness.* Annie's impassioned gaze had etched itself into her mind. *The Madness of Endurance. It's here again.* Tamra's skin prickled at the thought.

She needed some air, needed to get out of that place and get some perspective. Tamra thanked Hannah again and hurried through the lobby toward the entrance.

As the door closed behind her, its ornate beveled glass sparkled in a ray of sunlight. Crisp mountain air filled her nostrils, bringing respite from the foreboding. Perhaps this is how old people went loony. Living in close quarters, wasting away, watching your friends grow old, and left with only your regrets to ferment and poison your sanity. Was it any wonder that some of the folks at Marvale had become suspicious of each other?

The small tram that carried visitors and residents to and from the lower lot sat parked under its awning. Buzz hunched in the nearby booth, his pith helmet tilted to one side, whittling away at a block of wood. He cast a languid glance up at Tamra and, seeing she was not approaching, returned to his work. Leaves had begun to carpet the ground, a sure sign of fall's approach. Stevie Veigh, the grounds-keeper, stood over three colorful piles. His all-terrain vehicle sat parked nearby and, attached to it, the tractor cart with a load of leaves for mulch or incineration. Bev Beason, one of Nams's bingo partners, sat in one of several white wicker chairs along the porch, a paperback book lying upturned on her lap as she rested in the morning sun.

Rather than descending the steps, Tamra walked along the porch, drawing her hand along the wooden handrail, trying not to disturb Mrs. Beason.

An acute unease seeped into Tamra's bones. She looked past the pines and boulders toward the Endurance basin. From here, US 395 snaked its way up from Death Valley, a dark, glistening ribbon that coiled, rose, and disappeared in the Black Pass farther north. Tamra continued ambling along the porch as the northern Sierras came into her view.

These hills were full of tales. Indians. Miners. And Silverton, the ghost town hidden somewhere in the rugged foothills. Yet the most well-known of these tales was the one that placed the ninth gate of hell in an abandoned mine less than a mile from where she stood. Tamra stopped and set her gaze in that direction. Morning fog wrapped the distant foothills in its hazy tendrils. *Could it be? The Madness of Endurance. Could it possibly be?*

A breeze whispered through the pines.

As she gazed into the wild, a presence came near. The hackles on Tamra's neck bristled. She spun to find someone standing next to her. It was Mrs. Beason, staring off into the fog-shrouded foothills, her eyes as lifeless as a sidewinder's.

Chapter 6

Fergus Coyne's eyes sprung open. "Mum!"

But his mother wasn't there. She had never been there. And if she ever materialized, his first response might be to spit in her face.

Liquid pattered somewhere in the gauzy haze. Fergus squinted and shielded his eyes from the overhead light. His shoulder bore hard into a solid object, and his right leg lay twisted underneath him. Traces of mold and urine tainted the air. Where was he? How had he gotten here?

Fergus drew a deep, concentrated breath and forced himself to focus on his surroundings. A white formless object sat squat before him. Solid, unmoving. Tall panels rose on each side. The ground felt hard and smooth here, not like the shale and mossy granite of Otta's Rift.

Otta's Rift. Yes. He had been to the ninth gate of hell.

And someone had been there, standing over him.

Fergus planted his hands beneath him and pushed his body up. He straightened his leg and then collapsed again. His limbs were still rubbery, still weak, his mind as tangled as ever. The fetch always left him like this. The fetch always got their way.

And Fergus was growing weary of their abuse.

He sat for a moment studying his surroundings, recalibrating his senses. Smooth metal partitions scabbed with rust. Drab mosaic tile. Fergus knew this place. He dabbed moisture off his forehead with the sleeve of his flannel and fought to steady his gaze. Copper tubes glistening with moisture. Flecks of paper tissue. A ceramic bowl. No wonder it stunk in here—he was jammed into a bathroom stall.

"Ghaww!" Fergus clawed at the partitions and scrambled to his feet. He stood wobbling over the toilet.

The custodial restroom—that's where he was. Somehow he had made it back to Marvale Manor. Yet that realization brought its own set of terrors.

Blood thrummed behind his eyes. A blasted migraine was on

25

its way. He'd had his share of hangovers—cheap Irish whiskey did that—but nothing compared to the mallet of the rune. The trances. The blackouts. The screed of disembodied voices. When the fetch called, he had to answer, had to speak the words. Yet standing there, amnesiac and out of sorts, Fergus knew answering their call was beginning to take its toll.

Just like Pops had warned.

He massaged his temples with his fingertips until the throbbing ebbed into dull pressure. That's when he noticed mud on the floor and a single sheet of paper lying in it, sopping moisture. Fergus hunched forward, grimacing at the rush of blood in his head, and retrieved the wilted page. He stood, trying to decipher the soggy script.

...primitive metaphysical doctryne...

He had seen this before.

...counterparts and correspondences...

A wisp of breath died on his lips.

...assimilation complete.

Fergus stumbled backward, rattling the flimsy metal partitions. Pops's journal! It was a page from his father's spellbook...on the bathroom floor!

Fergus stared blankly at the page, searching his mind for recollection. How had it gotten here? He normally kept the journal in his locker, sealed behind a thick padlock. No one else had the key, nor would anyone dare to mess with his belongings. Crossing Fergus Coyne had consequences. Everyone knew that. Still, if someone were to get their hands upon the journal...

He forced the thought from his head, nervously folded the page, and jammed it in his back pocket. Fergus hurried from the stall and scanned the restroom. Near the entry lay his backpack, its contents scattered about the floor. *No!* It couldn't be.

Fergus snatched up the backpack and rifled through it. The scent of earth and pine clung to the material. He removed the flashlight and set it on the sink, followed by a bundle of waterproof matches and the sack of rune stones. Finally he removed the pistol, lightly kissing its barrel, as was his custom, and laid it near the other items.

But to his dismay the spellbook was missing.

The throbbing in his head returned. He grimaced, staggered forward, and let the pack drop to the ground.

This was not good. Not good at all. Fergus gawked at his greasy fingernails.

Perhaps he could retrace his steps—that's what he'd do. Follow the trail through Camp Poverty and Granite Bar, back to the Rift. People rarely went that way anymore. Superstition had gotten the best of them. On occasion hikers would pass through, working their way up the Pacific Crest trail. But they rarely ventured into the haunted mine. The documentarians had come and gone. Other than thrill seekers or amateur occultists, folks stayed away from the Rift. If Fergus had dropped the journal somewhere along the trail, there was a chance he could find it.

He forced himself to stop biting his nails, spread his hands on the sink, and hunched forward, cursing his amnesia.

Seer, seer.

Come hither yonder hill.

No! Not again! Fergus ground his teeth, wishing the words away. Why did the fetch keep tormenting him?

"Leave me alone," he growled.

To his surprise the spectral voice inside him evaporated.

Fergus exhaled in exhaustion. Water droplets echoed in the tiny bathroom, punctuating the silence like a ticking time bomb. However, something else had captured his attention.

A single bead of blood.

Fergus gaped at the white porcelain surface and watched the blood become a pink watery strand. Where had it come from? Another drop splashed the surface. He glanced at the ceiling. Once he'd caught a fetch on the ceiling, wings and teeth and fiery eyes, unfolding like hideous origami. But there was nothing there. He inspected his hands, then yanked his flannel back and scanned his wrists and forearms. No sign of cuts or scrapes. What was happening to him?

Perhaps the madness was starting. Just like it did with Pops.

The throbbing became a vise, wringing his skull with such force he wanted to bellow. Fergus clamped his hands over his head. Compressing his temples. Tighter. And tighter. He raised his eyes and glimpsed his reflection in the bathroom mirror. His heart leaped.

Dark rivulets coursed his jaw, bleeding from both ears, turning his face into a mask of glistening crimson.

ᘔ Chapter 7 ᘰ

The first time Zeph Walker considered himself a freak of nature, he was nine years old. By then his gift had blossomed. When he looked at people, he often discerned things about them. Random things. Sometimes awkwardly personal things. Back then the Telling came often; words meandered on the periphery of his mind like dandelion halos on the lazy summer air. With the encouragement of his mother, he learned to capture those intuitions, pluck them from the ether as a magician does a white dove. It didn't take Zeph long to realize he was not like the other kids. Not like them at all.

Leave it to Virgil Hedge to reinforce that uncomfortable reality.

Hedge hunted rattlesnakes and sold the venom to the lab in China Lake until the USDA stepped in and began regulating the business. He lived next door to the Walkers, would call young Zeph over to see the cages of slithering serpents, and then cackle at the boy's revulsion. One day Zeph innocently asked the man if he was illiterate, to which Hedge strummed his suspenders and declared, "I knows exactly who my daddy is." Shortly thereafter Hedge invited the young boy to see a freak of nature.

Zeph learned later on that multiheaded animals were not that unusual. The dictionary called them *polycephalics*, a word he never managed to successfully incorporate into his vocabulary. Supposedly some farmer near Dry Lake nursed a two-headed calf back to life and sold it to a circus. Nevertheless, when Virgil Hedge led Zeph into the barn that day and showed him a rattlesnake with two heads, it changed his world forever.

That day Zeph Walker came to believe in freaks of nature.

As he followed the detectives out of the morgue that late summer afternoon, he could not help but remember gaping at that reptilian curiosity just as he'd gaped at the cadaver on the guttered steel table. Even more unnerving was the sense that no polycephalic on earth could compare to Zeph Walker's own peculiarity.

28

The door whispered shut behind him, taking the cool formaldehyde-tinged air along with it.

"Albershart's dumbstruck." Lacroix put his sunglasses on and flapped the collar of his blazer. He and Chat Chavez walked toward the unmarked police vehicle with Zeph in tow. "He's bringing in an expert." Lacroix spoke over his shoulder. "Probably some lice-infested Berkeley grad with a degree in cryptozoology and an *X-Files* decoder ring. Nevertheless, while I am not inclined toward such soft science, I will readily confess—" Lacroix stopped and turned toward him. "—my complete astonishment."

The detective shrugged and proceeded to the car.

"Wait." The word escaped Zeph's lips before he realized it.

Both men stopped and turned to him.

Zeph swallowed back traces of bile. "So, what exactly's g–going on here? You can't just…I mean, that guy in there—w–what're we dealing with?"

Lacroix glanced at his partner. "At the moment we are dealing with a homicide. Plain and simple. And until forensics can perform an internal examination—if, indeed, one *can* be performed—revealing another cause of death, we have no choice but to conclude this is a homicide. You must remember, Mr. Walker, our expertise is criminal investigation. And until those fellas inspect the plumbing and tell us we are dealing with an extraterrestrial or a genetic muta-tion or somethin' comparable, whatever happened to that man in there—and whatever type of man he turns out to be—it was a single bullet in his chest that has set things in motion."

Zeph squinted. Ghost flames swirled off the tarmac behind them, turning the detectives into smoldering silhouettes.

"Nature's fulla freaks," Chat smirked. "Who knows? This might be one of 'em."

Indeed.

Lacroix circled the vehicle and took the wheel while Chat opened the back door and stood waiting. This man's rough persona disguised a tender heart. Zeph sensed that. However, he was not about to test his theory. He put his sunglasses on and slid inside without meeting the detective's surly gaze.

As he fired up the engine, Lacroix looked at Zeph in the rear-view mirror. "Our job is relatively simple here, young man. We are looking for the shooter." He put his seat belt on. "And you're sure that man at the diner, the one you assaulted, would not be seeking retribution?"

"I didn't assault him. It was in self-defense. And, no sir. That was almost ten years ago."

Chat leafed through a small tablet he had produced from his shirt pocket. "High Banton. That him?"

Zeph nodded.

"Very well." Lacroix readjusted the mirror. "Just remember, your cooperation could make all the difference."

"Of course. I–I'll do my best."

Lacroix's gaze lingered just long enough to indicate he was unconvinced.

They left the morgue, turning south on the highway, and headed toward the outskirts of town. Watching the shops go by—Maylene's Bakery, home of the best tarts in town; Bart's Bait and Tackle; and Cubano, a cigar store with a real wooden Indian stationed out front—brought back fond memories. It was years since he'd been downtown. Too many whispers, too many eyes. Too many High Bantons. Still, Zeph loved the city of his youth.

Why else would they have returned?

The downtown strip gave way to residences, large ranch-style pieces of property interspersed with roadside stands and family-owned businesses. Turning off the 395, they passed Carson Creek Park, with its sprawling shade trees and grassy knolls. Across the street stood the Vermont. Newly posted signs announced that the old playhouse was under construction, and the marquee now promised a "Word for the Day," today's message being: FORBIDDEN FRUIT CREATES MANY JAMS.

Clearly the new owner possessed the type of humor Zeph appreciated.

Farther down the car did a U-turn in the middle of the street and pulled to the dirt shoulder in front of Zeph's house. Next door Mila swept her porch, watching with interest. Several jars of cactus jelly, glowing warmly in lime greens and deep reds, were stacked on a wooden table in front of a white picket fence. Mila sold the best cactus jelly in town. Single jars for $3.50 were an awfully good deal, and Zeph always refused any discount she tried to give him. Fruit and nut stands were common in Endurance. Yet Mila's sticky rolls, breads, and jellies were unbeatable.

As far as neighbors went, Mila Rios was a saint. However, at the moment Zeph could not think about anything other than avoiding her probing gaze.

Lacroix put the car in park, turned, and handed Zeph a business card. "If you remember anything that might aid our investigation— a person of suspicion, an event—please contact us."

"Unless we're talkin' extraterrestrials," Chat added. "Then keep it to yourself."

Lacroix glanced at his partner, apparently not humored. "And until we get a handle on this, you'd best keep it under wraps."

Zeph sat pondering the detective's exhortation. "Please don't take this the wrong way, detective, but what're the chances you can get a handle on this?"

Chat slung his thick, tanned forearm over the seat. "Just watch yourself. Okay?"

"Yes, sir." Zeph opened the door and scrambled out of the car.

Chat looked past him through the open window of the passenger door. "Book Swap." The detective read the sign on the cottage next to Zeph's house. "You a reader?"

"Very much so."

"Figgers," Chat grunted.

As Zeph prepared to make a beeline for the front gate, he stopped. "One more question. Where'd you find that…where'd you find *him*?"

The men looked at each other, and then Lacroix said from the driver's side, "Not more than one hundred fifty yards from where you are standing."

Zeph straightened and looked up and down the street.

"One of your neighbors reported a commotion last night," Chat said. Then he aimed two fingers in the direction of the Vermont.

"Someone shot John Doe in the alley of the playhouse. Or stashed his body there." Lacroix put the car in gear. "We will be in touch, Mr. Walker."

Zeph peered at the old structure, the brick alley, and the gaudy red marquee with the word for the day. As the car pulled away, Chat called out the window, "Just watch yourself. Okay?"

Chapter 8

The Vermont, with its brick façade and crumbling mortar, had at one time been a hub of cultural arts. New tracts of homes opening in the north created the great downtown relocation, leaving the theater and its dwindling thespian community in its wake. After several unsuccessful attempts at revitalization, a new owner had taken over. Zeph did not know who that new owner was. And now, more than ever, his interest was piqued.

"Zeph?" It was Mila Rios. "Zeph, are you all right?"

Her words wrenched his gaze away from the old theater. Mila had stopped sweeping and squinted at him. He was standing forlorn on the side of the road. Zeph smiled sheepishly and waved. Mila waved back. A look of concern had replaced her usual sunny disposition. Which meant he could not escape.

Zeph turned, ducked past the row of hedges that separated their properties, and hurried to the front gate. It was open, and he suspected someone had visited the Swap. The wisteria vine on the arbor was going dormant, and dry leaves spiraled in his passing. Dappled sunlight shone through the towering Modesto ash, speckling the dirt with sunset orange. As he hurried down the footpath to his house, he could hear Mila's sandals slapping the hard dirt behind him.

He'd never make it.

"Zeph?" The gate rattled. "Don't you be running from me."

He stopped, released a deep sigh, and turned to face Mila Rios.

The gate swung open, and she stood with her arms folded, flowery yellow apron splashing color against the dried arbor. The woman's smile, as bright as the spring hues she often donned, conveyed genuine warmth. Shoulder-length black hair was tinged with gray, and the faintest wrinkles notched her kind eyes.

"You haven't gotten yourself into trouble, have you?" She cocked her head, lips crimped in a playful approbation.

"Mila, if I did, you'd be the last person to know."

"Oh, I'd find out. You know that."

"You're right."

She ambled toward him. "Well, unless you're dealing drugs or running a crime ring, I still think you're one of the finest young men in town."

"What I lack in good looks, I make up for in good nature."

"Oh, stop it." She swiped at him playfully.

"But now I'll have to dismantle my crime ring."

"Well, you can give all your proceeds to the shelter."

Mila served every Thursday at the downtown homeless shelter. She was one of those souls who put a lot more back into life than what she required from it. Which made Zeph feel all the more guilty for his disappearing act.

Seeing her master had hurried off, Jamie, Mila's Chihuahua, scampered along the dirt path and through the gate. The dog sniffed its way toward Zeph and began performing an extensive investigation of his pant leg. He could only imagine what exotic smells he had acquired in the morgue.

"Jamie!" Mila scooped up the dog. She rose, stroking the shivering rodent-like canine, and studied Zeph. "You look pale. Are you all right?"

His stomach muscles ached from vomiting, yet how could he explain the events at the morgue? And did he even want to?

"Honestly?" Zeph said. "I don't know."

She inched closer, a slight change in her eyes.

Something rich lay inside Mila Rios—he'd sensed that from day one. Most folks managed façades, carefully crafted personas cobbled together to hide their fears and insecurities. Not Mila. Kindness was too small a word for what lay inside her. As was *good nature* or *tolerance*. She loved without hesitation or qualification. Prodigals were always welcome in Mila's world. Standing this close to her, Zeph had to fight to keep from pitching forward in tears and contrition.

"Something is wrong." Mila's tone was full of concern. "Isn't it?"

Zeph melted under her motherly gaze.

She put the dog down, and Jamie skittered harmlessly after some chickens that had wandered from Zeph's backyard. "You need to get out more, Zeph. You stay locked up in that house too much. A young man like you, with all that talent—"

"Mila…" Zeph protested.

"Don't *Mila* me. You're too young. You should be out making friends, seeing people. Telling folks your story. And your paintings, Zeph. They're good. You can't hide forever."

Had anyone ever spoken so directly to him as Mila Rios did?

Her eyes relaxed as she studied his face. "Do you remember that question—you know, the one you said your father used to ask? It was about...*destiny*."

Zeph grimaced.

"That's right," she said. "Do you find your destiny...?"

He sighed. "Or does your destiny find you?"

"Yes. Well, whatever the answer to that question is, you're not gonna find anything without looking. And my guess is...that's the answer. Now—" She stepped back, straightened her apron. "Those two gentlemen had all the charm of law enforcement. Were they?"

"It was nothing, Mila."

She folded her arms.

"Okay," he said. "They were detectives."

She uncrossed her arms and her lips parted slightly.

"They just had some questions."

"Questions? About what?" The concern returned to her eyes. "Is something wrong?"

The thought of that crispy bug man in the autopsy room stalked his mind. *Until we get a handle on this*, Lacroix had said, *you'd best keep it under wraps.* But how could Zeph possibly keep something that bizarre under wraps? Especially with Mila Rios looking through him.

"I guess someone on the street called the police about a commotion last night." He let the statement dangle there in hopes that she might fill in the blanks.

"Commotion? Like what?" she said. "I know Jamie's been agitated lately. 'Specially in the evenings. I thought maybe the raccoons were back. But..." Her eyes narrowed. "Is something else going on? Something I should know about?"

Zeph glanced at Lacroix's business card and then stuffed it in his shirt pocket. "It's probably nothing, Mila."

She was peering at him, about to blow his cover, when a shrill buzzing sounded. Zeph flinched, still jittery from the Telling.

"My pies!" Mila said. Conflicted, she stared at her house and scrunched her lips. "Oh, I gotta run." She scampered to the gate, turned, and summoned Jamie, who came skittering under the hedges. As she looped her arm under the dog and closed the gate, Mila paused.

"Zeph Walker, if you need anything—*anything*—you give me a holler."

"I will, Mila." He meant it.

She smiled and then hurried home, her yellow apron billowing around her like a cloud of glory.

Chapter 9

She had lost too much time—maybe a lifetime. If being a senior citizen had any advantage, it was hindsight. However, the only way Annie Lane could envision making up for lost time was to speed things up.

Which is what she decided to do.

The pond inside the atrium sparkled, and the cattails drooped lazily. Yet no one was in the surrounding lounge to see. Annie turned the corner into the northern wing. They called it the Back Nine, mainly because of Easy Dolan. The wing consisted of twenty modest apartments, ten on each side, the last one having been gutted in favor of storage. The retired semi-pro golfer lived on the "nine side." He had been a resident of Marvale long before Annie arrived. Her interest in Easy, however, had nothing to do with his knowledge of fairways, chip shots, or nine irons.

The halls were empty again, a trend that had not escaped Annie's notice. Whatever was happening to people, it seemed to keep them indoors. At least, until the middle of the night. Despite the seeming desolation of the retirement home, she looked over her shoulder before tapping on Easy's door.

Her granddaughter was not going to like this.

The familiar thump of Easy's cane sounded inside. The door opened.

"Well, if it ain't Miss Annie!" The black man tipped his plaid cap and beamed a near-neon smile. "Back for more spelunking lessons?"

"Not this time," she said, worried about the decibel level of their conversation. "May I come in?"

"By all means." Easy pivoted away from the door with a sweeping, regal gesture of his hand.

A chemical smell struck her, and Annie waved her hand in front of her face. "Pheww! What do you have going on now?"

Easy's living room was more like an antiquities warehouse, the centerpiece being a large walnut rolltop desk surrounded by cluttered bookshelves, rolled-up maps, and a hood of chain mail fitted loosely over a half-mannequin. A gooseneck lamp illuminated a model car lying in parts on the surface of the desk, and nearby, an opened candy bar, half-eaten. A poster of a teed golf ball hung over the desk, and an iPod dock glowed, emanating soft strains of jazz music. Jars of liquid, cylinders, and tins of various sizes and shape lined the desk's shelves. Had one not known it was the twenty-first century, Easy Dolan might have been mistaken for an ancient alchemist.

"It's a '57 Chevy Corvette convertible." Easy went to the desk and proudly surveyed the parts under the lamp. "Banana yellow—my high school dream car." He smiled and shook his head in obvious nostalgic glee.

"It is a beauty." Annie entered the living room, grimacing at the chemical smell. "You have a regular laboratory going on over there."

Easy chuckled. "I suppose you could say that. Solvents. Wax. Glues. Love potions. Speaking of love potions, where's that raven beauty?" Easy winked at Annie. "She too shy to come?"

"Eugenia?" Annie's tone became grim. "I'm afraid she hasn't been herself."

"Do tell."

Annie had no reason to distrust Easy. At least, not yet. He seemed to be his gregarious, high-spirited self. Eugenia's change, on the other hand, had been abrupt, although it still required a keen eye to notice. Yet at some point, if she was going to find out what was going on, she would have to trust somebody. So Annie dove right in.

"How would a whole group of people change all at once?"

Easy squinted at her before a sly grin blossomed on his face. "You're talkin' about those rumors, aren't ya?"

Annie nodded.

"Mama Mae used to say that rumors were the only thing that got thicker when you spread 'em."

"Rumors or not, I've seen it firsthand. So you don't put any credence in them?"

Easy settled into the banker's chair and leaned his cane against the desk. "Pull up a chair, Miss Annie."

The only other chair in the room was the cloth wingback that Annie dreaded. Nevertheless, whenever he had visitors, Easy insisted they sit in that chair. Supposedly it had been passed down by his mother from the Civil War era. Easy's cat, Jezebel, usually occupied the chair. Now, the only evidence of the cat was a dusting of black fur.

"Where's Jezzy?" Annie asked, perching on the chair's edge.

Easy jabbed his thumb toward the patio. "She's been on hiatus for a while—two days, to be exact."

"Aren't you worried?"

"Pshh!" He waved his hand dismissively. "So, then—what's all this talk about people changin', hmm?" He leveled a cool smile.

"I was hoping you could tell me."

"I can tell you 'bout a lot—balsa wood aircraft, salt caves, possibly even the mating habits of North American fruit bats—but as far as why a whole bunch a people in a retirement home might be changin', well, that's a little bit outta my league."

"I know. It sounds so strange," Annie admitted.

"Ya think?"

"I first noticed it in Eugenia. We were bingo partners for the better part of a year, and all of a sudden she just lost interest. Stopped showing up. In fact, she pretty much stopped going out altogether."

"No kidding."

"I checked on her to make sure she was all right. But it was obvious—at least to me—she wasn't. I'm not sure how to put this, but I started to notice changes about her—the way she watched others, how she dressed. She started having trouble operating simple devices like can openers and the TV changer."

"You don't say."

"That's just the beginning. One day, at her apartment, I noticed the pantry was full of cereal. Eight, maybe ten boxes. And I don't mean granola, but the frosted, sugary kind of cereal. And showers—she took a lot of baths and showers. It wasn't long before she just stopped coming out at all. And at night…I can hear her late at night moving around."

Easy sat for a moment, squinting in thought. "You sure it ain't somethin' else? Maybe she had a minor stroke, or some sort a memory loss. Ya know, those things happen when you reach our age." He chuckled.

"Well, I suppose it could be. But what kind of stroke would make you obsessed with codes and strings of letters?"

"Huh?"

"That's right. More than once I caught her scribbling out odd sequences of letters, like a puzzle or cryptogram. Look." She unsnapped one of her Velcro pockets and produced an empty book of matches, which she handed to Easy. "Did I mention she burns a lot of candles?"

"Lotsa folks burn candles." Easy took the matchbook, looking slightly annoyed. "Ain't nothin' strange 'bout that.'"

"I suppose not. But look inside."

He opened the matchbook and squinted at the words scrawled there.

She asked, "Is that any language you're familiar with?"

"*Tau. Caph. Lamed. Ain.*" Easy shook his head. "Eugenia wrote this?"

"Yes."

"Ya got me. Somethin' Eastern maybe. Foreign. Hard ta say."

"I found that in her apartment one day." She pointed to the matchbook. "Took the liberty to *borrow* it."

Easy handed it back to her. "Like I said, Miss Annie, one of these days that sleuthin' of yours is gonna land you in hot water."

"I'm more afraid of *not* knowing the truth than landing in hot water."

Easy shook his head, looking more perturbed than humored by her stubbornness.

"Anyway," Annie said, stuffing the matchbook back in her cargo pocket, "she's been scribbling those kind of words, and others, everywhere. On tablets, inside books. She even carved something on the backside of her front door. I've never heard of a stroke causing someone to do something like that, have you?"

Easy lifted his cap and scratched at his thinning afro.

"It wasn't long before I started hearing similar stories," Annie continued. "Edie Lang said her husband was up all hours of the night, acting strange. And then Cecil Farmer called the police on his own wife."

"Now, I heard about that. Said she bit him!" Easy slapped his knee and guffawed. Then he folded his arms and looked at her. "Okay. I'll grant ya there's some strange things goin' on. But people are strange, Miss Annie. You know that. Heck, between our tastes in food, music, clothes—ya know, tics and whatnot—not a one of us is really normal. Besides, what exactly can you attribute it all to? Sounds to me like just a whole bunch a coincidences."

"Well, that's just it. I don't know what it could be. Something psychological. Maybe something..." She hesitated. "Something spiritual."

"Spiritual?" Easy snorted. "Like some mass possession?"

Annie shrugged. "Honestly, I don't know."

Easy pursed his lips and shook his head. Then he spread his hands in surrender. "I'm afraid I can't proffer an answer for ya, Miss Annie. In all my years I ain't encountered a phenomenon like that. 'Specially no mass possession." The derision in his tone was obvious.

They sat for a moment as the soft sounds of a saxophone from the iPod filled the in-between. The doors seemed to be closing on her, one after the other. Should she proceed any further? If finding the truth involved taking risks, perhaps this was another risk she should take.

Finally, Annie cleared her throat. "I do have a theory..."

"By all means."

"The Madness of Endurance."

Easy's eyes grew wide. "Now that's a theory! Don't think I'd ever o' come up with that one." He laughed again, his dentures gleaming pristine against his aged black skin.

"Silverton turned into a ghost town overnight." Annie's tone was weighted with inference. "Something happened quick to those people and sent them all off the deep end. At least, if the stories are true."

"You ain't suggesting..."

"I don't know." Annie stood, brushing the cat hair off the seat of her canvas cargo skirt. Then she started pacing. "I don't know what I'm suggesting." Easy watched her treading across his carpet, his brow furrowed. Finally he admitted, "That is where the legend started. Course, legends spring up everywhere, with or without factual basis. That ol' ghost story's no different. Findin' out the truth about the Madness is 'bout as hard as locatin' water in Dry Lake."

"Silverton is fact enough that something happened."

"But not enough to prove they'd opened a gateway to hell. Besides, how would that affect a bunch a seniors in a retirement spread, hmm?" Easy brushed at his slacks. "Listen, if you want my opinion, Miss Annie—and I'm assumin' that's why you're here—I'd be very careful. Very careful. You'll end up gettin' yourself in trouble, accusin' people of things that can't be proved. And if you place yourself anywhere near that old mine, I fear to think what kind a wrath you might incur. Nothin' good's come outta that place, and the folks that frequent it are a might unsavory. If somethin's really goin' on, if people's really changin', it'll come out in the wash. With or without your assistance."

Annie pondered his words. Suddenly she felt even more alone.

"I can't give up now, Easy. Not when I'm getting so close." Though she spoke the words with resolve, Annie's confidence was thinning. "God will protect me."

"Well, go on believin' that if you want. But if you land yourself in a mess, don't expect God to go bailin' ya out."

Any momentum Annie had hoped to generate was quashed by the finality of his assessment.

She thanked Easy and then escorted herself to the door.

"And next time ya come," Easy called from the living room, "make sure to bring that little sweet tart, Eugenia, with ya." He cackled and slapped his thigh.

Annie smiled, shook her head, and left the apartment, no more sure of herself than when she arrived. She had wanted Easy to side with her, to jump on her bandwagon and lend some credence to her claim. However, his response was probably a precursor to what she could expect from others.

Which meant that Annie Lane was on her own. Once again.

She stood in the hallway of the Back Nine, letting the reality of her plight settle in. All her talk about the Madness of Endurance and the ninth gate of hell—it must sound like lunacy. Had she told Easy too much? Anyone could be in on this. Even him. Then again, maybe she had not pressed the issue enough. Sending Tamra after the book would start a chain of events from which there was no going back. Had she moved prematurely? Perhaps her granddaughter was right and Annie was just overreacting.

Annie heaved a sigh of exasperation. Was this what senility felt like?

As she stood there, pondering her own sanity and the immensity of her theory, a sound drifted her way that caused Annie's skin to bristle. She angled her head, straining to discern what she was hearing.

It rose from the end of the hallway: soft laughter followed by a brief but frenzied gibbering in another tongue.

The voice did not sound human.

Chapter 10

As far as Annie Lane knew, no one spoke Latin in Marvale Manor. She stepped away from Easy Dolan's apartment, trying to distinguish the location of the obscure voice. If she was losing her mind, maybe she was also losing her hearing. Then again, perhaps her hearing was so good that she could detect television sets through the walls. If so, those sets were tuned to reruns of *The Exorcist*—for the voice she had caught wind of had all the garbled, frenetic anger of a demonized soul.

As Annie deliberated over the exact sound she'd heard, footsteps shuffled and a door slammed. She nearly jumped out of her walking shoes.

Now she was sure where the sound had come from.

The end of the hallway formed a T. One corridor led to the northern courtyard, the least-trafficked area of the Marvale facility. The opposite corridor led to the custodial area and boiler room, a dank block antechamber with an iron stairwell. She stared in this direction. What could be going on down there? Perhaps Fergus Coyne was talking to himself again. The skittish custodian was known for his schizophrenic rants. And lately he had drifted into a brooding, unpredictable melancholy. Fergus scared her. However, with everything going on, Annie wondered if she should brave an investigation.

Her answer was immediate.

A dull thud echoed up the corridor, followed by more rabid, incoherent words. Her heart was in her throat now. She turned and stared at Easy's door. Should she ask him for help? No. Easy had dissuaded her from further investigation. He was not supportive of her assumptions. But this was too much to ignore.

Lifting a silent prayer, Annie padded toward the custodial area.

She passed a bench seat littered with popcorn crumbs and crumpled gum wrappers. Were the folks back here turning into pigs, or what? She reached the end of the hallway. Annie looked to her right, where the set of double doors led to the courtyard. Then Annie looked the opposite direction, toward the boiler area.

A large Plexiglas sign cautioned STAFF ONLY. A smell of mold lingered. Two sets of iron stairs—one ascending, one descending—flanked the mineral-leeched block wall. One stairwell led to a boiler room in the basement. A confusion of pipes and ducts showed the way. She had heard the boiler room connected to a series of tunnels that ran the length of the facility. From there legends sprung into the fanciful. Having never ventured into this cellar, Annie could not substantiate those legends. Perhaps it was time she tried.

A large moth pattered against a single bare bulb overhead, sending shadows dancing about the cool enclosure. This looked like a scene straight out of an Edgar Allen Poe tale. On the landing above, a set of double doors led to the Yard, a fenced area where grounds equipment was stored. The custodial lockers were located directly across from these stairwells.

As Annie studied the poorly lit corridor, she noticed two things: muddy footprints descending from the Yard and a dossier of loose papers lying open at the base of the steps.

She stared, trying to fit the pieces together. Had someone dropped this, or had it been placed here? Annie leaned forward, squinting. Whatever this was about—the babbling voice, the muddy footprints, the scattered papers—she wouldn't find the truth just standing there. Annie drew a deep breath and entered the corridor.

The floor was sticky. Odd etchings marred the block in spots, incoherent words and mathematical equations, not unlike the ones Eugenia had scrawled. What was going on back here? She approached the dossier, fixated upon several loose pages. On one of them was a sketch that captivated her attention. It was an anatomical rendering of a man—arms, legs, torso. In place of a head, however, was a four-faced menagerie: the face of a raven, a serpent, a feral cat, and a man. And behind the torso spread two black wings.

What in the world?

She had seen this image, or something like it, before but couldn't place it. Annie looked at the custodial door. From somewhere behind her, in the Back Nine, came the muffled hum of a vacuum cleaner. The tortured voice and the Latin incantations were gone.

Annie returned her gaze to the strange sketch, then bent over and retrieved the dossier. She thumbed through ragged pages of symbols and mathematical equations, interspersed with memos, clippings, and photocopies. And words—pages of scrawled, illegible words, like the ramblings of some madman. Her insides were as taut as a banjo string.

Who in Marvale Manor would possess such a thing? Perhaps she should take this to the director. Or even the police.

That's when she noticed a droplet of blood on the concrete floor. Annie brushed back her skirt and hunched closer, scrutinizing the single crimson drop.

The moth beat the light overhead, sending soft shadows pulsating about the room. A low rumble emerged from the boiler room.

She straightened.

Something was happening here that she could not deny, a shadow in the atmosphere that she could not ignore. Whether or not Tamra believed her, whether or not Easy Dolan cared to join her investigation, a bizarre chain of events was in motion that she had been made privy to, events that she had long been waiting for.

She had prayed for confirmation, and this was it.

As one who believed in providence, her decision was swift and simple. She gathered the loose pages, stuffed them back into the leather journal, and whisked the strange documents to her apartment. Equally as swift was Annie's conviction that the owner of this book would come looking for it.

Chapter 11

Pops had warned him about this, said they were messing with things they ought not. The second sight had consequences—bad consequences. That's what Pops said. Course, that was after they'd awakened the fetch.

As Fergus stared at his reflection in the mirror, the blood trickling from each ear, it was not fear of death that gripped him. No. Standing there with his head pounding and the spellbook unaccounted for, Fergus was beginning to wonder if something else was playing out. Something that neither he nor Pops had foreseen.

Perhaps they were being used.

He leaned over the sink and splashed water on his face until the bloodstains were gone. Then he jammed a wad of toilet paper in each ear and stared at his reflection. He looked like he'd just stumbled out of a barroom brawl. And barely survived. What was happening to him? His jaw was swollen, his eyes jaundiced. A lattice of blue veins pulsed in his temple. However, he did not have time to fret over his condition.

Fergus returned the items to the backpack, but as he took the pistol, he paused. He had only used it once. Yet the way things were going, he would need to keep it handy. He slipped the gun under his flannel, into the belt of his jeans. Then he hurried from the restroom into the custodial locker room.

Just as he feared, a trail of muddy footprints led through the storage room out into the Marvale facility. However, the spellbook was nowhere to be found. Somehow, even in his catatonia, he had staggered back here. Had he dropped the journal along the way? Had someone taken it from him?

Then he remembered the dark figure in the Rift bending over him.

"Bad Fergus." A pitiful sob escaped his lips. "Hurry. Gotta h–hurry!"

Near the bank of lockers hung an 18x24 print of Jesus Christ in a nicked wooden frame. Miley, one of the day custodians, had placed it there. Fergus approached the picture. He'd scribbled out the image's eyes with black marker, and a web of cracks sheared the glass where he'd punched it. If he had to endure the holy man's gaze, he'd do so on *his* terms. Miley, remarkably, had taken little offense at the vandalism. Too bad.

Fergus glanced at the door. The day custodians were already gone, and except for the director or Stevie, the groundskeeper, the rest of the staff rarely ventured into the custodial area. Setting his backpack down, he moved the picture sideways to reveal an open section of crumbling drywall. The key to his locker lay inside on one of the braces. He opened the padlock and returned the key to its place, making sure to straighten the picture.

Rummaging past dirty overalls and aprons, he searched the locker for the journal. Removing a stack of *Popular Mechanics* magazines and a half-empty bottle of whiskey only confirmed his fear—the spellbook was gone.

He slumped on his haunches and remained there. *Blast it!* How could he have been so careless? The constant nickering of those old fools, the stench of dying that lingered there—it was finally getting to him. He kicked the lockers and growled.

There was only one thing left to do.

Fergus jammed his belongings back into the locker, along with the backpack, and snapped the padlock shut. He glanced at the digital clock on the shelf near his walkie-talkie. Dinnertime was fast approaching. If he hurried, he could scour the grounds and comb the fire trail while there was still light. They wouldn't miss him. Although the thought of venturing near the Rift at dark sent his heart racing, there was no time to waste.

He stepped from the custodial room into a dingy hallway. Muddy footprints smattered the concrete, and he traced them as they climbed the steps toward the Yard. He'd come this way, that much was clear. But it wasn't safe to go back. Not yet.

Fergus drew a deep breath, plastered his wet hair back with the palm of his hand, and hurried through the Back Nine toward Laurel House.

Marvale was situated on a large, stony terrace. Below it, separated by a dried creek bed named Servile Gulch and a wall of bristlecone pines, sat Laurel House. Warm. Glowing. And full of death. The convalescent home had been built after Marvale. It made sense, he thought, to put the facilities nearby. Retirement only lasted so long. After that it was wheelchairs, oxygen tubes, and diapers. How he hated Laurel House! If it wasn't for Pops, he wouldn't mind seeing the place burn.

A single walkway joined the properties, connected in the middle by a stairwell and a wheelchair ramp. At the back entrance a female attendant stood smoking a cigarette, probably between breaks. He kept his head down and hurried past.

As soon as he opened the doors, the stench hit him. Bedpans and disinfectants melded with the smell of cafeteria food. He bit back the revulsion and strode through the bright halls, a man on a mission.

Languid eyes stared from dreary rooms as he passed. A frail, balding woman looked away from her TV and followed him with her lonely gaze. A man lay murmuring, his right hand tapping aimlessly at the guardrail of his bed. Fergus grit his teeth. If there was a hell, Laurel House was it.

Room 708 was just ahead. He stopped abruptly at the doorway, his tennis shoes chirping on the vinyl flooring. Then he peeked in at Robert "Pops" Coyne. His father lay on his back, eyes closed, pale skin stretched taut over gaunt cheekbones, hands folded at his chest like a cadaver awaiting burial.

Fergus stepped into the room, trying not to disturb Pops. In the other bed Weltz lay curled in a fetal position with his back to them, the blankets pulled up to his ears. Perhaps Weltz had died and mummified. If so, no one would care. And Fergus wasn't about to find out.

He crept toward Pops, glanced at the doorway to ensure no one was watching, and cupped his hand over his father's mouth. Pops's eyes sprung open, and he recoiled from Fergus's overshadowing presence.

"Shhh!" Fergus hissed.

When the old man's eyes adjusted, Fergus slowly removed his hand.

"There we go, Pops. It's me, Fergie." Then he leaned in, his hand spread upon his father's bony chest. "Somethin' happened. Somethin' you should know about."

Pops's eyes grew wide, and he opened his mouth, struggling to speak. Only spittle and guttural grunts emerged. Then he summoned a burst of energy, seized the guardrails, and rattled them madly.

"Settle down!" Fergus gripped his father's shoulders. "It ain't Mum! Relax, 'fore you pee yourself."

Resistance dissipated from his father's body as quickly as it had come. Pops sunk back into the bed, panting and lethargic.

"I'm done tryin'," Fergus growled. "It's over. Just like you said. The fetch—"

The old man turned toward Fergus with wide eyes.

"Yeah," Fergus said. "They're tricksters. They're out to hurt ol' Fergie. Just look." He plucked the bloody tissues out of his ears and held them up. "They're in my head. They won't lemme go, Pops. They're eatin' old Fergie alive!"

He flung the earplugs to the floor and stood choking back emotion. He had to steady himself, or he'd start bleeding again. Finally Fergus said, "We gotta leave, Pops. It's gettin' worse. And the Rift...*it's changin'*."

Pops lay gaping. Then he lunged up and seized Fergus's wrist with such force the custodian yelped.

"I know!" Fergus wrenched his arm away and stumbled back. "I know ya warned me!"

He glanced over his shoulder at Weltz, who remained undisturbed under his cocoon of sheets. Then Fergus went to the end of the bed and began pacing. "It's the spellbook—I–I lost it. At the Rift or...or someone took it, I dunno. But it's gone. I'm sorry. I–I been careless. After this, it's no more. I promise. No more!"

Pops's eyes softened, and he seemed to drift in thought.

Fergus started pacing again. "I gotta go back. I can't leave it. Gotta go back to the Rift. But after that, we're leavin'. Back to Virginia, maybe. Or the old country. How's that sound, Pops? The old country." He nodded to himself with a hopeful smile. "But fer now, I gotta go back to that hellhole. Then it's over. I promise. It's over for us."

He cast a weak smile at his father. "And if I don't come back, have the Injun blow it up. The whole flippin' thing."

"That would not be advisable."

Fergus jolted at the words and turned to see who had spoken them.

Walther Roth stood in the doorway wearing his Burberry trench-coat, greasy black hair slicked back and shimmering in the lights. "Explosives rarely solve anything, Fergus. And if they do, it's always temporary."

A smarmy grin creased Roth's face.

Fergus spoke through gritted teeth. "Can't you people leave him alone?"

"People? Leave him alone? Good Lord! After all your father's done for us, and we're supposed to just leave him alone?" Roth stepped into the room and brushed his long, spidery fingers through the air. Then he adjusted his wire-rimmed glasses and stared directly at Fergus. "Why, you and Robert are still some of our most valuable commodities."

Roth approached and stood on the opposite side of the bed, his smug gaze traveling the length of Pops's body before meeting Fergus's glare. This government weasel was a reminder of everything Fergus despised. NOVEM had used Pops and then tossed him aside like a dirty rag. Fergus had his suspicions about Roth, the least being whether or not he was still human.

"Say your good-byes, Roth. 'Cuz we're leavin'."

"Is that so?" Roth's demeanor was one of indifference. He absently straightened Pops's gown. "I'm not sure we can allow that."

Fergus reached into his pants and exposed the butt of the pistol.

Roth's eye sparkled upon seeing the gun, a cool grin curling the edges of his lips.

Fergus returned the weapon to its place. "I'd just as soon take out the three of us than get dragged back into yer fun-n-games. What-ever's goin' on out there—" Fergus pointed in the direction of the mountains. "—it's turnin' ugly. Real ugly. I–I don't know what you guys are after, but it's c–comin' with a vengeance. And trust me, I will *not* stick around and let it come f–fer me." He was trembling again, and, if he stayed here, he was sure his head would start gushing blood.

Fergus strode to the doorway. He turned around and said, "I might be a monster, Roth, but at least I'm still the human kind."

Walther Roth only chuckled.

Fergus gnashed his teeth. As he prepared to leave, he saw that his father was watching him. A single tear tumbled down the old man's sunken cheek.

Chapter 12

She happened upon the picture by accident. It was buried behind her jewelry box, a framed snapshot of her father before he had gone AWOL. Tamra studied the photo. Thick sandy hair, tanned, firm shoulders. He looked so healthy back then. Which strummed chords of sorrow deep inside her.

A cold nose nuzzled under her pant leg, and she jumped.

"Shady!" She bent to pat the golden retriever. "You scared me, gal."

The dog fanned her tail, oblivious to the exclamation issued by its master. Tamra had rescued Shady Lady just hours before the dog was scheduled to be put to sleep. Being blind in one eye and having bad hips shouldn't be a cause for execution. If that were the case, a good chunk of humanity would be on the chopping block.

"Tam!" Dieter yelled excitedly from the other room. "Tam! Bunny's here!"

"Coming!" Tamra started to return the picture to its spot behind the jewelry box, then stopped. *Why not?* She stood the picture at the front of her dresser, stepped back, and admired it. What a handsome young man. If only Nams could remember her son *this* way. Tamra shrugged. Everyone needed a second chance. And if seconds were available, maybe thirds and fourths too.

"Ta-a-m!" Dieter was stomping in the other room.

"Okay!" Her jewelry case had a thin layer of dust on it. How long had it been since she wore earrings or a necklace? As much as she tried, Tamra Lane couldn't muster enthusiasm for the accoutrements of modern fashion. Give her a pair of jeans, some sneakers, a bandana, and an iPod, and she was set.

Tamra picked past a pewter crucifix and a Black Hills gold pendant until she found the library card. One of the highlights of her brother's week was going with Bunny and her foster kids to the Endurance library. Which was one of the things Tamra so loved about her brother—he was easily pleased.

51

A horn beeped out front, and the other dogs answered with a round of barks. Shady hobbled out to see the source of the commotion. Tamra took the library card and closed the jewelry box. It sounded as if a wrestling match had broken out in the next room. She followed the noise to find Dieter in the living room struggling to get a sweater on.

"You're gonna be too hot in that," she said.

"Uh-uh!" He tugged the wool sweater over his mop of red hair. "It's always f–f–freezing in there."

Tamra went to him and fluffed out his hair. "You said that last time, and Bunny had to take your sweater off."

"I know," Dieter said sheepishly.

She handed him the library card. "And be careful with it. You got your other books?"

He turned and snatched up three thin picture books and one encyclopedic volume on the animal kingdom. Although Dieter was twenty-one and could be mistaken for the little brother of Grizzly Adams, his reading level had never risen above third grade. And his social skills were little better. Which made him all the more precious in Tamra's eyes. Being entrusted to care for her little brother may be the highest calling of her entire life. And if that was the case, Tamra Lane would die a happy camper.

Dieter shoved the card in his back pocket, eagerly adjusted the books under his arms, and thumped to the front door. The screen door slapped the house as Dieter ran to the van with Shady Lady limping behind. "Bunny B! Bunny B!" he shouted, even though Bunny's last name was nowhere near the letter B.

Tamra stepped onto the porch, smiling, and waved at the plump, jovial woman in the driver's seat. Bunny cared for two foster kids and simply adored Dieter. Living next door, she had become a second mother to the handicapped boy. And with Tamra's work schedule, she often wondered if Bunny wasn't an angel in disguise.

Tamra walked to the fence. "I told him he was gonna be hot."

"Oh, he'll be fine." Bunny brushed her hand through the air.

The three dogs scuffled at the fence, all hoping for a bit of Bunny's attention.

"I'm working tonight," Tamra said. "Can you check on him?"

"Course." Bunny turned as Dieter opened the side door and

clambered into the van with the other kids. The door slammed, she waved, and they drove off. The dogs wandered over and surrounded Tamra as she watched, smiling as the kids broke out in ruckus celebration from deep inside the massive cargo van.

Across town the sun was drawing down on the mountain range. Tamra stared in the direction of Marvale Manor. She could not see the facility from her house, but the blue misty mountains stretched like a vast curtain before a playhouse stage. And suddenly she was an actor in some weird drama. The joy she felt hearing Dieter leave evaporated inside her. Tamra gazed at the snowy crags and the blue ravines. *Could it really be? Could something malevolent be lurking in the hills?*

She pulled the sticky note from this morning out of her back pocket. It was doubled over, and she had to flip it to read the whole title. *Mystery Spots and Magic Landscapes.* Annie was constantly sending her in search of obscure books about Bible prophecies and urban legends. It had become more than just a hobby or a diversion for her grandmother. Tamra was beginning to fear Annie's quest was becoming an obsession. She shook her head and put the note back in her pocket.

Tamra would look for the little book swap during her lunch break, just like she'd promised her grandmother. But this time Tamra could not deny the nagging sense of worry that had begun webbing its way into her thoughts. There was only one way to remedy this.

She went into the house, sat down at her desk, pushed aside some paperwork, and opened her laptop. She paused briefly, as if typing the words were a concession to something loony, before entering "The Madness of Endurance" into the search engine.

A Wikipedia article was the first in line.

Tamra hunched forward, staring at a grainy photo of an old mine captioned "Otta's Rift." She shifted uncomfortably in her chair and began reading:

> The Madness of Endurance is believed to be the mass suicide of an entire town in the American old west. Scant records are available for the incident. What is known of the event is attributable to two primary sources: the ghost town of Silverton and the journal of a traveling miner by

the name of Joseph Blessington. The journal was acquired by an area pioneer, one C. J. Hooper, who founded Gold Coast Prospectors' Museum, where Blessington's journal is displayed. Despite numerous urban legends having origins in the bizarre event, these two sources remain the only verifiable record of what occurred in Endurance, California, circa 1873.

Tamra settled back in her chair with her fingers steepled at her lips. Shady had returned and lay panting, probably exhausted from her jaunt with the other dogs out front. However, Tamra was hesitant to read on, feeling as if she was being drawn into something she did not want to know. Even more unnerving was the possibility that the Madness was rooted in historical fact. "Facts are stubborn things," Nams loved to say. Tamra sighed, leaned forward, and scrolled down the article:

Many factors commonly led to the abandonment of towns in the American West: depletion of natural resources, natural disasters such as floods or droughts, railroads and roads bypassing an existing town, disease, and sickness. However, the Madness of Endurance adds another entry to the catalog of possibilities: mass suicide.

Silverton began as a mining camp of little note following the discovery of silver in 1869 by a group of prospectors, namely R. L. Otta. The wealthy landowner purchased several properties along the southeastern Sierra Nevada range. (Otta died in a freak industrial accident in 1876.) Otta's Rift, as it was named, became the hub of operations, producing consistent silver loads and attracting hopeful prospectors. Silverton reached its peak in 1873 when, apparently, the mining operation ceased and the city was left abandoned. The reason for the inhabitants' actions remain a matter of speculation.

City records noted the discovery of unspecified artifacts in Otta's Rift, apparently those of a tribal nature. Unearthing burial grounds or cave dwellings was not uncommon for early prospectors. Nevertheless, the discovery at Otta's Rift was of such a nature as to immediately cease operations.

While the exact causes behind the standstill are unknown, records indicate great fear and superstition divided the miners, leading to several notable disputes among Silverton leaders. Scandalous charges of impostors, delusions, and soothsaying were made. The last recorded entry in the city records was in the spring of 1873, but no indication of Silverton's abandonment is mentioned.

Enter Joseph Blessington, a nomadic prospector of British descent who stumbled upon what he called a "field of skins." In a journal entry dated October 1873, Blessington wrote cryptically of the scene he had reportedly encountered:

Lord's Day, October 1873

On the southward leg of my journey, in departure through Miners' Meadow along the mule trail, I came upon the remains of the place therein known as Otta's Ryft. Equipment of such sort as possessed of mining operations were plenteous, though no living things manned such apparatus. This mystery drew me to investigate [illegible] an event of mass Extinction. It smote the eye, a sinister place, vile and decrepit in fascination. Regalia of unknown import bedecked the environs: altars, charms, and smoking fire-pits of unwholesome matter. On approach, fits and agonies of Mind assailed the author. Frightening displays of Workmanship most curious to the eye, as to be found in Cathedrals of religious origin, embellished the site. There rose before the ungodly gash a Bloodless mound of Limbs and gristle, corrupt and inhuman anatomies, such as to be henceforward believed the very Pylon of Hell. The landscape was charred as from great blasts, the mine entry piled of this field of skins. Said Figures [illegible] unencumbered by skeleton and rigidity, possessed of Beastly origin. I dared not approach closely to the remains, lest Plague or Terror smite me, and fled such wicked plot of ground, never to return.

After reporting his find to the nearest town, Joseph Blessington was never heard from again. The acquisition of his journal by C. J. Hooper remains a mystery. Upon his report, a search party was organized, which confirmed Blessington's findings. The remains had been scattered, most likely by animals, and were not considered human. When Silverton's abandonment was learned, great fear fell upon homesteaders and travelers. Rumor spread of the strange corpses, their incineration, and the disappearance of the entire city, and Otta's Rift fell into legend.

Though the ghost town has been administered by California State Parks since becoming a state historic park in 1962, it receives less than 300 visitors yearly, most likely due to the ignominious legacy it has left. Some have speculated an ergot epidemic decimated the city or drove its inhabitants insane, while others deem more conspiratorial forces. Otta's Rift was sealed, and the event eventually became known as the Madness of Endurance.

Tamra settled back into her chair. The words of her grandmother flitted about her mind. *It's the Madness of Endurance. It's here again.* How much did Nams know about this? This morning, Bev Beason had crept up beside Tamra. A chill swept over her as she recalled the woman's empty eyes. What could be happening?

Tamra shut the laptop and started to get ready for work. But she could not busy herself enough to remove the deep disquiet seeping into her marrow.

Chapter 13

At one time he'd fancied himself Robinson Crusoe. It was right after Zeph discovered a hardbound copy of the Defoe classic in Book Swap. The iconic literary figure brought him strange comfort, proof, as it were, that men could indeed be islands. If *that* Crusoe could survive on a remote tropical island with coconuts, goat milk, and solitude, then why couldn't Zeph survive on a ranch without a cell phone, laptop, or human interaction?

Daylight was fading. Autumn's approach was in the air, a dewy decay that lingered around the edges and tainted the daily chores with sadness. Fall had never been kind to him. The wind, the cooling nights, the dead leaves. If winter embodied death, then fall was its harbinger.

Zeph dabbed at a magenta sunset with his paintbrush, leaned back from the canvas, and gazed out from the back porch across the three-acre parcel. Carson Creek meandered just beyond his fence line, making its way along the foothills toward the aqueduct. Cutthroat and brook trout thrived in the icy waters. He fly-fished the area often, a regular castaway in his own little paradise.

Zeph followed the foothills with his eyes, the porch lights winking in the folds and clefts of the Sierras, up to the fierce and stormy peaks now wreathed in blistering sunset red. Yet despite the pristine setting, the image of the withered man at the morgue would not relent.

...*your darker self.*

Zeph shivered at the thought. It was a strange coincidence, that's all. Anybody could get a tattoo of the Star of David on their arm. But the scar, and those shriveled legs...it was just too weird. Maybe the detectives were right and High Banton was seeking retribution for getting beaten up, playing some cruel joke on Zipperface. Whatever it was, the police would uncover something. At least he tried to convince himself of that.

Jamie yapped next door, summoning Zeph from his thoughts.

The dog wasn't nearly as annoying as others on the street, particularly the Bagwells' hound who bellowed at the slightest noise. Zeph recalled what Mila had said about the Chihuahua's recent agitation.

He placed the brush in a nearby coffee can of water, rose, and wandered down the steps of the wooden porch, listening to the dog and following his instincts. His mother would have called this "walking by faith," although Zeph's faith presently seemed about as agile as a desert tortoise. He walked around the side of the house as a few stray hens bustled to their coop for the evening, and then into the front yard, where he stopped. The lamp across the street flickered to life. The smell of lemons and brown sugar drifted by, followed by the clamor of tins. Mila was busy at work, which brought a smile. Farther down the street the Vermont's marquee glazed the sidewalk in neon warmth and reminded him of the dangers of "hidden fruit." Jamie had now stopped barking, and an unusual stillness seemed to simmer in the dusky air.

That's when he noticed the door to Book Swap was slightly ajar.

Zeph stared.

The book exchange was self-service. People came and went as they pleased. The cottage set to the side of his property had an idyllic charm about it, he thought, and Zeph took care to cultivate the surrounding garden. Call him a preservationist. Yet in the age of digital readers, book exchanges had become a dying breed. Nevertheless, Zeph was quite happy to perpetuate Blythe McCrery's vision . . . even if it meant keeping his gate open to potential strangers.

Still, the open door struck him as weird.

Mint Wheaton was overdue for her sci-fi fix. Perhaps she had come when he was out back and simply forgotten to close the door. Nothing weird about that. And Timothy regularly drove down from Hunter's Lodge in search of maritime historicals. However, Zeph could not recall having heard the jangling of the bell on the door, which usually signaled guests.

The tree limbs grated overhead as a gust swept by, setting the porch swing rocking.

. . . *your darker self.*

He shivered at the memory of the humanoid husk at the morgue.

A twenty-six-year-old bachelor living alone on a three-acre parcel with enough money in various CDs and bank accounts to afford a suite in a gated community and a personalized bodyguard should not be in this predicament. That thought crossed Zeph Walker's mind more than once. At the least he should have a remote-controlled wrought-iron gate and two husky Rottweilers patrolling the property.

Instead he had chickens.

Mila's screen door rattled in the breeze. However, something other than her pear turnovers and oatmeal raisin cookies occupied his attention.

As far as Zeph knew, the thirty-by-twenty-foot adobe structure next to his carport had always been called Book Swap. He didn't particularly care for the name and on several occasions had thought about changing it. More often than not, shutting the place down seemed reasonable. Perhaps it was his gift—his love for words—that caused him to keep it operational. That and he just liked to read. Nevertheless, anonymity was a precious commodity to Zeph Walker. And Book Swap did nothing to further that goal.

Which left him utterly conflicted.

A small footpath divided his front yard, branching off through the picket fence that surrounded the cottage. Zeph followed it. A row of sunflowers tilted there, their dried seeds pecked clean by jays. He stepped to the front door and stood on the welcome mat. A breeze swept past again, rustling the dry sunflower husks. The wooden sign hanging from the fascia swayed with each gust. The door breathed open and closed.

This wasn't like Los Angeles, where dead bolts and security systems were a necessity. Nevertheless, the image of the reptile man at the morgue had poisoned his thoughts.

Zeph pushed the door open far enough to activate the motion detector. The light came on inside, and the bells jangled, but he remained on the porch.

"Hello?" He felt like a fool. "Anybody in here?"

He drew a deep breath and stepped into Book Swap. The smiling watercolor of Blythe McCrery greeted him. Zeph had painted it based off a Polaroid headshot of her he'd found in one of the books. The elderly widow had owned the three-acre parcel. Apparently the enterprise had started as a hobby and blossomed into a quaint watering hole for neighbors and local book enthusiasts. Blythe became known as an antiquarian sage of sorts, gathering books into her little silo as the dark digital age encroached. Friends and residents soon began dropping off all sorts of reads, from collectibles to disposables, which Blythe willingly accepted, building a dense but formidable library. Originally built as a guest house, she eventually converted the old cottage into a library where locals could come and exchange books at no cost. In fact, when the Endurance library went through its first renovation, they donated some of their old wooden bookshelves to Blythe. The monstrous shelves had to be dismantled and reassembled inside. They managed to squeeze seven into the cottage, all of which reached the ceiling. The event made the local paper.

When Blythe passed away, the city entertained prospects of making the home a historical site. But as much as she had contributed to the advancement of literary appreciation in Endurance, the city could not justify bestowing such an honor upon the widow. Or the inconspicuous piece of property. Blythe's son, a dreary, unemployed sign painter, had little intention of preserving the place or his mother's legacy. The house was sold as-is. So for the last eight years Zeph had nurtured Blythe McCrery's vision.

Outside in the yard another gust of wind rustled through the ash, and the weathered sign tapped against the house. The door rocked on its hinges.

...*your darker self.*

Perhaps it was the image of the doppelgänger that set him on edge. Yet something was not right about this place. Whatever it was, whether justified or not, Zeph could not deny that a new kind of fear had awakened inside him, as if the Telling had punctured a reservoir of untapped emotion. Suddenly he felt vulnerable, like he was prey to an unseen enemy.

Maybe destiny was stalking him.

The door yawned, and dirt spiraled into the room. He winced at the swirling grit. And then froze as a shadowy figure stepped into the doorway.

Chapter 14

She thought her hands were one of her best qualities. Sure, they'd never make the cover of *Bridal* magazine. And the tiny scar under the second knuckle of her right-hand ring finger was a painful reminder of how jewelry and carpentry don't go well together. However, Tamra Lane was not about to give up carpentry.

She glanced at the man who stood opposite the checkout counter. They called him Clegg. She didn't know if that was his first or last name. He blew in from the rim every couple of months sporting a grizzled beard and a disposition as agreeable as spoiled milk. Without so much as a nod of acknowledgment, he set to removing his items from a handbasket and laying them on the counter.

Tamra took the first item, watching that pale scar on her finger pass over the scanner. Her grandmother always said that a good woman worked with her hands. Annie even had a Bible verse to back it up. Of course, Nams could find a Bible verse for just about anything. Working in a hardware store may not be the best way for a woman to use her hands, Tamra surmised, yet with the economy the way it was and a city the size of Endurance, she felt blessed to have a steady job at all. Besides, where else could she use her knowledge of lithium-ion tools and hexagonal screws?

Clegg squinted through limp, shaggy hair as she scanned his items. A dead bolt, three industrial-size padlocks, a small spool of 17-gauge electric fence wire, and rat poison.

She looked up at him.

"And two boxes of shotgun shells." His gaze flitted nervously about the store.

"Twelve-gauge?" This was not a question she would ask her typical customer. Many of the locals hunted fowl, 12-gauge being the standard. Clegg, however, sometimes specified slugs—thick lead weights. Tamra was unsure why someone would prefer slugs, unless they were hunting rhinos. And she wasn't ready to ask him to explain. Today he simply grunted.

"You holin' up for the Apocalypse?" Tamra retrieved two boxes of 12-gauge and set them on the counter.

"Worse." Clegg stopped fidgeting and peered at her. "Lots worse."

Tamra glanced over her shoulder at Matthew, who looked up from rearranging sale items long enough to roll his eyes.

Clegg lived in the foothills of the southern basin near Breen's llama ranch. He'd been a stable hand there until he accidentally burned down a barn while attempting to build his own Taser device. Shadowmen prowled the wasteland, he swore, and he was only trying to stop them. The incident got him fired and made Clegg the butt of jokes around town. "You goin' *Clegg* on us?" people would taunt. Now the man lived alone on his ramshackle ranch and had apparently surrendered to his eccentricities.

"You ain't noticed it, I take it." Clegg ran his tongue over yellowed teeth.

"Um..." She bagged the items. "Ain't noticed what?"

Clegg passed her a fifty-dollar bill and snatched the bag.

"Just ask that boss of yours." He jabbed his thumb toward the service counter. "Or what's left of him."

She handed Clegg his change, and he shambled out the front door of Farner's Hardware without the slightest salutation. The door shut, and the bell jangled behind him.

"And you have a nice day," Tamra said dryly.

"Don't take it personal, Tam." Matthew rose, brushing his hands off on his work apron. "Everyone isn't as nice as me."

"Or as conceited."

"Aw. You know you like it."

She removed her apron and stuffed it under the counter. "I'm taking lunch. Can you cover?"

"Absolutely. But only if you promise to meet me at the Brandin' Iron after hours."

"Um, 'fraid not."

"Then how 'bout Dean's?" he called after her. "We can share a buffalo burger."

This time she ignored him. Matthew's advances were innocent enough. However, she occasionally entertained playing the sexual-harassment card just to cool his jets. But Tamra Lane wasn't one to admit surrender easily.

She went to the service counter, where she logged on to the computer and googled a city map. Mr. Farner sat at his desk, leafing through paperwork. The owner was a perpetual number cruncher. And with sales in a slump, Tamra could only imagine the anxiety going on under that hairless scalp. She returned her gaze to the computer, zeroing in on the Vermont. Several small businesses still existed in that area of town—a pawn shop and a laundromat, but no bookstore. Maybe her grandmother was mistaken. Whatever the case, Tamra had a half-hour to find Zephaniah Walker and commission him to secure a copy of *Mystery Spots and Magic Landscapes*.

She retrieved her helmet and backpack from the break room, put her flannel on, buttoned it up, and prepared to exit out the back door.

Mr. Farner was watching her.

Jonas Farner was a family man, a community icon. A gentleman, by all accounts. He'd never done anything remotely inappropriate to Tamra. Nevertheless, as their eyes met, something did not register. It was not daydreaming she saw in his eyes; there was nothing blank about his stare. In fact, there was something opposite, something anxious, almost ravenous about the gaze. She squirmed, but he did not look away. Just as she prepared to say something, to ask him if everything was all right, Mr. Farner set down his papers and said, "Tamra, are you okay?"

"Me?" The question startled her. "I'm...yeah." She nodded haltingly.

Farner peered at her. "The way you were staring at me. It reminded me of...of..." He shook his head and returned to the paperwork. "Nothing. I'm sorry."

Tamra stood gaping. Then she said, "Mr. Farner? It reminded you of *what*?"

He stopped and looked up. However, now she detected a hint of defensiveness. "It's nothing. I apologize."

People are changing, Nams had said. *They're not themselves.*

"Okay," she drawled. "I'm, uh, taking lunch."

Jonas Farner issued a slight approving smile and returned to his work.

She puzzled over the exchange. Then Tamra exited the hardware store.

Her scooter was chained to the gas meter in the alley, and she unlocked it. The afternoon heat had been replaced by a chill. In the shadow of the Sierras, temperatures could plummet quickly. An arid, ninety-plus-degree day could reach the low forties quickly. Fingers of clouds burnished by the sunset traced the dusky sky, and on the breeze was more evidence of summer's demise. She spotted an evening star twinkling over a brooding granite peak.

As much as Tamra cherished the scenery and the slow-paced, small-town atmosphere, she couldn't help but wonder if she had missed something. Twenty-five years old, minimal education, living with her brother, and raising three dogs from the animal shelter while working in the local hardware store. It wasn't exactly the stuff of reality television. To top it off, she had no love interests. And living in Endurance, the prospects of change on any of those fronts seemed distant. When her best friend Junie came up from SoCal every summer, she'd casually refer to Endurance as "the city that time forgot" and chide Tamra about not doing something more with her life. Tamra always conceded a chuckle, but, down deep, she knew there was truth to Junie's observation.

However relevant Tamra's disappointments were, they had been eclipsed by something far more troubling.

The Madness of Endurance was the stuff of childhood, and, indeed, growing up as a child in these parts elevated the story to mythic proportions. Adults would mention the mass suicide with a whisper, while kids vowed to explore the dreaded site and threatened their enemies with an overnight stay. Somewhere along the way rose the legend of the ninth gate of hell. "If there are nine circles," Junie speculated, "Then there must be nine gates." While never giving credence to such fables, Tamra could not help but feel spooked by the legends.

She strapped her backpack with a bungee, started the scooter, and drove into the mouth of the alley. Then she flipped on her headlight and turned southbound on 395. She navigated into the slow side of traffic whenever possible. Locals were rarely in a hurry. Which is why the scooter suited her just fine. She could go almost a month on one tank of gas, except when the rodeo came to town and she worked a concession stand the entire week.

The fire station, a stucco structure with an old bell tower, marked the official outskirts of the city. The streets bore the names of early settlers, like Johansson and Ware, before changing to minerals. The Vermont was just past Ore on Pyrite, where she turned.

A long and narrow street straddled by a collection of ranch properties on one side and old commercial buildings on the other, Pyrite wound its way up into the distant foothills. Porch lights had come on, and the aromas of dinner crossed her path. Across the street stood a boarded TV repair shop, Miller's Pawn, and then the Vermont. However, there was no bookstore in sight. *Could Nams have been wrong?*

She puttered down the street, looking from side to side. About halfway down a Chihuahua rushed the fence near a wooden table of breads and jellies. Tamra instinctively swerved to avoid the animal, even though it had not escaped its yard. That's when she noticed the house next door. It was a plain white wooden structure with a long patio and a porch swing. A mid-sized truck with mud splashes and a roll bar was parked under the carport. Off to the side of the property sat a smaller house with a sign reading BOOK SWAP tilting above an open door.

She pulled to the opposite curb and sat there with her scooter idling.

A white picket fence and a quaint garden surrounded the building. A light glowed through a laced curtain. Her first reaction was one of nostalgia. Book Swap hearkened back to an age when schoolhouses were actual *houses* and neighborhoods were educational enclaves. Perhaps at one time Book Swap served as a neighborhood library. Which meant Zephaniah Walker was probably some type of oddball antiquarian. Her second thought was to wonder if a hole in the wall like this could possibly have an obscure book called *Mystery Spots and Magic Landscapes.*

Then again, perhaps this was the exact type of store to find it.

She turned off the scooter and pocketed the keys. Removing her helmet, she hung it on the handlebar, unzipped the side pouch on her backpack, and located the sticky note. Then she crossed the street to the front gate.

The Chihuahua next door snuffled about the fence line, attempting to intimidate in the way only a dog ten inches tall could. Tamra stood with her hand on the gate, studying the property. *Where exactly had Nams sent her?*

She pushed the gate open and ducked under the dried arbor. A dirt footpath branched toward Book Swap. She followed it, her gaze moving from the darkened house to the cottage. She passed through the gate of a white wooden fence. A breeze rattled the leaves overhead. The door creaked on its hinges.

Tamra approached the doorway as another gust of dry wind coughed behind her and the door yawned open. Someone inside gasped, and several books thudded to the ground behind the figure. A lanky man stood terrified.

And something was wrong with his face.

Chapter 15

Fergus slung the backpack over his shoulder and left by way of the Back Nine, purposely avoiding Easy Dolan's apartment along the way. Fergus climbed the concrete steps, pushed the door open, and slipped into the cool evening air.

A faint trail wound its way through the Yard, past rusty storage bins, grounds equipment, discarded gas engines, and a wood chipper. A tractor, which doubled as a snowplow during especially fierce winters, sat like a decrepit dinosaur guarding a large water tank. Two halogen lamps perched over a sagging rock wall buzzed to life in the dusk. Fergus dreaded the path ahead of him. Yet the touch of the cold steel pistol under his shirt temporarily bolstered his confidence.

Fergus hurried through the Yard, scanning the ground as he went. But there was no sign of the journal. He ducked under the heavy chain barrier and trudged upward along the trail. The smell of manure signaled his approach to the grounds shed. Several mounds of compost and bark lay moldering under tarps, and against a large corrugated structure leaned tillers and shovels. Fergus reached the tottering stone archway and hunched over, panting.

The oxygen was thinning. At this rate he would hyperventilate before he reached the Rift, but there was no time to waste. Night was setting, and the Shadowfolk would soon spring to life. Fergus resumed his torrid pace.

The wooden sign announced his entrance into Camp Poverty. It lay under a grove of twisted sycamores, an ancient rock structure entombed in sediment and overgrown nettle. Warnings of toxic chemicals and dangerous conditions peeked between scrub and composting leaves. He'd found Roth here once. Yet Fergus did not linger. Camp Poverty gave him the creeps.

The trail narrowed, congesting with brush, until he reached the chain-link fence that cordoned the property. Sweat dampened his cheeks and forehead. Overhead the mountain loomed, its soft, cool silence hovering like a ghostly shroud. Fergus unlocked the gate and hiked up the rocky berm until he reached the mule road.

This broad, flat road traced the foothills for miles. Down below, Marvale's roof peeked above the canopy of foliage, and its lights winked through the thickets. The soft chirring of insects was interrupted only by a jay skittering through a nearby pine. He studied the road for any evidence of the journal. Ahead, the trail disappeared in shadowy twilight. Occasionally Fergus would encounter a hiker or fly fisherman along the way. But the trail was empty.

Otta's Rift lay approximately two-thirds of a mile from this spot. Fergus began the trek. Folds of canyon came and went as he studied the road for any sign of the spellbook. As the gloaming thickened around him, faint stars appeared overhead. He had to hurry.

Soon he spotted the scraggly birch grove and the werevane that served as his trail marker. Fergus left the road at that point and picked his way upward through blighted birch, rabbitbrush, and boulders, trying to retrace his normal route. At the hill's crest the barbed-wire fence stretched, cordoning the canyon from intruders. A sign speckled with buckshot warned against trespassing. But there was no one here to enforce those restrictions.

Besides, Otta's Rift needed protection from no one.

He reached the crest of the hill and looked into the gorge. A scree slope, one hundred feet of shale and rock shard, descended before him. A trail had been beaten hard, forming a series of switchbacks. At its base lay a gray meadow surrounded by sparse copse and diseased trees, now in deep shadow. Thick wooden joists framed the mine entrance, its mouth blackened long ago by some hellacious blast. From here he could barely make out the symbol spray-painted across jagged rock. It was the number nine.

He wondered why they hadn't blown this place up long ago.

Fergus located the spot where the barbed wire lay in a tangled knot. As he stepped over it, something caught his pant leg, and he tumbled forward. Shale rattled down the scree slope. He sprung to his feet and yanked the pistol from his pants. There was nothing behind him. Of course. The Rift did that to people. It set them on edge. Made them crazy.

He must steel his mind against the tricksters. Surely they knew he was coming.

Fergus inched his way down the scree slope, gun in hand. A cloud of dust rose as he navigated the loose expanse of rock, the echo of which sounded in the narrow gorge. Finally he reached the trail and followed it to level ground. There was no evidence of the journal.

The mine entrance loomed like a black gouge in the granite face.

Fergus dabbed sweat from his forehead. He slipped off his backpack and removed the flashlight. Flicking it on, he aimed it at the mine entrance. This was where it happened—the Madness of Endurance. He stood for a moment, allowing the flashlight beam to meander along the parched earth. An entire town committed suicide on this spot, burned themselves to death. The stench from that inferno still lingered. He could only imagine the tortured souls that haunted this place. He shook himself, slipped the backpack on, and stepped toward the Rift.

A dead pine, its uppermost branches charred by lightning, overshadowed the entrance like an ancient, arthritic sentry. The rock face towered above him. Long ago a vertical split had marred its face. Farther down the wall water trickled into stagnant pools. He swept a cloud of mosquitoes from his face and stared back into the mine. Cool air lapped at his ankles like an invisible shoreline demarcating an underground ocean.

Did he dare enter?

A series of crude stepping-stones, interspersed with lichen and matted buckwheat, descended into the mine. Picking his way down these hewn steps, Fergus reached the bottom and stood at the mouth of Otta's Rift.

Wind wheezed through the gnarled tree branches above him. And that's when he heard it—a whisper, rising from the bowels of the cavern, followed by a fully formed word.

Fergie. Ferrgggiiieeee…

The blood curdled in his veins.

It's me, Fergie. Lemme oot.

The voice glided on the breeze like a raven's feather. Bringing back memories. And pain.

Plink.

She hung herself with an extension cord on the balcony, over-looking a white-capped sea.

Plink.

"Mum," Fergus whimpered. "That you?"

Chapter 16

Before he realized it, Fergus was in the mouth of the mine. Shale broke free, creating a mini-landslide at his feet. He steadied himself as the clatter of rock echoed in the shaft. Dust wafted up the tunnel as the breeze swept past, carrying the stench of mold and the distant squeal of bats.

Yet the voice of his mother was gone, replaced by the susurration of subterranean air. She had been dead over a decade. Despite all the tears, all the pleading, she hadn't crossed over. So why now?

The fetch were toying with him. He should have known.

Fergus shook himself from the illusion and aimed the flashlight into the descending dark. Remains of track and railroad ties shone beneath the loose rock. Graffiti marred the blackened walls with epithets and mysterious glyphs. Tentacles of roots curled claw-like from the cave roof, and broken glass glinted in charcoal mounds. There was no sign of the journal.

His nerves grated like a blade on whetstone.

Then he heard something down below. Carried on the breeze was a soft patter of water droplets and with it, a shuffling sound. His flesh prickled with fear.

"Mum?" He worked his sweaty fingers along the pistol grip. "That you?"

His words died on the dank air.

Fergus tilted his head, straining to hear. Someone was down there—he could feel them. His pulse surged in his temples. The fetch were near. He could not surrender to them—never again! Yet he had to investigate.

With the flashlight in one hand and the pistol in the other, Fergus inched forward. Between the loose rock and the pitch black, descending the shaft was slow going. At the fifty-foot mark, the shale gave way to solid earth. The mine narrowed, intersecting several smaller tunnels. Down these adjoining tunnels he once spotted frame heads and pulleys, indicating that vertical shafts had been bored. Who knew what riches the miners had chased down these rancid corridors? A low moan issued from unseen granite chimneys. With it came the shrill bickering of bats jockeying for roof space somewhere below, stirring in preparation for the evening's aeronautics. As Fergus descended, the portal of twilight closed behind him, and the claustrophobia settled in.

Short, rapid breaths. The darkness was closing in, the shadow of the rune hovering in his brain. *Breathe, Fergie!* In the Rift a person could easily lose control of his most basic functions. Once Pops soiled himself. But that was before they learned the secrets of the mine.

Fergus crept forward. The flashlight beam trembled across dead roots and moldy crevices. Seventy-five feet deep. Eighty. The tunnel narrowed, and he had to duck to keep from hitting his head. One hundred feet. The track was no longer visible. He was having a hard time breathing again. A werevane tinkled ahead, telling him he was almost there.

The shaft abruptly opened into a sunken chamber. It was here that the legends began.

Fergus stepped onto a granite balcony, a precipice overlooking the chamber, and stared into this ancient subterranean hollow.

Stray fingers of twilight descended from granite flumes, casting a grayish hue upon the chamber. It rose fifteen, maybe twenty feet in height. At its center, braced against the smooth rock face, stood a dolmen, a crude megalith comprised of two vertical granite slabs supporting a third. Moss clung to the dolmen, as did dark smatterings of dried blood. Between the megalithic arch, framed therein, an ink-black aperture pierced the rock wall. A fissure, perhaps the height of a man, radiating ineffable darkness.

This was the gateway, the window between worlds.

"Mum?" His voice died in the dead air. "You down there?"

Only the soft patter of water answered him.

Fergus laid the flashlight down, aiming its beam at a nearby hurricane lamp. Then he wriggled the backpack off and retrieved some matches. As he struck one to life, he paused. Wedged into a cleft sat a bundle of dynamite. Pops had put it there for safekeeping: enough explosives to take down half the mountainside. Fergus's fingers trembled as he held the flickering match. The fuse was dangerously close. He could put an end to it all. No more bad dreams. No more regrets. No more monsters in his brain. The match's orange glow seemed to stoke his death wish.

"Ghaww!" Fergus dropped the match, his fingers blistering in fiery pain.

Pay attention, Fergie!

He hurriedly lit the lantern, capped it, and snatched his pistol. Then he spun toward the chamber. The glow of the lantern revealed images on the walls, glimpses of lithe figures and gangly humanoid sketches. Petroglyphs from some bygone era.

A shuffle of movement.

Fergus forced a dry swallow and stretched the lantern forth.

"Mum! It's m–me. Fergie."

There was no response.

The lantern sent shadows pitching around the perimeter of the chamber, wild arcing shapes.

Another sound. This time a dry sloughing.

Fergus gasped.

Could it be? He crept forward and teetered on the rock mezzanine, his gun hand trembling almost uncontrollably. Fergus extended the lantern. Makeshift steps had been carved helter-skelter into the stone, a black antediluvian stairwell. At its base was the dolmen.

They said it was a sacred site, that the miners had awakened something ancient in the roots of the mountain. Pops said it possessed *properties*.

Water trickled along the jagged rocks forming a pool nearby. A frail, otherworldly luminescence emanated from the crystalline spring, splashing fractals of light about the chamber like lunatic shadow puppets. Before the pool a shadowy figure knelt, staring into the water. Its body was the color of midnight, and its contours roiled like thunderclouds. Frail wings draped its sides.

"Mum?" The word slipped past his lips.

The figure straightened. Its wings arched in defense.

Fergus sucked air through his teeth and aimed the pistol in the direction of the fetch. It turned—its motions fluid, inhuman; shadowy limbs unfolding and refolding into itself—and looked up at him. Its eyes were without pupils and glowed fiery amber. The face, however, was human. It was a face he had seen many times before.

A face with an ugly scar across its mouth.

The Indian called this person the Great Branded One. Fergus simply called him *Scarface*. Whatever his real name, Fergus realized that the Shadowfolk must want this man. They must *really* want him.

As Fergus stood overlooking this unholy sanctum, watching the harpy morph before the megalith, something else sounded. A raspy slithering, a hive of disquieting motion. It came from overhead. Fergus gritted his teeth and slowly raised the sputtering lamp.

The ceiling of the chamber was alive with movement: dark, inhuman forms, an underbelly of dark sinews, contorting in anguish.

The rocks were alive with fetch. Grappling, clinging, suctioned to the ancient stone.

Had he not been so overwhelmed, Fergus Coyne would have blown up the mine then and there. Instead, he shrieked, dropped the lantern, and fled Otta's Rift, realizing what they had only once feared—the gateway to hell was opening.

Chapter 17

The door did not swing properly on its hinges. Having spent one summer as a construction apprentice on some new tracts of homes, Tamra noticed those things. The average person took it for granted that when a door opened, it didn't drag and it stayed where you left it. However, the door in front of her—the solid core door with minor ornamental trim, drifting open on Book Swap—had several things going against it, the least of which was bloated wood due to being left unsealed. However, at the moment, this ill-hung door was not nearly as interesting as the guy fumbling behind it.

A faint yelp escaped her lips as she stumbled to a stop in the doorway. The two of them stood, squared off, staring at each other.

Several books lay toppled at the man's feet. A large watercolor of an elderly lady hung behind him, and stacks of books teetered against wooden cases nearby. The place was musty, and she wondered if it had a water leak somewhere. Yet her gaze did not leave the young man. A disfigurement marred one side of his face, and, despite her best effort, Tamra could not keep from staring.

"I'm sorry." She finally shook herself. "I–I'm here for a book."

He peered at her for a moment, and then said with an embarrassed chuckle, "A book. Of course."

She followed suit, and they both laughed, the nervous, polite kind of laughter that people use to disarm tension.

"I'm sorry if I scared you." Tamra let her gaze drift about the cluttered little cottage, looking for evidence of water stains or crumbling plaster. "The door was open, and I—"

"No. No problem. I was—" He rubbed his hands up and down the front of his thighs. "Cleaning up. I–I was just cleaning up." Then he began randomly straightening nearby books. Moving excitedly, awkwardly.

It gave her a moment to try to identify what was wrong with his face. He had a deformity or birthmark—she couldn't tell. And she dare not be caught staring. As he aimlessly rearranged books, he

75

glanced at her. She smiled and quickly looked away. He was probably used to people staring at him, and Tamra felt guilty for being just like everyone else.

After watching him fumble between crates of books, she cleared her throat to get his attention.

"I'm sorry." He rose, brushing off his hands. "You're looking for a book."

Another round of shared, nervous laughter.

"Actually," Tamra said, "I'm looking for Zephaniah."

The name seemed to stun him.

A moment of clumsy silence passed. Then his face flushed, and his surprise gave way to annoyance. "Zeph," he said flatly. "It's Zeph."

That's when she saw it clearly—it was a scar that stretched from his left nostril to his right chin, a pale furrow that left his lips cloven at the intersection, revealing a moist glint of teeth.

She quickly returned her gaze to his eyes. Yet it was too late—he knew she was staring at him.

His defensiveness withered, and he looked away with his shoulders slumped.

She peered at him. "So are you..."

He nodded. "I'm sorry. No one calls me that. I just...I haven't heard that name in a while. Yeah." He straightened and composed himself. "I'm Zeph. Zeph Walker."

He extended his hand and offered a shy, apologetic smile.

She wanted to ask him why the name evoked such a hostile reaction. It was different, that was obvious. But not to the point of embarrassment. Instead Tamra stepped across the threshold and shook his hand, fighting to keep from letting her eyes wander to the ugly scar.

"So, uh..." He stepped back and scratched behind his neck. "Did someone send you?"

"It was my grandmother. She told me to come here."

"Your grandmother?"

"Annie Lane. She said I should talk to Zepha—I mean, talk to you." She cast an embarrassed smile.

"Annie Lane?" His eyes drifted in thought. "I don't think I know her."

"Well, apparently she knows you. She lives up at Marvale."

"The retirement complex?"

"Yeah." Tamra nodded. "She's been up there a coupla years. Quite the lady, trust me. She's lived around here all her life. And you?"

He nodded, but his gaze had grown distant.

Tamra shifted her weight. "I didn't even know this place was here. I usually go over to Spellbinder's."

"Most everyone does. But as you can see, this is no Spellbinder's. Heck, it's not really even a bookstore. More like a repository. Came with the place when I bought it. I've just kept the dream alive, I guess. Got a few loyal customers and, being that reading is such a dying art, I figured keeping the place open might earn me some humanitarian points."

"I could use some of those myself."

"Kinda runs on its own. The motto's simple." He pointed to a whiteboard and read the phrase written there. "Leave One. Take One. That's it. No money's exchanged. No orders placed. It's low maintenance. Runs on the good ol' honor system."

"Cool."

"Oops! I'm sorry." He pivoted out of the doorway and motioned for her to enter. "You wanted a book."

"Yeah." Tamra extended the sticky note. "Kind of an oddball title. But that's my grandmother."

Zeph took the note and looked at it.

She studied him as he did. He had a nervous way, she thought, like a dog who'd been kicked one too many times. She could tell he spent time in the sun, and even though his frame was lean, his upper body seemed sturdy. His features were rugged, intense, and if not for the ugly scar, he would be a handsome guy. She found herself wondering how it happened and what type of trauma and esteem issues Zeph Walker had endured. As usual, the urge to "fix" things stirred inside Tamra. Nams called her a "fixer," using the term derogatorily. And as Tamra had learned, fixing *things* was a lot easier than fixing *people*. She needed only look at her parents for confirmation.

Zeph stared at the note as if it contained a secret message. Finally he said, "*Mystery Spots and Magic Landscapes.*" His words seemed eerily detached.

"Kinda weird, huh?"

His lips parted, eyes passing through various shades of emotion. Then he slumped forward, as if he'd been punched in the stomach.

For a moment Tamra thought something might be wrong and instinctively reached to steady him. As she did, he looked up. The sinews in his neck were taut. A shadow had passed over his face.

"Look." He handed the note back to her. "I can't help you."

"Huh?"

"I said I can't help you."

Tamra took the note. "But my grandma—"

"Tell your grandmother it's over!" He curled his fists into balls, the veins in his neck straining.

She flinched at the rage in his tone and stepped back into the doorway.

But something else happened when he spoke, something she could not put a finger on. The air seemed to tingle, awaken with a static charge, as if his words had flipped a molecular switch that left the atmosphere thrumming. Had she not been so startled by his reaction, Tamra would have pulled back her flannel to see if the hairs on her arm were standing up.

He looked to the ground, shamed. Then he mumbled, "It's over, okay?"

Then Zeph returned to one of the nearby crates and sifted through its contents.

The bristling in the air had vanished—a figment of her imagination perhaps. She gaped at him and what had just transpired. After a moment, she shrugged. "Okay, then I guess it's...over."

She looked at him again. When he did not return the gesture, she turned to leave.

"When I was born," Zeph said, "my mother said I cried so loud I almost sent the doctor into cardiac arrest."

He was standing now, eyes unfocused, a nostalgic detachment glazing his features.

"She said my voice nearly blew a fuse in the house, almost short-circuited the entire block. That's when she knew I was *called*."

Tamra peered at Zeph Walker.

"Look." He seemed to return to earth. "I'm sorry. Really, I am. She means well—I'm sure she means well. Just go back and tell your grandmother I'm done with all that. It's over. It's past tense. Zephaniah Walker is dead. Tell her that. Tell her he's dead."

She looked at him a long time. Perhaps some people couldn't be fixed. Or rather, maybe they chose to stay broken. She wondered if Zeph Walker was one of those people. *The chosen broken.*

"All right." Tamra yielded. "I'll tell her."

He nodded.

As she turned to leave, Tamra added, "I work at Farner's. The hardware store. Swing shift. If you happen to find that book—or just get a hankerin' to intervene and help a seventy-two-year-old widow with two grandchildren and a really big heart—you can call me there. Or come by."

He remained stoic. Then a coy grin slowly crept across his face. "Okay," he conceded. "If I get a hankerin'."

"By the way, I'm Tamra. Tamra Lane. And I'm sorry for scaring you."

He issued a soft snort of laughter. "You didn't scare me, Tamra."

She left Book Swap with more questions than when she'd arrived. How did Nams know about Zeph Walker? How did he get that scar? And why did the mention of that book upset him so? Whatever the answers, Tamra could not help but feel that something much bigger than she could imagine was unfolding around her.

She closed the gate behind her. Dusk had drawn its dark lines around the alleys and trees. Tamra straddled her scooter and prepared to put her helmet on. That's when she noticed Zeph Walker was braced in the doorway, thumping his forehead with the heel of his hand.

She peered at him a moment, wondering what he was doing. Nams had said he was different. But as she drove back to work, Tamra found herself wondering if Zeph Walker's difference was more than skin deep.

Chapter 18

You will be a remnant. You will stand in the gap.

At the time Annie had no idea what those words meant. But for the last fifteen years they had sustained her. And now, both the *remnant* and the *gap* were becoming clearer.

Through the curtains of her bedroom window a wedge of sapphire revealed twilight's descent. Despite her granddaughter's concerns, Annie could not stop now, not when she was getting so close.

Especially after this new piece of evidence.

She reached under the mattress of her bed and produced the documents she had found earlier. The leather cover was warped and scarred. Annie released the braided strap, and the journal opened, swollen by its strange contents. She began leafing through the arcane volume and its documents, a mismatched collection of material: grainy photocopies, anatomical sketches, and medical examinations of someone named "Subject X." Diagrams and terms raced by her—*Planetary grids. Temporoparietal junctions. Catatonic schizophrenia*—jargon far beyond her understanding. Interspersed were sheets crammed with words in code-like facsimile.

Annie lifted a mimeographed page that bore a United States military seal. What in the world? She studied this page, wondering over its authenticity. This was more than just the personal diary of some senior citizen. But what was it? And what was it doing in a retirement home on the southeastern slopes of the Sierras?

The sketch of the multiheaded avian peeked from between the pages. Annie slipped the picture out and studied it, searching her mind for recollection. Where had she seen this before? Bat-like wings trailed behind a human torso, its four faces and angry black eyes unsettling. That's when it struck her.

She rose from the bed, went to her bookshelf, and removed a massive clothbound volume with cracked spine and fragile yellowed pages. This particular version of the *Enciclopedia de ángeles* had been translated into English. Tamra had tracked down the encyclopedia of angels for Annie, buying it online from a quirky New York book warehouse.

One could not read the Bible without encountering angels. Stories about angelic messengers, angelic warriors, and guardians of God's children filled Scripture. The heavenly beings had always seemed to retain their cultural mystique. However, Annie found Hollywood's fluffy portrayals of the mighty messengers hard to stomach. Likewise, much of the information in this volume veered into occult arcana and superstitious mumbo-jumbo. For this reason she always approached her study of angels with a degree of skepticism.

She sat on the edge of the bed and plunked the encyclopedia down next to the manuscripts. Opening the book, Annie coughed at the fog of dust and began turning the pages, trying to find the picture that had impregnated her mind. Past *archangels*, *baals*, and *celestial hierarchies* she went. Until her eyes widened. Staring at her was the image she had remembered: a crude picture of an angel with four faces.

Cherubs. One of the most powerful of heaven's angels, hybrid winged creatures with the face of a man, an ox, a lion, and an eagle. Annie lifted the sketch and held it beside the book. It was like looking at a negative. The sketch in this journal was a rendition of a biblical cherub. There was no mistaking it. Only this version was much darker. The foul, bat-winged, multiheaded cherub chilled her deep inside. She set the picture aside, almost out of necessity.

Amid the documents spread atop her comforter she spotted what looked like a blueprint. Its edges were brittle, and she unfolded it with care. It was dated 1928, and she quickly realized it was a topographical rendering of the Marvale property, well before the construction of the retirement facility. Several abandoned mines dotted the foothills, as did the Granite Bar aquifers. She located Servile Gulch as it wound into the foothills and intersected the old mule road, and then Quartz Creek, following the blueprint until she located Camp Poverty.

The ruins on the property's west end had supposedly been used by miners in the late 1800s as a camp, long before Silverton's inception. While the structure had been of some historical significance, it was not maintained, fell into disrepair, and eventually was barricaded when the Marvale facility was built. Now the rock and cement building was just a home to rodents and dusty memories. Symbols and notations had been scrawled on these blueprints, delineating particular areas in and around Camp Poverty.

Yet it was not the blueprint of these ruins that intrigued Annie most. It was what was underneath them.

A series of vaults and subbasements appeared on the map, branching into long perpendicular shafts before dead-ending in the distant foothills. She had been a Marvale resident for well on two years and had only heard rumors about such a subterranean complex. Of course, residents rarely went that far into the foothills. Camp Poverty was nearly a half-mile hike uphill. It was scenic but far too wild. Besides, Endurance started as a mining town. There were probably many unknown tunnels beneath the city. Still, she couldn't help but wonder if the military had actually been interested in the site. And with all that was going on in Marvale, her acquisition of these documents did not seem like a coincidence.

It made her decision easier.

She folded the blueprint, bound everything in the journal, and returned it to its spot under her mattress.

Sliding open the top drawer of the nightstand, she removed the Velcro cuff, then the mini-Maglite and her Swiss Army knife. Even though Tamra disapproved of Annie's sleuthing, her granddaughter had unwittingly become a great resource for gadgets. Annie lifted the hem of her skirt, a mid-length canvas La Rambla, and clasped the cuff to her thigh.

She had acquired the spelunker's cuff from Easy Dolan. The Velcro armlet was designed to hold tools for cavers, a hobby that Easy had undertaken in his youth, along with other exotic hobbies. Being that the sport required grappling, crawling, contorting, and the negotiation of precarious pitches, the cuff allowed the spelunker to do his thing hands-free and still have the necessary tools accessible in a pinch. While not nearly as strenuous as spelunking, Annie thought the device would come in handy for her own endeavors. With a little tweaking, she'd managed to make it fit her right thigh. Now, instead of a pickaxe or spike, it carried a pen light, a stainless steel multipurpose tool, and a blank sleeve for emergency purposes.

Miss Marple would have been impressed.

Annie quickly inserted the Maglight and the Swiss Army knife and let the skirt fall back into place. She went to the coat rack near the door and slipped into her favorite sweater.

Before she began stirring up any more commotion, Annie needed proof. And now she sensed she could get it.

As she stepped into the hallway, the aroma of cooked meats and vegetables confirmed that dinnertime was upon them. Perfect time for a little jaunt. The television blared from inside Vera's apartment. Perhaps the woman was going deaf along with whatever other changes she was undergoing. Annie glanced at Eugenia's door, but there was no evidence that her once best friend had recently come or gone. She hurried down the hall toward the Back Nine and the northern courtyard.

She passed Easy Dolan's apartment, reached the end of the hall, and stopped. Annie turned her gaze to the spot where she'd found the journal.

"Miss Lane?"

Annie jumped and banged her elbow against the wall. She spun around to see the director padding toward her from the opposite hallway.

"Miss Marshman." Annie massaged her smarting elbow.

Janice Marshman advanced. Her perfect posture and methodical movements gave her all the allure of a black widow. The silken red hair and thick eyelashes didn't hurt. She unnerved Annie. If the *Stepford Wives* ever needed a new model, the director of Marvale Manor could be Robot-in-Chief.

"An evening stroll?" The director's lips slightly curled at one edge—her signature smile. "A fine night for it."

"Yes." Annie adjusted her sweater, acutely aware of the tools underneath her skirt. "It is a fine night."

"Winter's coming early." The director cast a slow, drawn look at her, lashes glinting like flytrap pincers.

"Oh?"

"There's a chill in the air."

Annie shifted her weight. Miss Marshman had always been a cool one, hard to read. Efficient to the point of calculation, like a surgeon deciding where to make her first incision. Yet what the director knew about the strange happenings at Marvale remained a mystery.

As Annie debated broaching the subject, the director said, "Coyne—you haven't seen him, have you?"

"Fergus?" Annie could not conceal her surprise. She thought about the strange documents wedged underneath her mattress and whether or not Fergus Coyne had any connection. "I saw him earlier this afternoon. But..." She shrugged.

The director's gaze lingered. "Well, then. I'll keep looking. If you happen to see him, let him know he is wanted. Enjoy your walk, Miss Lane."

The director resumed her slow, catty gait. But this time she walked into the custodial area and began to descend the steps to the boiler room.

The tension left Annie's body, and she slumped forward. Only then did she realize how terrified she was of the woman. *You can't find the truth*, she'd boldly proclaimed to Tamra, *without risking something*. And here she was, as frightened as a jackrabbit.

Besides, what was the director doing down in the boiler room?

Annie cleared her throat and, before she realized what she was doing, called, "Miss Marshman?"

The director stopped at the third step and looked up. "Yes?"

Suddenly Annie found herself without words.

"I, uh..." Annie forced down a raspy swallow. She thought about Camp Poverty and the aged blueprints, about Eugenia's eerie transformation, and about Vera's son standing pale in the hallway. But all she managed was, "Is, um...everything all right here?"

The director tilted her head. Then she climbed the steps and walked back toward Annie, her black loafers whispering across the floor.

The director stopped directly in front of her. "You have questions."

Yes. Annie stared into those big gray eyes and flytrap lashes. *A lot of questions*.

"I am well aware of the state of this facility, Miss Lane." The director casually folded her hands at her waist. "And the sentiments of Marvale's employees. However, my primary concern is not to endear myself to those I superintend, but to ensure that the workings of this establishment aspire to our stated values."

Annie nodded dumbly.

"Whatever questions you have about the state of this facility," the director continued, "or whatever you may or may not have overheard from others about myself, I assure you I am here to provide our residents with the best of retirement living. Please know that whatever the—" Her eyes disengaged for a brief second. "—whatever *circumstances* may currently present themselves, I am privy to them and will dispatch of them to the best of my ability. So, to answer your question, no. Everything is *not* all right. It never is. Which is why I am here." Then she smiled again and issued a curt nod. "Do enjoy your walk. And...don't go very far."

Annie stood speechless. She watched the director glide away, down the stairs into the boiler room, in search of Fergus Coyne and whatever other circumstances might present themselves.

Chapter 19

While her demeanor would not win her a Miss Congeniality nomination, Annie had to admit that Janice Marshman ran a tight ship. The boiler room door thudded below as the director continued her endless inspection. But what did she know about the bizarre goings on?

Annie hurried down the hall into the north courtyard. She stood on the patio terrace, staring into the mountains. Fog coiled in the ravines, and squirrels tittered in a nearby pine. The vapor lamps were already on, casting a soft yellow hue across the rock pathway. Camp Poverty was not far. At least not by Annie's standards.

Her granddaughter was going to kill her, but Annie had to stay true to the remnant.

Passing through the courtyard, she turned westward and climbed away from the property. She passed a picnic area with tables and a gazebo into an unkempt terrace with a dried fountain before reaching a long rock wall. She was sweating now and bent forward with her hands on her knees to keep from hyperventilating. Either she was getting older or the altitude had thinned.

The grounds shed lay to her left, greeting her with the smell of manure. A sign warned of rugged conditions ahead. Yet Annie Lane had spent her whole life dealing with rugged conditions. She looked down the trail behind her. It disappeared in misty shadow. The chances of anyone following her this far were improbable. However, that thought was not comforting. If something devious was occurring in Marvale, being out here on her own was not exactly in the realm of genius.

As she prepared to continue her hike, someone emerged from behind the shed. Their eyes met simultaneously, and they both lurched to a standstill.

"Stevie!" she gasped, clutching her chest. "You scared me."

Stevie Veigh, the groundskeeper, stood holding a shovel, one half of his overalls unlatched, revealing a dirty T-shirt underneath.

Beneath a thinning mat of hair Stevie's forehead sparkled with sweat. He stared at her, as if trying to make her appearance register. Then he muttered something apologetic in his nasally voice and leaned the shovel against the shed. The man had a cleft palate and seldom spoke because of it. He seemed to genuinely love being out in the woods and working with the earth. And he was good at what he did. But Stevie was a loner, and everyone knew that. He turned, brushed his hands on his overalls, and wandered back around the shed.

Annie contemplated the encounter for a moment. She had no reason to fear Stevie Veigh, nor was it that unusual for him to be out here. Her being out here was another story.

Brushing aside concerns, Annie trudged upward. From what she understood, this trail meandered through the scrub to the edge of the property, where it met the old mule road. Like most residents she had never been this far. She crossed a wooden bridge beneath which Quartz Creek passed. Some fifty feet ahead she spotted a bundle of rusted wire and barrels stacked near a shed. A breeze swirled brittle leaves past the stone pathway. She hugged the sweater about her neck. The path was becoming less visible, and she debated producing her flashlight. Yet she did not want to be seen. So Annie continued forward, peering into the growing dark.

Just ahead she could make out the stone archway. She trekked under it and spotted a rock chimney amidst huge rambling sycamore branches and a stone wall, half buried, with rusty wrought iron bars over a frosted window. The Camp Poverty ruins. Signs posted reading KEEP OUT rattled in the breeze. Behind her the final vapor lamp glowed like a ghostly orb in the distance.

She did not think she could go much farther. The old ruins hardly evoked a sense of relief.

Annie slogged along the trail until she reached a gated gravel road. At its base lay Camp Poverty. The incline was steep, interlaced with roots and water-torn crevices. Annie wiped sweat from her brow. *Was she really up to this?* She could break an ankle making the descent, and in the dark the chances of that happening were multiplied. Tamra always said Annie was too impulsive. And standing there on a dirt trail under the shadow of the Sierras, all alone, she couldn't help but think her granddaughter was right.

All that crazy stuff about military experiments and sketches of demented cherubim returned to mind. Perhaps she should just turn the journal over to officials. But why? She possessed no evidence of wrongdoing by anyone. And if people were changing, whatever the cause might be, bringing more of them into the picture would be the last thing to do. She peered at the shadowy ruins, deliberating.

Finally Annie lifted up her skirt, retrieved the flashlight, and turned it on.

Camp Poverty sat in a geological horseshoe, a natural amphitheater hewed by wind and water. She allowed the beam to wander through this eerie hollow. The structure was made of crude stone and mortar and appeared to be nothing more than a large box embedded in the earth. A door sat below ground level in deep shadow.

As she let the flashlight beam wander about the mysterious structure, she noticed a fresh rut at the base of the gate—and footprints, coming and going.

A jay whipped through the trees overhead, sending pine needles showering. She lurched at the sound, dropped the flashlight, and it spiraled down the gravel road until it came to rest at the base of the rock wall.

Then she heard footsteps—heavy footsteps—barreling down the path toward her.

Annie instinctively spun toward Marvale. She would never make it there in time. Perhaps Stevie was still at the shed. She could cry out for his attention. Whoever was approaching was coming fast. She had to hide. If she was caught out here, at this time, there was no telling what might ensue. The flashlight lay below, casting a long yellow beam across the gnarly terrain.

She had no other choice.

Annie forced the gate open. She squeezed through and inched her way down the steep incline. Before she knew it, she was skidding. Flailing at the air, her foot caught something, and she tumbled forward. Her hands broke the fall but could not prevent her from doing a somersault. Fabric ripped and rocks tumbled as she thudded against the base of the wall.

She bit back a yelp. Pain seared Annie's lower back, but she didn't have time to waste. Scrambling to her feet, she stared up at the trail from which she'd fallen. Twilight sky shone through the canopy of trees. She listened. Not only were the footsteps approaching, but a voice now accompanied them.

She grabbed the flashlight, wincing as she rose, and switched it off. Annie stared breathlessly into the dark. Branches crackled as the figure approached. Standing there with only a Swiss Army knife and a flashlight hardly bolstered her confidence. She glanced behind her at the darkened ruins.

Annie heaved herself up on the rock wall, banging her shin in the process, and slung her leg over the other side. She did not have time to negotiate a soft landing or calculate the distance of her fall. Luckily it was minimal. She dropped to the other side, nearly screaming in pain as she did.

Annie pressed her back against the cold stone wall, fighting to contain her breathing. The blackness enclosed her. She listened. Crunching gravel sounded on the trail above her, as did a voice wrought with frenzy.

"—quit before they eat ya!" It was a man's voice. "—I told ya, didn't I?"

The voice sounded familiar, and she strained to identify it.

The footsteps slowed then grew silent.

The chirring of crickets filled the quiet.

Annie cupped her hand over her mouth to muffle her panting. An owl hooted somewhere nearby, and the glade seemed to come alive with insect chatter. Had the person left? If not, what was he doing up there?

She sat listening for a moment, but there was no evidence of the stranger.

Annie stood and slowly peeked over the wall.

On the trail directly above her, glistening with sweat, a man stood staring into the foothills.

She dared not move. Who was this person? Where had he come from? And what was he doing out here?

Annie's pulse thundered through her body. She was sure the man was aware of her, would turn and see her petrified in the dark. Instead he muttered something and plunged back down the trail toward Marvale. As he went, the glow of the vapor lamp revealed the unshaven jaw and untrimmed hair. It was Fergus Coyne.

Annie remained there in Camp Poverty, listening to Fergus's angry conversation fade into the lull of the foothills. Her shin throbbed, and the pain in her lower back lanced along her side. The chill crept in, and she tightened her sweater around her shoulders.

She sat for a time in that dark wilderness place. Praying, thinking about the immensity of it all. Finally she turned the flashlight on and aimed it at the ruined structure. Camp Poverty. What had gone on in this ancient quarry? What secrets lay beneath the moldering earth? The door's dull metal had been battered from the inside, and its surface was splattered with brownish liquid. Hanging from the drawn bolt was a shiny padlock, looking very new.

Suddenly, two fiery yellow eyes glinted in the beam.

Annie gasped and pinned herself against the rock wall.

A cat bolted from the shadows, followed by several others. It was Easy's cat, Jezebel. The felines leapt into the night, mewling out their lonely complaints.

She switched the flashlight off and remained in the dark, listening to the whistle of the breeze through the pines. Feeling the thrum of her heart.

The shadow had returned to Endurance. Something evil was afoot. She was sure of it. All her preparation, all the waiting, had brought her to this moment. Now their only hope was for the prophet to rise again.

But if their hopes were tied to young Zephaniah Walker, then they were in great danger.

Chapter 20

Her eyes were the color of autumn, with freckles to match.

Stop it, you idiot!

Zeph snapped the sheets back, slung his legs over the bed, and ran his fingers through his hair. He would never sleep; in fact, he wondered if his world would ever be the same. The girl had brought something more with her than just a cute tomboy swagger. Tamra Lane had delivered the one thing he most dreaded.

He switched on the lamp next to his bed, and his thoughts went to the girl's note: *Mystery Spots and Magic Landscapes.* He'd rehearsed that title in his head a thousand times over. There was no denying it—the insanity was beginning again. What a fool to think he could run from it. Even Robinson Crusoe was found out.

The shade on his bedroom window flapped, drawing his attention. In the distance a dog barked. Zeph listened. Normally he found solace in the night sounds, deriving strange comfort from the midnight hours. People recovered strength now, prepared to meet the waking world. However, Zeph liked the night because he could be alone; the prying eyes, the whispers, the taunts were all retired. Tonight the barking dog tugged at the tethers of his rational mind.

Something was happening in his world, a string of events far beyond his comprehension. In the morgue lay something of another order, a second self. *A darker self.* Where it had come from, he couldn't say. What it wanted, he didn't know. If that weren't enough, along with the eerie duplicate came a message. And now a messenger.

He left his bedroom, followed the hall into the kitchen, and went to the back door. It was not locked. Zeph never locked it. Psychopaths and thieves were big city problems. Here in Endurance people slept with their doors open and talked to strangers. There was no reason to wonder what went on next door. But after today Endurance seemed...*different.* And the unlocked back door seemed unnervingly inviting.

He opened the door and peered through the screen. The barking

91

had stopped, replaced by the throaty croaking of toads. The land lay still. He pushed the screen open and stood in the doorway, looking out.

His property stretched toward the foothills. It was more than enough for his needs. The faint cadence of Carson Creek lapped at the evening's stillness. Just past the copse of trees, the mountains rose black, speckled with lights from ranches and homes.

He turned on the light and stepped softly onto the porch. Its wooden planks creaked under his weight. The empty easel sat nearby, and next to it, a rocking chair. This was his favorite spot for painting. For reading. For pondering the shambles of his existence.

Zeph descended the porch steps.

The house sat on a raised foundation. Below the back porch was a screened-in access panel, which Zeph went to and unlocked. Removing the screen, he got on his hands and knees and peered into the pitch black of the crawlspace.

It was there, just as he'd left it.

He sat on his haunches, breathing the cool night air.

You can't hide forever, Mila had said.

Zeph drew a deep breath, reached under the porch, and dragged out the wooden crate. It contained a jewelry box, several letters, a monogrammed Bible, and other assorted items, each one evoking a different memory. He'd never had the guts to throw them away. Stashing them underneath the house seemed like the next best option.

Brushing aside cobwebs and insect husks, he removed a framed picture and wiped the glassy surface. Angling it toward the porch light, Zeph stared at the image of him and his mother. She wore her long-sleeved church dress, cheeks blushed and rosy, eyes as deep as water wells. Her hand rested on young Zephaniah's shoulder. He was in his suit, hair slicked into a pristine wave, his face as fair and unblemished as an infant's. With one hand the young boy gripped the Bible, and with the other he pointed toward the camera in judgmental fervor, a pubescent Billy Graham.

They had called young Zephaniah Walker *the Prophet of the Plains*.

He stared numbly at the picture. At one time, it would have produced rage inside him. Now he wondered where that innocent little boy had gone.

Returning the picture to the crate, he rummaged through the

contents until he found the object he sought. Zeph removed it and brushed the dust off. He held the book out, and its gilded title glistened in the light.

Mystery Spots and Magic Landscapes.

It was a testament to his conflict that he kept this junk. He should have burned it long ago.

A distant keening rose. Zeph straightened, and goose bumps rippled across his forearms. He'd spent plenty of time on the back porch listening, drawing peace from the stillness of nature. He knew the sounds of the coyote, the black bear, and the marmot. This eerie wail was none of those. Zeph gazed into the pitch-black foothills. Again the cry sounded, shrill and inhuman. A bark that morphed into a lonesome bay.

Something was happening. No amount of denial or deliberation could change that fact. Something dark sought him, stood between him and the land.

The Telling never lied.

There was only one way to put an end to it. And whoever Annie Lane was, she was not going to like it.

Chapter 21

Annie stumbled into her apartment, locked the door, and leaned against it. Her shin drooled blood and her back ached. Perhaps she needed to rethink her theory about finding the truth and taking risks.

"You should lock your door."

Annie gasped.

A figure leaning near the dinette table said, "In times like these we can never be too cautious." Then the figure crossed into the living room area, went to the end table near the rocker, and picked up Annie's Bible.

"I was in a hurry," Annie said, the tension leaving her body. "But you're right—I have been careless."

A studded belt sparkled between the girl's black leather jacket. A bleach streak partitioned one side of her hair, which she brushed aside as she leafed through the old Bible.

"Sultana!" Annie studied the girl. "You've grown up."

Sultana glanced at Annie and offered a slight smile. "I keep hearing that."

"Are you and Earl still in the Pass?"

"He's never leaving that place, you know that. It's his mission in life to preserve the prophecy." She closed the Bible. "Besides, he likes the tourists."

Annie limped to the dining table and plopped into the chair with a hiss. She'd probably have a bruise the size of Texas on her rear end.

"You hurt yourself." Sultana's eyes were creased with concern.

"Nothing fatal." Annie took a napkin from the table and dabbed at her shin. "Although I'll probably get another lecture from my granddaughter."

Sultana chuckled. "That's what Earl always liked about you—you were a tough one."

"Wasn't always," Annie said, "but I'm getting there."

Sultana ambled across the carpet and stood before the faded

color picture of Annie and Harold, her deceased husband. "Earl said things are in motion—however he does that."

"I've sensed it as well."

Sultana traced her thin finger along the picture's wooden frame. She looked over her shoulder. "He said the Rift's active again. That the remnant's been warned."

Annie nodded grimly.

"You've sent for the prophet, then?"

"Yes," Annie said. "Whether or not he will come is another story."

Sultana moved away from the picture. "I was—what?—nine, ten years old when you sent me to him. He was pretty surprised. I guess anyone would be. Kid shows up on their porch with a book, who wouldn't be skeptical? I remember he asked a lot of questions. I told him, 'Just keep it safe. Whenever someone returns for it, you'll know it's your time.' I left him on the front porch with his mouth open. So, do you think he kept the book?"

"I don't know." Annie stopped swabbing at the wound and set the bloody napkin on the table. She removed the Velcro cuff from her thigh and brushed her skirt back into place. "My granddaughter went there today. I'm assuming that she delivered the message. Now it's a waiting game. We can only pray he hasn't surrendered."

Sultana approached and stood near Annie. Though her skin was fair and youthful, Sultana's eyes bore the look of one who'd seen great suffering.

"There's someone else," Sultana said. "I can't say he's one of us, really. Earl said he's part of *another tribe*, whatever that means. Little Weaver's his name. He's not very little, though. Been up to Meridian a couple times. He knows about the Rift, lots more than Earl ever knew."

"And these changes—whatever is happening to people—this Little Weaver knows what it is?"

"Earl and him don't see eye to eye on it. But they both agree—it has to be stopped. He's had an eye on the prophet, just like us. Been watchin' him for quite a while, I guess. Longer than we've been around. Funny how these things work, huh?"

"Yes."

"And the prophet," Sultana said. "What kind of move do you think he'll make?"

"If I had to take a guess—he's hoping for a stalemate."

Sultana seemed to ponder Annie's words. Then she said, "Either way, Earl sent me to tell you the remnant's ready."

Annie smiled weakly. "Let's hope that the prophet is."

PART TWO

THE PROPHECY

This is he, and he speaks not.
This one, being banished, every doubt submerged.
—Dante's *Inferno*

What you call riddles are truths, and seem
riddles because you are not true.
—*Lilith*, George Macdonald

He woke with Austin Pratt on his mind. It was not the first time Zeph's childhood friend had tormented his dreams. Tamra Lane's visit last night had sent him into this nostalgic tailspin. Ozzy, as they had affectionately called him, was a small boy beset with numerous physical maladies. A musical prodigy, Ozzy manned the piano during school plays, occasionally interspersing rockabilly riffs with the children's choruses just to anger Miss White, the cranky schoolmarm. His feet were clubbed, which consigned him to leg braces during school, but it never seemed to hinder his stints at the piano. Schoolmates were unusually accepting of Austin Pratt. He was the kind of underdog most folks rooted for rather than picked on. Zeph and Ozzy had been best friends, which made his memory so heartbreaking.

Austin Pratt was the first recorded instance of child abuse in Endurance. Even more haunting was the grim, persistent reminder that Zeph Walker could have stopped the boy's murder.

Zeph washed his hands at the kitchen sink. The dust from chicken feed had a way of mucking up the drain, so he made sure to run the water a little longer. As he dried his hands, he glanced at the book on the kitchen table.

Mystery Spots and Magic Landscapes.

He'd never forgotten about that book. How could he? Ever since that kid showed up, out of the blue, entrusting him with that quirky volume, Zeph knew he was a marked man. He knew someone was watching him closely. Whoever these people were—these *believers*—they just could not seem to let the Prophet of the Plains go. They always wanted another word, another miracle. All he wanted was to slink into obscurity.

For the last eight years the book had lain under the house like a carcass, decaying alongside Zeph's calling. However, after the man at the morgue and Tamra Lane's inquiry, he could not pretend this was going away. He had to confront these wackos, put an end to their obsession.

Perhaps that would also lay his darker self—whatever that was— to rest.

So that morning Zeph Walker did something different. He did not buy a hot, sticky cinnamon roll from Mila Rios. Of course, she would notice. Creatures of habit make themselves conspicuous by their absence. Instead he slung his corduroy jacket over his shoulder, grabbed the book, and, for the first time in years, locked the front and back doors as he left.

There was a subtle change in the air, the deep chill at the onset of a hard winter. Geese were honking, skating over the foothills like a pearly banner, and the smell of tilled earth was in full bloom. Mila had not yet assembled her cactus jelly and pastries on the stand out front. The house was strangely vacant of the clanging of tins and baking sheets. She'd probably raced out on a sugar or cinnamon run, which would make his escape easier.

Zeph peered down the street to the Vermont. What connection did the old theater have to the body, if any? And why would someone have shot his dead ringer? Despite his determination to rid himself of the stigma of his prophetic past, he feared what he might find if he probed too deeply. But hiding hadn't solved anything.

Someone had changed the marquee overnight. Today's word for the day read: NOTHING IN THE WORLD IS SMALLER THAN A CLOSED MIND.

As he pondered those enigmatic words, a faint snuffling sounded from somewhere nearby. He went to the fence and peered over the hedges to see Jamie digging frantically behind Mila's coops. She'd said the dog had been acting weird lately. He watched it scrabbling and scratching at the earth.

Zeph went to the carport. A layer of dust and leaves had settled atop the truck. He turned on the water and hosed off the vehicle. It'd been several weeks since he'd fired up the trusty Ford four wheeler. He tossed his jacket on the passenger seat, followed by the book. Then Zeph started the truck, let it warm up, and opened the gate.

The wound festers. The land awaits. Between them stands your darker self.

Whatever it all meant, Zeph was determined to stop it. People could change their destiny. Neither DNA nor divine intention could force a man to do what he chose not to do. If Jesus really stood at the door and knocked, then leaving Him standing there was the soul's prerogative.

As Zeph drove away, he hoped that Jesus and Austin Pratt would forgive him for what he was about to do.

Chapter 23

Tamra dropped her helmet and backpack onto Annie's sofa. She removed the laminated library card from her back pocket and extended it to her grandmother. "Dieter went to the library yesterday. If you want that book, you might—" She stopped in her tracks. "My gosh!" She gaped at Annie's leg. "What'd you do?"

Annie yanked her sock over the scabbed, gnarly bruise on her shin. "I hurt myself...playing shuffleboard."

"Huh?" Tamra stuffed the card back into her jean pocket and put her hands on her hips. "You don't play shuffleboard!"

"Shh!" Annie glanced at the front door. "Someone'll hear you."

"Listen." Tamra went to the table, spread her hands on it, and peered at her grandmother. "At this point I don't care if someone hears me. This is not going well. You're not sleeping—I can tell. And all this talk about people changing is totally nuts."

Tamra felt ashamed for speaking this way, but after seeing the wound on her grandmother's leg, she felt desperate. She had to get her point across. In the back of her mind, what she had learned about the Madness of Endurance haunted her thoughts. She inhaled deeply and then said, "You wanna know what, Nams? The only one who's really changing is you."

Annie's jaw grew slack, her expression moving from shock to hurt. As she prepared to speak, Tamra held out her hand.

"No, Grandma. You *have* been changing. Maybe you haven't seen it, but you're not yourself. You've been short-tempered lately. Testy. Almost like...like I'm the problem, or something. That stupid ghost story about that old mine—it's all you can think about anymore. I almost dread coming by."

Annie winced and then looked away.

Their relationship had always been a little chippy. Not that Tamra intentionally kept it that way. They were both cut out of the same cloth. Stubborn. Resilient. Outspoken. Usually, out of respect, Tamra gave in to Annie's wishes and tried not to butt heads. Her grandmother had been through a lot. Between her son's addictions, the collapse of their business, and her husband's sudden death, Annie Lane could not be blamed for being so serious and unyielding. However, after seeing her bruised, bloodied shin, Tamra couldn't help but believe things were heading down the wrong track. Really fast.

"Something's going on with you, Nams. There's more than you're telling me."

Annie returned her gaze to Tamra, before folding her hands on the table and staring straight ahead.

"There is, isn't there? And now look at you." Tamra walked around the table and put her hand on her grandmother's shoulder. Her tone softened. "You're all banged up. Grandma, you're scaring me. If you keep this up, you're gonna kill yourself."

Annie rose from the table, slipped from Tamra's touch, and went to the window. She put her hand through the curtains, and a ray of morning sun gleamed into the kitchen. Annie stared out the window for a moment. Then she let the curtain fall back into place and turned.

"You're right, dear," Annie said. "I have been snippy with you. I'm sorry."

Tamra tried not to appear surprised by her grandmother's admission, even though she was.

"But you have to believe me. Something really *is* going on here."

Tamra groaned and slumped forward.

"I'm sorry," Annie said. "That's not what you want to hear, I know."

"You're right. That's not what I want to hear."

They stood for an uncomfortable moment, with Tamra measuring the lay of the land. Finally, by way of concession, she said, "I ran into Mrs. Beason yesterday on the front porch."

Annie's eyes sparked to life. "Beverly has not been herself."

"I also spoke to Hannah."

"And?"

Tamra exhaled sharply. "They've been having complaints. Some of the residents have been acting strange."

"I could have told you that."

"It doesn't prove much of anything," Tamra quickly added. "Especially about that old folk tale."

"Old folk tale or not, then my observations are corroborated. Other people have noticed the same things. And Zephaniah, the boy?" Annie's tone became hushed. "Did you see him?"

"Yeah. But he's hardly a boy, Nams. And he doesn't go by that name. In fact, he got kinda defensive when I called him that. He wants to be called Zeph."

"Zeph." Annie looked off, spacey, as if the name meant something to her. "Then you saw him. And the book—did he find it?"

"I dunno what's so special about that book. But when I gave him the note, he got weird. He said to go back and tell you that it's over. That it's over and Zephaniah Walker's dead. That's what he wanted me to say—he's dead."

Annie's gaze faltered. Then she meandered back to the table and plopped into the chair.

Tamra studied her, then asked, "Do you guys, like, know each other?"

"It's been a long time." Annie's words were detached. "I don't expect he would remember me."

"And that book. Why would it make him so upset?"

Annie shook her head.

"He seemed so...timid," Tamra offered. "Broken up inside. And when he got mad, I don't know how to explain it—it was like...something happened. His words..."

Annie perked up and scooted to the edge of her chair. "Go on. He said something, and what happened?"

"I don't know. It was just weird. And how'd he get that awful scar?"

Annie settled back in her chair. "Someone close to him surrendered to hell and took his heart with her."

Tamra gazed quizzically at her grandmother's words. Finally, she said, "Sad. Well, whatever you wanted from him, he's not cooperating."

"No. Apparently not. Not unless there's another miracle."

No sooner had Annie spoken than several loud raps sounded at her apartment door. They gasped in unison and turned that direction.

"They're here!" A raspy voice shouted in the hallway. "Reinforcements have arrived!"

Chapter 24

Tamra cut Annie off at the pass and flung her grandmother's apartment door open. An old man in a wheelchair with an unevenly chopped gray beard blocked the doorway. A worn army cap sat cock-eyed on his head. He held a cane at his waist, which he coddled like a machine gun, and in his lap laid a pair of binoculars.

It was the General. Behind him stood Zeph Walker.

After meeting Zeph last night and seeing his reluctance to help, Tamra could only gape in surprise.

"I found'm in the lobby," barked the General. "Lookin' like part o' the lost brigade."

"General." Annie pushed past Tamra. "Shh!" She pressed her finger to her lips. Then she looked at Zeph.

"I'm sorry to bother, but—" Zeph glanced nervously up and down the hallway. "Your granddaughter said I could—"

The General reached back with his cane and thwacked Zeph across the chest.

"Listen up!" The old man rolled back in his wheelchair, jabbing his cane haphazardly in Zeph's direction. "Whatever she says, you abide. Understood?"

Zeph nodded, flinching at the General's every movement.

"Good! We can use all the help we can get. Now go on, young man." He tapped Zeph on the behind with his cane.

Zeph stumbled forward, holding a book at his waist.

Across the hall Vera's door opened slightly, and someone peeked out.

The General's gaze snapped that direction. "Can I help you?"

The door promptly clicked shut.

The old man snarled, then settled the cane on his lap and looked at them squinty-eyed. "They're everywhere, Lane. The hills are alive with 'em. Shadow ops. Lookin' for a beachhead, I reckon." Then he leaned forward in his wheelchair and whispered. "Ain't no time for cowards."

Annie looked back at Tamra with an I-told-you-so glance.

Tamra scrunched her lips in disdain. The last thing her grand-mother needed was some old coot fueling her fascination.

"Ain't nothin' get by the General. You can count on me." He punc-tuated the statement by slapping the armrest of his chair. Then he saluted them and began wheeling himself down the hall, jabbering to himself.

Zeph leaned back and watched the General go. "Wow."

"He can get a little loud," Annie agreed. "At least he left his handgun at home."

"Yeah?" Zeph said. "Those two don't seem like a good combination."

"They're not."

"Is he really a general?"

"He was in the military, one branch or another," Annie said. "He has a lot of medals. The General is our resident watchdog. Can't slip much past him."

"I guess not. I was in the lobby, going through the directory." Then Zeph looked at Tamra. "Your granddaughter mentioned you lived here. I hope it's okay that I..."

"Of course," Annie said, clearly elated to have the young man at her doorstep. "I'm glad you came."

"Then I'm assuming you're—"

"Yes. I'm Annie Lane."

Tamra watched them politely shake hands and wondered what kind of history had brought them to this point. Annie glanced up and down the hallway and quickly motioned Zeph inside. She closed the door behind him, and they stood awkwardly in the entryway, Zeph with the book at his waist and Annie with a nervous enthusiasm.

"I wanted to apologize to you for yesterday." Zeph looked squarely at Tamra.

After the initial shock of seeing the scar on his face last night, Tamra was much more able to look at him without distraction. He had an outdoorsy look shared by many locals, a tanned complexion and an unkempt ruggedness that spoke of lazy days along the creek or chopping wood near an orchard. His eyes were green, and she could see in them that his apology was genuine.

Tamra glanced at her grandmother and shrugged. "Apology accepted."

Zeph nodded, as if he'd completed his first order of business, then turned to Annie. "And I wanted to personally give you this." He handed her a cloth hardbound book, emerald green, with sweeping gilded lettering across the front.

"Then you *did* keep it." As Annie took the book, her wide eyes glistened.

"And now I've returned it, just like that girl said."

"It's been almost ten years." Annie riffled through the yellowed pages of the book, glancing up at him as she did. "This is encouraging, you know."

"It's a fundamental weakness of mine," Zeph said. "A soft spot for my childhood roots."

Annie smiled, clearly buoyed by his words.

"No doubt it'll be my eventual undoing."

As quickly as her countenance had risen, it fell. "Please, let's sit down." She motioned to the living room.

"I'd rather stand, thank you."

"Well, then. Do you know what's in this?" Annie extended the book and patted its cover.

Zeph's posture did not betray hostility. In fact, he seemed to be slightly conflicted, almost nervous, as if the words he was about to say came with great labor.

"Let me put it this way, Miss Lane. When that book was delivered, I was just a kid myself."

Annie nodded, her attention rapt upon the young man.

"I was comin' out of a really bad place in life," Zeph admitted. "I was confused. Hurt. My mother'd passed away suddenly several years before that. My father remarried right away. Pearl was her name. We left Endurance and moved to Los Angeles. After living here all my life, it was quite a shock. But you know all this, right?"

Tamra peered at her grandmother. Annie nodded slowly, as if she had reservations.

"Then you know Pearl was a psychopath," Zeph continued. "She hated everything about me. Especially this."

He reached across his body and pulled back the sleeve of his print T-shirt to reveal a tattoo of the Star of David. Tamra had seen enough tattoos to know this one was amateurish, probably inscribed in a garage or back-alley parlor.

He let the sleeve fall back into place. "I got it as a tribute to my mother. I was the young prophet she'd always wanted me to be. Pearl couldn't stand that, you know? She hated my mother for what she'd made of me and said I'd been brainwashed." He looked away. "Sometimes I wonder if Pearl wasn't right."

Annie shook her head. "Please, don't—"

Zeph stretched out his hand to silence her. A hint of derision seemed to rise in his voice. "Pearl left me with something." He pointed to the scar on his face. "It was a really dull letter opener. Went right to the bone."

Tamra pressed her hand to her mouth, unable to stifle a gasp. Yet her surprise did not elicit a response from Zeph Walker. He just stared forward, intractable, as if he'd rehearsed the story a thousand times over.

"Pearl's in a nuthouse in Los Angeles now. She wanted to shut me up, and I guess you could say it worked." He sighed deeply, and his features softened. "Anyway, when the girl delivered the book, I was confused. Lost. We'd just moved back from LA. I received an inheritance, bought the Carson Creek property. I was in and out of the hospital. They tried to reconstruct things cosmetically but weren't able to do much, as you can tell. Which has put a serious damper on my career as a male model."

He glanced at Tamra, but acknowledging his humor seemed inappropriate, if not profane.

"Anyway," Zeph continued, "when the book showed up, all I wanted to do was bury everything. I stashed it with the rest of the junk my mother'd left me. And, to be honest, Miss Lane, I wonder if I shouldn't have burned this stuff a long time ago."

Annie's attention remained fixed on him, as if trying to decipher some hidden script in his story. Finally she said, "Then you don't know about the prophecy?"

"Let me put it this way, Miss Lane."

"Please, call me Annie."

"Okay, Annie. I don't know about the prophecy," Zeph crossed his arms, "and I really don't care."

Chapter 25

It was as if a silent communiqué passed between Zeph Walker and Annie Lane. Every twitch, every gesture seemed infused with the weight of some unspoken message. Tamra watched them carefully, trying to read their inner exchange.

"Okay," Tamra finally blurted. "What's going on here, huh? Do you two know each other or what?"

"I haven't a clue," Zeph said.

Annie's brow furrowed. "You're serious?"

Zeph nodded.

Her grandmother's lips formed a thin crease.

Tamra knew how stubborn and strong-willed Annie could be, and after seeing Zeph's outburst last night, she could only imagine what kind of collision they might be heading for.

"Wait right here." Annie handed Tamra the book, turned on her heel, and hurried into her bedroom, limping noticeably as she went.

The sliding of drawers sounded down the hallway, followed by soft thuds and the rustling of paper.

While Annie scavenged for some mystery object, Zeph and Tamra exchanged nervous glances.

"I—I'm sorry," Tamra said. "She can be pretty obsessive."

"I know the feeling."

A louder thump jarred the picture frames on the wall.

Tamra tapped her fingernails atop the cover of the book. "I feel like I'm caught in the middle of something."

"Believe me—you are."

Annie hurried out of the room with a large scrapbook. Setting it on the dining room table, she turned on the overhead light and motioned them over. Zeph did not budge. Annie leafed through pages of yellowed newsprint, faded Polaroids, bookmarks, obituaries, and pressed flowers until she came to several clippings.

Annie spread the pages, stepped back, and said, "See if this jogs your memory...*Zephaniah*."

Tamra glanced at Zeph. He did not quell at the mention of his full name as he had yesterday. In fact, he maintained his distance, as if he knew what was about to be revealed.

Tamra turned her attention to the scrapbook. It was the *Desert Daily*, a weekly paper that covered the not-so-exciting happenings of the Inyo County basin. Even the age of twenty-four-hour news blogs could not seem to kill off the old rag. It was still going strong, probably due to a sizable amount of local oldsters who refused to surrender to technological advance. Tamra cast a suspicious glance at her grandmother and then studied the news clippings. The heading of one page read "Prophet of the Plains," and below it was a large picture of a young boy on a stage surrounded by all the regalia of an evangelistic crusade. Men and women looked on as the young boy strode on the stage, Bible in hand, preaching to the fixated congregation.

Tamra read the subtitle aloud: "Boy prophet preaches to packed houses."

She looked from her grandmother to Zeph, who still refused to make eye contact.

Tamra returned to the newsprint, now fascinated by the unraveling history.

"Miracles." Tamra read another headline. "Young Zephaniah Walker wields the power of God."

"Oh, my." Tamra gaped at Zeph. "This is . . . *you?*"

"Unfortunately."

Tamra leafed through several pages of newsprints containing pictures of young Zeph Walker praying, kneeling, and posing under the smiling gaze of his mother. *Prophecy. Healing. Deliverance.* The words emblazoned the pages, kindling fantastical images in her mind of tent revivals and wild-eyed evangelists.

She looked at Annie. "So this is how you two—"

"I attended several of your crusades," Annie said to Zeph. "I was at the end of my rope. My son—Tamra's father—was an addict by that time. Meth. Diet pills. Whatever he could get his hands on. I retired early from teaching, but our business dried up, and my husband fell into a terrible depression. His health withered before my eyes. Everything we had worked so hard for seemed to crumble. I felt like a failure. I needed a miracle." She stepped forward. "Zeph, you changed my life."

He looked away and ran his fingers through his hair. "That was a long time ago, Annie. Like I told your granddaughter—"

"And you can call me Tamra."

His gaze lingered on Tamra, as if vocalizing her name would push him over some psychic precipice. "Like I told *Tamra*, that part of my life is over. I was a kid. I—I didn't really know what I was doing."

"That doesn't mean what you were doing was wrong," Annie challenged.

"Maybe not, but I know what I'm doing now."

Annie stared at him for what seemed like a long time. Finally, she said, "Zeph, we need your help."

"I can't help you."

"How do you know?"

"Okay. I *won't* help you."

"Zeph." Annie stepped toward him slightly, her hand extended. "You don't know yet what you can do. You haven't even begun to—"

"Can't you people leave me alone?"

Tamra glanced at her grandmother. "Hold on a second. What people are you talking about?"

"Please," Annie said, ignoring Tamra's question and motioning toward the living room. "Let's sit down."

"I am *not* going back there, Annie." He pointed at the scrapbook. "That part of my life is over. Don't you get it?"

"Please." There was softness in Annie's tone. "Let's sit down."

Zeph pursed his lips and looked at Tamra, as if waiting for her advice. All she could manage was spreading her hands in a *what-could-it-hurt* posture of surrender.

He sighed heavily. "Okay. But that's as far as this goes." He pointed a cautionary finger at Annie.

By the look on her grandmother's face Tamra could tell Annie had won a strategic advantage.

Zeph and Tamra sat on opposite ends of the sofa, while Annie angled the rocking chair toward them. Tamra laid the old book between them, its gilded lettering sparkling in the lamplight.

"Now, let me tell you *my* story." Annie straightened her cargo skirt and settled into the rocker. "I've lived here in Endurance all my life. Harold and I always loved this place. It was so rich in history. Well, long before you were born, there was a belief about this land.

The basin, the mountains, the Black Pass. The Indians called it the Valley of Enchantment. And for good reason. They believed it to be a place of magic."

Knowing her grandmother, Tamra could only imagine what kind of florid story would soon emerge. She braced herself.

"Mind you," Annie said, "I'm not one to give credence to doctrines of devils and pagan mythologies. It took awhile for me to even concede the notion. But the more I looked into it, I had to conclude they were on to something. Especially after...the Madness."

Tamra groaned. "How did I know you were going there?"

"You didn't."

"Well, it went there."

"Maybe it *should* go there."

"Nams, do you remember what we talked about?"

"And do you remember—"

"All right!" Zeph glanced angrily at both of them. "So what does this story and that book and that crazy old suicide have to do with me?"

"I was getting to that." Annie glanced sternly at Tamra. "When you showed up and started preaching, I was skeptical. I've seen my share of hucksters and snake oil salesmen. But the more I watched you and talked to folks, the more I knew there was something about you." Annie leaned forward, her voice hushed. "Son, God was in you."

Zeph shifted uncomfortably.

"That's when Earl told us about the prophecy. Earl lives up there in the Pass, at Meridian."

"That kooky tourist dig?" Tamra said.

"That kooky tourist dig is one of the most famous roadside attractions in the United States. In fact, you'll find a detailed chapter about Meridian and the Endurance Valley mythologies on page forty-nine." She pointed to the emerald green book. "We'd hoped it would have piqued your interest, nudged you our direction. Anyway, Earl told us about a prophecy written in the rocks. He didn't think anything of it. Until you showed up."

Zeph tapped the toe of his boot on the carpet, looking more and more perturbed. "Maybe I should just go. Like I said, that part of my life is over. I'm glad I was able to help you, Annie. Really. But prophecies written in the rocks? C'mon."

Annie had moved to the edge of her seat. "The prophecy foretells a darkness that will spill out of the earth, poisoning the land and its people. It tells about a prophet who will rise up to stand against that darkness. And we knew that you were that one. The people, the land...it was *waiting* for you."

His agitations stopped, and Zeph squinted at her. "What did you say?"

She furrowed her brow. "I said we knew you were the one."

"No. The other part."

"You mean, that the land was waiting for you?"

His gaze turned blank and he said dully, "The land awaits..."

"Yes," Annie said, expectation rising in her voice. "*The land awaits.* It always does. God gave His people a promised land. Prosperity, produce, famine—it was all tied to the people. If they obeyed, if they followed, the land flourished and evil was restrained. The land always awaits. It awaits the reign of the righteous. It awaits redemption. It awaits those who will stand in the gap."

Zeph gaped at her. "You've really thought about this."

"I told you she was obsessive," Tamra offered.

Annie ignored their comments. "The prophets were always called to the land, Zeph. Moses was called to Egypt. Jeremiah and Ezekiel were called to Babylon. Jonah was called to Nineveh. When you moved back to Endurance, we knew it was true. You were called to *this* land."

Zeph closed his eyes and massaged his forehead with his fingertips. "I get that people believed I was a prophet. But how does this connect with that mass suicide? That was, like, over a hundred years ago. And what kind of *darkness* am I supposed to be fighting?"

Annie lifted her Bible from the end table, settled back in the rocker, and began leafing through its pages.

"She thinks people are changing." Tamra's words felt like a guilty admission. "That something is...possessing them. Replacing them. It's the same thing that happened back then, I guess. Something just made everyone go crazy all at once. No one knows for sure what it was. But Otta's Rift was right in the middle of it."

"It's all here." Annie tapped her open Bible. "Spelled out way ahead of time."

Zeph looked sideways at her.

"In the last days," Annie said, "they will find the key and open the abyss."

Zeph squinted. "You're not suggesting that the old mine—"

"And out of it," Annie continued, "will emerge hideous creatures from the pit which will torment those who did not have the seal of God on their foreheads."

"Wait a second—"

Annie extended her hand to hush him, and she read, "Their hair was like women's hair, and their teeth were like lions' teeth...the sound of their wings was like the thundering of many horses and chariots rushing into battle. They had tails with stingers, like scorpions... *and their faces resembled human faces.*"

"You've gotta be kidding."

"She's not." Tamra smiled curtly.

Annie gazed at him and closed the Bible. "Revelation, chapter 9."

Zeph stared and then said, "As in the *ninth* gate."

Annie nodded. "According to the legends, on Planet Earth there are nine gates to hell. Most of the gates are scattered across America—insane asylums, cult clearings—"

"Retirement homes," Zeph deadpanned.

"People can open those gates through lots of ways," Annie said, apparently undeterred by Zeph's warped sense of humor. "But when all nine gates are opened, there will be hell on earth. We don't know how it happened, but we believe that mine up there—the spot of that suicide—is one of those gates. Even worse, someone has the key to it."

"I thought you didn't believe in pagan mythologies."

"Well, I don't." Annie laid the Bible on the end table. "But whatever happened up there—and whatever might be happening now—it's evil. And it's predicted right here." She moved to the edge of her rocker, her eyes piercing. "Something unnatural is up there in that mine, Zeph. Someone has a key to it. We think you've got the ability to stop it."

He settled back on the sofa and became quiet.

Tamra had grown used to Annie's tales about apocalyptic doomsday and a colorful cast of villains, both visible and invisible, that would rise to the fore. While Tamra took her grandmother's ravings with a grain of salt, she could only imagine how this sounded to a stranger like Zeph Walker. Although, having led evangelistic crusades, he had probably encountered his share of ravings.

"This is insane," he finally said. "So I'm supposed to hike up to that abandoned mine like Moses up to Sinai and—what? Bring the mountain down? Command fire from heaven?" His tone was full of sarcasm. "All that gift has ever brought people is pain."

"But I—"

"I don't care!" He lurched to the edge of the sofa.

Annie gasped.

The atmosphere bristled as he glared at her.

Then, by increments, he sunk back into his seat. "You can have your book and your prophecy and all those pagan mythologies you said you don't believe in. All I want is..." The anger drained from his eyes, his gaze faltered, and he hunched forward. "Just to be left alone."

Tamra had sensed it all along. His outburst confirmed it. Zeph Walker was a broken soul. His scars were more than skin deep. She worried about what her grandmother might say to the troubled young man.

Annie studied him, and then her courage seemed to return. She scooted forward on the rocker. "What is it, Zeph? You know something about this, don't you? You've been expecting this, haven't you?"

Zeph shook his head and looked to the floor.

"You can't keep running, son. The pain, it's poisoning you."

He rocked forward and back, staring blankly, wrestling with whatever demons possessed his soul.

"I can't..." He rose to his feet. "Listen, I can't do this."

Annie opened her mouth, ready to object.

"You seem like nice folks," Zeph said. "But you don't understand. With the Telling, there's always a price. Someone always gets hurt. Someone has to pay. I can't let that happen again."

He stood, staring at the carpet.

Whatever strange energy had filled the room moments ago was quickly replaced by a cloud.

"Promise me," Annie finally said, "before you make a decision, before you do anything, you will go up there. To Meridian. Zeph, you need to see the prophecy for yourself."

He continued looking at the floor, chewing at the inside of his cheek.

"Please," she prodded.

"I had a friend once," he said to no one in particular. "His name was Austin Pratt. We called him Ozzy. It was the strangest thing because whenever we were together, I would sense certain things about him. That's part of how it works. But with Ozzy, it was hurtful things. Violent things. Things that most normal folks would cringe at. I was just a kid, seven or eight. I didn't know how to process that, you know? Every time I was with him, I felt like he was in danger, that he needed to run. But how do you tell your kid friend he needs to run away from home? What exactly do you do?" He looked up, his eyes glistening with moisture. "I did the only thing I could. I just watched."

They were both staring at him.

"Ozzy was beaten to death by his father. Technically, I guess, he died of a brain hemorrhage due to head trauma. They think he was kicked in the temple. Apparently he'd been abused for years. Picked on by some drunken old man who hated the fact that his only son was lame. So I guess all I'm sayin' is," Zeph smiled sheepishly, "even if I am a prophet, I guess I can't save everyone."

His words distilled into the silence.

Then Annie rose and limped to him. She stood directly in front of him, but he did not meet her gaze.

"Zeph," Annie said. "You saved *me*."

Chapter 26

Plink.

The fairy kingdom is but the germ of a larger mythology, a dimension of superior intelligences, which some call *fetch*.

Plink.

Suppose a formula existed to access that dimension.

Plink.

Seer, seer.

Fergus woke with a start. He snatched the pistol from his lap and forced his eyes to focus.

Yet no one was there. He'd fallen asleep outside again.

Fergus heaved a sigh of relief. He kissed the barrel of the pistol and settled back into the ragged vinyl seat. Steam fogged the truck windows, and the windshield glowed with golden morning sunlight. He sat for a moment, recalibrating his senses, when he realized he was freezing. With a little nudge from his shoulder, the door ground open and he stepped out, groaning with stiffness.

He couldn't close his eyes anymore without the fetch haunting him. The way things were going, there was no telling where he'd wake up next. All the more reason they needed to leave this place.

Fergus stuffed the pistol into his pants and checked to see if his ears were bleeding again. Thankfully they weren't. Nevertheless, something was happening to him. His body was changing. His head and joints ached. Running away was no guarantee things would change, that he would get better. They had done something wrong. Really wrong. No matter how far he ran, running would never change that fact.

A ribbon of smoke rose from the Williams's ranch on the property below. The other campsites were vacant, as usual. There were eleven small plots in all, each containing electric hookups, fire pits, and water. Initially designed to house ranch laborers and grounds crews, the Williamses had scaled back, allowing rural areas of their property to fall into disrepair. Fergus had been given permission to park his trailer there long ago in exchange for shooing off trespassers and marauding coyotes. Occasionally he was called upon to stack firewood or fix the irrigation for the orchard. Now, virtually forgotten by the Williamses, the isolation had seeped into his psyche. The foothills were his, just the way he liked them.

The morning sun cast a long orange glow across the Owens basin, illuminating pockets of fog below the snowy peaks. A jackrabbit darted from the brush nearby, followed by another. Fergus's teeth chattered from the cold. He rounded the truck and passed under the makeshift awning. A six-cylinder engine sat on blocks of wood surrounded by greasy tools. He had allowed the junk to pile up: old computer parts, keyboards, braided cable, and motor parts. Nothing much was worth keeping, just Pops's medals and Fergus's tools. The rest could rot.

He entered the trailer. It stunk of alcohol and tuna. Fergus walked into the kitchenette, massaging out the crick in his lower back. He removed the pistol and slid it onto the table next to beer bottle caps and stick matches. Opening the refrigerator, he reached past a crusty sandwich for a carton of milk, which he gulped down. Despite the cool liquid, his throat hurt with every swallow. Then he went through the narrow hallway and squeezed past a stack of cardboard boxes into the living room.

"Moon Dancer."

Fergus stumbled back and slammed into the wall, sending the trailer rocking.

Little Weaver sat in the recliner, his carved javelin leaning nearby. Biker goggles hung at his chest, and beneath his army jacket, tools and instruments lined his belt. The Indian was so large that his knees were practically up to his chest.

"Ghaww!" Fergus stood with his heart pounding. "I t–told you ta stop followin' me!"

"I have not forgotten."

"Well then...*stop!*"

"Perhaps you should be thankful I am following you." Little Weaver's small charcoal eyes remained intense.

Fergus squinted. "Then it was you in the Rift last night."

Little Weaver's gloved hands draped the armrest like the talons of an old dragon. "There is a story told of a great bird."

"Please," Fergus spat. "Not another story."

"The greatest of all birds. Revered by all other creatures. Majestic! But she grew proud in herself, so proud that she fancied to fly to the sun. 'If I can but drink of that golden bowl,' she said, 'I will live forever. The Creator Himself will not outshine me.' She flew upward with her great wings, past the clouds and the stars. Onward to the sun! But as she drew near, her wings were burned. She had been deceived by her *hubris*. Her once-powerful wings turned to ash, and she plummeted to earth as a serpent. There she was forced to crawl on her belly. From the greatest of birds to the most despised of creatures. Such is the story of all those who misuse their power."

Fergus stared at the Indian.

"You have brought great evil upon yourself and your people, Moon Dancer."

"Stop calling me that. I'm no dancer."

Little Weaver raised an eyebrow. "You grow tired of my tales. Ah! Sad indeed is the soul who forgets the great stories."

"Your riddles bore me, Indian. The only story I care about is the one I'm writing now. And it has nothin' to do with stayin' around here."

Little Weaver scrutinized him. "Destiny can always be reclaimed. It's *irrevocable*, as you would say. The prophet never loses his calling, only his way."

"Yeah? Well you can have yer destiny," Fergus muttered. "We're leavin'." He strode across the room and snatched a cardboard box from one of the stacks. Setting it on the end table, he began packing random items, in seeming disregard for the Indian.

Little Weaver pulled his coat around him and heaved himself from the chair. The tools in his belt clanked as he rose. The man seemed gargantuan in the small trailer, his shadow spreading across the yellowed ceiling like a wraith. Tightening his jacket about him, he scanned the cluttered room.

"The dark angels roam freely now," Little Weaver said. "Like a great bear awakened from her slumber. Hungry, they are. Consuming! Someone must pay for this."

"Them ain't no angels. Besides, that hellhole was there a long t– time before us."

"Yes, but there is still time. You can stop the march of the shadow."
Little Weaver approached and stood at Fergus's side, towering over
him. He smelled of wood smoke and raw venison. "You have the
power, Moon Dancer."

Fergus stood rigid and spoke through clenched teeth. "I told you,
we're leaving."

"Where will you go?"

"Does it matter?" Fergus looked sideways at the Indian.

"The shadow will not allow it."

"They can't stop me."

"But your father—he cannot be moved."

"Then I'll leave 'im!" Fergus bellowed, separating himself from
Little Weaver's intimidating presence. "Give it a break!"

As he did, a sound rose inside him.

Plink.

Fergus winced, and then he clasped his hands over his ears and
stumbled backward, sending the lamp careening off its stand.

Seer, seer.

"Ghaww!" He doubled over, gripping fistfuls of hair in an attempt
to force the fetch out of his brain. "Make 'em stop!"

As the presence subsided, Fergus rose to see Little Weaver's pene-
trating gaze upon him.

"The poison of the underworld runs deep in you, Moon Dancer."

"Kill m–me," Fergus whimpered.

Little Weaver's brow furrowed.

Fergus squared his chest and yanked open his flannel, sending
buttons flinging across the room. "Then kill me!"

Little Weaver peered at him. "I cannot harm the prophet. Nor the
land. The dark angel alone is my enemy. You insult me with your
foolish charge! Bah!"

Little Weaver snatched his javelin. He brought the end up and
ran the metal delicately through his gloved fingers as if it were a fine
sword. With that end raised, he approached the corner of the room.

Hanging from the ceiling was the skin of a fetch, nothing more
than an empty sack. Fergus had hung it there as a trophy. The only
time Fergus had used his pistol, it was to kill this one. He had
stopped it mid-metamorphosis. While it still had wings. The creature's face, or what was left of it, looked identical to Fergus Coyne.

It had been trying to imitate Fergus.

Little Weaver took his javelin and poked at the dry, withered epidermis. Reaching the single bullet hole in the chest, he inserted the tip and looked over his shoulder.

"Next time," Little Weaver said, "you won't be so lucky."

"There won't be a next time," Fergus growled. "We're leavin', I said. By tomorrow I'm outta here. I'm takin' 'im and...and we're goin'. I'll just keep drivin'. Get as far away from you people as possible."

Little Weaver stepped back and settled the end of the javelin on the floor.

"The shadows gather, Moon Dancer. Many eyes are watching. You have the power to speak the word. While there is light, you can speak the word."

"I've spoken enough," Fergus said. "It's time for someone else to start talking."

Chapter 27

Maybe this was a bad idea.

The cashier slid a perspiring bottle of orange juice across the counter, trying hard not to stare at Zeph's scar. He'd missed his morning cinnamon roll, so this would have to suffice. However, the way this woman was looking at him, Zeph knew she had something she was dying to say.

"They call him Earl," said the woman, scrounging his change from the register. "He's an oddball. But anyone who lives up there's gotta be."

"Thanks." Zeph took the bottle, regretting that he'd stopped along the way.

As she plucked coins from the tray of an old cash register, she looked sideways at Zeph before finally asking what had, apparently, been on her mind.

"Ain't you that kid? The one that used to perform?"

Zeph glanced out the door of the market as a diesel barreled past. "I'm afraid so."

She gasped. "I read about you! Terrible how that happened."

"Yeah, well—"

"Hey! I don't wanna be rude, but can you predict something for me?"

Zeph adjusted his sunglasses. "Listen, I–I don't do predictions."

"Well, can you tell me my future? Like, if I'll get married again? Or when I'll die?"

"Can I have my change?"

She shouted into the back room. "Johnny! Johnny, come 'ere! Hurry!"

"Keep the change." Zeph headed for the door.

"No! Wait, kid! You gotta meet my Johnny. He's got the gift too. I swear it. He can predict things. Johnnyy-y-y-y!"

Zeph hurried out of the country store. If he needed a reminder of why he rarely went out, this was it. He tossed the bottle onto the seat, climbed into his truck, and backed onto the shoulder. Any second Johnny would probably shamble out with a cigarette dangling from his lips and his gut showing, hoping to catch a glimpse of the phantom of the opera. Instead Zeph plowed across the gravel, fishtailing, and he swerved onto the asphalt highway aimed at the Black Pass.

The Endurance basin was a sixteen-mile oblong granite bowl, bordered on its northern end by a narrow granite pass. At its pinnacle sat the rickety tourist stop named Meridian. As Zeph left town, warm air beating him from an open window, the residential homes became more scattered, yielding to stretches of farmland and rock outcroppings.

Meridian loomed now, a beacon to something Zeph had always feared.

The land awaits.

The Telling had always been his own private burden. He had the scar to prove it. Yet the notion that others had a stake in him, that Zeph's gift, that his well-being was somehow tied to the land seemed preposterous. And terrifying.

He passed the aqueduct and then the small adobe mission. Jesuits came to Endurance in the late eighteenth century on their trek through California, hoping to convert the Indians to a higher form of religion. The mission was a decaying testament to their spiritual impotence. Now Zeph wondered if they hadn't run into something more powerful than all their icons and imagery.

The land awaits.

It wasn't a coincidence that Annie Lane had used that phrase. The magic was stirring. He used to believe it was everywhere, that God never slept. That every leaf, every circumstance was infused with His divine presence. What a fool to think he could run from Him! He couldn't just settle down and seep into the woodwork like normal folks. Zeph Walker was not normal! He was a freak of nature. A regular polycephalic. Why couldn't he get that through his thick head?

He wrung the steering wheel, his thoughts grinding bone against bone.

He should not have left his house this morning. That was where everything went wrong. If he would have just left the book under the porch, bought a cinnamon roll and freshly squeezed orange juice, and returned to his house, none of this would have ever happened. Now here he was, driving to some silly roadside attraction to see a cave painting about the Prophet of the Plains.

Perhaps it was her eyes that got under his skin. And her little laugh.

You're a fool!

Zeph stared through the bug-splattered windshield across the dry flatland to the dark, volcanic peak at the highway's end. His stomach churned as he watched that dark, fabled monument approach.

However, it wasn't his decision to go to Meridian that most troubled Zeph Walker. Nor was it the possibility that something inhuman had broken free to possess people's souls.

It was what he knew about where this was headed. He had seen it in their eyes.

Annie and Tamra Lane were headed for a collision with darkness. He knew there would be casualties. There always were. Just ask Austin Pratt.

Chapter 28

The early afternoon sun cut an orange swath across the basin, and boulders hugged the highway, casting elongated shadows. As the road ascended, Zeph's truck passed a billboard with the word *Meridian* spelled in a groovy sixties font.

He couldn't remember the last time he'd been this far out of town.

Ahead the Black Pass rose, a cleft in the mountainside framed by two uneven rock columns through which the 395 passed. At its peak a dirt turnout ringed by brittle piñon pines overlooked the vast northeastern wasteland. The tree roots grappled the rocky soil like gnarled witch's talons, and between it perched a sign proclaiming the dusty outcrop a scenic lookout.

He turned off the highway, stirring dust, and came to a stop in front of the roadside attraction.

Meridian was a chain of irregular wooden structures—cubes, spires, and boxcars—joined by a long narrow porch with a sagging overhang. A wooden rocker listed in the breeze near a weathered statue of a mermaid that appeared to be sculpted in sand.

Shutting off the ignition, Zeph sat with his hand poised on the keys.

He believed in prophecy. And prophets. Yet believing in a prophecy about himself posed a whole set of problems. Especially the kind of prophecy found at a roadside attraction.

He finished the bottle of orange juice, opened the door, and stepped onto the gravel shoulder. Behind him, the entire Endurance Valley spread. Patches of rich green farmland interspersed with dwellings, framed by the rugged mountains. No wonder the Indians considered this landscape magical.

Across the highway rose the rocky columns. Apart from graffiti chiseled into one, the spires appeared almost lunar, like alien obelisks puncturing the earth's crust. In person, the Black Pass seemed much bigger. A plaque embedded in a stone pedestal at the base of the nearest column outlined important details of the Endurance archway, as well as geological information.

Out of the corner of his eye a figure moved into the doorway of the shop.

Zeph turned as a gust of wind sent nearby chimes tinkling.

"Mornin', son." A thick man with wild, overgrown sideburns and red suspenders stood in the doorway. "Welcome to Meridian."

Zeph squinted against the glare of the cresting sun. "Morning, sir."

"Name's Earl." The man lumbered onto the porch with a noticeable limp, stood on the edge, and peered down at Zeph. "We been expectin' you."

Again Zeph wondered why he had come up here. He cleared his throat. "My name is—"

"Don't bother!" Earl rumbled. "I know who ya are and why you're here."

"Why am I not surprised?"

"You're here for the tour!"

"Of course." Zeph folded his arms. "So, what's the tour?"

Windows framed either side of the doorway, draped with lace curtains, displaying shelves of curios and pottery. A fleet of pale green flying saucers dangled from fishing line near the wind chimes at the entrance, no doubt the glow-in-the-dark variety.

"There's a coupla tours," Earl said. "The House of Gravity's popular. The Pueblo City tour is a buck-fifty. You can take it yourself out back. Just follow the red footprints. There's some genuine pottery and mannequins all dressed up and propped in the windows. Like Indians. And there's petroglyphs in the cave—we still ain't found the bottom—and lotsa arrowheads scattered. You can collect 'em for a buck each. But the barricaded areas are off limits. Some fella got lost down there awhile back. Wandered out three hours later, glassy-eyed and spacey."

Zeph shifted his weight. If the traveling circus was looking for a new barker, Zeph might have discovered him.

Earl slipped his thumbs under his suspenders. "But most folks just wanna see Ginny."

Pinching sand off the bridge of his nose, Zeph asked reluctantly, "Who's Ginny?"

"You mean, *what's* Ginny? She's just a coupla parts. A mummified hand, two legs from the knees down, and what appears to be a wing. Well-preserved and not at all human."

Dust swirled at Zeph's ankles. How the man knew Ginny was a female was a discussion Zeph did not want to broach. Instead, he asked, "So, *what is* Ginny?"

The saucers wafted at a passing gust, followed by the tinkle of the chimes.

"There's a coupla theories. Some say she's a spaceman. Ya know, an extraterrestrial. Can't be sure. The one that keeps people comin'— from as far away as Alaska, matter of fact—is that Ginny's an angel."

Before he had time to steer the conversation away from Ginny, Earl continued.

"Course, some think the Paiute—you know, the Indians that lived 'round here—preserved the remains for one reason or the other. But if you ask me, I think it's residue from those government experiments. Probably some farmer caught a whiff of radioactive fog or somethin'. Anyway, the parts are in the caboose, and you can view 'em for two dollars. Or with the purchase of ten dollars or more, you can see it for free."

Zeph stared at the man for a moment.

A pickup truck carrying a load of pickers from one of the outlying farms crested the hill, and the driver made the sign of the cross as they passed between the stone arches. The slow-rolling dust cloud swept past, and the vast silence of the mountain pass returned.

"You said I was here for the tour."

"Indeed, I did." Earl strummed his suspenders. "Follow me!"

Earl turned and limped back into Meridian. Zeph remained, listening to the floorboards creak inside. The foam saucers fluttered in the breeze, and the wind chimes sent harmonic fractals dancing along the porch. Zeph climbed the steps and entered Meridian.

"Feel free to take a look around," Earl said, waiting for him at a glass counter. "I'm sure you'll find something to your liking."

Thick timber framed the structure with each end leading, rather perilously, into another dimly lit antechamber. Every possible nook was displayed with random arcane items. A long glass counter, cluttered with magic paraphernalia—card tricks, locked rings, wands—stretched before the entryway. Road signs hung helter-skelter on the rustic wooden walls, some with buckshot and rusted acne, announcing the historic Route 66, Four Corners, and Sunset Blvd. Crucifixes of all shapes and sizes adorned the walls. A massive snakeskin spread across a plaque above the counter, displaying what was purported to be the largest diamondback ever encountered in the Owens Valley. A poster of Raquel Welch in her animal skin outfit from *One Million Years B.C.* stretched across the ceiling, as did an assemblage of album covers, license plates, and tins. Rattle-snake eggs sat on the counter, but Zeph knew enough to not inquire.

"This is Jim." Earl nodded toward a slender young man at a desk hunched over disassembled electronic parts.

"Heyah, Cap." Jim saluted Zeph before returning to work.

"And this is Sultana." Earl motioned to a girl dressed in black, tipped back on a stool reading a paperback. A bleached streak traced a geisha-cut hairdo.

Sultana righted herself, slid off her stool, and extended her hand. "Pleased to meet you. Finally." Her smile was gracious.

Zeph removed his sunglasses and slipped them into his shirt pocket. He shook Sultana's hand. "Ditto. I guess."

"She's also part of the remnant."

"The remnant?" Zeph asked.

"Annie didn't tell you?" Earl's overgrown eyebrows knotted.

Zeph shook his head.

Sultana hoisted herself back on the stool, using her booted foot to lightly push off from the glass counter. "It's a loose-knit group of religious fanatics who believe in Armageddon, the Great Tribulation, government conspiracy, and a variety of political intrigue."

"Oh, is that all?" Zeph offered.

Sultana smiled. "We also happen to believe that, when you came back here—what, a decade ago?—you triggered a series of events that unequivocally prove you are the one spoken about in the prophecy."

Zeph wrinkled his nose. "Um, maybe you can just show me the tour."

"Right!" Earl slapped the countertop with his thick hand.

Zeph followed Earl through an aisle of geodes and crystalline spikes before ducking through a beaded curtain into a dim hallway. A series of wooden steps descended steeply to a door.

Earl lumbered down the steps with considerable difficulty, leaving Zeph to surmise that either Earl was not the tour guide or the tours were rather infrequent.

Sunlight burst into the stairwell as Earl opened the door onto a dusty landscape. Zeph winced at the glare, following the store owner into a sandy cove in back of the buildings. A calico dog looked lazily from its bed, flies agitating its crusty eyes. A wall of granite, veined with quartz and sandstone, towered along the backside of Meridian. A cobblestone trail traced the side of the mountain, cordoned by a rope walkway, before plunging into a squat cavern some fifty feet below the store.

"That's where it all started," Earl said reverently, staring toward the cave. "The legends, you know, about the prophet."

Another gust of wind swirled at Zeph's feet, and a low moan rose from the cavern.

He could not say why, at that moment, he thought about Jonah's whale, its jaws opened wide, preparing to swallow the wayward prophet. Yet somehow Zeph realized that if he walked into this cave, there would be no turning back.

Nevertheless, Zeph turned to Earl and said, "Lead the way."

Chapter 29

A rickety string of bare bulbs crackled to life inside the Meridian cavern. Earl followed the roped walkway into the sloping subterranean grotto. Zeph remained behind him, unsure of what he would find.

"When they first found this place," Earl's voice echoed in the cavern, "there was leftover pottery and arrowheads everywhere. Whoever lived here got beamed up or somethin'."

The string of lights wafted in a rising breeze, descending into a smooth, twisting corridor of rock. A series of archways disappeared below. The slope was gradual, but when he reached the first archway, Earl was sweating. He turned to Zeph, his face glistening in the artificial light.

"Most people have never seen what you're about to see. So be careful, young man. For your eyes only, ya hear?"

Zeph nodded. "My lips are sealed."

The dog had managed to rouse itself and loped along behind them. Earl ducked under the rope and held it up so Zeph could do the same. A series of carved steps branched off the main tunnel. The cool breeze disappeared, and dank, listless air took its place. Earl navigated down these steps into an adjoining corridor of smooth, graceful, sandstone-type walls. The further they moved from the main trail, the darker it grew. If there were not another light source ahead, they would quickly be in complete darkness.

The memory of the doppelgänger ignited, striking dread inside him. How did Zeph know this stranger could be trusted? Here he was, miles from civilization, in a dark cave, following a guy wearing red suspenders into a hidden chamber. What if Zeph was being led to his death? After all, the detectives assumed someone was after him. Why else would someone shoot his look-alike? Why not the remnant? It wouldn't be the first time religious fanatics committed murder. Perhaps it was all an elaborate scheme to get him here. Alone. What better spot to off a wayward prophet with a bankload of money than in a lightless tunnel behind a roadside attraction?

Zeph's breathing was labored, and a claustrophobic terror seized his thoughts. His mind squirmed under the weight of the horrific possibilities. He wondered what lay ahead of him.

Then, in the dim yellow light, symbols and etchings began to appear on the tunnel walls. They were timeworn and prehistoric. Zeph stopped to marvel at them.

The passage elbowed and opened into a dark chamber. Particles glistened faintly on a sandy substrate. Earl disappeared inside. Zeph attempted several steps but had to stop. He stood listening. Earl wheezed somewhere, and his footsteps scraped the floor. Muffled reverberations indicated he had entered a small chamber with a low ceiling.

A flashlight beam snapped on, aimed straight at Zeph. He shielded his eyes.

When he opened them, images, slight and pale, filled his field of vision. Winged creatures and dancing men—an immense sandstone storyboard stretched before him. It was an oval chamber with a crude fire ring in the middle and no other apparent exit. A dead end. Earl's flashlight passed over the faint images painted on the wall—a collage, a Mesolithic coloring book—that Zeph strained to comprehend.

"This is it." Earl's voice died in the chamber. "They excavated the site decades ago, said it was some migrating tribe going south, but they up and vanished. This is all they left us." He steadied the flashlight beam on the wall. "They reckoned it was discovered by some early miners. Creeped 'em out, so they left the place untouched. But it's where the story started."

Zeph's eyes roamed the menagerie of pictographs, but he could not make sense of the images. "Story," Zeph murmured in disbelief, still wrestling against a rising dread. "What story? And what does this have to do with me?"

Earl peered at him, perhaps detecting the submerged skepticism in Zeph's tone. "You really don't know?"

Zeph shook his head.

"Look here." Earl traced the beam across a long green serpentine body, perhaps eight feet in length, which seemed to be the centerpiece of the panel. "It represents the earth. That's how they saw it. A great, graceful thing. But dangerous! And notice the wound."

The beam rested upon a dark gash in the serpent's side. From it there rose a black cloud and dark winged things with yellow eyes.

"The earth was wounded," Earl said reverently. "Profaned or defiled. From it spewed evil. Like Pandora's box—somethin' wretched was released."

Zeph stood mesmerized over the crude prehistoric paintings. He glanced back the way they'd come and did a double-take. The calico dog sat at the mouth of the chamber, its eyes glistening like tiny moons. Sultana and Jim stood on either side of the animal. Either Zeph was cornered or what he was about to see really interested them.

Earl swabbed sweat off his face and turned his gaze back to the petroglyphs. "They believed one would rise to heal the land, a great prophet. And this would be the sign."

He swung the beam to the next panel of rock where, etched in the cave wall, stood a pale figure with an oversized head. Instead of a mouth was a thick vertical line—as clear and unmistakable as the scar on Zeph's face.

He could not stifle a faint murmur. Zeph took a step back. Then another.

Earl said, "They called him the Branded One. It's all over their prophecies and legends. It's who they waited for. A wielder of wild magic. A great sorcerer who would heal the land. This one, with a mark on his face."

Earl kept his light trained on the figure. However, Zeph's head was buzzing. The musty underground air seemed to bristle with energy.

"When you returned from the city," Earl said, "you came with the scar. And then we knew you were the prophet, this Branded One who would heal the earth's wound."

Everything seemed to go mute as Zeph studied the antediluvian caricature. The fear that he felt at that moment was unlike anything he had ever felt. It was the fear of destiny.

Nausea tightened his gut. Zeph realized he was touching his scar and dropped his hand to his side. It was just as Annie had said. Something long ago had been set in motion. Something that he had no control over. The tumblers of some vast universal combination were falling into place, and there was nothing Zeph could do about it. Nothing except wait for the vault to swing wide.

Or run. Which is what Zeph instinctively did.

He turned and pushed past Sultana and Jim. The calico dog yelped as he stepped on its paw and stumbled up the corridor like a madman. Earl called after him, but Zeph ignored the man and barreled through the ancient tunnels into fresh air. He hurried through Meridian, knocking a tray of polished stones to the floor as he passed. Zeph ran onto the porch and stood there in a stupor, swaying, squinting in the daylight. He wondered if he might vomit.

Behind him, the floorboards thumped under Earl's approach. "Zephaniah! Zephaniah!"

"Stop it!" Zeph spun about, facing the storeowner. "Would you all just stop calling me that?"

The glow-in-the-dark UFOs fluttered on a gust of wind.

Sultana emerged behind Earl and stood in the doorway, gaping at Zeph.

Zeph's gaze dropped, and a wave of regret yanked him back to earth. "I–I'm sorry, sir. I shouldn't have—"

The dog pushed past Earl's leg, loped toward Zeph, and sat at his feet, staring up at him. The chimes tinkled in the dry air.

After a moment, Zeph heaved a sigh. "Look, I'm...I'm pretty confused right now."

Earl stepped toward him. "I was there when you killed that man."

Zeph looked up. "I didn't kill him."

"Ol' Duty probably deserved it, lyin' to the Holy Ghost like that."

"I should've never come here."

"You can't resist the hounds of heaven, son. I'd say they're mighty on your trail."

Zeph shook his head and wandered back to the truck. As he put his sunglasses on and opened the door, Earl called to him.

"*Weaver.*"

Zeph looked up.

"*Little Weaver,*" Earl said. "He owns the Vermont. Got Indian blood 'n him. Right knowledgeable man. And storied! Been keepin' an eye on you, like the rest of us. He's been here, seen the prophecy. Don't know about his theories, though. Says he's part of the remnant now, and I can't deny him that. Anyway, he can help you, son."

Zeph stood for a moment looking at the owner of Meridian. The Vermont. It figured. But could anybody really help him? Even this Little Weaver?

"Thank you, sir," Zeph said. "And I'm sorry about—"

"Don't mention it!" Earl brushed his hand through the air. "Just know this." He stepped to the edge of the porch. Jim and Sultana came to opposite sides of him. "We're the remnant, son. We been at this a long time. And trust me, we will see this through."

If the words were intended to produce confidence in Zeph, they had the opposite effect.

Zeph nodded, got into the truck, and spun a U-turn on the highway. He did not look back at the billboard or the Black Pass, or the cloud of dust spreading in his wake.

However, he did wonder if the smallest thing in the world really was a closed mind.

Chapter 30

"T he prophets were an odd bunch," Annie said.

Tamra looked up from the scrapbook. Their conversation with Zeph Walker had left her mind numb. She still had a hard time comprehending that the boy in these pictures was the man who had just sat next to her on her grandmother's sofa. "It's just so hard to believe. A modern-day prophet?"

"Why not?" Annie came to Tamra's side, and they both gazed at the news clippings of the Prophet of the Plains. "God didn't just suddenly stop speaking. And if He still speaks, He can use anyone He wants, including Zeph Walker."

"Yeah, but he seems so...confused."

Annie nodded ruefully. "Just like the prophets of old. They were often troubled. Conflicted. Sometimes disobedient. Look at Jonah— he ran from the call of God. Elijah fled to the wilderness and lived in a cave. Moses argued with God. Yet God used them. They were flawed, but they still had incredible power."

"You're not suggesting that Zeph's got some type of *power*, are you?"

Annie hesitated. "I'm saying just that."

"Pfh!" Tamra brushed her hand through the air. "That's crazy. What kinda power?"

"Like making it rain."

"What?"

"You heard me." Annie closed the scrapbook and snatched it from the table. "He made it rain."

Tamra folded her arms and cast a skeptical gaze at her grandmother.

"I know you don't believe me," Annie sighed, somewhat dramatically. "You've resisted everything I've had to say."

"That's not true," Tamra objected. "I went to Zeph's yesterday, didn't I?"

Annie strummed her fingernails atop the scrapbook.

"Listen, I'm trying to figure this out too, Nams." Tamra relaxed her posture. "So what happened?"

Annie continued tapping her nails atop the scrapbook, as if debating whether to tell her story. Then she nodded to herself and laid the scrapbook back down on the table.

"It was probably fifteen or more years ago," Annie began. "We were in the middle of one of the biggest droughts of the decade. They'd begun rationing water. The farmers were arguing with the DWP about it, but there was so much politics. Eventually farms started drying up and going out of business."

"I remember Grandpa talkin' about that."

"Yes. It hurt our business. As you can imagine, folks turned to the Lord in droves. Churches were crowded. At the time Zephaniah Walker had risen to some acclaim. He would visit local churches with his mother. He was only nine or ten at the time. I was there the day he spoke the prophecy at Bethel. He walked through the crowd, as if he were tuning into God. Finally he went back up on stage and sat down. And didn't say a word. This was a little odd. Usually he would stop and talk to someone. Speak a word of encouragement or say something. Not this time. He just walked up to the stage and sat back down.

"People whispered amongst themselves. Reverend Wade and Sister Hitchens didn't know what to make of it. They looked at each other, decided to sing another hymn, and, to everyone's dismay, prepared to dismiss the assembly. That's when the boy stood.

"His face was flinty, radiant. As if the glory of God rested there. You could hear a pin drop. He took off one shoe, and then the other. Then he rolled up the cuffs on his pants. This leg," Annie mimicked the motion, "then that leg. Everyone was spellbound. Then he said, 'God has heard your prayers. Go home, before the rain stops you.'

"The church cleared out. People got in their cars and raced home. That night a storm rolled in from the north, covering the mountains with snow and filling the aqueducts. The weathermen were confounded."

Tamra gaped at her grandmother.

Annie cleared her throat and said dismissively, "It happened just like that. The boy said God had heard our prayer, and that night the drought was over."

Tamra continued studying her grandmother before lowering her gaze. "What am I gonna do with you?"

"With me?"

"All this stuff about the gates of hell. Prophets. People changing. And now a rainmaker? We must sound like fanatics."

"I'm prepared to go this alone, young lady."

"Oh, I bet you are." Tamra put her hands on her hips. "But that's the last thing I'm gonna let you do."

Annie arched her eyebrows.

Tamra strode to the front door.

"Where are you going?" Annie asked.

"Not me—us. We're going next door to talk to Eugenia."

"But she's—"

"Don't!" Tamra spun around and faced her grandmother. "If you expect me to believe all this crazy talk, then I'm gonna have to see it with my own eyes. If your friend next door has really changed, then let me be the judge." Tamra returned, squeezed Annie's hands, and pleaded, "Nams, you have to realize what this sounds like. You're scaring me."

Annie appeared shocked by her granddaughter's boldness. Her stubbornness quickly returned. "Doubting Thomas needed to see for himself too. And the Good Lord obliged." Annie went to the door, opened it, and stood waiting. "Lead the way, *Doubting Thomas*."

Chapter 31

Tamra knocked on Eugenia Price's door and took a step back. Perhaps it was an unintended indication of what she feared she might find. Annie stood right behind her, deferring to her granddaughter's momentary act of boldness.

Annie whispered, "They don't seem to move around much during the day."

"Who?" Tamra asked over her shoulder.

"The Others."

"Oh, they have a name now?"

"Shh!"

No one answered the door.

Tamra glanced up and down the hall. She was having second thoughts about her impetuousness. What exactly would she say if Eugenia opened the door? *Hi, are you human?* Tamra clucked her tongue.

"Maybe she's gone," Tamra said.

"Eugenia doesn't have a car."

"Well, then maybe she's sleeping."

"It's almost noon."

As Tamra debated whether she should knock again, Annie stepped around her and rapped on the door.

"Nams!" Tamra hissed.

"You're the one who wanted to investigate."

"Yeah, but..."

Still, no one answered.

"C'mon," Tamra said. "Let's go."

"Wait." Annie tried the door handle.

The door popped open.

Tamra gasped. "What're you—"

Annie pressed her index finger to her lips. She inched the door open enough to reveal the darkened room. Apparently Eugenia Price did not like the bright afternoon sun. Either that or she had, indeed, turned nocturnal.

"Genie?" Annie called into the room. "Hey, you in there?"

"Grandma!"

Annie shushed Tamra and bent her ear toward the apartment.

There was no answer.

They glanced at one another, but before Tamra could pull her grandmother away, Annie had opened the door, slipped inside, and yanked Tamra along with her.

"What're you doing?" Tamra resisted her grandmother's tug.

"Shh!"

The configuration of the room looked the same as her grandmother's room—a kitchenette to their immediate left, a modest living room space that opened onto a tiny patio, and a hallway into the single bedroom. Except for an orange crevice of light revealing the fold of thick curtains, the room lay entombed in thick shadow.

"Genie?" Annie called again, drowning out Tamra's muffled protestations.

As Tamra fumbled for the light switch, Annie gripped her hand. She was staring in the direction of the living room. Tamra followed her gaze. A figure stood motionless in the corner of the dark room.

Tamra slapped her hand to her mouth to keep from screaming.

"Genie?" Annie said. "Genie, is that you?"

Tamra clung to her grandmother like a little child, fixated upon the shadowy form. Yet even stranger than Tamra's display of fear was that the person standing stiff in the corner showed no evidence of movement.

"Let's go!" Tamra pleaded.

Annie motioned for quiet, then separated herself from Tamra. She crept toward the living room. Then she removed something from under her skirt, and the next thing Tamra knew, the beam of a flashlight cut through the darkness, shining directly into the face of Eugenia Price. The woman's lips moved silently, yet her eyes were closed. She stood in a catatonic stupor.

Tamra issued a slow gasp.

"Genie?" Annie's voice was laced with caution. "Are you all right?"

Tamra crept forward, watching with breathless fear. *What in the world was going on?* Part of her was astounded by the brashness of this seventy-two-year-old woman. Part of her wondered why her grandmother was carrying a flashlight under her skirt.

The rest of her could not imagine why Eugenia was sleeping standing up.

Annie stood directly in front of Eugenia. Her flashlight beam splashed eerie, elongated shadows across the ceiling.

"Psst!" Annie motioned Tamra over. "Come here!"

Tamara could not believe she was doing this. The resolve she'd had just moments ago had evaporated like the fog on a summer's day. She tiptoed across the carpet to her grandmother. Her eyes did not leave the elderly black woman standing stationary in the corner. All this talk about people changing struck Tamra with the force of a ton of bricks. What could Eugenia be doing? Could her grandmother have been right all along?

Tamra inched her way past the dinette table into the darkened living room.

That's when she noticed the writing on the walls. Like some mad scientist's chalkboard, crude sketches, unfamiliar words, and equations were inscribed, seemingly helter-skelter, throughout the living room. Pictures and shelves had been removed, replaced by scrawled lengths of text. Why would someone do this? Tamra stood dumbfounded before turning back to Eugenia Price.

Annie allowed the beam to search the features of the woman. Dressed in a nightgown, Eugenia's eyes were shut, and there was no REM. Her skin possessed an unusual pall, not quite dry but unreflective of light. Acne stippled her forehead, and a small, moist lesion glistened on her cheek. Her breathing was faint, slow, and almost indistinct. Tamra wondered if she might be paralyzed or experiencing some psychological condition. Despite the flashlight beam in her face, Eugenia remained unmoved.

Annie leaned toward Tamra and whispered, "Do you believe me now, Doubting Thomas?"

As Annie said this, two things happened simultaneously. Eugenia's eyes sprung open, and a second figure emerged from the shadows behind them.

Chapter 32

Annie fumbled the flashlight, recovered, and spun the opposite direction.

It happened so quickly, the only conclusion Tamra could reach was that her eyes were deceiving her. She blinked hard and steadied her gaze.

Janice Marshman rose from the sofa, holding a digital pad. Its screen cast a soft glow upon her sharp features.

"She's been like that for hours," the director said.

"Oh, my!" Annie trembled. "What're you doing here?"

The director spread her hand before her face, squinting in the light. "I suppose I could ask the same thing of you, Miss Lane."

A rush of adrenaline tore through Tamra's body, and close behind it followed a chill. She turned to see Eugenia's glazed eyes staring at her.

Just like Bev Beason's.

Tamra took a step back. Something crunched under her feet, and she glanced down to see an overturned box of cereal, its flakes ground into the carpet. What was going on here?

"I was worried about her," Annie said to the director. "That's what *I'm* doing here."

Tamra returned her gaze to Eugenia. Despite the darkened room, nothing seemed noticeably different about the woman. Short-cropped, wiry hair, thick lower body, and arthritic knuckles. If someone was swapping bodies, Eugenia Price's was not exactly a prime model.

"It's me." Annie stepped toward Eugenia. "It's Annie. Are you all right?"

Eugenia's lips had begun to move silently. She opened her palm and, with her opposite hand, began scrawling invisible figures with her fingertips.

"What's wrong with her?" Annie said with a note of panic in her voice. "And why is it so dark in here? Maybe we should turn on a light and—"

141

"No!" the director blurted. "No. You might hurt her eyes."

"Her eyes?" Annie turned back to the director. "She's never had problems with her eyes."

"Please, Miss Lane," the director urged. "You have no idea what this is about."

Annie allowed the flashlight beam to trace the cluttered floor, past gum wrappers and overturned soda cans, until it came to rest on the far wall. Strange angular symbols were etched in ink and pencil. Jumbled combinations of letters trailed off into incoherent scratch.

"You're right," Annie said, staring at the wall. "I have no idea what this is about."

Then Eugenia brushed past them and meandered to the couch. The director stepped aside as the woman passed. Eugenia sat down and stared forward listlessly.

"*Parasomnia* is the clinical term," the director whispered, glancing at Eugenia. "It's a sleep disorder. Involves nightmares, sleepwalking, and unpredictable arousals. Miss Price asked me to chronicle her episodes, which I obliged. I did not, however, expect other residents to *intrude*." She lingered on the last word, erasing any doubt as to her anger.

Then the director motioned them to the front door.

Waxen blobs marked the remains of candles here and there. Cereal bowls were stacked on the kitchen sink, along with crumpled cigarette packs and half-eaten squares of toast capped with butter. Either Eugenia had suddenly lost interest in cleanliness or she was aiming for the slob-of-the-year award.

The director led them out and closed the door behind them, leaving the shadowy figure unmoving on the sofa. Tamra winced in the hallway light.

"I've been suspicious for a while now," the director said, looking at her digital device. "As you may have detected from our last conversation."

Annie nodded, but Tamra could see the wheels of her mind churning.

"She reported it to me several weeks ago," the director said. "Waking up at odd places. Unable to sleep normal hours. For fear that she may injure herself or others, Eugenia asked me to look in on her."

"I had no idea."

Tamra cleared her throat. "I'm sorry, Miss Marshman, but if Eugenia's got something *that* wrong, shouldn't she be seeing a doctor? And all that weird writing on the wall—that's more than just sleepwalking."

The director's lips curled at the edges. "I see you have your grandmother's spunk. But who said she is *not* seeing a doctor? Parasomnia is hardly terminal, unless, of course, the victim wanders onto the highway or off their balcony. And, for the record," she turned the electronic pad and aimed the screen at them, "that is exactly what I am chronicling for her health care provider."

Tamra felt her face flush with embarrassment. "Oh."

"As far as the scribblings," the director continued, "we are far more concerned with Miss Price's mental well-being than our walls. She is currently undergoing tests, at the request of a distant in-law, for a variety of possible conditions."

The director gripped the device politely at her waist. "While I appreciate both your concern for Miss Price, I feel compelled to remind you about our policies. Entering the apartment of other residents uninvited, at the least, looks suspicious. At worst, it may constitute a criminal offense."

Tamra could see her grandmother's body tense at the director's words.

"Excuse me," Annie objected, "but we're friends, ma'am. I've known Genie since I moved here. If she was suffering from some condition, I didn't know about it. And as far as a criminal offense, if being concerned about my friend is against the law, then I'm guilty as charged."

The director remained steely. "Indeed. I appreciate your concern. But from now on I would suggest you leave any further investigation of individuals or this facility up to me or a trained investigator. While I do appreciate your concern for Miss Price, in the future I would suggest more...*discretion*." She smiled. "Good day, ladies."

Annie and Tamra watched the director move lithely down the hallway.

Finally, Tamra said, "You don't believe her, do you?"

"I don't know."

Tamra shook her head. "We need to report this. Go to the police or something."

"What are the police going to do? So my neighbor has a condition that forces her to sleep standing up."

"And write all over her walls? C'mon, you don't believe that, do you?"

Annie raised an eyebrow. "Now who's the one believing all this *wild* stuff?"

Tamra drew her fingers through her hair. "I'm not sure what to believe anymore."

"Well, before we go anywhere—especially to the police—we need more evidence."

"Uh-uh," Tamra said sternly. "You've gathered enough evidence for today."

"Excuse me? You're the one who wanted to investigate."

Tamra took her grandmother by both shoulders, turned her around, and nudged her toward her apartment. "Well, I'll take over from here. No more investigating for you. And what're you doing with a flashlight under your skirt, anyway?"

Chapter 33

He considered himself a *modified realist*, although Zeph Walker understood the incongruity of those two words. His unbelief was really a carefully constructed rationalization, a dismissal of his own culpability in some universal formula. God could do His thing, Zeph reasoned, and nothing on earth could stop Him. Which meant that any refusal to act on Zeph's part was a component of that universal formula. That's how destiny worked, wasn't it? Even your *resistance* was predetermined.

Yet as the pieces were aligning—the man at the morgue, the ninth gate of hell, the Meridian prophecy, the remnant—Zeph's resistance was eroding as fast as sandstone in a rainstorm.

The morning sun had yielded to dry afternoon heat. As Zeph raced away from the Black Pass, the image of the Meridian petroglyphs and the prophetic figure with the slash on its mouth smoldered inside him. Those cave paintings had to be 150 years old! What ancient hands had squeezed the blood of berries and cacti onto that rock? This was more than coincidence. This was destiny.

Sweat stung his eyes, and he hunched forward at the wheel, his mind careening down corridors he had long feared to tread.

The screeching of the tires jolted him back to earth. Zeph took his foot off the gas and yanked the truck back into its lane. Driving off the cliff would not put him out of his misery. He may have shed many of his childhood convictions, but Zeph's belief in a place called hell was not one of them.

He slowed the car, fighting to still his mind.

The Endurance basin spread before him, swatches of farmland laced with the Owens River and its crystalline tributaries, the entire valley ringed with the Sierras' rugged blue peaks. How long had it been since he witnessed this sight? He could not imagine a landscape more beautiful.

The asphalt rippled with serpentine heat waves, invisible tentacles rising toward the cobalt blue. He traced the thin black runway with his eyes, following as it sloped in a series of low rolling hills before spilling into flatland. As the mill wheels of his mind turned, a building appeared on his left—at first nothing more than a pale speck against the dry earth. Then the white wooden bell tower rose into view, weathered into decay.

Zeph slowed as the church came into sight. It had been so long since he'd come this way, he'd almost forgotten about Shiloh Church of God in Christ. Seeing the place had the effect of a scab being ripped from a wound.

It was here that he knew his life would never be the same.

A white picket fence, though sagging in sections and brittle with age, surrounded the property. How many times had he run the perimeter of that fence, chasing monarchs in spring while singing church hymns? One time the entire congregation did a Jericho march around the whole seven acres. Now tumbleweeds and old newspapers dotted the empty expanse.

He slowed the truck and veered onto the shoulder. The plywood sign out front tilted haphazardly while announcing a revival. Zeph looked away from the marquee to the boarded-up white structure. The image of the neolithic cave painting had scarred his mind and left him off-kilter. Which was the only explanation for his next move. He parked and turned off the ignition.

Zeph sat grinding his teeth, peering at Shiloh. Finally he nudged the truck door open and stepped onto the gravel. Several cars whooshed past, kicking up dust, but his gaze remained on the tiny church.

He walked cautiously along the fence. The afternoon sun throbbed upon his back, and in the distance a hawk wheeled against the blue sky. He prepared to vault the fence, but finding the gate unlocked, pushed it open. Dry leaves skittered across a rock-lined path. Far off the droning of a semitruck warbled to life, merging with the unseen chatter of locusts to form a low-level monotone soundtrack to the proceedings.

Adjusting his sunglasses, Zeph walked to the church building. The porch creaked terribly, and he worried that it might collapse under his weight. He faced the thick wooden doors. With their braided wrought-iron handles, the doors always seemed excessive for the little country church. How many times had he marched through these doors like a king into his court, all eyes fixated on the boy wonder?

Zeph took the handles in both hands and shook them firmly. Something thumped inside, and the doors creaked open.

Dust motes exploded, and he stepped back coughing. Hazy light drifted through the doorway, casting a foggy sheen about the wooden pews. Zeph glanced at his truck, inhaled, and strode inside.

A smell of urine and feces struck him. Shiloh was probably home to vagrants and hitchhikers. Had he woken someone with his rude entry? Except for a broken stool and some tattered hymnals, the stage was barren, so different from the last time he saw it.

Zeph proceeded up the center aisle. He climbed the steps, stood on the stage, and turned to the empty pews. Cobwebs draped sections, and the light cast gauzy silhouettes about the abandoned church. Zeph's gaze settled on a spot on the carpet.

Blaise S. Duty had lain there. Right there.

Yes, that was when everything changed.

Chapter 34

He was well respected, that insurance salesman. Of course, behind closed doors the boy prophet had heard the deacons snicker and refer to the man as B. S. Duty, with an emphasis on the B. S.

Which may or may not have affected the outcome of the man's life.

"Zephaniah!" His mother tugged at the cuff of his suit. Then she tapped her temple with her forefinger. "Pay attention!"

Her eyes were so blue. And by "pay attention," she meant he should not allow his surroundings to distract him from ciphering. That was one of the terms she used for the Telling. Her brother, a seven-foot-tall math wizard, had coined the phrase. She knew twelve-year-olds were easily distracted. Especially from ciphering.

The basket swept through the crowd for the second time. Brother Miller beamed his ultra-white smile at Zephaniah. It always made him uncomfortable, and the boy prophet looked away, wriggling in his seat. The word "bury" always came to his mind when talking to Brother Miller. But Zephaniah could never calculate what it meant. Bury what? Bury where? Or maybe it was berry—as in strawberry, blueberry, and, his favorite, raspberry. No matter. Zephaniah never spoke a word of it to Brother Miller.

In fact, there was a lot he'd never spoken. Even to Belle, his mother.

From the stage he could survey the whole congregation. Mother called this the Measurin', the part of the service where he should settle in and watch for God's presence. Just like those tongues of flame rested above the early disciples, when the Lord moved upon someone, He often set His mark upon them. Sometimes Zephaniah could see that mark. But mostly it was a knowing that the boy prophet could not shake.

"The Lawd is here!" Brother Miller shouted after the collection had been received. "He shall speak!" Then his tone descended into abrupt, dramatic hush. "And we shall listen."

"Amen!" The congregation sounded their approval.

The Lord will speak. The boy prophet believed that. The Lord *did* speak. Zephaniah had heard Him. Yet being His spokesperson was not something Zephaniah cherished.

Out of the corner of his eye Zephaniah could see his mother staring at him. She had her way of prodding. Thankfully he had graduated from the Pit, from the darkness and the mold and the rats. The boy had learned his lesson. Mother was proud of Zephaniah for that. She could not take losing another son to his own sin. It pained her to have to shut him up in the Pit, she told him. But the Lord was even there, she said, just like He was with Daniel in the den of lions.

Still, Zephaniah never, ever wanted to go back to the Pit.

It didn't take much to train his mind. He looked out on the collection of farmers and migrants mixed with the well-to-do ranchers and city folk. Despite their smiles and shouts of praise, the boy prophet could sense their emptiness. Their longing. So many lost souls. So many people yearning for something more. The scary part was they all looked to him for hope.

He scoured the audience, ciphering, his spiritual antenna up like the tower at the Mighty Z. They watched him, faces full of fear and anticipation. That's when his eyes came to rest on Blaise S. Duty.

A large man, disproportionate at the waist. His face was thin, gaunt, in direct contradiction to the bulging waistline. He wore his shirt in such a way as to camouflage his size. Flowery Hawaiian prints, opened at the collar to intentionally display expensive jewelry.

As the boy prophet looked at Blaise Duty, a familiar sound rose inside him.

It reminded Zephaniah of a Geiger counter over precious metal, an emotional sonar that pinged something deep inside his soul. Although this sound did not register in his ears, it seemed to drown out the outside world, a switch that he could not control, only witness.

And sure enough, the Telling arrived and took his breath away.

Mother reached out her hand as Zephaniah twitched at its reception. She knew when the connection came. If Zephaniah turned to look at her, she would have probably been smiling proudly. However, the words emblazoned on his mind prevented him from doing anything other than study Blaise Duty.

Zephaniah rose from the large wooden chair and yanked the hem of his coat down, as his mother had showed him. The congregation became as still as the sky before snow. He descended the steps. No doubt Brother Miller was beaming, anticipating a second offering.

Blaise Duty did not possess the normal tan one would get working outdoors under the Death Valley heat. His was the kind movie stars acquired indoors, under strange orange lights. He fanned himself with a brochure and nodded aimlessly. Until he saw the boy prophet measuring him. Zephaniah could almost smell the man's fear ooze from the pores of his body.

You're lying, Blaise. That's how Zephaniah heard it. *You can't hide. This day the wife of your youth, My little lamb, is freed.*

The words were not full of hate or anger, although that shifty newspaper reporter liked to describe the boy prophet as always angry. If anything, the Telling broke his heart.

Zephaniah walked down the aisle, gazing at Blaise Duty and thinking about that little lamb that would be set free. Before the boy prophet even called his name, Blaise Duty lurched to his feet.

"Mr. Duty." The world seemed to wait for Zephaniah's words. "The Lord has this for you."

The congregation drew a single collective breath. And held it.

Zephaniah spoke the words just as he'd heard them.

Blaise Duty looked like he'd been punched in his soft, spongy gut. The color drained from his orange-tinged skin, and his bottom lip began to tremble. Then he pushed his way out of the pew, stomping May Bristol's foot, and stumbled into the center aisle.

Blaise Duty opened his mouth to speak but didn't. He wiped perspiration off his forehead and did a slow rotation, staring at the gaping congregants, his lips twitching.

"I—" He swallowed. Then coughed. "My wife, she..." Fumbling at the collar of his flowery print shirt, tears welled in his eyes. "God, I'm sorry," he whimpered. "I am so sorry."

Then his features grew placid, and his skin turned hideously ashen.

"Loree-e-e," was the last thing he said before spinning like a corkscrew onto the carpet and falling flat on his back, as dead as a possum on the center line of the 395.

Chapter 35

A gust of wind flung the church door wide, whipping sand into the dilapidated sanctuary and snapping Zeph from his daydream. He stared at the spot where Blaise Duty died.

By the time the ambulance arrived, the insurance salesman was already losing color. That's how fast it went down. The congregation refused to touch the body, although Zeph doubted that any amount of resuscitation could have altered Blaise Duty's arc into the afterlife. Some congregants openly recalled the story of Ananias and Sapphira in the Bible, claiming it was the judgment of God. Others believed it was the precursor to a great revival. The coroner claimed it was simply a massive heart attack. Nevertheless, when it was learned that the man had a mistress, as well as an elaborate plot to stage his wife's death and collect the insurance, they looked at the boy prophet differently. How could they not?

Zeph stared at that patch of faded carpet. Did Detective Lacroix know about the Prophet of the Plains? Had they uncovered the sad story of Blaise Duty? Could they even fathom the weight Zeph had carried all these years?

He left Shiloh, the mold and urine, and stood under the weathered sign, staring back into the afternoon sun. The Black Pass rose like a monument to mystery.

Do you find your destiny, or does your destiny find you?

Yesterday the answer to that question was obvious. The detectives arrived on his doorstep unannounced. Could they be part of some universal scheme? Then there was the man in the morgue who'd set everything in motion. Who was he? *What* was he? And why was there a bullet in his chest? And there was Annie Lane and the remnant—could he really be the fulfillment of some ancient prophecy? Whatever the answers, one thing was clear: destiny had finally come knocking for Zeph Walker.

He removed his keys and cast a long look at Shiloh. A man died in there because of something Zeph said. Now more than ever it confirmed what he had once only wondered.

Zeph got into his truck and drove back to his property. Perhaps he should have never left. When he arrived, he parked the truck under the carport and closed the gate. Then he did something he hadn't done in years. Zeph removed a cardboard placard from inside the Book Swap and taped it on the door. It announced the store was closed.

Like Crusoe, if God really wanted Zeph Walker off his lonely island, then He'd have to come and rescue him.

Chapter 36

"Take a look at this," Annie said.

Easy Dolan watched as she dumped the dossier on his desk.

"Good Lord, Miss Annie!" He snatched a package of powdered doughnuts from the path of cascading papers. "Whatcha got here?"

"I was hoping you could tell me."

Easy retrieved his glasses, turned the gooseneck lamp on, and began sifting through the strange documents.

"Have a seat, Miss Annie," he said, already enthralled in the assemblage of paperwork.

She glanced at the antique wingback chair. Jezebel was still missing from her usual spot. Annie recalled seeing the cat at Camp Poverty last night, but Easy seemed unconcerned with the feline's wandering ways. However, the way her lower back ached, Annie would not be able to stand that chair. She declined Easy's offer and remained standing.

The retired golfer's eyes seemed to widen with every page. He studied one of the anatomical sketches. "What'n the world is this?" Easy held up the sketch of the winged, four-faced man-beast.

"An angel, I think. A cherub, to be exact."

"Angel? Ain't like no angel I ever seen!"

"You've seen an angel?"

"You know what I mean—the Precious Moments kinda angel."

"That is definitely not a Precious Moments angel."

Easy mumbled something and hunched forward, continuing his inspection of the dossier. Finally he leaned back in his chair and scratched under the bill of his cap.

Annie folded her arms. "So, do you believe me now?"

Easy swiveled toward her and read from the folder: "United States Army." He tipped his head and peered at her over the top of his glasses. "Now, how in the world'd you come by these?"

Annie hesitated. After seeing Fergus last night at Camp Poverty and the director huddled in Eugenia's darkened apartment, paranoia seemed to be seeping into the crevices of Marvale like fog in a marsh. Could she trust Easy? He didn't possess any of Eugenia's recent traits: reclusion, emotional distance. There was no bizarre writing on his walls, either. Yet if the devil appeared as an angel of light, perhaps he could disguise himself as anyone. The thought sent her stomach spiraling. Nevertheless, with the documents now in Easy's possession, she was probably past the point of no return. Eventually she would have to trust someone. Which was not one of Annie Lane's strong suits.

Finally she said, "I found it in the custodial area, by the boiler room."

"Found it?" Easy squinted at her. "What were you doin' down there?"

"Following a hunch."

"Obviously you ignored my word of caution."

"I'm sorry. But yesterday, when I left here, I heard something strange."

"Strange? Like what?"

Annie shook her head as she recalled the throaty language. "Like moaning, in some odd dialect."

"You sure it wasn't the Higginbothams?" Easy issued a wry smile. "They've been known to have some exotic vices."

"It wasn't the Higgenbothams," Annie said dismissively. "I followed the sound to the custodial area. That's where I found it. It was scattered on the floor, as if someone had dropped it."

"Dropped it? Someone like Fergus?"

She shrugged. "It was his shift. No one else goes back there except Stevie and the custodial crew. And then last night..." Annie hesitated.

Easy peered at her. "Last night *what?*"

Annie met his inquisitive gaze. "I saw him up near Camp Poverty."

"Fergus?"

She nodded.

"Now, what on earth were you doin' all the way up there?"

"There's a map of Camp Poverty in there, Easy—maps of this whole area."

"Ya don't say." Easy turned back to the desk and brushed through the papers absently. "I just can't imagine what Fergus could be doin' with somethin' like this. Or what the government wanted here."

"I was hoping you could tell me. With everything going on, it just didn't seem like a coincidence."

"Coincidence or not, if this stuff is Fergus's and he finds out, you'll be in a world of hurt, Miss Annie. That young man gives me the creeps."

"That makes two of us."

Easy examined the documents, his brow alternately furrowed in disbelief and wonder.

Annie massaged her lower back with her fingertips as she watched him. The knot of blue on her shin peeked from under the lip of her sock, evidence that her investigations were taking a decidedly risky turn. And if these documents were any indication, things would only get worse. Perhaps the most perilous thing she had undertaken was finally to involve Zeph Walker. Up to this point the remnant had remained observant but uninvolved. They had watched the prophet from a distance, kept a close eye on the happenings in the city. Now Annie was having second thoughts about her actions. It would not be the first time her foolhardiness had gotten her into trouble. However, it was the effect it would have on Zeph Walker that most concerned her. They could not afford to lose him. Not again. Nevertheless, as long as he had free will, losing him remained a possibility.

"So, what do you think?" Annie motioned to the spread of documents. "Do you have any ideas what that could be? Or why it's here?"

"Let's see." Easy randomly snatched a paper from the pile. "Words. Lotsa words. Perhaps some type a code." He retrieved another page and studied it with the same eager intensity. "Here we got a diagram regarding what looks like...magnetic fields. And here's a medical examination of some sort. *Hyperplasia. Cellular replication. Assimilation. Subject X.* Almost like they was experimenting on someone. Odd." He thumbed through several more papers before stopping.

"Well, will you look at this!"

"What is it, Easy?"

He adjusted his glasses and peered at a single page. "So it is true."

"What's true? What're you talking about?"

"You wanna know where these documents come from?" He swiveled toward Annie. "Try Robert Coyne."

He passed the page to her, tapping the bottom. "*R. J. Coyne.* Signed right there."

It was a photocopied memo on Department of the Army letterhead. Annie stared at the scrawled signature. "As in *Fergus* Coyne?"

"It's Fergus's father. I'd bet my life on it. It'd been rumored that Robert Coyne was a physicist of some repute. Worked for an independent firm before being recruited by the government for some top-secret experiments. But that was a long time ago. He showed up around here with only a rumor of greatness. Not sure if Marvale Manor is the best retirement home the government can get ya. Anyways, he's down in Laurel House now."

"You're kidding." Annie returned the paper to him.

"Used ta be a resident here till he had a stroke. I remember him." Easy leaned back, drifting in thought. "Wife passed away—killed herself, from what I recall—left him all messed up. Never talked much, but when he did, it was always ramblin', pseudoscientific nonsense about interplanetary travel and other dimensions. Got his son on staff. How he managed to get that one past the director, I'll never know. The both of 'em used to get on people's nerves somethin' fierce. Then one day he just stopped talkin', laid there like an overstuffed hen. They called in Doc Beauchamp, who deduced the old man'd had a stroke. And that was that. Hasn't uttered a word since, from what I understand."

"And you're sure that's his signature?"

"R. J. Coyne—that's what they called him. *Pops*, for short."

"And he was involved in...military experiments?"

"Well, that was the going theory. But this," Easy tapped the page with his fingertip, "this seems to corroborate that."

"So, what was the military doing here?"

"Whatever it was, it had a name." He sorted through the documents and passed her a single sheet.

"Project NOVEM," Annie read.

"*Novem.* It's Latin for the number nine."

Annie gasped. "The ninth gate. *They were studying Otta's Rift.*"

"Well, let's not jump to conclusions. Whatever they were studyin', Project NOVEM was terminated. Says here, R. J. Coyne signed off September 1948. Apparently Uncle Sam shut 'em down."

"So, why would he come back here? And what would the military want with that old mine?"

"That's assumin' they were studyin' that god-awful place." He shook his head. "But I suppose I can proffer a theory."

"Please do."

Easy settled back in his chair, hands folded on his lap, as if he were an old sage preparing to spin a yarn.

"Death Valley's got a fairly rich geologic history," he said. "As well as the Sierras. Fact, the whole basin was once submerged, they say, covered by some sorta prehistoric swamp. Imagine that—Endurance underwater." He cackled. "Either way, it leaves the whole Owens Valley awash in riches. And geological oddities."

"I'm not following," Annie said. "What does that have to do with the military?"

"I'm getting' there," he said with a raised finger. "The eastern Sierras were not exactly a hotspot for the gold rush. But once things got goin', camps sprouted up all along the range, from Lone Pine to Tahoe. Camp Poverty's evidence of that. Silver. Ore. Enough to draw in a few families near the turn of the century. Course, the Madness put an end to all that."

Annie shook her head. "We used to scare ourselves silly with stories about it when we were kids."

"Well, it's worth being scared about. A hundred-and-some folks settin' themselves afire. A regular Jonestown Massacre."

"I've always wondered about that event. But how are they connected? Why would the military care about the site of a mass suicide?"

"Maybe they weren't. Maybe there was somethin' else up there that caught their interest."

"Like what?"

He retrieved a wrinkled map from the assemblage of paperwork. "I ain't an expert, but this is a topographical map of this area. Follows the roads up along the foothills—Cyril Loop and Lower Thermal Mine Road. Locations of pits and aquifers. And also geomagnetic coordinates."

"Huh?"

"Magnetic fields. They cover the earth, and wherever they intersect, strange phenomena tend to occur—optical illusions, gravitational disorientation. Bermuda Triangle type a' stuff. You've heard of the Oregon vortex, right?"

"I'm afraid not."

"Nothin' but a tourist trap now. But they claim the area possesses certain properties, anomalies. Ya know, brooms stand on end, objects roll uphill, compasses go whacky. And if you look closely," he traced his fingers along the map, "there appears to be unusual intersections all along the foothills, especially—" His bony finger came to rest on the page. "—at the Rift."

"You're saying Otta's Rift is a...magnetic vortex?"

"Don't know. But whatever it was, the military mighta been conductin' a scientific analysis of the disturbance. They've been known ta take interest in such phenomena. Remember, that was the middle of the Cold War. The government was looking for any leg up they could get. Antigravity devices, mind control, invisibility."

"Invisibility?"

"Sure. The military'd been experimenting with invisibility since the early thirties. Quantum physics was in its inception, opened up all kinds of possibilities. You don't think Uncle Sam would miss an opportunity to exploit that, do ya?" He issued a sinister chuckle.

"Invisibility? Quantum physics? I'm officially over my head."

"Ya think?"

"So, whatever was going on here," Annie said, "Robert Coyne returned for it."

"And if this stuff was in Fergus's possession," Easy passed his hand over the spread of documents, "there's a good possibility somethin's still goin' on. And that Fergus will be lookin' for this."

Easy Dolan settled back with a contented smile. "I take back what I said, Miss Annie. I do believe you have landed somethin'. If the Lord's really guided you, as you suggest, then maybe it's time to jump in with both feet."

He issued his broad white smile.

Which was all the confirmation Annie needed.

Chapter 37

"You're lucky we didn't get a ticket." Tamra dismounted her scooter and gave her grandmother a stern eye. "I could've fired up Old Glory if I'd known you wanted a ride."

Annie massaged her lower back and grimaced, then glanced at the scooter. "It's not very kind on the buttocks, is it?"

"Probably because it's only meant for one person." Tamra hung her helmet on the scooter. "Now, tell me again why you were in such a hurry to get here."

They both turned and gazed at Zeph Walker's house.

Wisps of orange clouds showed neon against the twilit sky. Cricket songs awakened in the evening. Along the streets, porch lights cast long shadows while families huddled inside over steaming plates of food and around their television sets. However, Zeph Walker's ranch lay dark, entombed in shadow.

"This place is just like I remembered it." Annie gazed at the house.

"So you *have* been here."

"Not really. When we learned he'd moved back, we used to drive by, just out of curiosity. And concern." Annie straightened her braids and looked squarely at Tamra. "Call it a hunch. But I'm afraid that young man is in grave danger."

After discovering Eugenia in an upright coma and the director sitting in her darkened apartment, Tamra had the feeling she should start trusting her grandmother's hunches more.

"Haven't we bothered him enough?" Tamra said. "I mean, he's either gonna get the message or he isn't. You probably scared him off with all that talk about the ninth gate of hell."

Annie raised an eyebrow. "Do you mean to tell me, after what you saw today, that you're not scared?"

Tamra could not shake the feeling that she was being cornered. She cleared her throat. "I told you, until this thing gets figured out, you're moving in with us."

"Moving out of Marvale is not going to stop anything. If Zeph doesn't come to his senses, this thing may never get figured out. Now, come on."

Annie unlatched the gate and led them under the dry arbor. The huge ash tree made the area unusually dark, and after what she'd seen that day, Tamra's emotions were already on high alert.

"Hey, that's weird." Tamra stopped and peered at the Book Swap.

"What's weird?"

"His bookstore." She wandered toward the cottage. "There's a closed sign in the window."

Annie was right behind her. "So?"

"He told me he never closes that place. Let's it stay open all the time, just like the previous owner wanted. Hmm. Maybe he left town or somethin'." She stopped and listened. The dried sunflowers scraped against each other in the evening breeze, and somewhere in the foothills coyotes began yipping. "Somethin's wrong, Nams. Maybe we should leave."

There was no response.

"Nams?" Tamra turned around. Her grandmother was gone.

"Nams!" Tamra spun, frantically scouring the shadowy yard for any sign of her grandmother.

"Shh!"

The sound came from the porch. Annie Lane was standing at the front door.

"What're you doing?" Tamra hissed, and hurried across the yard. "Let's get outta here."

Despite her granddaughter's admonition, Annie rapped on the door.

A dog barked somewhere down the street.

Tamra held her breath, strode up the steps, and took hold of her grandmother's elbow. They stood breathlessly, listening for a response. The porch swing creaked at a passing breeze, yet the house was silent.

"C'mon." Tamra tugged Annie away from the door. "I can come by tomorrow. When it's light."

Annie yanked free of Tamra's grasp and knocked on the door again. "Zephaniah! I know you're in there."

"What're you—"

"He's in there, I know it." Annie's eyes glistened with intensity. Or madness. "Zephaniah! Open up!"

Annie tried to open the door, rattling the handle and nudging it with her shoulder.

"Would you—" Tamra looked across the street to make sure they were not being watched. "C'mon!"

As Tamra prepared to drag her grandmother off the porch and down the steps, Annie froze. As did Tamra.

A soft but evident thud sounded inside the house. They looked at each other.

"Something's wrong." Annie pounded on the door with her fist. "Zeph! We're here!" Then she turned. "Tam, do something."

Another thud sounded, this time followed by what Tamra could only describe as a dry whistle, followed by a titter. The sound was so foreign, so inhuman, that they looked at each other, stunned.

Tamra's first reaction was to cover her ears and run. Her grandmother was right. Something was going on in this city. Something quite outside the realm of ordinary. Despite the possible consequences of breaking and entering—for the second time today—running would be even worse. Besides, Zeph Walker was in trouble.

She quickly sized up the situation. Her gaze swept across the front porch, then raced to the window, but she was unable to see through the curtain into the darkened house. Pressing her palm against the glass, Tamra attempted to open the window. It was locked. Breaking it would only draw attention to them. Thumping past the porch swing, she squeezed in front of Annie, studying the door in the dim light. It was a standard spring-loaded lock, and atop it was a dead bolt. If the dead bolt was drawn, there would be no way to enter apart from ripping the door off the jamb.

"Hurry!" Annie implored.

"I need a credit card or somethin'." Tamra looked at her grandmother, then at her scooter. But she'd left her backpack at Nams's apartment because they'd ridden double.

"I don't have one," Annie hissed. "Hurry!"

Tamra glanced at the door, then the window. Then she remembered.

"God bless you, Dieter," she said, removing the plastic library card from her back pocket.

Her hands trembled, but she slid the card straight inside and gently wiggled it.

The house had gone quiet again.

"Hurry!" Annie said again, this time patting Tamra's thigh.

"I'm trying!" Tamra snapped.

She could feel the clip behind the card and wriggled it between the plate until a click sounded. The dead bolt was not secured because the door popped open.

The room was dimly lit. Tamra stepped in, trying to shield Annie from entering. A thick, musky odor immediately struck her. Light from another room cast a long beam across a wooden floor. Directly ahead of her, she could make out a step-down den. A large painting hung above a sooty fireplace. And before it writhed a large, indistinct shape.

Annie squeezed past Tamra, and they stood trying to discern the dark roiling object no more than fifteen feet away.

"Zeph?" Tamra spoke timidly, stepping toward the darkened shape. "Is that you?"

A raspy susurration sounded that made her stop in her tracks. Her skin prickled. The odor was coming from there, and now she could see there was more than one person. Her field of vision was obscured by an unwholesome dark shape straddling Zeph's body on all fours.

Annie whimpered something. As she did, a pale face rose from its feeding and turned toward them, two phosphorescent eyes radiating hate and unspeakable malice.

Tamra may have screamed. She fumbled for a light switch near the door and found one.

Even if she'd had time to gather her thoughts and find the words to describe what she saw hunched over the body of Zeph Walker, Tamra knew it would have sounded like gibberish. Zeph was on his back, eyes open in a frigid paralysis. Whatever had hunched over him rose, its torso—if it could be said to have possessed a torso—elongated, like some maniacal jack-in-the-box. A soft curtain of shadow rippled behind it, and a head—a very human looking head—turned upward to glare at them.

That's when Tamra realized that she and Annie were shrieking.

For the thing unfolding before them had the face of Zeph Walker.

Chapter 38

Belle Walker dropped dead when Zeph was thirteen years old. At that age most boys have exchanged their love of toads and toy soldiers for a newfound interest in girls. But unlike the rest of his schoolmates, Zephaniah Walker did not have toads or toy soldiers. Aside from feeling like mush when Kim Daschle passed by, any interest he had in girls was kept strictly under wraps. His mother would not tolerate crushes, even of the adolescent kind.

So when Belle collapsed at the kitchen sink holding a colander of greens, the boy prophet was left with little to fall back on. Their ministry had already hit on hard times. His mother complained that that's what happened during times of prosperity—people forgot their Maker—although Zephaniah wondered if there were other reasons the Prophet of the Plains was losing his following. Belle's unexpected passing nurtured his growing suspicions. Sudden deaths were reserved for adulterers like Blaise Duty, he believed, not women of God like Belle Walker. However, what he believed had never really been his own.

The doctor surmised she died from a brain hemorrhage. Yet the rumor around town was that she had pushed her son too far and reaped the consequences. Either way, the old man was finally free from Belle's iron fist. He quickly took advantage.

And all the magic on earth could not prevail against the destiny that was bearing down on Zephaniah.

They buried her at Moncrieff's, near the fence line. His father said she'd have liked the view. Zephaniah could not dispute that, and neither could he prevent his father from selling the ranch and moving to Los Angeles. Zephaniah came to believe it was in response to the trust she'd left for him. Between almost a decade's worth of "love offerings" and an uncanny financial intuition, unbeknownst to them Belle had amassed a small fortune and left it to her only son. It irked the old man. But if her death was a body blow to Zephaniah, leaving Endurance was the ensuing uppercut.

It was hard enough for him to cope without his mother. Now he had to deal with Pearl.

The marriage remained a mystery. Had his father previously known Pearl? Where did they meet? And how could he gravitate to someone so *different* from Belle? Zephaniah's questions remained unanswered. Pearl was introduced and moved into their apartment, bringing her cigarettes and stainless steel demeanor with her.

But it was Pearl's hatred that ultimately sealed his destiny.

"She ruined you," Pearl would sneer at Zephaniah, oozing malice. If words could carry poison, Pearl's were lethal. "You won't last, kid. Ain't no such thing as prophets."

If only his mother was there to guide him, to help him navigate the waters of Pearl's disdain.

But he had the Telling. And when it finally came, he would rue that day.

It was the stuff of folklore, a standoff between boy prophet and queen of the damned. Only, in his case, the damned won.

"You've been weighed in the balance," Zephaniah declared to Pearl, bristling with the energy of the Telling. "And you've been found lacking."

Those words had barely left his lips when his stepmother snatched a nearby letter opener and brought it down across his face. Even worse than the gash was that she cackled as he rolled on the floor, clawing his face, blood spraying everywhere.

Pearl was institutionalized, and her words officially came to pass. That was the final time Zephaniah prophesied.

She cursed him, Pearl did. And he returned the favor. Now, staring into those phosphorescent eyes, he knew this was the echo. The aftermath of his regret and bitterness. The shadow he had nurtured had become a living thing…a thing that now sought to absorb him.

And Zephaniah couldn't resist it. Nor did he want to.

So he fell into the shadow…

Chapter 39

Had Zeph's attacker appeared human, Tamra may have rushed him in an attempt to separate his kneecap. However, by the look of things, this person did not have kneecaps to separate. In fact, this person did not look human.

Its torso was fleshy in appearance. Soft flumes of atmosphere rippled behind the being, as if an invisible cape or winged appendages buoyed the body. Yet its limbs seemed pixelated, comprised of something other than solid matter. Its extremities amassed and folded within themselves, columns of fog churning and reshaping. The face glared at them, its evil eyes blazing, and as it did, its mouth yawned open, slinging drool. Then it returned and hunched over the body of Zeph Walker, like a vampire preparing to dine on its prey.

Tamra stood dumbfounded. Calling the police seemed so feeble, so inconsequential in light of the anomaly before them. And breaking the thing's kneecaps was out of the question.

As they watched the awful thing blossom over Zeph, as Tamra fumbled within herself for a plan of attack, footsteps thumped up the steps behind them, wrenching Tamra from her thoughts.

"Brother Walker!"

A tall, barrel-chested man, biker's goggles hanging from his neck, thumped through the door in heavy boots and stood menacingly with a crossbow positioned at his waist. His eyes were small, set deep in a large ruddy head. He wore leather gloves of the construction variety and a canvas jacket with camouflage markings. Beneath the jacket, Tamra could make out a thick army belt and various accoutrements dangling from it.

"For the land!" the man bellowed, and aimed the crossbow at the creature.

Tamra and Annie stumbled to opposite sides of the room, their eyes wide with shock. She did not have time to worry about the man's aim. The bow twanged, and a silken strand trailed the arrow into the den. A soft *pop* was followed by a hideous cry, a shrill avian caw. The creature was driven off Zeph's body in a blur of motion.

Zeph dropped limp as the entity whirled in a tortured, indistinguishable mass to the corner of the den. Meanwhile the man had dropped the crossbow and seized the cord attached to the arrow. He wrapped it around his gloved hand and leaned back as if fighting some great marlin in a tropical sea. But the thing on the end of this line was not nearly as graceful. It rose toward the ceiling, battering the walls and sending pictures and mantelpiece objects clattering about the room. Garbled titters and chirps emerged. Wing-like appendages pummeled the air, as if some great bat had been harpooned. Glimpses of its face contorted in the pale light. It struck one wall. Then the other. Then it finally slumped to the base of the fireplace, life draining from its shadowy frame.

The man tugged on the rope, which now hung limp. The thing at the other end lay in a discolored, crumpled heap. Other than the fleshy face and upper torso, it could easily be mistaken for a pile of filthy laundry.

The man loosed the cord from his gloved hand and let it settle to the floor.

Tamra's mouth hung open. She had backed into a small, overstuffed bookcase and stood with her spine wedged there. Across the room, Annie looked similarly flabbergasted. One of her braids was frayed, and her shin appeared to be bleeding.

Zeph moaned and sat up. Upon seeing the dead creature and the thick man with the biker's goggles and crossbow, Zeph scrabbled backward and pushed himself to his feet, gaping and wobbling.

The stranger thumped along the floor, down into the den, and toward the body, where he remained, studying it. He poked it with the point of his crossbow. Apparently satisfied that it was dead, he turned to Zeph.

"*Vocal Memnon,*" he said. "Ever heard of it?"

Chapter 40

Tamra was too stunned to move. She watched as Zeph stood incredulous, his gaze drifting back and forth between the man and the entity he had harpooned.

"*Vocal Memnon*. One of many great tales! A statue—two of them—side by side on the Nile." The stranger's voice was thick yet contained an exuberance, a gaiety, that enthralled Tamra. He spoke with the flair of a storyteller, but the lines on his face suggested a wisdom worn by age and a joy carved from sorrow. "It was commissioned by one of the pharaohs. Colossi carved out of sandstone. Wonders! An earthquake destroyed one of them—split it in two. Every morning, they said, at the break of dawn, it made a sound: a moan or a whistle. Temperature change or evaporation? Most likely. Yet they believed it was something sacred. Ancient man—aha!—'twas all sacred to him!"

Tamra swallowed hard. Adrenaline and fear coursed through her body. *Who was this wild man talking in riddles?* His skin was the color of cocoa, and Tamra was sure he had Indian blood in him. How had he joined their story? And what in the world had he killed?

She looked at Annie, but her grandmother was as still as one of those sandstone statues, peering intently at the man. She had risen to her feet and stood braced against the wall.

"Pilgrims flocked there," he continued in his lithe baritone. "They said the lucky ones, the ones who heard it, were healed. Their prayers were answered. For hundreds of years it went on singing at sunrise, healing the lame and downcast. Ha! And then one day it just stopped." He clapped his gloved hands and then said, "Never uttered another sound."

Zeph stood panting, shades of emotion knotting his eyes. Finally he swallowed hard and managed to ask, "What is that thing?"

"The real question, Brother Walker, is—" The man leaned forward, as if he were whispering a secret to Zeph. "Why does the singing stop?"

Zeph looked at Tamra, but all she could do was shrug.

The man stepped back, the tools under his jacket jangling as he went, and nudged the body again with the tip of the crossbow. "It is a dark angel, a soul eater. Vile ones of the Third Column."

Zeph blinked at the words. Then he steadied his gaze. "You're Little Weaver."

"You know of me. Aha! I must hear the tale of that telling. Yes." He spread his gloved hand on his chest. "I am Little Weaver, heir to Big Weaver, guardian of the gate. Friend to all who are friends of the land."

They looked among themselves. Finally Annie stirred and stepped cautiously toward Little Weaver. She stood at the step of the den and, even then, was only eye level with the massive Indian.

"An angel?" Annie's face was pinched in skepticism. "That's no angel, Mr. Weaver."

"Lilies that fester smell far worse than weeds. As do beings." Little Weaver turned toward Annie and bowed his head slightly. "Annie Lane, I am pleased to finally make your acquaintance."

Annie glanced at Tamra, and then said to the man, "You're one of the remnant, the one Sultana talked about."

"Ah. The remnant. Fine folk! Did they tell you how we met? Of course not. Such tales require days to tell, and, at the moment, time is our enemy. Onward then!"

Little Weaver reached under his coat, removed a gunnysack, and turned toward the twisted carcass. He bent down and then stopped. He rose and remained standing with his back to them, as if in thought. Then Little Weaver turned.

"You have questions," he said. "Many of them. Mystery is good for the soul, friends. How else can we trust? Pity those who have all the answers. But alas, I shall answer what I am able." He set down the gunnysack and, on top of it, the crossbow. Then he knelt beside the corpse and turned to them.

"It is a sad tale, indeed." Little Weaver motioned to the crumpled remains. "Once of the First Column, they left their estate. Driven by envy. By a lust for power. And jealousy. Craving light, they relinquished the light they had. All that which is evil begins as something good."

Tamra could hear Zeph's breathing from across the room. She was worried he might hyperventilate.

"If y—you're tryin' to make sense, it's not working." Zeph wiped sweat from his forehead.

"Does the tale of the fallen ones trouble you, Brother Walker?" There was a hint of rebuke in Little Weaver's tone.

Zeph opened his mouth to speak, looked at the dead thing, and remained silent.

Meanwhile Annie took two steps back, as though fearful she might tumble into the den and land next to the ashen angel. "What do you mean it was *jealous?* And why does it look like him?"

"Ah! The dark angel craves one thing—to be like man. And to be like man, it needs but one thing—the breath of life. If this one had finished its feast, Brother Walker's body would have been disposed of—a fully formed ectype would have developed, an angel become man. It would have blended into your society without notice. In the case of Brother Walker, few would ever know it."

A long silence passed between them.

"Then this is what's happening at Marvale." Annie seemed to be thinking aloud.

"There is much to speak of and little time," Little Weaver said. "The world is growing dark. Soon the night will fall when no one can stand. All will become enemies. Friend and foe. I must take this specimen to my lab while it is fresh. You will be safe there."

Little Weaver retrieved the burlap sack and knelt before the withering, hollow body of the dark angel.

"Hold on a second." The color had returned to Zeph's face. "Maybe I deserve to die—did you ever think of that?"

"Brother Walker." Little Weaver's tone was full of compassion. He leaned back on his haunches and peered at Zeph.

"This is all because of me, isn't it?" Zeph drew his fingers through his hair. "Monsters. It makes sense. That's...that's what I am, isn't it? A freak of nature." He forced a dry, humorless laugh. "Maybe I'd have been better off getting stabbed through the heart than slashed across the face."

After a long moment Little Weaver spoke. "Brother Walker, you should sit down. You do not look well, and you must save your energy for the—"

"I'm not your brother!"

The moment the words left his mouth, Zeph winced. He took a step back and reached for the wall. He drew his fingertips across his forehead and wobbled dizzily.

"Zeph!" Tamra hurried to him. "C'mon. You need to sit down."

She took him by the shoulders and steered him to a nearby chair. He was taller than she had remembered from last night. A good eight to ten inches taller than her. He did not have the soft shoulders of a bookworm or a video gamer. There was resilience and strength in his body. She helped him into the chair, where he sat trying to gather himself.

Tamra knelt to get eye-level with Zeph. "It was Nams. She called me. She was convinced you were in trouble." She glanced over her shoulder at her grandmother. "I don't know how she knew it, but she did."

Little Weaver cast a brooding gaze at Annie.

"When we showed up, everything was dark—the bookstore, the house. We heard something inside. We decided to break in. Zeph...it was tryin' to kill you."

Tamra turned and studied the remains. Its limbs had now become dry husks; only the torso and head remained that of a human.

"Moon Dancer calls them the fetch," Little Weaver said solemnly. "It is the lore of his people. An evil twin or double who is sent from another world to *fetch* one's soul."

Zeph fixated upon his double.

"When a person sees their counterpart," Little Weaver continued, "it's said to be a premonition of their death. In the case of the soul eaters, such is true."

A moment of silence passed. Zeph seemed to be weighing the implications of Weaver's words.

Finally Zeph said, "It was in the shadows. Just standing there, as if it was part of them. I don't know how long it was there, or how it got in, but I sensed it. I knew it was there. I was drawn to it. Don't know why, but I couldn't r–resist it." He looked at Tamra with a shamed expression. "I went to a bad place, a dream. A nightmare. It was...*feeding on me.*"

"It is the only way they can live," Little Weaver intoned. "They gorge upon human souls, your regrets. Your bitterness gives them life. And once they have your breath, they are complete."

"Then it's the same as the one at the morgue." Zeph straightened. "Isn't it?"

"The morgue?" Tamra said. "There's one of these at the morgue?"

Little Weaver nodded. "Yes. That one escaped my lab."

Zeph looked slightly humored. "You mean *the Vermont?*"

"The old theater?" Tamra glanced between the men. "Okay. So what else is going on that we should know about?"

"I had no choice but to kill it," Little Weaver said. "Someone was passing in the street. I hid myself. The police came. Now we are being watched by more than just the Third Column."

"Escaped?" Zeph protested. "What do you mean it escaped?"

"Brother Walker, we're wasting time. We must hurry."

"Hurry?" Zeph seemed to gather strength, his defensiveness returning. "Why shouldn't we just call the police?"

"I agree." Tamra's voice faltered. "Why shouldn't we j–just call the police? Besides, if they have one of these at the morgue…"

Little Weaver peered at Zeph. "Truly, the shadow is deep in you, Brother Walker."

"Well, why should we trust you?" Zeph asked. "How do we know you're not part of this? Maybe you're one of them!" He pointed at the grisly angelic corpse.

Little Weaver closed his eyes. He drew a breath and straightened. "My name is Little Weaver, heir to Big Weaver. He guarded the gateway to the underworld, heir to those before him. Long before the miners came with their tools and their lust for wealth. Long before the scientists with their calculations and careless tinkering. We watched. We waited for the wielder of wild magic. The Branded One who would close the gateway forever."

Little Weaver stepped toward Zeph, his boots thumping with his approach. Tamra stumbled back.

"Another prophet has arisen, Brother Walker. His intentions are twisted. And if he succeeds, the columns will be fused. A gateway to a world of evil! The land will be defiled. And the soul eaters will consume you like the cancer feeds upon its host. The seeds of madness already take root. And like that great madness, the end can only be destruction."

Zeph stared at the Indian. "We've met before, haven't we?"

"Ha!" Little Weaver clapped his gloved hands. "A shred of sanity!" Then he leaned toward Zeph. "At some point, Brother Walker, you will have to trust again."

Zeph's eyes were locked upon the Indian. Then his shoulders slumped. "That's what I was afraid of."

Cool night air seeped in through the open door. Somewhere in the distance a howl sounded, echoing in the foothills. Little Weaver stood.

"We should go."

And without further dissent the three watched Little Weaver stuff the remains of the dark angel into the burlap sack, and they followed him down the street to his lab, otherwise known as the old theater called the Vermont.

Chapter 41

The dry night air seared Zeph's nostrils. Little Weaver walked ahead with the sack containing the hideous remains of the soul eater slung over his shoulder. His bootsteps were swift, clicking across the sidewalk, and he stayed to the shadows. Overhead the autumn leaves rustled, as if chattering with expectancy at their arrival.

Tamra was at Zeph's side. He knew she was studying him. And he knew something else about her, something that he had never felt from a woman. Something that scared the wits out of him. But her feelings could not drown out the surreal experience he had just survived. Looking into the eyes of that creature was like looking into hell itself.

The same hell that existed inside him.

The marquee in front of the Vermont cast a neon glow across the sidewalk. The Indian led them into the brick alley. On the hood of a mud-splattered jeep curled a cat that followed them with its green eyes. A vapor lamp hung low over a metal door, and trash clung to the dank corners. A thick padlock hung open on the latch. Little Weaver pulled the heavy door open with ease. The man had to be six foot seven, with considerable muscle to back up every inch. If he was *Little* Weaver, Zeph could only imagine what *Big* Weaver looked like.

The metal door grated open, and Little Weaver motioned them inside before clanking the door shut behind them. The Indian led them through a roll-up door that opened into a backstage area, a dark cavernous expanse draped by burgundy curtains, pulleys, and dangerously frayed ropes. Wooden crates laden with cobwebs tottered against moldy plaster walls.

"Despite what you may have heard," Little Weaver said, "I have no interest in theaters. Or renovating them. I needed a place close to you, somewhere where I could observe. Watch your movements."

"Sounds exciting," Zeph snipped.

"And conduct my research."

"Research?" There was ridicule in Zeph's tone.

"Yes."

Annie said, "You're not part of that military project, I hope."

Little Weaver stopped and cast a discerning gaze at Tamra's grandmother. "Why would you say that?"

Annie opened, then closed her mouth.

"You know of NOVEM," Little Weaver said. "How?"

The three looked at Annie.

"I–I found something at Marvale."

"You found something?" Tamra put her hands on her hips and glared at her grandmother.

"Go on." Little Weaver stepped closer to Annie, his dark eyes overshadowed by thick brows.

Annie cast a hesitant glance at Tamra. "A file or journal of some sort, on military letterhead. It contained documents and charts, some of them medical, maps of the mountains. And Otta's Rift. There's notes, sketches, things I don't understand."

"You promised me you'd stop snoopin' around," Tamra said angrily. "Why didn't you say something?"

"Because I wasn't sure what it was." Then Annie returned her gaze to Little Weaver. "There was also a picture of something that looked like..." She swallowed hard. "A cherub."

"A what? Nams, you said you'd—"

Zeph touched Tamra's arm to calm her. Apparently her frustration with her grandmother was reaching overload.

"You mean," Zeph said to Annie, "an angel?"

Little Weaver seemed neither humored nor mystified by the reference. His features remained resolute, fixed on Annie.

"I showed them to Easy Dolan," Annie continued. "He said he thought the documents were Fergus's father's, that he'd been part of that military project."

"Fergus?" Tamra said with surprise. "The night shift guy at Marvale?"

Annie nodded.

"And these documents," Little Weaver said. "Are they still with Mr. Dolan?"

"No. They're back at my apartment."

The Indian's gaze dropped to the floor. "They are not safe. Follow me."

He led them through the backstage area to a section of rooms that Zeph surmised had been used as dressing rooms. Little Weaver flipped a switch, and two large overhead lamps flooded the space with light.

Large tables arrayed with glass tubes and stainless steel instruments stood between cluttered aisles. Two large cages were in one corner, objects of similar size draped with sheets, and nearby, more gunnysacks. An apparatus of some sort with pulleys and gears hung from the ceiling. Either Little Weaver was a Native American incarnation of Doctor Frankenstein or he was the most incognito scientist in North America.

They followed Little Weaver past the workbench. A large javelin with an ornate wooden grip hung above shears, goggles, and a long thin blade. What kind of research was this man doing? Zeph stopped to gaze at a tin of perfectly round polished balls, about the size of marbles but made of a strange material. He picked one up and let it rest in his palm.

Little Weaver had stopped to watch him. "Wood from Sacred Tree. It will stop a dark angel in its tracks."

Zeph peered at Little Weaver. "Who are you?"

"Ha! Such a tale would take ages." The Indian turned on the heel of his boot. He led them to a dull metal table. Setting his crossbow aside, he emptied the contents of the sack. The carcass of the soul eater thudded in a moist, grotesque heap.

Zeph kept his distance, and Annie and Tamra clung to each other, gaping. A thick, rancid odor struck them. Little Weaver switched on a surgical light and swung its arm over the corpse, where he fixed the blazing beam on the hideous form.

Zeph stood there, enthralled and repulsed.

The upper torso was fleshy and quite human in appearance. Its limbs, however, were now little more than casings devoid of meat, charred papery husks that dangled from the table. The head turned their way, its scarred mouth and lifeless face a haunting effigy. And trailing from its back, now hanging limp, were leathery appendages. As one who'd spent his life enjoying fictional worlds of island castaways, hobbits, and talking animals, the entity lying before him was unlike anything Zeph Walker had ever imagined.

Little Weaver studied the remains.

Zeph swallowed. "And this is an angel?"

"A dark angel," Little Weaver said. "Banished from the First Column."

"First Column?" Zeph did not conceal his annoyance. "Do you only talk in riddles?"

"To the hard of hearing, all truth is riddle." Little Weaver's eyes sparkled with a mischievous delight. "Brother Walker, ancient theologians believed that the universe consisted of three pillars, three parallel columns: heaven, earth, and hell. Existing side by side, but separate, distinct. Closer than we can ever imagine, but infinitely distant."

"And you're saying that thing," Tamra pointed to the dark angel with a grimace, "was banished from heaven?"

"The First Column. Indeed! Myriads of such beings live there—powers, principalities, thrones, dominions. It was believed that Lucifer, the greatest of all angels, was once a cherub. Ah, the saddest of all tales."

"Angels..." Annie peered at the thing on the table. "Here in Endurance? Looking like that? How is this possible?"

"And what does it have to do with me?" Zeph asked.

"Aha! Another tale!"

"Great," Zeph said sarcastically. "Do we really have time for more riddles?"

Little Weaver scowled. "Aren't you a storyteller, Brother Walker?"

"Me?" Zeph felt his skin flush. "I–I guess I was. Once."

"And you stopped?" Little Weaver shook his head. "Friends, we should mourn such an admission."

Zeph wanted to ask the man who he was again, but the effort would be futile.

"They came, just like the miners," Little Weaver began. "But instead of picks and shovels, they wielded equations and theories. They had charted a vortex—pools of electromagnetic energy in the hills. At the Rift."

"I knew it," Annie said. "It's where they're coming from, isn't it?"

Little Weaver nodded grimly.

"Otta's Rift?" Zeph said, unbelieving. "A magnetic vortex?"

"An unstable field of energy." Little Weaver spread his arms with dramatic flare. "It affects all things within its reach. Gravity and light, plants and animals. The ancients feared the place. As well they should! They believed it was a gateway to the underworld, the place of the dead. A portal to hell."

The three listened, spellbound at the Indian's tale. Zeph had long ago dismissed the legend as simple folklore. Silverton was nothing more than one of many ghost towns strewn throughout the American West. And the old mine was just a convenient way for wackos to explain the city's abandonment. Nevertheless, as he looked at the moldering remains of the winged creature that bore his face, his mind swirled with fantastical, horrific possibilities.

"Such areas are considered highly sacred," Little Weaver continued. "The Great Pyramid. Stonehenge. Superstition Mountain. The men of science believed they could harness its power."

"It's paganism," Annie exclaimed. "Good Lord! Our own military was invoking the dark side."

"Such is the quest for knowledge, Annie Lane. NOVEM theorized that the Madness had a scientific explanation. They believed it was contact with this vortex that produced changes in people. Drove them mad. Soon they came to believe another irregularity was occurring."

"An irregularity?" Zeph looked away from the dark angel. "What does that mean?"

"A spatial tear," Little Weaver said. "A wormhole."

"You mean," Zeph squinted skeptically, "a passage between dimensions?"

"Don't discount such wonders, Brother Walker."

Tamra's eyes were riveted on the Indian. "You're saying that...there's a dimensional gateway of some sort in Otta's Rift? A portal to hell?"

Little Weaver nodded.

"And the United States government knows about it? They've done experiments? And that these things," she pointed at the creature, "these dark angels are being released?"

"The breaching of the columns." Little Weaver slashed his hand through the air, as if demonstrating. "Summoned from the Third Column, seeking embodiment in your plane."

"Summoned?" Zeph asked. "By whom?"

"Long after the military left," Little Weaver said, "the great shaman returned—Father Coyne. Fergus's father. He lives in Laurel House now, an invalid. He returned with great sorrow. He sought to exploit the Rift for his purposes, to summon from the underworld someone who had passed away, someone lost in grief."

"His wife!" Annie gasped. "She committed suicide."

"Yes." Little Weaver nodded.

Zeph wondered aloud. "And he believed he could use a dimensional gateway to call her back from the dead..."

Little Weaver arched his eyebrows. "Perhaps there is hope for you, Brother Walker."

"Perhaps," Zeph deadpanned.

"Ha!" Little Weaver stepped toward him and slapped Zeph playfully on the shoulder, sending him stumbling into a nearby table. "Father Coyne peered into other dimensions, such places forbidden for men to see. Intelligences lived there, cool, filled with malice. They watched, yearning for this place. Yearning to possess what you have." Little Weaver turned and spat at the corpse. "Father Coyne knew the power to summon such entities was within the realm of the possible. The soul eaters had waited for such a time."

The silence of the vast, dark theater encroached upon them. *Dark angels peering into their world, waiting to be called forth.* The thought sent chills deep into Zeph's marrow. He shifted uncomfortably and unraveled his thoughts.

"You're saying that this scientist, this old man in the convalescent home, is summoning dark angels from," Zeph glanced at Tamra and Annie, "from Otta's Rift? How is that possible?"

"All tribes have the belief in ones so gifted," Little Weaver said. "Mediators between the two worlds. Shamans. Prophets. Those gifted with words."

Little Weaver cast a long gaze at Zeph.

"Wait a second." Zeph held up both hands. "Just like I told them, I hung up the robe and sandals a long time ago."

"You underestimate yourself, Brother Walker. Father Coyne knew it was not one of machines, but metaphysics. The military eschewed such nonsense and promptly terminated him and NOVEM. Yet so great was his grief that he returned. Relentless. He believed that words spoken in the proper order could alter the fabric of the world—a formula, if you will. He sought such an incantation. And a seer. Father Coyne discovered that his son, Moon Dancer, was gifted with the wild magic."

"You mean," Zeph said, "there's another prophet?"

Annie placed her hand over mouth in surprise. "Fergus."

"Moon Dancer," Little Weaver said. "He has learned the incantations that rouse the soul eaters, that summon the dark angels from their prison. He now holds sway over the Third Column. And the one who controls this gateway has great power."

Zeph stood numb. His mouth was dry, and for a brief second he thought he might pass out. Or get sick. He could see where this was going. The footsteps Zeph heard in his head was destiny barreling toward him. He licked his lips and muttered, "What kind of power?"

"The dark angels have one purpose," Little Weaver said. "To create symmetry. To fuse the columns. To bring hell to earth. Even now they plot their way, moving amongst us in the shadows. Friends. Neighbors. Kin. They know no boundaries. Gorging on human souls and swapping out the remains. If Fergus is assimilated by the dark angels, there will be symmetry. Something from that dimension—a great shaman, a being of inexplicable might and majesty—will cross over and stand as a conductor between hell and earth. The columns will be fused."

Zeph closed his eyes and massaged his temples. The nausea had taken hold of him. He looked for a place to sit.

"You have that power, Brother Walker." Little Weaver approached him, commanding his attention. "Call it what you will—prophecy, forth-telling. The ancients called it wild magic because it cannot be harnessed. Unless you close the Rift, speak the dark angels back to their place, it's only a matter of time before you are consumed by hell. It is your silence, Brother Walker, that keeps the portal open."

Little Weaver's words were like an intoxicant, driving Zeph toward inevitable delirium. He lifted his eyes to the Indian, knowing full well the implications.

"This is why they seek you, Brother Walker." Little Weaver stepped back and motioned to the dark angel. "You are the only one who stands in their way."

Chapter 42

Irish whiskey was the best.

Fergus drained the pint, drawing his tongue across the rim of the bottle for good measure. He winced as the liquid fire seared his throat. Then he lobbed the bottle into his locker and tossed his wadded apron in behind it.

The throbbing in his head resumed, spikes of white-hot metal piercing his temples on a beeline to his brain. Fergus stumbled forward and slammed into the metal lockers, writhing against the deluge of pain in his cranium.

The night was waiting. He could feel it. The fetch were calling him, beckoning him into their cool, dark clefts. A forest of limbs and minds, waiting for his command, yearning only for escape.

Be with us, they moaned. *Come stay and be our king.*

Fergus clawed at his ears. If only he could rip the thoughts from his head.

"Leave me alone!" He flung himself into the center of the custodial room, where he stood panting. From behind the picture's shattered glass Jesus watched him.

"I'm s–sorry," Fergus whimpered, staring into the image's placid blue eyes. "I just c–can't stop 'em."

But there was no response to his plea, only the dull thud of blood behind his ears.

Fergus drew his hand across his clammy forehead. He had to move. Get away from there. The fetch would be calling, and once they did, he knew he would never come back. But even if he ran, could he ever escape their grip upon him? How could you run from the voices in your head?

Either way he had to try. He had lost the spellbook. If the authorities found those documents, they would surely trace it back to Pops, and Fergus's secret would be out. All that blood. All those bodies. He whimpered at the thought.

The clock read 10:57 p.m. His shift was over. He would

go down to Laurel House and start packing Pops's stuff. They couldn't take much, just whatever he could fit in the camper shell. But how would he care for his father? *Medication. Diapers. Wheelchair. Oxygen.* It sent Fergus's mind into a tailspin. How would they manage?

He was biting his greasy nails again.

Fergus spat a shredded cuticle and forced the details out of his mind. He touched the pistol grip positioned underneath his flannel. It bolstered his confidence. If worse came to worse, they would go together, him and Pops. One bullet in each brain. That would show them.

Then, maybe then, they would finally see Mum.

Fergus left the custodial area and hurried toward Laurel House. A cool breeze whispered through the bristlecone needles, and somewhere in the foothills a coyote yelped. The stars shimmered behind pockets of stray clouds. This time of night the facilities were slowing down. The night nurses were making their rounds, and the slumber of death coiled its tentacles around all who tread here.

"Hey, Fergus."

The custodian lurched as the figure emerged from the shadows near the back door of Laurel House. It was Jared, one of the night nurses, grinding a cigarette out under his tennis shoes.

"D'you hear about—" Jared stopped and gaped at Fergus. "Dude, you don't look so good."

Fergus wobbled forward and steadied himself. "They ain't s–started, have they?"

Jared shook his head, looking pale. "Naw, they ain't started the night rounds yet. Man, you been drinkin'? And your face...it's, like, swollen."

Fergus reached up and felt drool trailing down his jaw. He wiped it away, mumbled something, and hurried through the entrance of Laurel House, leaving the nurse staring.

It was shift change, so the nurses should be at their stations. Hopefully he could begin packing some of Pops's stuff without interruption from those busybodies. His footsteps echoed down the corridor. The rooms were alive with shadows. There were more than just withered bodies and tired souls in there. Something was watching them, dining off the stench of death and regret. He could feel them—the fetch. Wherever there was darkness and dying, they made their home. Longing, waiting. Cursing the light.

Fergus hurried on, refusing to look into those portals of death. He arrived at Pops's room. Weltz lay in his usual spot, wrapped up like a mummy with his bony spine peeking out from the sheets. Pops lay on his back, snoring gently with his mouth open. A nightlight near the bedstand illuminated his spindly arms resting limp at his sides. How would Fergus ever manage to care for his father? The old man was so frail. They might scrounge up enough money to find an apartment in Reno. Maybe get as far as Montana. Then what?

Fergus stood gnawing his nails.

He had to try. It was the least Fergus could do. Pops hadn't gotten a fair shake. Between Mum killing herself and NOVEM kicking him to the curb, the old man was devastated. Fergus had the gift. He was special. At least that's what Pops always told him. If only Fergus could use the second sight to save both of them.

He slid open the drawer of the nightstand and removed Pops's wristwatch, which had long since died; some fingernail clippers; and a bib. He would gather a few of his father's belongings tonight and start loading his truck. No one would suspect. Then tomorrow they would leave, never to be seen again. The plan was doable and brought temporary hope into Fergus's otherwise gloomy imaginings.

"Fergus." A voice from the shadows.

Fergus spun about, sending the objects on the nightstand clattering across the floor. Roth leaned against the far wall in his trench coat, wire-rimmed glasses glinting in the night light.

"Ghaww!" Fergus growled.

"The spellbook," Roth said, seemingly unflustered by Fergus's rage. "You've kept it safe?"

Hate welled inside Fergus like molten rage. "I thought I told ya to leave him be."

"Leave him? Robert is one of our trophies. A man of genius—far ahead of his time. He served his country well, Fergus. You should be proud."

"Yeah? Then why'd you do him like that? Everything you learned, you learned 'cuz of him."

"It wasn't him, Fergus." Roth stepped out of the shadows, a sleazy grin on his face. "It was you. You were the real one we wanted. You were the gifted one. Your father knew that; that's why he brought you back with him. He couldn't have done it without you."

The thought snatched the rage right out of him.

Roth was right. It was Fergus's gift, the second sight, that had changed things. Once Fergus discovered the rune, learned the words that opened the Rift, everything was different. That's when they knew Fergus was special. He was the key to NOVEM's success, not his father.

But Pops wouldn't use him, not like NOVEM had used them. Pops would never do that.

"You're the lore master," Roth droned. "You're the chosen one. Not everyone can summon the fetch. Why, you're special, Fergus. That's why we left the book with you. You knew its value. You could unlock its secrets."

Fergus squinted. "You didn't leave the book with me. Pops kept it. He hid it from you. The secret was ours!"

Roth chuckled. "Really, now. Do you think we didn't know about his experiments? About the rune? About...*your mother?*"

"I'm done with it!" Fergus shook his head defiantly. "Mum ain't comin' back. She never was. And I don't care 'bout the fetch, or whatever you call 'em. That was NOVEM's doin'." Fergus stepped toward the man and sneered. "They're tricksters, Roth. Dark fairies. They been usin' us, just like they're usin' you. But it's over. We ain't stickin' around to see that hellhole bust wide open. We're outta here!"

Fergus pushed away from the bed and hobbled to the tiny bathroom, where he splashed water on his face.

Roth's footsteps sounded behind him. "Stay here, Fergus. We can make it worth your while."

Fergus hunched over the sink, staring into the porcelain basin. "Yeah? How so?"

Roth stepped into the doorway of the bathroom. Fergus raised his eyes and studied the man's reflection in the mirror. Roth's eyes glistened behind his glasses. "We've learned how to make it go away, Fergus. The voices in your head—we can stop them."

The statement nearly made Fergus gasp. The voices—could they really make them stop? After all these years? The headaches, the blackouts, the taunting voices? Could they really silence the fetch? A wisp of hope curled its way inside him. Fergus looked in the mirror.

What he saw snatched that frail hope from inside him.

His skull was swollen to one side, and his lips sagged from his jaw, revealing gray gums and crooked teeth. Faint trails of blood trickled from his ears. He was changing, now no longer a man but the elephantine offspring of some sideshow freak.

His heart plunged into a new cold darkness.

Roth smiled and stepped away from the bathroom, back into the shadows of the room.

Fumbling under his flannel, Fergus removed the pistol. His skull seemed to encumber his body with immense pressure. He managed to aim the gun at Walther Roth.

"Whadda they done?" His hand trembled so bad he thought he might drop the firearm. "What's h–happening ta me?"

"There, there," Roth said unnervingly. "Shooting me will not stop the metamorphosis."

Fergus stumbled forward and fought to steady his gaze.

"Your old self is dying, Fergus." Roth gazed darkly. "You're becoming one of us. Part man, part angel. Imagine the possibilities!"

Fergus's mind was growing gray. A noxious odor snatched his breath from him, and he lurched upright, struggling to remain lucid.

"All we needed was the parts." Roth wandered to the other side of Pops's bed and stared down upon the gaunt sleeping figure. "DNA, cell strands. The rest is adaptation. Who would've thought it? Angels cloning humans. Partaking of the plasma pool. Neurons and taste buds. Glorious! We've had eons to tinker. To experiment. And *feed*. Did you know that memories have a distinct taste?"

"Ghaww!" Fergus managed to aim the pistol at Roth's head.

Roth grinned. "That won't stop us. Do you realize how many of us are down there? Just waiting for the right person. Waiting to get back at Him! Waiting for *symmetry*. You see, once you're swapped, we will have complete control. Legions of fallen ones—can you imagine? Cast into outer darkness, now set free upon the earth. Shooting me won't stop the process. I'll migrate, find another body. There are so many to choose from." He chuckled.

"No." Fergus panted and let his arm dangle to his side. "Shooting you won't stop the process. But shooting *me* might."

Fergus kissed the barrel of the pistol and put it to his temple.

As he did, Fergus noticed that Pops's eyes were wide open. His mouth was forming unspoken words, and his trembling hand grappled forward. Pops wasn't staring at Fergus, however, but at some point behind him.

A rustle of movement sounded nearby. Fergus spun about to see Weltz's bed vacant, the sheet thrown to the side. A figure rushed at him.

It was not Weltz, but something dark and inhuman. Something with a face like Fergus's and eyes that blazed amber.

Seer, seer.

He could not move. Nor did he want to.

Come hither yonder hill.

Its breath was foul, reeking of eons of decay.

Where the hollow waiteth.

Its mouth lolled open, jaw unhinged and gaping, an ancient crypt seeking to swallow the living.

And the word is yet unhewed.

The unhewed word. Maybe he could speak that word and banish this demon.

As Fergus opened his mouth to speak, a faint scream left his lips. That utterance was snatched by the fetch. As the cat draws the baby's breath, so Fergus's vitality drained from the pores of his being. His lungs deflated, and his breath left him. Its cold hands touched him, caressed him. Every cell in his body yielded as the fetch—Fergus's look-alike—gorged upon him as a tick does a mule deer, feeding not on blood but on breath, memory, and regret.

Roth had walked across the room and gently closed the door. His eyes now shone with a newfound glory, like glowing embers in black sockets. His smile gaped, wide and insatiable.

"I told you we could make the voices go away," Roth said gleefully. "Now NOVEM will be complete. Now we have a prophet of our own! The world that would be, now is." Roth raised his hands, a hideous triumph in his face. "My kingdom come, my will be done!"

And then Fergus Coyne was no more.

Chapter 43

After lengthy debate, most of which involved Zeph interrogating
Little Weaver about his pseudoscientific assertions, the three
agreed to return to their homes rather than remain at the Vermont.
Little Weaver was adamant about the danger that now prowled in the
shadows and crevices of the city and encouraged them to reconsider.
Looking at the bizarre corpse, it was hard to dispute the Indian's
claims. But the thought of spending the night in that creaky old
theater with people he didn't know was equally disquieting. Especially now that Zeph was expected to save the world.

Tamra's grandmother, while seeming quietly suspicious of Little
Weaver, also appeared enthused that her longstanding theories were
finally finding some validation. She remained fixated upon Zeph,
intense and critical. Which could not help but remind him of his
mother.

"They are extremely fragile in their transitory state, and they
hate the light," Little Weaver said, instructing them how to defend
themselves if they were to encounter a dark angel. "In transition
between dimensions, shadows becoming substance. Little more than
ghosts, they require humanity to complete themselves. Foul beings!
Pah!" he spat. "Indeed, the pure of heart are their worst enemy. The
soul eater's strength lies elsewhere. It captivates its double by sheer
madness, paralyzing its victim with fear and wonder. Whatever you
do," the Indian warned, "do not look in their eyes. No! Seeing one's
double is, truly, the harbinger of death."

"How can we tell them apart?" Annie asked. "How can we know
who's who?"

Little Weaver's eyes narrowed. "Like their lord, they are deceivers.
Be on your guard!"

The cryptic answer seemed to set them all on edge.

They left the Vermont near midnight. The lights of the city and
the black swath of mountain were infused with an ominous new
mystery. Annie had agreed to stay at Tamra's for the night, although

186

she vowed she was not afraid of the devilish fetch and would return to her apartment in the morning to gather more of her belongings. Tamra seemed encouraged by her grandmother's concession.

Zeph loaded Tamra's scooter into the back of his truck. They squeezed into the cab with him and drove to Marvale, while Little Weaver followed in his jeep. At the retirement facility Annie scanned her key, the door opened, and the odd foursome tiptoed through the quiet hallways. Thankfully Little Weaver had abandoned his crossbow for what looked like a black powder pistol with a long barrel and a flintlock trigger mechanism, a piece straight out of the seventeenth century. It only steepened Zeph's questions about the hulking Indian and his mysterious body of knowledge.

Annie went through her apartment turning on lights, and then she retrieved the leather journal they had discussed. Little Weaver quickly strapped it into a canvas pouch and slipped it under his army jacket.

As they parted, Little Weaver exhorted them again. "The light— the dark angels hate the light. Go home and turn on every light in your house. The shadows are their essence, and the Holy One is their bane. When morning dawns, open all the blinds. And in your hearts—aha!—unfurl the shutters." He laughed. Then he turned to Zeph, his features rigid with intensity. "Tomorrow, at sunrise, we shall go to the Rift, my friend. Perhaps I can cull their secrets." He tapped the place where he'd stuffed the journal under his jacket. "And maybe the prophet can summon his strength."

Yet Little Weaver's steady, mirthful gaze evoked a newfound fear in Zeph.

Tamra lived on the eastern edge of town near Hooper's trout farm in a modest newer tract of homes surrounded by chain-link fences and quaint brick planters. An older model turquoise sedan sat parked outside the garage and appeared to be collecting dust. Zeph pulled along the curb, directly under the street light, as a chorus of barking erupted.

"Hush!" Tamra tapped the truck window in an attempt to silence the dogs. It didn't work.

The screen door flung open, and someone lurched onto the lighted porch. A bearded man wearing just pajama bottoms stood there staring.

"Tamra!" he blurted, in the rambunctious voice of a child. "You're late!"

"Oh, dear." Tamra hurried Annie out of the truck. "Dieter! Quiet."

The dogs nuzzled up against the fence, barking, pawing, and flinging saliva as they eagerly welcomed their master.

"Grandma!" Dieter shouted, clomping toward Annie with his arms open wide and hugging her over the fence.

"Deets." Tamra tapped her finger to her lips. "It's late. Quiet." Then she turned to Zeph and said, almost apologetically, "He's my little brother."

"Little brother?" Zeph glanced at the young man while unloading Tamra's scooter from the back of the truck. He brushed off his hands and turned to meet Dieter. The dogs snuffled excitedly as Zeph approached the fence.

"And who is this?" Dieter tromped over, straining to see in the dim light.

"His name's Zeph."

"Zeph? Uh-uh! No one's named Zeph." Dieter gawked over the fence and then pointed frantically. "Tamra! His face! What's wrong with his face?"

"Dieter!" Tamra scolded. "That's not nice."

Zeph brushed his hand through the air. "It's all right."

"Well there is somethin' wrong with his face!" Dieter protested. "Just look!"

"Deets, please. We know."

But Dieter ignored Tamra's protests and seemed supremely interested in Zeph's scar. He slung his arms over the fence, and his tongue squirreled around in his mouth like a little kid. Dieter definitely weighed more than Zeph and had more facial hair, yet Tamra's little brother seemed to have the innocence of a six-year-old. For that reason Zeph obliged the inspection.

"What happened, Zeph?" Dieter's words were laced with wonder.

"Well, Dieter," Zeph glanced at Tamra. "Do you believe in monsters?"

"Course I do!" Dieter snorted. "Everybody believes in monsters, silly."

"Of course. Well, I got attacked..." Zeph lowered his voice to a whisper, "by a monster."

"Did you win?"

"Actually," Zeph straightened, "she's still chasing me."

Dieter gasped and began scanning the street.

"Okay, big guy." Tamra stepped between them. "It's way late. Grandma's staying the night. So why don't you and her go inside? I'll been in, in a minute."

"Grandma!" Dieter did a little skip in the grass, which excited the dogs and set them barking again. Then he marched to the porch, chattering to himself.

Annie closed the gate behind her and stood with her bag of night-clothes. The crickets chirped. Behind her the stars twinkled like pinpricks in a nuclear canopy.

"I'm so glad you're back," Annie said to Zeph. "This is your time. It's what we've been praying for."

Zeph looked away. "I wish I shared your confidence."

"Nams," Tamra objected. "Give him some space, okay?"

"I'm not crowding him," Annie said. "No more than anything else."

"Listen," Zeph looked at Annie. "I have no idea what I'm supposed to do here. I'm just going along for the ride." He closed the lift gate of his truck and dusted his hands together. "Besides, after seeing that thing at Weaver's, I don't know if I have a choice."

"We always have a choice," Annie said. "That's what makes us human."

A cool breeze blew past them, and a night bird twilled overhead. The three stood in an awkward silence. Finally Tamra said to Annie, "Go ahead, Nams. I'll be in in a sec."

Annie nodded but seemed reluctant. She walked toward the house, stopping midway to look back at them.

"You can use the extra room," Tamra said.

"C'mon, Grandma!" Dieter yelled from behind the screen door. "Nice ta meet ya, Zephy!"

Zeph smiled. "You too, Dieter."

She and Zeph stood on the sidewalk. Tamra slung her helmet over the handlebars of her scooter and patted the seat. "Thanks for giving Silver a lift."

"Silver?"

"That's what I call 'er," Tamra licked her thumb and dabbed at a spot on one of the mirrors. "Silver. As in 'Hi-ho, Silver.'"

Zeph laughed.

"I'm sorry 'bout that." She jabbed her thumb toward the house.

"About your brother? That's no problem."

"He's a little slow, as you could probably tell."

"Aren't we all?"

"We've been on our own a lot. Dieter's twenty-one. He can take care of himself just fine. But the lady next door checks on him once in a while when I'm gone, just to make sure. Other than that, he's really sharp in other areas. He's great with numbers. You'd be surprised. But my mother was a drinker and all, so..." Her gaze drifted.

"I'm sorry."

"Oh, I'm not."

Zeph did a double-take.

"No," Tamra said. "I mean, of course, I'm sorry that my mother did that. But he's a blessing. Plus he helps me keep my priorities straight."

Her admission struck a chord of guilt. What most people would use as an excuse to curse their existence, Tamra Lane came to see as a blessing. Instead of renouncing heaven, perhaps Zeph should have used his disfigurement to help him get his priorities straight.

Zeph put his hands in his pockets and pretended to look down the street. Out of the corner of his eye he could see her hair shining under the street lamp, a silky champagne glow. One didn't need a supernatural gift to know that Tamra Lane was full of grit and tenacity. However, intuition told him that her toughness was fueled by something tender.

"You sure you guys'll be all right?" He motioned to the house.

"Yeah. Unless those dark angel things can mimic dogs. I doubt anyone could make it past them without causing a ruckus." The three dogs were back at the chain link, watching expectantly, dark eyes glistening. "I volunteer down at the animal shelter once a week, which probably doesn't help. I have a soft spot for strays. Probably because I am one." She reached over the fence, and the canines tussled for her attention.

Zeph chuckled and gazed down the street.

"Did you really do that stuff?" Tamra asked, with hesitation in her tone.

"What stuff?"

"You know, that stuff in the paper. Miracles. Healings. That stuff."

Something inside him shrunk back.

"Let me put it this way, Tam. If anything really happened, it didn't come from me. But if you're after a performance…"

Tamra frowned. "That's not nice to say. I don't want a performance."

She turned away. He had offended her.

"I'm sorry. I—" Zeph shifted his weight. "It's just that all my life, ya know, people find out you have a gift, and suddenly they want to deify you. Or treat you like a pet monkey. Then when you fall or mess things up, or don't perform on cue, suddenly you're a wannabe. It's a no-win situation."

Tamra seemed to ponder this. Finally she said, "Yeah, but that doesn't mean you don't have a gift. I mean, just because people take advantage or misunderstand you doesn't mean you don't have something to offer."

He had heard this before, and the reminder seemed to carry a divine nudge.

Zeph allowed his gaze to drop to the ground. "Are you trying to fix me?"

"Ha!" Tamra waved her hand. "Just tryin' to help, that's all."

"Well, I'm nothing special. I only wish your grandmother knew that. They act like I'm the savior or something."

"They just see more in you than you do yourself."

She was sounding more like Mila Rios every minute. Zeph shrugged. "I dunno. I just have always had a sense about people. And sometimes—this is gonna sound weird—these words pop into my head. Prophecies. Premonitions. I'm not sure what you'd call them. I've always called it the Telling."

"The Telling." She issued a tiny little laugh, not in derision but amazement.

"I've had it since I was a kid. Sometimes it'll come as a word, or a string of words. Sometimes it won't come at all. But whenever it does, things seem to happen."

Tamra eyes widened slightly, anticipation glimmering in them. "Like what?"

Blaise Duty flashed into Zeph's mind, laying gray and lifeless on the church carpet. How could he explain something like that without seeming like a freak?

"It's hard to explain," Zeph said. "My mother, she had a lot of beliefs. Strong beliefs. She told me I could develop an ear for it. Become proficient. That's what the prophets did, she said. They learned to listen to the still, small voice. I dunno, it just seemed wrong. Like trying to train a tiger or a killer whale. Some things are best left wild."

Tamra watched him intently, as if she were the one intuiting his soul.

"They named me Zephaniah because of the prophet. 'Not by might nor by power, but by My Spirit, says the Lord.' That's how it reads in the Bible, in the Book of Zephaniah. Apparently my mother was infertile. They tried for years and finally gave up hope. After much soul-searching, my mother abandoned hope. Shortly after that, she was impregnated with twins. She believed it was a total miracle."

"So you have a twin brother?"

"Well, I *did*. He died when he was young."

"I'm sorry."

"Me too. Being an only child ruined me for life."

She smiled and shook her head.

They stood for a moment listening to the crickets, watching the fog gather under the glow of the street lamp.

"Well," Zeph rubbed his hands on his thighs, "I suppose I should go."

"So you're really going up there tomorrow?"

"I don't know what else to do, Tam. I've done my best to hide, and obviously that hasn't worked. In a way, I just don't feel like I have a choice."

"Like my grandma said, we always have a choice. But if it's any consolation, I think going up there is probably the right one."

"Well, if I come back all glassy-eyed and zombie-like—"

"Don't say that." Then she opened the gate and started to walk her scooter through it while Zeph turned to leave.

"Hey," Tamra said.

Zeph turned.

Her hair was shimmering again. "Be careful, okay?"

"Thanks."

Zeph fired up the truck and watched Tamra walk to the house. He was feeling a little buzzed from their conversation. Yet something else was brewing inside him. As Zeph prepared to drive away, he could hear Dieter from inside the house, yelling with gleeful abandon. "Tamra's gotta boyfriend! Tamra's gotta boyfriend!"

But at the moment Zeph wondered whether or not either of them would live to test that theory.

eph arrived home from Tamra's after 1:00 a.m. The silver moon had arced its way into the western precipice and peeked sporadically from behind a net of slow-moving clouds. The wind had died, leaving the air still and pockets of fog roiling in the shadows. He parked the truck under the carport, got out, and stood listening.

The foothills loomed dark and mysterious, and the downtown lights cast a luminescent afterglow across the belly of the cloud cover. It felt like any other night—the chill of a dying summer, the smell of mold and decaying blossoms, fireplaces springing to life, the barking of toads as they prepared for winter hibernation. Yet the world had changed, changed in ways no one could imagine. He thought about the residents of Marvale sleeping soundly, the deserted streets, the lonely truckers hauling their loads along the 395. Did any of them know what was going on, what lurked in the shadows of Endurance? Perhaps a better question... *how many of them were still human?*

Zeph sighed deeply. It sounded so loony! He thought about Silverton and Otta's Rift, once nothing more than legends to him. How could he possibly be connected to these tales? The anticipation of hiking to the old mine in the foothills, and what he might encounter, had diffused a nervous energy inside him. If he had not seen it with his own eyes, Zeph would dismiss it as madness. But he *had* seen it with his own eyes, which made him all the more confounded.

Zeph walked into the yard, his mind careening under the weight of it all, when a voice sounded from behind him.

"You ever tried her jelly?"

Zeph spun to see two dark figures on the porch, one rocking in the swing, the other leaning against the house.

Oddly, at that moment, Zeph realized it was finally time he fixed his porch light.

"Cactus jelly, in particular, is one of my favorites." It was Detective Lacroix. He motioned to the area where Mila's fruit stand stood.

"Who knew that such a cantankerous organism could yield such a delicacy?"

Zeph's heart pounded. He peered at the shadowy forms. Seeing the dark angel had impregnated his imagination with questions and innumerable horrid possibilities. How did he know these men were who they said they were? Zeph forced himself not to look away.

But all he got was static.

"Mila's cactus jelly's wonderful," Zeph said. "And reasonably priced."

"Yum!" Lacroix smacked his lips. "Ain't nothin' like a well-made cactus jelly."

Zeph did not reply. The other figure on the porch was large. An ornate belt buckle reflected a glimmer from the streetlight. Chat.

Nevertheless, Zeph sensed something had changed about the detectives.

"I don't know what strings you have pulled, young man—" Lacroix rose from the swing with a grunt. "—but we are officially off your case."

"What?"

Chat spoke from the shadows. "The Feds got jurisdiction. Took the body and told us to take a hike."

Zeph shook his head dully, trying to comprehend this information. Was this some ploy, some sort of misdirection? "I–I don't understand, sir. Why would they do that?"

"Our question exactly." Lacroix walked down the steps into the dim moonlight. He smelt of liquor—peppermint schnapps—and his cologne had given way to the funk of day-old dried sweat. "Our superiors are mum on the matter. However, this would not be the first time the United States government did something that left me thoroughly baffled."

Chat harrumphed. "Prob'ly won't be the last, either."

Their conversation with Little Weaver about NOVEM and the military's interest in the electromagnetic anomaly immediately came to mind. Yet Zeph played dumb.

"I don't—" Zeph ran his fingers through his hair. "Why would they take the body? And what does the government have to do with this?"

"They ain't sayin'," Chat growled.

Lacroix nodded. "And ridin' in on horseback to snatch away such evidence, in mid-investigation, leaves one wondering as to the government's underlying motivations. Or complicity. Especially when so much else is unfolding."

Zeph peered at Lacroix. "Like what?"

Lacroix stroked his chin. "Somethin' along the lines of hysteria has affected a sizable portion of the populace. Seems that not a few folks believe that a relative or significant other," he glanced at Chat, "has changed. And whoever—or *whatever*—that person at the morgue actually was, the remains have been taken by a rather shifty-lookin' agent who thanked us for our professionalism before discarding us like an empty bottle of whiskey. Now all traces of the acquisition of said remains have been expunged from our records. Which means, unless you have a hotline to some bureaucrat or military big-shot and know somethin' you ain't sayin', that thing that went down the other day—" Lacroix shrugged. "—it never happened."

Zeph shook his head. "I had nothing to do with this, sir."

The detectives studied him.

"Truth be told," Lacroix said, "I believe you."

The detective reached the gate and turned around. "We did, however, manage to salvage one piece of evidence before the Feds snatched John Doe." He reached into his coat pocket and produced a clear plastic bag with a small item wedged in its corner.

Zeph wasn't sure if he could handle any more revelations. Nevertheless, he approached the detective, peering at the small, round object.

"Apparently it was not a bullet that killed your twin." Lacroix handed the bag to Zeph. "It was this."

Even in the dim moonlight Zeph could tell what he was looking at.

"For lack of better words," Lacroix said, "it is a wooden musket shell, a projectile from a small powder firearm. Unlike anything I've ever seen. Our forensics guys swear that the material comprising this slug," he retrieved the bag from Zeph and gazed at it, "is not from this planet."

Lacroix returned the bag to his coat pocket, motioned to his partner, and opened the gate. "And here I was looking forward to a speedy, if not slightly ambiguous, resolution. But as it stands, mass delusions are sweeping our fair city, the doppelgänger at the morgue never existed, and we are back to investigatin' domestic abuse, cannabis possession, and shoplifting."

Zeph watched them leave, feeling rather lost. He didn't know what was worse: having a government official suddenly inserted into this process or having A. J. Lacroix and Chat Chavez removed from it.

As Chat passed, he stopped and eyed at Zeph from under his cowboy hat. "And in case you haven't figgered it out, someone's got their eye on you."

"Someone pretty powerful, at that." Lacroix squinted. "Roth's his name. Gotta boatload of credentials and a scowl that could kill a Gila monster. Keep an eye out. Just don't say we warned you."

Lacroix held the gate open as Chat ducked under the arbor and left. "And if you would be so kind, young man, as to tell your neighbor over there that I will return to secure a jar of cactus jelly at a future date, I would be obliged." Lacroix pointed to Mila's house.

Zeph followed the direction of his gesture and was startled to see Mila Rios standing behind her screen door in her nightgown.

"I–I'll do that," Zeph muttered, fixated upon Mila's presence.

The detectives left the yard and crossed under the lamplight. Zeph had not noticed their car parked across the street. They got in, turned on the lights, and drove slowly back through a growing fog, straying in front of the Vermont before speeding off.

Mila remained unmoving behind her screen door.

A great foreboding grew inside him. Mila was never up this late. By 6:00 a.m. her oven was on, and the smell of pastries greeted the neighborhood. Yet this wasn't like her. Without thinking, Zeph wandered out his gate, past the white picket fence, and entered Mila's yard.

Jamie was nowhere to be found.

"Mila?"

She stood ghostlike, her pale figure silhouetted behind the screen door.

"Mila, are you all right?" Zeph wandered past the empty fruit stand and climbed her front porch. He stood at her door, gazing at her.

Mila spoke, her voice but a wisp. "It was like a dream, Zeph."

"What was like a dream?" He took hold of the handle and drew the door open.

Down the street a dog barked.

"Like part of me just drifted off. Like I was disappearing before my very eyes."

"Mila, you're scaring me. " Zeph pulled the screen all the way open. "What are you talking about?"

"I looked in the mirror, just to make sure." She gazed at Zeph, but her eyes were flat. "And she was gone."

"Mila, it's late. You're tired, or—"

"I'm wide awake, Zeph. In fact, I've never felt more alive in my life." A smile grew across her face, stretching her cheekbones to the point of clownish mockery.

Zeph's stomach dropped.

"Mila, listen to me. Do you remember yesterday, you said if I needed anything, you'd do it?"

Her smile remained fixed, but her eyes disengaged.

"Mila, right now I need you...I need you to hold on. The shadows, they're...you can't listen to them. Hold on. Do you hear me?"

He seized her arm. Its coldness shocked him. The dark angel writhing atop him sprung into his mind. He gasped. Whoever this person was, it was not Mila Rios.

She looked at his hand gripping her and then smiled. "Hold on." The words seemed nonsensical in her mouth. "Hold on. Do you hear me?"

She was mocking him.

And as she spoke, her breath struck him, vile and foul. A rancid gust of air wheezed from the woman's mouth. Then she smiled, and her eyes gleamed phosphorescent amber.

Zeph stumbled back. "No! God, no!" He let the door slam, flailing to steady himself lest he topple off the porch.

Mila—or the thing that was her—laughed.

"Hold on. Do you hear me?" Her voice was mocking, oscillating through her vocal range. "Do you hear me? Do you hear me? Hold on."

Zeph stumbled down the steps and ran from the dark angel.

He stammered through his gate and fell to the dirt, sobbing.

Jamie was howling in back of Mila's house. Zeph knew what was buried there. He staggered to his feet and stared at his darkened home. What lurked inside? Another demon perhaps, waiting to pounce upon him? The shadows seemed to pulsate pure evil.

He found his keys, unlocked Book Swap, and staggered inside like a drunken man.

Insane with grief.

He turned on the light, locked the door, and fell, crying, as the gray ceiling wheeled overhead, turning his world ever darker.

Part Three

THE TELLING

It is not in the stars to hold our destiny but in ourselves.
—SHAKESPEARE

But if I say, "I will not mention him or speak any more in his name," his word is in my heart like a fire, a fire shut up in my bones. I am weary of holding it in; indeed, I cannot.
—JEREMIAH 20:9

Mother! It's not like that!" Zephaniah wrestled the tie loose and whipped it out from under the stiff collar. He hated those starched shirts, but he couldn't tell Belle that. In fact, there were a lot of things he couldn't tell Belle Walker.

Like about Kim Daschle.

She was twelve, like Zephaniah, and did not seem fazed by his extracurricular activities. Boy prophet or not, Kim saw Zephaniah for what he was—a boy. That was something other folks just seemed to miss. If they weren't looking cockeyed at him, they were wanting a performance. Not Kim. Her eyes were blue, like his mother's. But that's where their similarities ended.

His mother closed the door to the church dressing room and stood with her back to it. "Son, there's people out there that have come for God's Word. We can't just leave them."

Steely. Intense. Zephaniah got lost in those eyes. Yet behind them was something else…something he feared.

He dabbed sweat off his forehead with a handkerchief. Acne dotted his forehead, evidence of adolescence. He had spoken healing to a girl with a fever once. Then there was Lance McGrew, the Archer's farmhand, whom Zephaniah once watched cough out a spirit of fear. Yet despite these miraculous events, Zephaniah couldn't keep himself from getting acne.

He did not want to look at his mother, so he turned to the vanity.

"It isn't there." He removed his cuff links. "The Telling is not there, mother. I can't just—I can't just make something up."

He looked at her reflection in the mirror.

"Of course not!" She scowled, and then her features softened. "But sometimes, son, you can say what you *think* it might be."

Zephaniah peered at her for a long moment, letting that notion register. Finally, he shook his head. "It's not the same. They'll think what I'm saying is God's Word. And it isn't. It's…*my word*. Or somethin' like it. I can't—we can't—go that way."

She walked over, knelt next to him, and took his hands in hers. Her fingers were long and agile, like those of a watchmaker or artisan. Indeed, she was able to adjust and tinker with the machinery of his soul. She squeezed his hands and summoned his gaze. Belle did this when she wanted her son's attention. Zephaniah had begun to wonder if it was manipulative, even though he felt guilty thinking that.

"Zephaniah, you know I'm not asking you to lie. I would never do that." She glanced at the door. "But son, we have to eat. Your father, he...you know we can't rely on him. You know that. And the Good Lord, He doesn't want us to starve. Now, does He?"

He shook his head.

"Of course not! Now, look at me. Pastor Wyler is a good man. You can sense that, can't you?"

Zephaniah nodded.

"Yes," she said. "He is a good man. And he tends to a good flock. These are hardworkin' folks. But tonight they're here to see you. You, Zephaniah. You can't just walk away. You can't just leave them with nothing. You've got to tell them *something*." She stood and straightened, looking very stately. "Even if it's not the Telling. Even if the heavens are silent. Somethin's still got to be said."

Zephaniah stared, not wanting to concede.

She could sense his resistance. She always could. "Pastor Wyler has to stand up and speak God's Word every Sunday, son, whether or not he got the revelation."

"That's not the same, mother." Zephaniah pushed himself away from the vanity. "They think I'm...I'm perfect. That everything I say is God's Word."

Her gaze flinched, and she glanced at the door again.

"Son, word is going around that the boy prophet has lost his power. We just ain't getting the folks in like we used to. You noticed that."

He nodded.

"That church in Red Creek—word is getting 'round that you walked off the stage."

"What was I supposed to do?" He rose from the chair, nearly toppling it in his haste. "The Telling wasn't there!"

"Yes, but...but now people are believin' that you no longer have it. That God has up and abandoned us." Her voice trembled, and he thought, for a moment, that she might cry. "And that's just not the case. Is it?"

Zephaniah stared at his reflection in the mirror.

He looked like an old man, as if the ministry had drained him of his childhood. He'd missed playing down at the river and riding his bike up to Lost Lake. And despite his mother's stern warnings, more than once he thought about Kim Daschle and her strawberry blonde hair.

"Is it, son?" His mother stepped closer, her eyes pleading. "The Telling is still with us. Isn't it?"

Zephaniah unbuttoned his shirt and, without looking at her, said, "I don't know."

Chapter 46

Zeph woke with a start, although sleep was hardly the realm he had left. He was leaning against a bookshelf in the romance section, with his knees pulled up to his chest and fallen paperbacks scattered around him. The light was still on in the Book Swap. He shivered against the cold and worked a nasty crick out of his neck. Kim Daschle was on his mind, and, close by, the memory of his mother's stern gaze brooded like a ghostly apparition.

Then Zeph remembered Mila, her vacant stare, her mockery, her sulfurous breath, and the emotion welled inside him like a poison spring.

He stood, hastened to the door, and opened it.

The sun had yet to rise, but its presence had turned the horizon a gray pall. The chickens wandered the dewy yard in search of grubs. Mila's house was dark. Maybe it was all a dream. Perhaps the last few days were just part of a psychological breakdown. That's what happened when you lived alone for so long—fact and fiction blurred. Even Robinson Crusoe feared he would go mad on the desolate island. In this case, however, Zeph wondered if insanity would be a welcome option.

Despite being a modified realist, Zeph knew it was all real. The dark angels. The petroglyphs at Meridian. Little Weaver. The Rift. And now Mila Rios. This wasn't a dream. It was reality catching up with him.

Once again he was the object of wonder. All eyes were upon him. It was the destiny he always feared.

Something brushed Zeph's feet. He yelped and slammed into the door. Images of reptilian angels with tortured features snapped into his brain.

Jamie looked up at him, shivering.

Zeph scooped up the animal.

"Hey, little guy." He stroked the dog while peering at Mila's house. It was silhouetted against a hazy dawn, looking as dreary as

Bates Motel. Although even Norman Bates and his mother could not compare to the evil that lurked inside Mila's house. Two days ago he would have scoffed at the notion. Now he was on the other side of the looking glass.

You need to get out more, Zeph. That's what Mila had told him yesterday. *You stay locked up in that house too much.*

Mila was right—the other Mila, the one with emotions and compassion and humanity. Staying locked up in his house hadn't prevented anything. Destiny had found him, and now everyone was being steamrolled by his silence.

Just like Mila.

Zeph patted Jamie, and the dog licked his hand.

Little Weaver would come for him soon. It was almost sunrise. Together, they would hike to the Rift. Was there still evidence of the mass suicide up there? And what did a dimensional portal look like? Perhaps the Indian had discovered a formula in the pages of Annie's journal. If not, at least Weaver could spin him a tale to humor him. Meanwhile one of the best people Zeph Walker knew had been swapped by something inhuman. Rage and regret gripped him.

He'd already dragged too many people down. They were in danger because of him. Tamra. Annie. And now Little Weaver. He could not afford more collateral damage.

If there truly was a gateway to hell in those foothills, a portal into some infernal realm, and if he could do something about it, then Zeph had to take the chance.

And he had to take it alone.

Zeph hurried into the house and grabbed his down vest. Then he set out a bowl of water for Jamie. As the horizon paled to overcast skies, Zeph got in his truck and drove toward town. He stopped at the convenience store, found Lacroix's business card, and used the pay phone next to the ice machine. He left a voicemail for the detective.

"I realize you're off the case. But you should know something. My neighbor, the lady with the cactus jelly—something's buried in her backyard. I think you need to check it out."

Chapter 47

Crusoe believed the storm was providential, punishment for his sins. Shipwrecks didn't happen by accident, so why should his? No, it was judgment for his sins. As Zeph drove north along the 395, blinking back tears, watching the sky go from iron gray to ash, he wondered whether or not the events around him were, like Robinson Crusoe's, the result of his own transgression.

If so, Zeph was determined not to see anyone else drown.

In the distance the Black Pass rose like an incision in the pallid sky. He didn't need a GPS to navigate his way to Otta's Rift. Everyone around here knew the general location, even if they'd never visited the legendary site. Like most, Zeph's conceptions of the ninth gate of hell were built around rumors and innuendo. He had seen the documentaries and the fanciful tabloid pieces. But in spite of his love for this land and his familiarity with its features, visiting the Rift had never been high on his bucket list.

Eight miles past the turnoff for Marvale, a sheep road named Dawson's Rut cut a beeline across flatland into a ridge of manzanita and ragged groves of gray pines. The dusty road gave way to rutted clay before he passed a water tower and arrived at Silo's Bridge. Zeph allowed the truck to idle there. The fishing was good here, mostly native trout. He looked past the cool mountain stream into the ridge. Just beyond it, in the crook of a sparsely timbered bluff, were the remnants of Silverton.

Zeph sat there, staring up into the lonely hills, listening to the cadence of the brook. They called it Miner's Meadow. Dilapidated shanties strangled by tumbleweeds and rubbish were all that remained of Silverton, the community that had sprung up around Otta's Rift. Silverton remained one of several authentic ghost towns across the basin. But the legends about the Madness of Endurance had prevented the place from becoming a vibrant tourist destination.

Up ahead Dawson's Rut joined the fire road. That road traveled the foothills for miles. He had traveled it many times and knew it

208

would take him past Otta's Rift. Zeph crossed the bridge and turned south on the fire road, heading back in the direction of Marvale. The truck sidled along the trail, leaving a fog of dust in its wake. Zeph stared past the tree line to the ridge. Was there a trailhead, a distinguishing feature that identified the spot? He sunk into himself, letting his mind roam.

If he could walk by faith, maybe he could also drive by faith.

The truck rumbled along, Zeph glancing from the dirt road into the distant mountains. But there was no sign of Otta's Rift. Perhaps this was a bad idea. Maybe he should have waited for Little Weaver. His valiant plan to march into Otta's Rift and save the world had hit a snag—before he had even arrived. Zeph knew his way around Endurance; he'd hiked the trails and fished most of the creeks and streams. He also knew that if he dared venturing into the mountains recklessly, he could find himself wandering the foothills for days.

A scraggly thicket of birch rose on both sides of the fire road, littering the area with dead leaves. Suddenly a figure bolted from the brush, and he slammed on the brakes. A doe stood panting in the middle of the road, staring at him. Zeph's heart pounded as he met the gaze of the startled animal.

As the fog of dust caught up and drifted by, directly behind the scared creature, he noticed something hanging from a nearby tree.

Zeph peered at the object, trying to make sense of what he was seeing.

The doe hurried off into the stand of birch, but Zeph remained fixated on the strange object. It looked so familiar. He pulled the truck as far off the road as possible, got out, and locked the door.

The sky was formless, a sea of gray that seemed to cast a malaise about this place. Dawn had revealed a vast canopy of gloom. The trees dripped moisture and the earth was still. Zeph slowly approached the tree, crackling dead leaves as he went. Its limbs were stripped of foliage, and it bent haggard, as if some great weight had laden the birch. Approximately ten feet up hung a curious object. He crept forward. At first Zeph thought it was a dreamcatcher, the handmade charms used by some Native Americans to protect sleeping children from nightmares. By the looks of it, this object might be intended to have the reverse effect—to invite night terrors.

It consisted of the traditional willow hoop, but from it hung several bones and the dried carcasses of small animals.

He had seen things like this before. Once, in Liberty, his mother had taken him to the home of a woman whose daughter they believed was possessed. Outside their house Zeph recalled seeing such a talisman. It gave him the creeps back then, as it did now.

He stared through the trees here. The ground was matted with leaves, as if the area was diseased. Past this matchstick forest, over the berm, fog shrouded the foothills. Could this be the place?

A breeze rose, and the bank of fog rolled over the berm like a spectral tide, drawing rock and brush into its cloak.

Plink.

It was a dry, hollow sound. Zeph looked around, trying to identify its source.

Plink. Pa-plink.

It came from overhead. He looked up to see the bone chimes dangling in the breeze, emitting an odd, hollow tinkling among the cancerous forest.

Cold creeps scampered across his flesh. This was it! He knew it. However, something else, something equally as sure, kept him unmoved. Zeph knew that if he crossed this point, he was passing into a realm unlike any he had ever experienced. This was sacred ground. Or rather, *un-sacred* ground. How many generations of mystics and thrill-seekers had invested this area with its own unique ambience? And if there was any truth to Weaver's claims about this befouled place, Zeph could be stepping into a war zone beyond his imagining.

Nevertheless, he could not turn back, not after what had happened to his dear friend, Mila. Emotion swelled inside him at the thought, but he swallowed it and reset his resolve.

God, help me.

It was closest thing to a prayer that he could manage. And perhaps it was also the most genuine. With those words Zeph stepped off the road, under the bone chimes, and into the dead wood.

The smell of fall's approach was thick. As he went, he churned decaying leaves underfoot, awakening the stench of mold and rot. Zeph picked his way through the blighted birch. There were no birds or animals, nothing but a dead silence. He looked for more signs of strange paraphernalia but found none. The thicket cleared, and the rocky berm rose before him. Fog hovered like a spectral curtain, and behind it towered steep granite walls.

He picked his way through the scrub to the base of the berm, inhaled deeply, and trudged upward. At its crest he stopped and stood panting. The fog drifted by, clearing enough to reveal a barbed-wire fence sagging across a dark ravine. Several signs riddled with buckshot warned against trespassing. Zeph stepped toward the fence, peering into the misty canyon below.

Could this be it? He strained forward, looking for any evidence of Otta's Rift. As he did, the murk parted just enough to make out a dark gap at the base of the mountain. A mine entrance.

Otta's Rift—the ninth gate of hell.

The revelation begat an eerie repose inside him. *Do you find your destiny, or does your destiny find you?* Zeph settled back, gazing into the gloomy gorge.

For a moment he thought about destiny, about what brought him here. He thought about Tamra Lane, who had a soft spot for strays and a cute patch of freckles across her nose. He thought about Annie and the remnant, watching him all these years, wanting him to play the prophet. He thought about Little Weaver, the guardian of the gateway, protecting him from the demon spawn.

And Zeph thought about the day he stood at his mother's grave and denounced the Telling.

Something struck out from the brush behind him, and he spun about.

Several blackbirds barreled from the trees below, screeching past him before plunging into the foggy ravine. His heart raced, and a wave of fear washed over him, drowning the frail resolve Zeph had mustered. Who was he fooling? He couldn't just wander into some prehistoric cave and expect ages of incantations and evil to snap to attention at his command.

The breeze swept by like invisible fingers, stretching the mist into phantasmal shapes. It carried a voice.

He cocked his head, straining to hear the wisp of words.

Fallow and fruitless.

Were these words in his head, or was someone calling from the gorge?

Be thou withered, O son of silence.

Zeph straightened. Terror spiked his body to the dewy earth.

How could he forget that voice? He hadn't heard it in ten years, but he would never forget it. And her prophecy—it had draped him like an emotional anvil.

See, I have touched thy lips...

Zeph found himself touching the scar on his face. Rage welled inside him, followed by regret. The voice, though repulsive, had a hypnotic allure. It was coming from the Rift.

Nearby a section of the fence hung limp. Below it a trail switchbacked through a scree slope to the floor of the ravine. He wandered to the open section of fence. Snippets of weathered fabric clung to the barbed wire there. Before he realized it, Zeph had slung his legs over the sagging wire and teetered at the edge of the scree slope.

Fruitless and mute. A deep, throaty chuckle. *Fruitless and mute.*

He stumbled forward into the gorge, following the trail as it descended into the fog. Others had come this way. Cigarette butts and empty whisky bottles scattered the rocky path. Along the way he stopped to wipe sweat from his brow and study the mine entrance. The number nine had been spray-painted on the rock. A withered tree stood sentinel, spectral and brooding. A thin spine of rail protruded from the dark entryway. Yet there was no one there. Perhaps the voice was just an illusion, some psychological echo seeking to finally escape his tortured mind.

Finally he reached level ground and stood sweating in the damp coolness.

A barren swath of earth spread between him and the mine. Gray and blasted. Cursed ground if ever there was. He'd seen it in the documentaries and the tabloids. This is where it happened—the Madness of Endurance. How many had died here, set themselves afire before these god-awful ruins? He could see the ghoulish pile in his mind's eye. Women and children, a smoldering heap, cauterized in their own agony.

Zeph gasped. He had stopped breathing for a moment.

What sort of devilry possessed this place?

He hurried forward, remaining focused on the mine entrance. Broken glass shown dully in the gravel, and a crude lean-to made of gray wood rose nearby. A single barren pine stood before the charred entry to the mine. Runes and glyphs notched the surrounding rock. The stench of herbs and spoiled meat lingered.

Zeph slowed. Then stopped. Perhaps twenty-five feet away. In living color.

The ninth gate of hell.

Zeph swayed, dreamily. Then caught himself. At least he was still breathing. He slowly approached, peering into the dark aperture. A magnetic vortex. Isn't that what Weaver called it? A portal into the Third Column.

Inside the mine the haze coiled, coagulated, thickened. And seemed to take shape.

Someone was in there. They'd been expecting him.

And who better than Pearl?

"You…" Zeph said.

You aren't a prophet, the phantom hissed. *The blade proved it.*

Sadness. So much of it inside him. Her words seemed to reawaken the venom of bitterness. Zeph swayed back, overtaken by a great darkness looming on the periphery of his mind.

You're the son of silence. Sickly glowing eyes peered at him from deep inside the mineshaft. *And now you've gone and killed someone.*

Mila.

What a fool to think he could stand before the gate of hell! He could barely stand before his own mirror without regret and rage oozing forth. Zeph tried to run, but his legs would not work. His body felt leaden. Voices, so many of them, called from the Rift, pining for freedom. That dark breeding place, that cell, that tomb of regret and waste. It was calling him. The others were expecting him.

Zeph doubled over, gripping his skull.

He had let them down—all of them. Annie and Tam and Little Weaver. They were wrong to have trusted him. God had no choice but to remove the Telling and abandon him in this defiled place. Zeph had renounced heaven, and this was its echo.

He crumbled to the wet earth.

Plink.

Death. So much death lay here. He could smell it in the moss and the mold.

Plink.

How many souls had died on this spot, driven to madness by hell and their own pain? Well, one more wouldn't matter.

Plink.

Fallow and fruitless, barren but for the sorrow he had brought. Indeed, he had become the son of silence, just as his stepmother had prophesied.

Plink.

He opened his eyes enough to see a shadow descending upon him. A great winged thing with phosphorescent eyes. The darkness roared toward him, a wall of hate. Pearl cackled from inside it.

And Zeph descended into shadow.

Chapter 48

I'll be fine." Annie unlocked the door to her apartment and turned to Tamra. "I'm just going to pack a few things. Call me when you're ready. I'll take the tram down, and you can pick me up in the parking lot."

"Okay. That's it." Tamra's words were stern and cautionary. "I don't want you going anywhere else. Or talking to anyone. Even if it *is* daylight, we have to be careful."

Annie did not like being talked down to. But her granddaughter was right. Nevertheless, Annie Lane had other plans.

"Nams?" Tamra peered at her with suspicion. "That's it, okay?"

Annie knew better than to lie to her granddaughter. Perhaps she should be thankful for that. Tamra was not gullible, nor was she afraid to challenge what she considered deceptive. Annie derived a certain satisfaction from knowing that her Tamra was not naïve or easily snookered. That's the kind of woman who could make it in this world. No, she couldn't lie to Tamra.

Misdirection, however, was another story.

"I want you to check on him," Annie said.

Tamra stopped chewing her gum and gaped. "Huh?"

"Zeph—I'm worried about him."

"I thought you were gonna let this go? I mean, what more can we do…besides go to the police? The evidence was right there. Either he's gonna do what Weaver said or he's not. Nams—this is what you wanted, isn't it? He got the book, he went to Meridian—he knows about everything."

Annie looked away.

"Look," Tamra said. "Little Weaver's gonna pick him up, and they're going up there. It's out of our hands at this point."

"He's been running and hiding for years," Annie said. "Old habits are hard to break."

Tamra shook her head, eyes drifting in thought. "He's had a hard life, that's for sure. Either way, this whole thing is creeping me out.

This place is creeping me out. All this talk about miracles and prophecies. And dark angels. Whatever's going on in this city, whatever that thing was that attacked Zeph, people have to know. I don't care if we look like a buncha kooks. And if one more thing happens, I promise you I'm calling the police." Tamra yanked her phone out of her pocket and waved it at Annie. "I don't care who finds out. There's plenty of normal folks around here still."

"Are you sure about that?"

Tamra cast a long gaze at Annie. She stuffed the phone back in her pocket and said, "Okay. Even if *some* of the police are in on this, they're not *all* in on it. Other people know what's going on here. They have to."

Annie did not concede Tamra's point. Instead she said, "If we're really dealing with some type of spirit beings, no police force in the world will be able to stop them. And who knows how far they'll go to make sure they aren't found out?"

Tamra chewed her gum slowly. Her eyes revealed that she shared Annie's fear.

"I'm not sure I believe Weaver," Annie said flatly.

"I could tell. But why would he want to trick us?"

Annie shook her head. "I don't think he wants to trick us. I'm just not sure about his motivations. Or whose side he's on. I'm just not sure. Hopefully he'll decipher something from that journal and whatever formula he thinks it contains. Maybe they'll uncover a way to stop whatever is happening up there. But I'm skeptical, I can't deny it. We're dealing with demons here, Tamra. Fallen angels who want to become like us. Weaver can talk all he wants about parallel worlds and wormholes and that scientific mumbo-jumbo. This is something spiritual. All the theories and computations in the world can't change that fact. I don't care who Weaver thinks he is. Only the prophet can stand before the gates of hell."

Tamra sighed. "Okay. I'm running by work to tell Mr. Farner I need a couple days off. I'll stop by Zeph's and check on him and make sure everything's all right. Then I'll be back here in an hour or so. Just lock your door, and don't open for anyone but me."

Tamra stared at Annie and then leaned across and kissed her on the cheek. "Love ya, Nams."

Annie watched as Tamra slung her backpack over her shoulder and walked down the hall.

Seeing her granddaughter and Zeph talk together outside last night had rekindled something in Annie, something she'd believed had died long ago. All she had ever wanted was to make a difference, to leave behind a godly lineage. After watching her son play the prodigal, squander his gifts, and give himself to drugs, Annie had all but abandoned her dream. Yet standing there watching Tamra, a sense of hope flickered to life inside her.

And hope was not something Annie Lane had been used to lately.

She hurriedly gathered up a week's worth of belongings into her only suitcase. Before she could leave Marvale, however, there was one thing she had to finish. In fact, completing their mission might even depend on it.

She slipped the Velcro cuff on her thigh, inserted the Swiss Army knife, and checked the flashlight to make sure it was working. Then Annie stepped into the hallway, gently pulling the door shut and locking it. Behind her another door clicked shut. Annie turned to see Vera's son standing across the hall, two large black plastic bags lying on either side of the doorway. The last time she had seen the young man, he was ranting that his mother had changed.

They exchanged glances, and then he did a double take.

What conclusions had he reached about Vera? And what else had he uncovered in his search for the truth? Perhaps he could be a comrade in their resistance.

"Pardon me." Annie approached. "Your mother, how is she?"

He straightened and studied her, eyes roaming along her features with an inquisitive calculation. "She's better now." His eyes sparkled. "We're both better." Then a hard smile crept across his face.

Annie stumbled back and gasped. "What happened? Where are they?"

He tilted his head, retaining the chilling smile. "*They?* I have no idea who you're talking about."

Down the hall Violet left her apartment and approached with her handbag draped at her elbow. She looked from Annie to Vera's son.

He said, "She wants to know how *mother* is."

Violet turned to Annie and looked at her, studying her features as the man had done. When she spoke, her tone was defiant. "Vera's fine. You know," she tilted toward Annie, lowering her voice to a whisper, "you really should watch yourself, Annie dear."

Then Violet leaned back and nodded to the man. She bent and picked up one of the trash bags. The man picked up the other. Then they turned and walked back down the hall, side by side.

Annie watched dumbly as her heart thudded in her temples.

How could she have missed it? The world was changing. The people she had lived among, laughed with, and shared memories with were no longer there. In their place was something alien. It was happening all around them—it *had been* happening without her notice. Subtly. Imperceptibly. How long before the whole facility—the entire city—was swapped by hideous *others?* Dark angels disguised as humans, plotting an invasion the likes of which the world had never seen.

She meandered to the nearby reading area and dropped listlessly into the chair.

There was no way to stop this—what kind of fool would ever believe that? Hell does not yield to peons. And that's what Annie Lane was. An impotent, undependable peon. Perhaps it was infused into her DNA. You can't escape your destiny. She was destined to fade away, to find hope only to lose it. To leave the earth without leaving so much as a thumbprint, much less a godly lineage.

Stop it!

Annie straightened. This is how it starts: a slow surrender that becomes a complete sellout. She had to fight it! How else could she stand in the gap?

Annie rose and looked back down the hall. Monsters or not, she had a mission to accomplish.

She would start by recruiting Easy Dolan.

Chapter 49

Why, if it ain't Miss Annie!"

Easy stood with his apartment door open, but upon seeing Annie, his bright smile faded. "You look like ya done seen a ghost."

Annie pushed her way inside, closed the door, and leaned against it, panting.

Easy was wide-eyed. "What'n the world—?"

"Something's happening, Easy. Something terrible." Annie strode past him into the living room, where she started pacing.

"You didn't git yerself into trouble again, did ya?"

"I think we're all in trouble," Annie gasped. "Big trouble."

"Oh, come now—can't be that bad."

"Oh, yes it can." Annie said firmly, "I need your help, Easy."

He peered at her, then walked to his desk. "Have a seat, Miss Annie."

She barely noticed the chemical smell and, without resistance, wandered to the Victorian wingback and sat.

Annie inhaled deeply, hoping to compose her thoughts and sound as persuasive as possible. Convincing Easy to assist her could be the difference between life and death. "Everything we talked about—the Madness, the Rift, the ninth gate of hell. It's all true, Easy."

He remained standing, strumming his fingers on the back of his chair. He looked long and hard at Annie. "I encouraged you ta dive right in. So, I take it you have."

"Last night I saw one."

"One what?"

"This is going to sound crazy," Annie said. "They're dark angels."

"Angels?"

"Fergus calls them the fetch. It's some sort of Irish folklore concerning elves or dark fairies that come to fetch someone's soul. But these things aren't fairies, Easy. They're...monsters. Real-life monsters. Fallen angels of some sort. They want to duplicate us. It's how they cross over to this side."

Easy shook his head and scratched under his cap. "And you saw one of these things?"

"It was awful." Annie stared blankly, recalling the hideous mutation. "Whatever they are, Fergus is the one who opened the way. I'm not sure how. His mother killed herself, just like you said. And they thought they could bring her back. You were right about his father. It's part of some military cover-up. And it's still going on." Annie scooted to the edge of the chair. "Easy, they opened a door to another dimension. A place we weren't supposed to go. It's necromancy!"

Easy stared, incredulous. "I've believed some far-out tales in my time, Miss Annie. But this takes the cake. Either you got a wild imagination, or somethin' mighty odd's goin' on 'round here."

"It is mighty odd. But I've seen it with my own eyes. You have to believe me! Genie, Vera, Violet. And then last night..." She shivered. "People are being swapped, murdered. They're bodies are disposed or hidden. I can't believe I'm saying this." She slumped forward, exhausted from the weight of it all. "I don't know anymore."

Finally, Easy said, "I dunno, either, Miss Annie."

Taking a nearby rag, he poured some liquid on it and dabbed at a model lying on his desk. Over his shoulder he said, "It's quite the conspiracy, that's fer sure."

"It must sound crazy."

"You got that straight!" He chuckled. "And you're sure about all this?"

Annie nodded. "I'm sure about it. I've seen it with my own eyes. And you saw those papers. We need to do something."

"Like what?" He stopped his work and looked at her with his eyes creased in suspicion. "Call the cops, or the military? Why, if it's that bad, what *can* we do?"

She hesitated and then said, "There's a young man. He has...*powers*."

Easy raised one eyebrow. "Like Superman?"

"Not quite. He's a prophet."

"Pshh!" He brushed his hand through the air.

"No, really. I believe God has put him here. He has the power to control the Rift, to stop whatever they started. In fact, I think he has more power than even he can imagine."

"And you believe that?"

"I do. It was predicted a long time ago. Someone with a brand, a scar on his face, would heal the land." She nodded, as if to reenergize her confidence. "They're going up there today. We can only pray they stop it."

"Up where?" Easy turned and looked at her quizzically.

"To the Rift," Annie said. "I'm just afraid Fergus will find out. That he'll do something and try to stop them. I mean, if he's tied in with this, if he's conjured some power, some evil, who knows what kinds of things are on his side? We need to stop him, Easy. Keep him from trying to thwart this."

"We?" Easy uncorked a brown jar, poured some of the liquid onto the rag, and corked the bottle.

"You and me. We can...we can do something to keep him from going up there." She inched forward on the chair. "I've been thinking about it. Maybe we can orchestrate something to distract him. You know, a diversion."

"You sound like a regular sleuth, Miss Annie." Easy laughed and held the sopping rag out. "And as much as I hate ta say it, I believe you done stumbled onto somethin'."

"Thanks to you."

"Me? I tried ta warn you." The liquid sweetness struck her nostrils. "So I figured, well, if curiosity done killed the cat, then maybe settin' out some milk'll speed the process."

She squinted at him. "What're you talking about?"

Easy walked toward her.

She wanted to ask him why he was walking without his cane. He approached her remarkably fast, the rag extended.

Had she not been caught off guard, Annie Lane could have given the old man a fight. But as usual it was the element of surprise that won out. Any respect Miss Marple had for Annie would have vanished that instant. Easy Dolan stuffed the sweet-smelling rag over Annie's face and held it in place with very little resistance.

"Chloroform," he said, as Annie's world faded. "Makes a great solvent."

Rather than attack, her body surrendered to the sweet liquid. As her world went black, a strange amber glow tinged Easy's eyes.

Chapter 50

At the time Annie had no idea what it meant.

You will stand in the gap. You will be a remnant.

Her life was in shambles back then, and the words seemed to be senseless. What *gap* was she supposed to stand in? And what kind of *remnant* was she to be a part of? At first there was confusion. Then resentment. She expected something more specific. When God spoke, you knew it. This word had none of that specificity. Still, it had lingered in her brain.

After years of angst and second-guessing, Annie realized those were the exact words she needed to hear. They had given her hope. From that day on it became her mission to find the remnant, to be part of that remnant. And to stand in the gap with them, whatever that gap might be.

She woke to nausea. As she did, that word was on her mind. And she wondered if she would ever live to fulfill it.

Her lower back was throbbing again. Annie tried to rise, but she couldn't. She fought to call out, but her mouth wasn't working. Something was stuffed in it. Instinctively she flailed in panic. Her feet were free, and she managed to hoist her torso into a sitting position. A small, dark space swirled around her. It smelled of bleach and moisture. Where was she? Pain seared her wrist, and she realized her hands were tied behind her. Then she attempted to scream, but only a garbled yelp emerged.

She was bound and gagged!

Panic streaked through her, and her mind struggled to reassemble the pieces.

Her suitcase was packed and lying on her bed. Waiting. Waiting, just like Tamra would be waiting. She remembered Vera's son, his chill gaze, and Violet carrying out the bulky black trash bags alongside him. Then there was Easy, his eyes glowing like fire pits in a volcanic flume.

Above it all Annie remembered Tamra's warning to stay inside.

A beam of light fingered through an open doorway. She could make out boxes against the dim contours of walls. Wads of fabric or clothing littered a concrete floor, and a broom or mop tilted in the corner. The scab on her shin had been torn open again, and fresh blood glinted darkly in the light.

The fetch! They were coming for her. It was finally her time.

Annie bit against the gag and tried to wrest her hands free, but she could not.

Muffled voices rose, and a shape passed in front of the light. The door opened, and a figure stood silhouetted against the bright rectangle.

Easy Dolan flicked on the switch, and Annie squinted as a bare bulb came to life overhead. He stood smiling with his golfer's cap tilted upward, revealing a widow's peak of gray.

She was in the washroom. A washer and dryer sat to her left, detergents and cleaning supplies on the opposite wall. The floor was hard and cold. Was she still in Easy's apartment? Annie focused her eyes on him—or the creature who now looked like him.

Easy took a step toward her, bent in inquiry.

"No, the light don't faze us now, if that's what you're thinkin'." He straightened, looked up, and blinked rapidly, as if to demonstrate. "Chalk it up ta adaptation! That's what organisms do, in the strictest sense. Besides, we had lotsa time ta learn how to adapt."

He cackled his familiar laugh. But now she detected something malevolent in his tone.

"Deception's such a useful mechanism, ya know?" He smiled smugly. "Why, it's the only way some animals survive! S'ppose ya could call us chameleons, in that sense. 'Cept you're the ones we learned to copy. DNA, chemical compounds, genetic sequencing— heck, it's all just info. Any half-wit computer programmer can duplicate the chemical makeup of your species. The rest is just details. Brains, bones, and electrical impulses. That's all you are. Fer the most part, I know just about everything that old golfer knew. His kids' names. His favorite food. Just data stored in his noggin. I even know how he felt about you, Miss Annie...just don't count on me exercising his sympathy."

Easy leaned over her, showing his pearly whites.

"I'm surprised at you, Miss Annie. Ya know, I thought you was more discernin'. But you missed it all. I tried to dissuade you at first. Not outta pity. No, sir! Pity's such a useless emotion. When did pity actually advance a species? No! It ain't pity." He rose and spread his arms. "It's survival. Mountains. Mines. Fields of undeveloped land. Death Valley's the perfect place fer our endeavors. And then there's Poverty. They'll be hard pressed to find ya once we strip you of the essentials. We just didn't wanna ruin such a fine vessel." He drawled the word fine, eyed her up and down, and a lustful gaze sparkled in his eyes. "Ya know, for a woman your age, you have kept yourself in wonderful condition."

Annie bit at the gag and fought to free herself. She kicked toward Easy, hoping to land a heel in his kneecap, but struck nothing and fell back onto the floor.

"I told you to just leave it, didn't I? You were just too stubborn." His brows creased, and he gazed at her, the edges of his eyes framing pure hatred. "It's that faith o' yers that's got you into this mess, Miss Annie. Why, not a few souls have gone on to destruction for that foolish belief. But I must say, it played right into our hands.

"See, when we learned ya found the old man's journal, we had to lead you on. Fergus been careless with that book, yet we had no choice but to leave him with it. He's a sorcerer, ya know? Big things in store for him. Big! If only ya hadn't gone snoopin' round, perhaps it wouldn't come ta this. But it's played to our advantage. Ya see, we needed to get Zipperface to the gateway. With your assistance, we've done sealed the deal. I do believe he's on his way to the Rift as we speak. And you were the ones that wooed him there, Miss Annie. If he's swapped, a powerful thing will happen. Powerful! A black cherub, the rarest of all beings, will control the gateway. Then there will be no one that can stop us. Not a soul."

Annie turned her head away from him. Zeph was in no condition to stand against something of this magnitude. Little Weaver and the boy prophet were heading into a trap! And Annie was partly to blame.

She heaved herself upward again, biting at the gag. Finally, she thudded back to the concrete in exhaustion, tears clouding her eyes.

"Save yerself, please." Easy chuckled. "And if you're lookin' fer this..." He pulled Annie's Swiss Army knife from his pocket and shook it before her. "Don't."

She looked down at her skirt.

"Hope ya don't mind. We'll just go ahead and stash it somewhere for good keepin'."

He stepped into the washroom, bent, and huddled over a dark form that lay on the floor.

It was Easy Dolan's—the real Easy Dolan's—body, lying crumpled next to her.

Annie released a garbled yelp.

The man stuffed the knife into Easy's pocket.

"Someone'll be along for the both of you shortly. You wouldn't wanna go ruinin' yerself before we get a chance to use ya."

She could smell the stench of his breath, a dry rotten flume of hot air.

Annie scooted herself into a sitting position with her back against the washer. She frantically scanned the room. Unless she could manage to free herself, there'd be no way to escape. She glared at the man, her face now wet with perspiration.

"I know what you're thinkin'." Easy held up his finger. "But we ain't demons. No, sir! We like ta think of ourselves as messengers. Messengers of a better way. We were special, Miss Annie. A new order, you could say. But before we even had a chance to spread our wings—so ta speak—we was incarcerated. Learned too much, apparently. Got too powerful to suit Him. So He locked us up! Ya see, that's no parallel dimension ya'll pierced. That's a prison. You done unlocked the madhouse of the universe!" He cackled.

Annie's mind was spinning. They were demons, fallen angels. Hellish organisms that could, somehow, duplicate human bodies. She tried to steady her breathing and fought to keep from swooning in the presence of such evil.

"We've had plenty of time to tinker, and now we're on the verge of symmetry." Easy's eyes glistened. "A sustainable fission between two worlds. Pops woulda been proud! All we needed was the right person. And ta think he was here all along. But you don't need me to rattle on. You'll understand soon enough." He nodded. "Trust me, you'll understand."

Annie glared at him and shook her head, as if to deny any part of this.

"It's not somethin' ta fear, Miss Annie. You'll become part of us, somethin' new. That awful Dictator of yours ain't the only one who can create. No, sir! He made you in His image, but we've made ourselves in yours. Ain't never been somethin' quite like us." He spread his arms and beamed proudly. "Genetically human. Metaphysically divine."

A shadow moved in the hall beyond him. Annie's gaze was frozen upon the approaching figure. Eugenia stepped into view.

She smiled. "We're changin', Miss Annie. Just like any new species. Evolving."

Annie looked at Eugenia with pleading eyes.

"Eugenia's gone," the woman sneered. "I got the sequence and what's left of her. It'll do for now. When the time's right, I'll find another."

Then the woman walked in and put her hand affectionately on Easy's shoulder. He turned, slipped his arm around her waist, and they kissed.

"Ah, the flesh!" Easy turned back, smiling with delight. "It's no wonder ya'll get addicted. Touch, taste, smell. It's a whole new world! One that we been refused for eons."

Then his demeanor grew grim.

"In a bit, I'll have to conk ya out again. Stevie, the grounds guy'll be by, and he'll take you up. There's tunnels in the boiler room, just like you said. Go all the way up to Poverty. It's a bit of a walk, but that's what happens when you give up your wings. Anyway, there's someone dyin' to meet you."

He licked his lips, his red-rimmed eyes little more than creases.

"And I do believe you'll be dyin' ta meet her."

Chapter 51

After the events of last night, even this gray morning felt glorious.

Tamra parked her scooter under the shade of the ash tree, removed her helmet, and stared at Zeph's house. Chickens wandered the front yard, pecking away, and pigeons cooed somewhere in the hazy daylight. Other than that, the neighborhood was still.

She had not slept last night. How could she? Visions of dark angels had niggled into her mind. Now every corner and closet seemed laden with some dreadful presence. Tamra could not close her eyes without seeing the face of the wretched entity hunched over Zeph. She and Annie had lain awake in Tamra's bed, reminiscing about broken dreams, occasional triumphs, and the fantastical world they had stumbled into. Two days ago Tamra's life was boringly normal. Suddenly she was a sidekick to a rebel prophet on a mission to save society from fallen angels and dimensional fusion. Who knew?

She walked along the front of the fence, opened the gate, and started down the path to Zeph's house. Two things immediately caught her attention, and she stopped in her tracks. Zeph's truck was gone, and the front door was open.

As she stared through the darkened doorway, the memory of the fetch riffled through her mind, and she came to an immediate halt. She looked down at the Vermont. Had they left already? If so, why would they leave the front door open? Tamra glanced at the Book Swap, but the cottage was dark and the CLOSED sign was still in place. What was going on?

She went to the porch and stood at the base of the steps.

"Zeph," she called out. "Zeph!"

There was no answer.

The thought of that hideous creature hypnotizing Zeph, entwining itself around him, drew chills along her spine. But she couldn't just stand there. She slowly climbed the steps, staring into the darkened house.

Moisture pattered the ground, dripping from the dewy rooftop.

The porch creaked with her weight. She stood before the front door and called out his name again, but there was no answer.

Something scampered from inside the house, something small and dark, aimed straight at her feet. Tamra gasped, danced out of the way, and stumbled into the porch swing. She fell into it and lay swaying wildly.

A Chihuahua licked frantically at her ankles.

A wave of relief rushed over her. She sat up and reached toward the dog. It leapt into her arms, knocking her back into the swing. The Chihuahua was on her chest, lapping at her face. Tamra wrestled the dog away, laughing.

"What's wrong, guy?" Tamra stroked the shivering dog. "Zeph didn't tell me about you."

As she sat trying to calm the nervous critter, a thud sounded inside Zeph's house, and she bounded out of the swing. The dog leapt from her arms and tumbled across the porch. It skidded to a stop, scrambled to its feet, and stared into the house, growling. A ridge of hair bristled along its spine.

Tamra's heart was practically in her throat. Should she run? If it was a dark angel, there was no way she could compete. Little Weaver had assured them the wicked angels could not stand the light. They were fragile in their transitory state, he'd said. But the thought of hand-to-hand battle with such a hideous thing made the impulse to flee more immediate.

Yet if Zeph was in trouble, as her grandmother had feared, Tamra had to risk it.

"Zeph!" She stepped to the doorway. The dog scampered behind her. "Zeph! It's Tam. Are you in there?"

But there was no response.

She called out again. Again there was no answer.

From here she could see the den where Zeph had wrestled last night with the creature.

Then something happened inside Tamra. The dreadful fear that only moments ago threatened to yank her heart out of her ribcage now seemed as far away as the stars were from the earth. Had she been asked to explain it, Tamra Lane would have needed a dictionary, a thesaurus, and a lot of time to think about it. At the moment she didn't have any of them.

Only the sensation of assurance.

Yesterday's discussions about miracles, healings, and prophecies had left Tamra's head spinning. While she conceded the miraculous, until last night she had never witnessed anything she considered to fit that category. Nevertheless, she could not deny that what was stewing around inside her right now was unlike anything she had ever experienced.

And that sensation was so profound, she could do nothing but respond.

Tamra Lane knew, without a shred of doubt, that Zeph Walker was in trouble. Equally as strong was the sense that she was called to protect him.

"Zeph!" She strode through the front door with a newfound confidence. "Zeph! Is that you?"

No answer. Dim light shone through thick curtains. What was she supposed to do? She remembered Zeph describing the Telling and how he would have to be still and listen. Maybe it would work for her. So she listened, hoping for some still, small voice.

Instead the Chihuahua scuttled in behind her and hurried toward the hall where it stopped, turned, and gazed up at her with its big, wet eyes.

"What's up, fella? Whatcha want?"

The dog skittered down the hall.

Tamra guessed that she had her answer.

She followed the dog into the hallway. It passed a kitchen. A combination of smells came from this room. A bottle of meds sat on the counter. Uncapped. Empty. The dog was not here. The hallway ran to the back of the house, and several doors stood open along the way. The dog stepped from one of those rooms and looked anxiously at her.

"What is it, boy?"

Tamra followed the animal to a darkened bedroom. She felt for the light switch and turned it on. A small lamp whose shade sat cockeyed on a crate cast an oblong shadow across white walls. The room looked odd, disorienting, something that she could not immediately identify. She stepped into the room.

Sheets of paper plastered the walls. Individual pages of print.

Hundreds of them! The room, from floor to ceiling, was one big collage.

She wandered to the wall closest to her with her hand outstretched. With her fingertips she brushed the Bible pages. Genesis, Psalms, Mark, and Revelation plastered randomly, in overlapping seams. Some pages were large print. Some yellowed and torn. Tamra removed her hand and did a slow, 360-degree turn.

Zeph Walker's entire bedroom was wallpapered with pages from the Bible.

As she gawked, allowing her mind to absorb this oddity, a rustle sounded and she turned to see someone standing in the doorway.

Chapter 52

Little Weaver stood in the doorway to Zeph's bedroom, his features sullen, his gloved hands hanging limp at his sides.

Tamra's voice was wedged in her throat. The bad vibes were capering in her mind again. Annie was suspicious of the Indian, and standing alone in the bedroom with him, Tamra couldn't help but share her grandmother's wariness.

"What's going on here?" She motioned to the walls pasted with Bible pages. "Why'd he do this?"

She said this partly as a way to stall and, even as she watched him, begin contemplating a plan of escape. If they'd gotten to Weaver, there was no telling what he might do. Take her back to his lab for some god-awful experiments? Maybe run her through with his javelin. Her throat felt like sandpaper. Perhaps there was something nearby she could use as a weapon. If it came to brute strength, there was no way she could overpower him. But she couldn't think about that. If she was really supposed to protect Zeph, then God would watch over her. Even if it meant hand-to-hand combat with this mammoth Indian.

"A sad story indeed. But one that must wait." Little Weaver glanced down the hallway.

She swallowed dryly.

"It is worse than I feared," Little Weaver said. "Brother Walker has gone to the Rift. Alone."

Tamra stared at him, emotionally unyielding.

Little Weaver cocked his head. "You do not trust me."

"Should I?"

"Perhaps I could say the same about you."

They squared off, eyeing each other.

Then he looked to the ground and drew up strength. "I am Little Weaver, heir to Big Weaver. Guardian of the gate." He raised his head, and his eyes flashed with fury. "Those of the Third Column have no part of me!" The atmosphere seemed to resonate at the force of his words.

Tamra took a step back but continued staring at the man.

Then a kind smile crept across his face.

She sighed and slumped forward. "He's in trouble. I know it."

"Yes. The journal reveals far more than I imagined. Brother Walker's heart has turned for the good. We should be thankful. You have helped him find his way. But he has no idea of the power of the Rift and those who dwell there."

Tamra's gaze drifted about the room, the walls and ceilings plastered with pages of Scripture. What kind of angst and torment could have brought the young man to do this? Something else stirred inside Tamra, something more profound than dark angels and mad professors—the possibility that she had really played a part in helping Zeph Walker find his way.

"I must go to him," Little Weaver said. "If there is still time."

"I'm going with you."

"There is great danger involved."

Tamra shrugged. "Well, yeah."

"Ha! Then let us go, Warrior Soul!"

He nodded, and they hurried out of the house together with the little dog at their heels.

A dirty white car was parked behind Tamra's scooter. It sat inches from her tail light. A large man with a cowboy hat and a scowl leaned against the hood of the car with his arms folded, watching them descend the steps. A second man wearing a rumpled white blazer circled the vehicle.

"I trust we have not been summoned here without good cause." This man had a southern drawl and a head of white hair that would have made Colonel Sanders envious. "Especially this early in the morning."

"You can say that again," the cowboy grumbled.

Little Weaver glanced at Tamra, as if he were trying to communicate telepathically. Then he lifted his gloved hands as if in surrender. "I had nothing to do with it."

"I am aware of that, Mr. Weaver." The white-haired man ambled to the front gate. "Question is, what brought you to this house at this ungodly hour of the day? Especially when you have heretofore professed no connection with the young man who resides here."

Tamra was so enthralled with the detective's linguistics she did not see Little Weaver's reaction.

As the white-haired man reached the gate, the Chihuahua charged the fence, yakking fiercely. Tamra hurried to the dog, lifted it, and attempted to calm the animal in her embrace. It remained snarling at the men.

The detective curled his lip at the dog. "Irritable little things, aren't they?"

"You're...*cops?*" Tamra cast puzzled glances between the men.

"Detectives, ma'am. A. J. Lacroix. And this is my partner, Detective Chavez."

The cowboy was staring at the neighbor's house and nodded sternly without looking at her.

"And I take it you are Ms. Lane." Lacroix tilted his head.

"How did you..."

"As I alluded to, we received a phone call this morning, the content of which I am not permitted to divulge. It was, however, rendered by the owner of this house."

"Zeph?" Tamra said. "He called you?"

"You sound surprised," Chavez said. "Was he not *supposed* to call us?"

"Well, I—"

"He inside?" Lacroix motioned to the house.

Tamra looked at Little Weaver, wondering what signal he'd been attempting to send her. As she did, he took her arm.

"Something has happened," Little Weaver said, motioning toward Zeph's house. "A struggle of some sort. We're worried, Detectives."

Chavez pushed himself off the car, glaring at the house, while his partner opened the gate and ducked under the arbor.

Tamra had to fight to keep the Chihuahua from leaping out of her arms and assaulting the detectives. Either this dog had a thing against cops, or these cops were not what they seemed.

Lacroix squinted at the animal. Then he stepped back and scanned the property. "Despite the dissuasion of our superiors, we have been following your escapades with interest. And until this morning, I would have thought they could get no more queer. But at the moment, my suspicions are growing exponentially."

"Huh?" Tamra puzzled over the statement.

"He thinks yer in on somethin'," the cowboy said, ducking under the arbor and removing a handgun from his boot.

Tamra gasped.

"We're gonna have a peek inside," Lacroix said. "After which we will have a few questions for the two of you. So, if you would, please." Lacroix motioned them toward the street. "Wait right here, and let's see if we can extract some answers about what is goin' on between the three o' you. Hmm?"

Chat walked up the steps with his firearm clasped at the ready, Lacroix following behind him. They crept into the house, disappearing into its shadow.

"What're we gonna do?" Tamra whispered, stroking the shivering dog. She looked at Little Weaver for a response, but his eyes were focused elsewhere. She followed his gaze to the house next door.

The screen was slightly ajar, and a woman stood behind the mesh, watching them.

Last night they had asked Little Weaver how to recognize a dark angel in human form. But at the moment Tamra needed no instruction.

Little Weaver nudged her arm and pointed across the street. "My jeep. Hurry." He started to move that direction.

"But—" She glanced back at Zeph's house. She had never received a speeding ticket, been fined for loitering, or run from the police. And she hated to have her streak broken.

You can't find the truth without risking something.

"What about him?" Tamra lifted the Chihuahua.

But Little Weaver was already jogging across the street in the pale morning light.

She set the dog down. "I'll be back, buddy. And be nice to those cops, okay?"

Chapter 53

They buried Belle Walker at Moncrieff's, near the fence line overlooking the northernmost edge of Death Valley. It was spring then, and after an especially wet winter, the folks in Endurance were calling it the bloom of the century. How fitting, he thought, that his mother would die when the world was alive with color. Rivers of wildflowers coursed the dry landscape, veins of lavender, crimson, and gold fingering their way through washes and ravines. And when the breeze rose, it drove the fragrance through the old cemetery like a wisp of heaven itself.

But standing at his mother's graveside, no aroma on earth could replace the stench of hell the boy prophet felt. And maybe that's when hell took root.

At thirteen years old Zephaniah Walker did not possess the emotional mechanisms to accurately process such an event. Perhaps it was due to the special relationship he and his mother shared. At first Zephaniah felt somehow complicit in her death. He had been doubting his own gifting, questioning those around him, most notably Belle. And then came thinning crowds. The Telling was growing distant, coming less often. The Plains Prophet was conflicted.

Now, five years later, he returned to that cemetery. So much had changed. Not only was his face cloven, but a fissure had left his faith sundered and shipwrecked. Meanwhile his father's disregard had gone to seed. Turned out the old man thought Belle was a wacko all along, but he never had the courage to say it when she was alive. He played the game, bowed his head at the dinner table, and looked the other way when Belle locked the door on her only son.

How could God let this happen? Pearl got three meals a day paid for by the state, his father slouched back to Endurance, and Zephaniah was scarred for life.

"I didn't want this!" Zephaniah's words echoed past the headstones into the flower-laden landscape. He stared through tears at his mother's grave, clenched his fists, and turned away. "No more words—I'm done with You. I'm done with everything! I don't want to hear the Telling ever again."

So it was, at eighteen years of age, near the graveside of his mother, that Zephaniah Walker died. To some he became Zipperface. To the rest he became only Zeph Walker. Recluse. Outcast. Sad, sad story.

He turned and left the cemetery. He deserved to be struck by lightning. Instead of lightning, however, the sweet smell of blossoms met him, a slap in the face of his rage. As he walked past the large, marble angel that guarded the entrance, a voice called to him.

"It'll make a fine story some day."

Zeph stopped in his tracks and turned to see a young Indian man, stout and tanned, leaning against the wall, watching him. Probably another vagrant, hitchhiking his way along the 395. But what was he doing all the way out here?

Zeph peered skeptically at the man. "What's a fine story?"

The young man just smiled. A gust of dry wind cast his hair about his face.

Zeph pursed his lips and turned to leave.

"A prophet never loses his calling," the man said, "only his way."

Zeph studied the man's deep-set eyes. Pain was etched there, as was wisdom. His face seemed familiar. And his voice...

"Brother Walker!"

The shadow inside of Zeph flinched. Uncoiled.

"Brother Walker!"

It was the voice of that same man. This voice wasn't inside him, dredged from the mud of his memory; it was outside him. And when he heard it, something came alive inside of Zeph Walker.

And he remembered the magic.

Chapter 54

"Brother Walker!" Little Weaver's voice echoed in the foggy canyon.

Tamra leaned into the sagging fence, feeling the prick of the barbed wire in her palms. "Maybe he didn't come here," she wondered.

Hiking through the ragged stand of birch had left her panting. However, part of her breathlessness was the rush of finally looking down upon the mythical ninth gate of hell.

Little Weaver gripped his javelin and peered into Otta's Rift. Seeing him standing there with the sleek metal implement and its ornate handle conjured images of primitive hunters in prehistoric wastelands. Although Tamra seriously doubted that any primitive hunter brandished a pair of motorcycle goggles like Weaver did.

"Brother Walker!" The misty shroud seemed to swallow the sound of Little Weaver's voice.

She returned her gaze to the gorge, staring forward in hopes of spotting Zeph Walker. Suddenly Little Weaver touched her shoulder and pointed into the ravine. A trail had been forged through the scree slope, and at its base the mist cleared enough for her to make out the mouth of a charred, timber-framed shaft in the granite wall. And before it lay the pale form of a man.

Tamra pressed forward. "Zeph! Something's wrong with him." She pushed past Little Weaver, trudging toward an open section of the fence. "He's hurt. Zeph!"

As she prepared to sling her leg over the sagging barbed wire, Little Weaver grabbed her with his gloved hand and yanked her back. She nearly slipped on the moist earth and fought to steady herself.

"What're you doing?" She glared at him. "He's in trouble!"

Little Weaver met her gaze with equal ferocity and, for a moment, Tamra glimpsed in his eyes the same fiery intensity she had encountered at Zeph's house. However, she didn't back down. Instead she clenched her fists and stared up at him. "I'm going down there. And you can't stop me."

He studied her, his eyes clouding over with curiosity. "Brother Walker is not the only one in danger, Warrior Soul. The land is poisoned. The dark angels grow strong. The Rift bleeds its magic into root and rock."

Tamra swallowed hard. Then she stared down into the gorge. "It's just a hole in the mountain—that's all."

Little Weaver seemed surprised by her assessment. Then his eyes widened and a grin creased his ruddy features. He laughed, a sound that rose in such crescendo its joy seemed to shear the foggy veil before them. He laughed until the canyon boomed with the sound. So incongruous was his joy in that gloomy place that Tamra couldn't help but laugh along with him, even though she wasn't sure what was so funny.

"Indeed, you are the Warrior Soul!" Little Weaver playfully slapped her shoulder, sending Tamra scrambling for footing. Then the glee drained from his face and the sternness returned. "If I tell you to stay here, I know you will not. The Warrior Soul follows her heart, not the commands of others. And you have already determined to rescue him. You now feel a kinship with his pain."

She fought to stifle a flush of embarrassment, and then nodded, as if a great secret had been exposed.

"Ha! This is how the great stories are made!"

"Hopefully we'll live to tell this one."

Little Weaver's eyes glistened and he said reverently, "The great stories never end, even though one dies. Follow me! But guard your mind. The dark angels feed on your fears. That which you lock inside, they will find and exploit. Move with caution, Warrior Soul."

Little Weaver stabbed his javelin into the earth on the opposite side of the fence. He brushed the moisture off his goggles, strapped them on, and then climbed over the barbed wire in two great strides. He reached across and helped Tamra over. Then he plucked the javelin out and followed the trail toward the mine.

"Brother Walker is in the shadow slumber," Little Weaver said over his shoulder. "He is not dead. Though some never wake from such sleep."

She wanted to ask him what shadow slumber was but feared she might provoke a riddle, so Tamra remained silent.

As they worked their way into the gorge, she trained her eyes on Zeph's form. Though she could see no wounds on his body, he remained motionless. Nevertheless, despite her concern for him, the charred mine wooed her attention.

She recalled Joseph Blessington's journal entries: the abandoned mine equipment, the field of skins, the pits of burning debris, the carcasses of animals strewn about the area. What had happened here? Could the miners really have unlocked some great subterranean evil? And if so, how in the world did Little Weaver expect Zeph to stop it?

The granite wall rose above, a deafening curtain that disappeared into misty gray. The temperature seemed to dip with every step. Tamra was not sure she believed in haunted places. But if they existed, this place was a perfect candidate.

Broken glass crunched under their feet as they neared the floor of the ravine. Small animal bones dotted the gravel. Ahead a lean-to of twisted branches tilted near a crude fire ring. As they passed, Tamra slowed. Inside of it lay a mound of debris, soiled pornographic magazines, and wooden bowls. A rotten stench brought her to an immediate stop. She peered into the decrepit dwelling. A soft rustle emerged. Was someone inside? She glanced toward Little Weaver, who continued on, oblivious to her wonder. Overhead a crow cawed, and she traced her eyes up the towering rock face.

Fear shuddered through her, and with it came a staggering sense of vulnerability. Tamra was not used to this feeling. She turned and stared back up the scree slope into the shrouded foothills. All alone. They were all alone. A perfect setup. Perhaps they'd been coaxed here. But by whom? Whoever it was, something could happen and no one would ever know.

A faint buzzing sounded, and she turned back to the rickety structure to identify its source. A slight breeze rustled the pages of one of the magazines, and she glimpsed what looked like photos of a surgical procedure. Sutures. A wound. Bloody gauze. She stepped closer. Who would be reading such a thing out here?

The buzzing intensified.

As did her unease.

She could not say when her parents had stopped caring or when their addictions eclipsed the welfare of their own children. Self-reliance had sprung up in her not from active cultivation but as a means of survival. She could fend for herself. That was one thing Tamra Lane could do. Nevertheless, it was her self-sufficiency that seemed so pitiful; in the murk of this defiled canyon, before this ancient maw of madness, her confidence was exposed for what it was: a glaring façade.

She crept forward. A dark, filmy liquid filled one of the bowls. Was it blood? Flies ringed its rim, and as she approached, they buzzed with agitation but did not scatter.

A shadow fell across the earth.

She thought about Dieter. What would happen to him if she died? But why must she die? Tamra Lane could fend for herself. That's what she'd done for most of her life. She'd learned to do the laundry on her own and make meals for the family. At sixteen she got her permit, and every weekday before taking her mother to the crack house, she took her brother to school. And at night she tucked Dieter in with a story, whether or not Dad was lucid enough to care. Yes, Tamra could take care of herself. But in the shadow of this chasm, on the very ground of the Madness, she wondered if she could stand against the evil that dwelt there.

It was the same evil that took her mom and dad.

"Warrior Soul!"

Perhaps hell fed on people like her, those too strong-willed and stubborn to see their abject poverty, too independent to need the truth. That's what Otta's Rift was—a graveyard. A graveyard for the once self-sufficient.

The shadow advanced.

"Warrior Soul!"

Little Weaver's voice startled her.

Tamra stopped and stared blankly at the wooden shanty. There was no shadow. Nor were there any bloody pictures. The lean-to was empty.

She gasped and quickly located Little Weaver. He stood over Zeph's body, peering at Tamra through his goggles, shaking his head. Then he spiked his javelin into the earth.

She glanced back at the wooden structure before hurrying to Zeph and Little Weaver.

"A north-south terraline that oscillates east and west." He pointed to the Rift and drew imaginary directional arrows in the air. "It intersects an east-west terraline that oscillates north and south. There is a spot inside the mine, which, if you stand on it, you will sway with a rotary motion, usually in a counter-clockwise fashion. Unless, of course, you are left-handed."

Tamra studied Zeph and, without looking at Weaver, said to him, "I take it you've been here before."

"I am the guardian of the gateway."

"Right." She knelt at Zeph's side. He appeared to be coming to.

Little Weaver continued, "The phenomena is caused by the alternating movement of the east-west, north-south lines. But there are other effects of this confluence of coordinates."

"Like hallucinations?"

"I warned you."

Tamra returned her attention to Zeph. "Is he all right?"

"For now, yes."

Little Weaver bent down, scooped his large hands under Zeph, and helped him sit up.

"Pearl," Zeph muttered, shaking his head and blinking hard to adjust his vision. Then he stared into the Rift.

Tamra followed his gaze.

Zeph said, "She was in there."

Little Weaver did not look into the mine. Instead, he stared at Zeph through the thick goggles. "Greater demons than your step-mother inhabit that foul place. Can you stand?"

Zeph nodded. Tamra positioned herself on one side, Little Weaver the other, and together they helped Zeph to his feet. Tamra continued to steady him while he wobbled for footing.

"More is at work than I have imagined." Little Weaver plucked the javelin from the ground. "The journal—I have learned much. Quickly. We must not delay. We will return again to this foul place. But before we do, other battles must be fought."

Zeph steadied himself and stood upright on his own. "I think I know one of the battles you're talking about."

Chapter 55

They hurried through the ragged birch grove, as if some dread phantom was on their heels. Zeph's head was in a fog. He was ashamed about being found in a fetal position—especially after such a courageous effort on his part. Perhaps going it alone was the wrong thing to do. But after eight years of going it alone, it was a hard habit to break. His stepmother's ghostly presence wandered the dark periphery of his mind, as if the Rift had awakened her buried remains inside him. What manner of evil could extract such memories from a person? He shivered at the thought of returning to the dreaded mine but knew he must.

Little Weaver led the way, his javelin doubling as a walking stick. He was unusually quiet, and Zeph wondered why the Rift had not affected the man. Or had it? Tamra walked beside Zeph, and out of the corner of his eye he could see she was watching him closely. He remembered their brief talk outside last night but forced himself to not wander that lonely road of possibility. Through the trees Zeph saw Little Weaver's jeep parked in front of his truck along the mule road. The atmosphere was so dank and depressing here, he half-expected his vehicle to have been vandalized or stolen by mountain men. Nevertheless, it sat untouched where he had parked it.

Plink.

Zeph halted at the sound, skidding in the decaying mat of leaves.

Pa-plink.

Tamra gasped and reached for him. "What is it?"

Little Weaver spun about with the javelin hoisted at half-mast. His goggles dangled at his chest, and his eyes surveyed the thicket.

Zeph looked nervously at the dream catcher swaying gently from the tree.

Plink.

Little Weaver followed Zeph's gaze, exhaled, and lowered the javelin. "A *werevane*, harbinger of dark tidings." He spat. "Look not upon it!" Then he turned and hurried through the trees.

Little Weaver went to his jeep and wedged the javelin into place while Zeph and Tamra plodded out of the decrepit woods. They went to Zeph's truck. His clothing was soaked from lying in the damp earth, and his boots were equally full of muck from the hike to and from the Rift. He leaned with his back to the vehicle, closed his eyes, and massaged his temples.

"Are you okay?"

Zeph peeked through one eye. "Other than feeling like my brain's been blowtorched, I'm terrific."

"What happened out there?"

Zeph winced at the reminder of his foolhardiness. He had achieved the opposite of what he'd intended: drawn them here. Now he looked like a wimp. "It's hard to explain," he said. "I thought I could..." He looked away, shaking his head. "I don't know. I just didn't want anyone else to get hurt."

Little Weaver stopped rummaging through his jeep to watch them.

"The police were at your house," Tamra said. "They said you called them."

"I did. It's my neighbor. I'm afraid she's been..." His voice cracked with emotion, but he quickly composed himself. "She's dead."

Tamra gasped.

"One of those things..." Zeph's gaze drifted to the gorge, its sheer face rising above the fog. "They buried her body out back."

"Do the police know?"

"If they aren't part of this, they know now."

"Which means they know that we know."

Zeph nodded.

"They wanted us to stay," Tamra said. "But we ran. They'll be after us, Zeph. They'll come looking."

"And they'll bring others."

Little Weaver clomped over in his muddy boots, his tools clanking underneath his camo jacket. Even in these defiled woods he seemed to be alive, impervious to the unfolding darkness. He carried Annie's journal, approached Zeph's truck, and assembled some of the documents on the hood. They surrounded the Indian, mystified over the strange archive.

"It is worse than I feared," Little Weaver said. "The journal is not only a scientific record but a rune to open the black mirror. A spell-book to summon the dark angels."

Zeph bent closer to see symbols, cuneiform scripts, hand-drawn letters comprised of lines, angles, and stars.

"An angelic alphabet," Little Weaver said. "Once thought only fable."

Zeph squinted, trying to make sense of the symbols and words. He read haltingly, "*Grimel. Nun. Va—*"

"Silence!" Little Weaver thundered. His voice echoed through the foothills.

Zeph stumbled back from the truck.

"Speak not those dread words, Brother Walker."

"They're just words," Tamra said defensively. "You scared the heck outta me."

"Just words?" Little Weaver mused. "Just words. Ha! Was it *just words* that formed your world, brought light from darkness? Was it *just words* that awakened the Great Serpent? Is it *just words* that loose the soul to forgiveness or bind it to perpetual grief? No, Warrior Soul. There is no such thing as *just words*."

Tamra glanced rather ashamedly at Zeph. After his encounter before the Rift, he wondered if a scolding wasn't appropriate for both of them.

Little Weaver turned back to the documents. His tone was stern. "These are more than just words. Hewed from darkness by Father Coyne. Dictated by the seraphim, it is the rune to open the ninth gate of hell."

Zeph could not hide the incredulity in his tone. "You're saying that those words, those documents, were dictated by *angels?*"

"It is the script of the seraphim," Little Weaver said. "Dark angels. They made contact with the other side, just as Father Coyne predicted. A code for unlocking the Third Column."

"Can't we just destroy it?" Zeph asked. "Burn it or something?"

"Indeed. Such texts deserve burning. But it cannot stop what has begun. The formula is found. And the Teller of it grows strong. Those who have deciphered this and possess its secrets wield untold might. More than they imagine." Little Weaver grew still. "The dark angels walk among us. They prepare the way for a great one—a being of such might, were it to cross, no one could stop it." Little Weaver leafed through the papers, located one, and laid it before them. "A black cherub—the most insidious of all entities."

Zeph took the sketch and studied it. "Annie warned us about this."

"One of the mightiest of all angels," Little Weaver intoned. "The cherubim were guardians of the throne of the Almighty. But some turned. Now they seek to obtain symmetry, to merge the two columns and so control the worlds. The black cherub could harness such power. All the seraphim need to complete their plan is one so gifted—a shaman, a prophet. When he is found, the black cherub will emerge."

After a long pause Zeph said, "That prophet has been found. Hasn't he?"

Little Weaver nodded. "The Rift has remained open because of him. He holds sway over the land."

Zeph stared blankly. He sensed what was coming.

"Ha!" shouted Little Weaver. "There is time for this tale, Brother Walker!"

"Go for it," Zeph sighed.

"A man once had a dream," Little Weaver began. "In his dream the man was carried away by a great eagle, far into the future. They arrived at an island—a violent, flaming volcano. The man asked, 'What is this thing?' And the eagle responded, 'This is a word you once spoke, gone out into eternity and crystallized in this form.' And then the eagle snatched up the man and flew on for a great distance until they arrived at another island, this one cool and green, covered with fountains and fruit trees. And the man again asked, 'What is this thing?' The eagle replied, 'This too is a word you once spoke, which has gone out into eternity and crystallized in this form.' And the dreamer awoke."

Zeph looked long and hard at Little Weaver. Finally, he said. "So this is my fault, isn't it? This is my *volcano?*"

Tamra scowled. "Why're you always so hard on yourself? How could this be your fault?"

But Little Weaver was honed in on him. "Go on."

"The wound festers," Zeph recited the words. "The land awaits. And between them lies my darker self."

Tamra's annoyance appeared to be growing. "What're you talking about, Zeph?"

"When this all started," Zeph said, "I received a word. That word. It was the Telling. It'd been years—"

"A prophecy?" Tamra said. "About all this?"

"Yeah. That's the day the detectives came, showed me that thing at the morgue. The same day you came. Then I went to Meridian, like your grandmother said. There's a cave painting up there. It shows a person with..." He swallowed hard. "With a mark on their face."

"The Branded One," Little Weaver said. "He will heal the wound and save the land."

Tamra's incredulity was obvious. "And you believe it's about you?"

"I have no other choice. I came back to Endurance eight years ago. I–I didn't know it then. I thought it was just...coincidence. I was wrong. It was all foretold. But instead of coming back to do something good, I went to my mother's graveside and renounced everything—my calling, my gift. I cursed heaven, Tamra." Then he said to Little Weaver, "And that word has crystallized, hasn't it?"

The Indian nodded.

"Now people are dying," Zeph said. "And hell is feeding off my inaction."

Tamra reached out to touch him, but Zeph shrank back.

"You were there, weren't you?" Zeph pointed at the Indian. "Way back then, you were there. You were watching me."

A slight smile creased Little Weaver's ruddy features. "You are returning to yourself, my friend."

"Do you remember how you said the dark angels feed on our regrets, our disappointment? It's like the darkness inside us is their magnet, their lifeline. Well, if they feed on unforgivingness and regret, then I'm like a twelve-course meal. As long as I hold onto this garbage, let this fear, this bitterness eat me up—as long as I keep runnin'—they have power here. I can't stand before them." He gestured toward Otta's Rift. The memory of the shadowy winged thing swooping upon him sent chills over Zeph. "Don't you see?" He turned to Tamra, almost pleading. "They don't want me going in there, into that rotten mine. Whatever I'm supposed to do when I get there can put an end to this." He stepped back.

The stillness of the mountains encroached, as if the world—the land he had been called to—was waiting for the words Zeph was about to say. "But if I'm gonna do this, there's something I need to get off my chest."

"Now?" Tamra looked cock-eyed at him. "Can't we just get this over with?"

Zeph pulled his car keys out of his pocket. "I'm sorry."

"It is as he says, Warrior Soul." Little Weaver's countenance was grim. "Meanwhile, I shall go to Marvale, to Camp Poverty. I must stop Fergus's advance. He cannot be allowed here, for the soul eaters march with him. Dark forces will align against us in forms you have not conceived." He faced Zeph. "Take heed! You must return here for one last match." His eyes sparkled. "Surely it will be a tale for the ages!"

Chapter 56

*Z*eph told Tamra he was well enough to drive, although now behind the wheel he had second thoughts. Pearl's words stalked the borders of his mind, threatening to tug him back into an infernal malaise. He was fallow and fruitless, just like she'd said. His twenty-six years were a virtual road map to existential barrenness.

Tamra pulled out her cell phone and rested it on her lap. She drew her fingers through her hair. "This is all so crazy."

"Which part?" Zeph peered out the dirty windshield, navigating back down Dawson's Rut toward the highway. "Are you kidding? The whole thing."

"Maybe you shoulda listened to your grandmother. She seems to have figured it out." He smiled to himself.

"Don't get me started about her. And Little Weaver doesn't help matters."

"I know what you mean," Zeph said. "Half of what he says I don't understand. And the other half I'm not sure I can trust."

"That makes two of us."

"But he did come for me, so that's gotta count for something."

They reached the highway, and Zeph sat with the truck idling, looking south past town.

"What's wrong?" Tamra asked.

Zeph shook his head. "Nothing."

Tamra stared at him. "You're not having one of those..."

"Prophecies? No."

He continued to let the truck idle, contemplating his next move.

Then Tamra said, "You said there was something you had to do before we go back there, something you had to get off your chest. You're not having second thoughts, are you?"

Zeph was beginning to feel that Tamra Lane was reading him a lot faster than he was reading her.

"Okay," she said. "If you *are*, you *shouldn't*."

"How do you know I'm having second thoughts?"

"I'm just guessing."

"You're good. Maybe you'd make a better prophet than me."

"No thanks."

Zeph turned the truck onto the 395 heading south, to a ramshackle community outside Endurance named Blister.

"I was right," she eventually said. "Wasn't I?"

But Zeph was too busy thinking of what waited ahead to answer.

Tamra dialed a number and put the phone to her ear. After a minute or so, she hung up and sat staring forward. "It's Nams—she's not answering."

"You dropped her off at her apartment, right?"

"And I was supposed to pick her up there. She was worried about you, ya know? That's why I went to your house."

Zeph stared at the passing landscape. "What do you want me to do?"

"Maybe I should do what I shoulda done a long time ago," Tamra said.

"Which is?"

"Let her go."

He cast a quizzical glance at her.

"Our folks—me and Dieter's—are both addicts," Tamra explained. "I couldn't even tell you where they live anymore. Or if they're alive. When they bailed on us, Nams stepped in and helped. She was a godsend. But I couldn't help but feel it was out of guilt, mostly. She took it personally that her son, my dad, had turned out that way. Anyway, she eventually bought us that house. I dunno, I suppose I just feel her pain. And I feel obligated to watch out for her, especially since her own son is AWOL. Maybe I've just been too protective. But something tells me I need to trust her to find her own way. And hopefully not kill herself in the process."

Approximately seven miles south of downtown Endurance, past Loomis's farms, the llama ranch, a honey stand, and a billboard touting the health benefits of alfalfa, Howard Walker lived. The lawns were dead here, just as they'd been for the last twenty-some years. Located at the southernmost point of Endurance, Blister received the worst of Death Valley's wrath. Built cheaply during a brief economic upturn, it remained a community of drywall boxes, decorative rock yards, and serious down-and-outers.

Zeph turned off the highway and drove slowly down a ragged asphalt road.

Endurance was not the Capital of Nice, but this area made Zeph's house look like a Bel Air mansion. A man in an undershirt stood outside a dingy yellow house smoking a cigarette. He followed them with a leering gaze. Near the end of the cul-de-sac Zeph parked in front of a ranch-style property. A screen door hung cockeyed on its hinges, and near it was a broken window with its pieces held in place by black electrical tape.

The house was even worse than he remembered.

Zeph looked down a dirt driveway to the old Triumph. The red convertible sports car sat dull and dusty, sagging on flat tires. After he received his inheritance, Zeph fancied the vehicle the car of his dreams. But by then his dreams had already started to sour. For the last five years the sports car had sat there gathering rust and memories. This house was like a monument to everything he had fled.

He turned off the truck and sat there. The gray afternoon draped the neighborhood in its gloom.

Tamra said, "This is your dad's place, isn't it?"

Zeph nodded. He knew she wanted to ask more, but she refrained. It was a sacred moment for him, and Tamra Lane seemed to respect that.

He got out of the truck, closed the door, and walked toward the driveway. Zeph stared at the house. He could still remember returning here from Los Angeles, scarred and lost, feeling like a prodigal. The heartache swelled inside him, just as it had before the Rift. What had occurred at this house, he now knew, was as hellish as the Madness itself.

A voice roused him.

"I figure we're in this together, huh?"

Zeph turned to see Tamra at his side.

He nodded. "I guess you could say that."

A row of cyprus trees bordered a dirt driveway and stretched deep into the property. Corrugated metal stitched the back fence together, and several stacks of bald tires teetered there. A tire swing hung from a dead tree out back, evoking childhood memories.

He straightened his jacket vest and walked down the driveway to the back gate. Tamra walked beside him. As they passed the

Triumph, she drew her finger along the dusty driver's side window. Even though Zeph struggled against embarrassment, Tamra did not seem put off by the home of his youth. He reached the gate and stopped, looking into an overgrown field of grass left dried by summer's passing. Through the dead meadow he could see the cellar. Zeph opened the gate and walked through the waist-high grass, which rustled in the breeze.

Zeph reached the cellar and stood over a stone stairwell that descended to the tiny door. "This is where it all started."

"Where what started, Zeph?" A hint of fear laced Tamra's words.

He looked at her and said matter-of-factly, "This is where I lived, Tam."

She gazed at the door and looked at him with brows creased. "Down there?"

He descended the steep, narrow steps, which could only be managed by walking sideways. The wooden door was warped by moisture and age. Almost unconsciously he traced the initials carved into the wood with his fingers. It had become a ritual of his and, even now, before proceeding, it seemed to bring consolation.

"Zeph," Tamra said gently from the top of the steps, "what is it you have to do here?"

"I need to see him."

"Someone's in there?"

Zeph nodded. He put his shoulder into the door, and it scratched the surface as it opened. He smelled the must. How many years had it been since anyone had been down here?

He stepped inside. Tamra descended the steps and entered behind him.

Thick cobwebs overlaid empty canning jars that lined several sagging wooden shelves. The floor was dirt. Slits of gray light poured through broken windows. The memories swirled around him like mist from a graveyard.

He went to a wooden box, not much bigger than a produce crate, with a lid. A dried bouquet of flowers lay scattered there.

"He's in there," Zeph said.

"In the box?" Tamra's breathing halted. "Zeph..."

"My brother. We were twins. He died at birth. My cord—" He turned. "My cord strangled him."

"Oh, Zeph." She touched his arm.

"Mother sent me down here to learn. Life's fragile, she said. I should think about that. For days, weeks sometimes—I don't remember. And the Telling, she said I should listen for it. God spared me for a reason, gave me the gift, and took him. So that's what I did—I sat here in the quiet, and listened."

He let his gaze drift around the room.

Tamra stared at the tiny makeshift coffin. She was growing pale. And angry.

"Zeph," she finally said. "This...this isn't right."

Something rustled at the stairwell, and a shadow passed into the entryway. Tamra gasped. Zeph stepped between her and the looming figure. And he knew this was the final darkness inside him he needed to slay.

Chapter 57

It smelled like...

Annie awoke with a gasp.

"What was that?" a voice echoed.

She was still gagged and swallowed rapidly in an attempt to keep from choking. Still, Annie clamped her jaw, stifling any further noise. Her eyes burned and a sharp, acidic smell stung her nostrils. As did a stench of rot and spoilage. Water droplets pattered out a sludgy murmur. She was on her back in a dark, moldy place. Her hands were still tied behind her, and the pain was so sharp she knew that something serious was developing. Perhaps her circulation had been cut off or her wrist was broken. Either way, she dared not move.

"—s nothing."

"...er...have to wait until...the others..."

The voices trailed off into the musty din. Whoever it was, they were near.

She stared into a dark void overhead and what appeared to be timbered beams laden with webs and rusty pipes against thick plaster. Where was she? She turned her head slightly to try to identify her location. Pain lanced her temple, and she clamped her teeth on the gag to avoid from crying out. It felt like the side of her head was swollen.

Then she remembered. *Camp Poverty!* Easy had said they were taking her there. It was here they were planning to swap her. Which meant that somewhere nearby...

Panic tore through her.

She would not become one of them. Whatever it took, Annie refused to surrender to these devils.

Her eyes were watery from the pain in her head. She rolled onto her side, blinked back tears, and waited for her gaze to clear. Her surroundings came into focus. A single bare bulb wafted above an antechamber and a semicircular stone bench. Below it a tiered basin dropped into shadow. Nearby stood an uneven row of barrels with stenciled numbers on them and a red skull and crossbones.

A dark, discomforting mound lay across from the basin. She forced her eyes to focus, and what she saw made her heart freeze. Bodies, bruised and sunken, rose in a decrepit drift. At their base she could barely make out Easy Dolan's emaciated carcass, a cusp of white teeth showing between his sagging jaw.

This time Annie could not withhold a gasp.

Something scurried across her field of vision. And another. Then there were footsteps. Large roaches fled from an approaching figure. Annie forced herself to remain as rigid as possible.

"It *wath* you."

Someone stood over her.

"We thought maybe he'd killth you, hittin' you in the head like that. Here."

The person grabbed Annie by the shoulder and propped her up. Then stepped back and stood before her. She stared at a pair of black rubber galoshes splattered with fleshy particulate matter.

She could make out a pair of grubby overalls beneath a thick apron.

"We thought you'd be twouble. And then when I cawth you back here, we knew it."

Annie did not look into the face of Stevie Veigh's dark angel. Instead she stared at the bank of bodies. How many of her friends lay in there? Eugenia? Vera? Now a mass of rotting flesh. It wouldn't be long before Annie's body was next to them. How had it come to this?

"You probly been wonderin' how we do it, where the bodies hath been goin'." Stevie walked around the basin and sent more roaches skittering from his boot steps. A cat hissed and emerged from the back of the pile. It was Jezebel, most likely standing guard over her master's remains. "They had it figured out a long time ago. The scientiths. Couldn't have all these dead angel bodies lyin' round. They had to hide their trackths, you know."

Stevie approached a large open-faced barrel and wriggled on a thick pair of black rubber gloves. "Hydrochloric athid. They dissolved 'em, poured 'em right down the drain. When we took Roth, things changed. Now the tables hath turned. He's got *connections*, ya know?" He smiled, his cleft pallet revealing a triangle of gums. "Now we're doin' the disposal."

He twisted, reached into the pile, and yanked on a leg.

She groaned and looked away.

"What?" Stevie stopped. "You don't wanna watch?"

"She'll see it soon enough."

Annie squirmed, adjusting her body to see where the second voice came from. A man stood deeper in the subterranean shadows. He emerged into the naked light wearing a long coat and wire-rimmed glasses. His face was long, gaunt. Annie had seen this man before and tried to place him.

"Walther Roth," he said in answer to her thoughts. "Guardian of the gateway."

Stevie bowed clumsily. "On earth ath it is in hell."

Roth waved his hand through the air dismissively. "Save it, you fool." He approached Annie, looking into the basin. "By the time anyone really figures it out, they'll be swapped. We calculate we can take the whole city in twenty-six days. Twenty-six days. All a matter of critical mass. And once the black cherub comes through, the world as you know it will fundamentally change. The Third Column will be fused."

"So mote it be," Stevie snickered.

"Shut up!" Roth's eyes flashed amber, and a tittering sound escaped his throat. "Get to work! There'll be more on the way."

Stevie slobbered something and continued extricating one of the bodies from the stinking heap.

Meanwhile Roth stood directly before Annie. "You've been a thorn in our side, Annie, but night is almost here. And when it comes, the shadows dance. The hive awakens. That's when our power is strong."

A dry slither sounded from below. Something was moving in the dark tunnel. What darkness had gestated below? Annie might as well have stopped breathing, such was her dread. She peered into the black maw of the ancient stone chamber.

A bat-like squeal was followed by raspy chatter.

Roth watched her with cool intensity. "It's in the dark places that we live—your fears, your lusts, your despair gives us life. And that pitiful thing inside you called hope. Its dying brings us life."

Behind him Annie glimpsed Stevie struggling to hoist a body over his shoulder.

She was too far away from Marvale to cry out for help, and Tamra would have no idea to look here. Annie was supposed to have stayed in her apartment. This creature named Roth was right. That pitiful thing inside her had finally met its match. Annie Lane wouldn't stand in the gap. Her life had been one huge, disappointing waste.

"The darkness comes. The hive awakes." Roth motioned down the tunnel. "Soon your little resistance—your remnant—will be swapped, devoured by the seraph. Even now, the hive is on their way. The trap is set." He chuckled, then laughed, a laughter that rose in a maniacal crescendo. "The Prince is on his way. The Seer! And with him is your guardian angel."

The vat sizzled and sputtered, and a sickly gray cloud of acid filled that place of death.

Metallic rustling sounded: the grate of a metal hinge. Gray daylight cast a languid stream from an upper chamber of the room.

Roth clapped his hands.

A misshapen figure plodded through the door, its steps ponderous, its frame malformed. Heavy breathing interspersed the scratching of gravel. It was dragging something.

Annie looked away.

Roth's glasses glinted in the overhead light as he watched the figure on the platform above with apparent glee.

That stuff about taking risks and finding truth seemed like a joke. Her stubbornness and pride loomed before her, mocking her. *God, forgive me!* She had taken risks, all right, and now she would die with her risks.

The acid splat and sizzled. Roth laughed again. The bare bulb swung wildly in the rising acidic cloud.

They were soul eaters, that's what Weaver had called them. And this was their operation. Swapping souls and liquefying the remains. Annie was about to experience firsthand what that process was like.

She looked up, trying to make sense of what was happening above her. The figure had stopped and released its load. A wedge of light revealed a gray curtain outside. She could not tell what time of day it was. But through the open door Annie could make out the rock wall where she had crouched several nights ago. She was in the bowels of Camp Poverty.

How long had this been going on? How could no one have observed these hideous impostors? How many of these dark angels walked among them, protecting this little secret?

The figure stood on the platform with its back to her, hunched forward and panting like some simian cave creature. It turned its elephantine head toward her, and Annie saw the monster that once was Fergus Coyne.

His head was massive, disproportionate to the size of his body, and lolled from its sickly girth. Tiny eyes were embedded in the swollen cranium and glowed with a savage radiation.

"Look who I just found." Fergus slurped drool.

"An angel," Roth chortled. "Guardian of the gateway, wasn't that it?"

Fergus issued a garbled yip, and Stevie rose from the pile of cadavers cackling and jigging. Their hideous laughter echoed in the chamber.

Fergus stepped back enough for Annie to glimpse someone lying at his feet. It was the body of Little Weaver. Blood splattered his jaw, and his arms were bound behind him.

At that moment any hope Annie had mustered vanished.

Chapter 58

Z? That you?"

Zeph stared up the cellar steps. Dust motes swirled through that gray aperture. He could see the familiar leather sandals and, circling the calf, the tattoo of a viper peeking from under cutoff sweat pants.

His heart leaped at the sight. Zeph looked sideways at Tamra, who had returned to staring at the makeshift coffin. Then he said, "It's me, Dad."

"You shoulda called, son."

"Sorry, sir."

His father descended the steps, bringing the stink of nicotine and liquor with him. The man stopped when he saw Tamra.

Howard Walker had grown a gut in the years since Zeph's departure, but he still maintained that military look. Apart from the gray around the temples, his crew cut retained its meticulous sheen. Except for a manicured strip of mustache, he was well shaven. Zeph recalled how, after his disfigurement, he became jealous of his father's rugged smooth jawline and wondered if the man shaved just to mock him. Howard Walker stood with impeccably upright posture, open-chested to the point of cock-surety. Apparently the man had kept up his daily push-up routines. He tended toward flower print shirts and always wore them unbuttoned to reveal his stellar pecs. Nevertheless, any real connection with the military had been jettisoned upon discharge. *Unsuitability* and *substandard performance* were the terms used often by Belle Walker, which seemed to send the old man further into his world of disdain and cold indifference.

He took the last step and looked from Tamra to Zeph.

"This is Tamra Lane," Zeph said.

She turned, but her demeanor had soured. And by the looks of it she was prepared to unload on this wannabe military man.

Before either of them could speak, Zeph said, "She's a friend," answering the question he knew would have followed.

Howard grunted and then swayed slightly. By this hour of the day he was probably four drinks deep. "You come for your car?"

Zeph shook his head. "No, sir."

"Well, it's right there if you ever want it."

Zeph nodded. However, he knew that the chances of the rusty red Triumph ever leaving these premises would require a flood, a cyclone, or some other act of God.

"It's been awhile," Howard said.

"Eight years."

"I mean since I've come down here."

"I don't blame you."

Howard studied the musty tomb, and then his features grew still. "It wasn't my idea, Z."

"No, sir."

"I told her it was wrong. But your mother—that woman was nuts."

Zeph could not corroborate that fact and remained silent.

"All that religious mumbo-jumbo." Howard pursed his lips and appeared to bite back a rising tide of anger. "You know, once she said that God would kill me if I didn't change my ways. Well, guess who the last one standing was."

He thought about Blaise Duty spinning to the floor. Zeph's perception of who God needed to strike dead had changed. Truth be told, there wasn't a single one of them who didn't deserve a lightning bolt from the Almighty. Everything else was straight mercy.

His father reached into his shirt pocket and fumbled for a pack of cigarettes.

Zeph needed a second to gather his nerves for what he was about to say. He watched his father remove a cigarette with trembling fingers, his face flushing. There was no way to ease into this, and Zeph didn't have time for diplomacy.

"I've come to tell you something, sir."

"That a fact?" A hint of defensiveness cast an edge to his father's tone.

Zeph shifted his weight. "Dad, listen I . . . "

His father managed to stuff the pack into his pocket and stood, tapping the cigarette on a nearby crate like a judge bringing a court to order with his gavel. His gaze grew steely. Zeph knew what usually accompanied that gaze and fought to keep from recoiling.

"Go on, boy. What is it?"

"I…" Zeph swallowed. "I forgive you."

His father stopped tapping his cigarette. "Me?"

"Dad, I forgive you."

Howard Walker looked surprised. "You forgive… *me*?" He glanced at Tamra, who did not share his amusement. "You forgive *me*? After eight years you came all the way over here to tell me you forgive *me*?"

However, at that moment, Zeph could not take affront with his father's growing resentment. There were logical reasons for the man to have resisted. However, after having spoken that word—and what seemed like eons holding it in—Zeph relished the sense of peace that accompanied the surrender.

"You just show up and…and what? Absolve yourself of guilt? *I forgive you, Dad.* After eight years? Eight years, Z! And you just roll in to indict me."

But Zeph would not be drawn in. He had seen this before. Rather he thought about all those people over the years who wept at the Telling and found hope in his words. He wondered how *this* word could have such an effect. Wouldn't most people want to be pardoned? Wouldn't most people pine for absolution? Apparently Howard Walker was not one of them.

"All those years I just stayed out of your guys' way. I let you go off and do your thing, prophesy and preach it up. Jostle around like some ghetto revivalist. Buncha baloney, if you ask me. And now you wanna come back and *blame me?*"

His father jammed the cigarette behind his ear, his face now red and twitching with anger. He aimed his thick forearm up the stair-well. "You get outta here, boy. You and your girlfriend. You got your money, and I got stiffed. If anyone needs forgivin', it's Belle and what she did to me. And what she did to you."

He studied his father's tanned smooth jawline. Zeph had his chin. And his short temper. Yet despite the rage in his father's eyes, Zeph's temper was not aroused.

Howard Walker flinched. "It was her idea, Z. When your brother died," he looked away, "she thought you was to blame. It was her way of making things right. And she believed—" He shook his head. "—she really believed that locking you up would purge the evil. And I wasn't about to argue with that nut job. 'Sides, a man needs discipline." His pectoral muscles rippled. He retrained his gaze, and his antipathy, upon his son.

Zeph nodded at his father, sadly, and turned to Tamra, who had pushed past his father and was almost halfway up the stairs before he noticed. Then he turned and looked one last time at the crate that housed his brother's body.

Zeph left the cellar knowing he would never return. Tamra waited just long enough in the grass for him to know she was angry and she was leading the way off the Walker property. The overcast sky had been sundered by a ray of light that rested on her auburn hair, giving Tamra Lane all the appearance of an angel.

As odd as the feeling was, at that moment, everything seemed right. He might have conceded it was even his destiny to have come to this awful place with Tamra Lane.

Zeph followed her through the gate, down the driveway, to his truck. Tamra's fingerprint in the dirty window of the Triumph was the last thing Zeph would see of Howard Walker's house. They got into the truck and sat there.

The anger was rolling off her like heat waves off the August asphalt. But something else had possessed him.

"Okay," he finally said, with a deep sigh. "Now I'm ready."

Chapter 59

Tamra barely spoke to Zeph on the way to Marvale. Her silence was not out of spite or fear, and she guessed he knew that. Seeing the crate with his brother's body in it and the cellar where a young boy had been locked sent her emotional sensors into overload. She thought about Dieter and Nams and Shady Lady limping around with her bad hip, rescued from inevitable death. How could anyone—much less a parent—lock a child in a cellar? Suddenly the Bible pages plastered across his wall made perfect sense—he was simply trying to reconcile truth with its abuse.

She tried to call Annie again but received her answering machine. Where could she have gone? Different scenarios unraveled in Tamra's mind, none of them good. Hopefully Little Weaver had reached Marvale and rendezvoused with Annie to stop Fergus.

Upon Tamra's urging Zeph drove his truck through Marvale's lower parking lot and climbed the service road to park closer. Buzz spotted them and immediately got on his walkie-talkie. Zeph parked near the delivery dock, and they got out and hurried to the front doors. Bev Beason was on the deck, in her usual spot. Out of the corner of her eye, Tamra could see the woman staring.

"Well, what's the fizz, biker chick?" Hannah sat at the reception desk gawking as Tamra and Zeph hurried past.

Tamra slowed but was unsure how, or if, she should engage the woman. What more did Hannah know about this? Several days ago, the girl had the skinny on the Marvale invasion. By now she could be part of it.

"No hurry," Tamra said as they bustled past.

"Well, be on the lookout."

Tamra stopped, leaving Zeph marching down the hall. "For what?"

"You mean, for *who?*" Hannah glanced both ways and then whispered, "Mother Superior's on the prowl."

After having caught the director in Eugenia's apartment, Tamra was beginning to wonder if there wasn't good reason for the staff's dislike for the woman. Perhaps Janice Marshman knew more about the happenings at Marvale Manor than she was letting on.

Tamra said, "So, that stuff we talked about..."

Hannah glanced at Zeph, who stood in the lobby waiting for Tamra. "Oh, that stuff? It appears to be catching." An impish smile crept across Hannah's face.

Tamra took a step back. "I'll make sure to keep an eye out."

Hannah fluffed at her hair. "Do that, Easy Rider." She chuckled, a slow rumble that escalated into a near guffaw.

Tamra joined Zeph without bothering to look back at the receptionist, and they hurried to Annie's. "So, how can we tell?" she asked.

"Huh?"

"If someone's one of them. I mean, how can we tell?"

"Um, we can pour water on them and see if they melt."

"Funny."

"I'm not sure there is a way to tell. Weaver said they were genetic duplicates—clones. So any differences would not be external. It'd have to be behavioral or emotional. Even if we can tell, we can't just start knocking people off. Whatever it is, we're going to have to stay on our toes." He paused. "And trust each other."

Tamra cast a sidelong glance and arched her eyebrow.

"I know," Zeph admitted. "I have to do more of that."

They arrived at Annie's apartment, and Tamra began searching her backpack for the keys. As she did, Zeph tried the handle and discovered the door was open.

"What the—" Tamra squeezed between Zeph, pushed the door open, walked in, and stood gawking.

Annie's apartment had been ransacked. Drawers lay on the floor, their contents emptied. The sofa cushions had been removed and strewn about the place. Even the refrigerator door was wide open.

"Nams!" Tamra marched through the apartment, from one room to the next. "Nams!"

In the bedroom the mattress had been removed, sliced open in spots, and boxes of picture albums lay scattered across the carpet.

Tamra stood incredulous

"They were looking for the journal," Zeph said, staring over her shoulder.

"Weaver has it."

"Yeah, but whoever was here doesn't know that."

"What if she was kidnapped?"

"In the middle of the day? In public? Your grandmother doesn't strike me as someone who could be carted off without some kinda commotion."

"Unless the entire facility is in on it."

Zeph pursed his lips in thought. "What else would she do, Tam? Is there somewhere she would go, someone she would want to see before leaving?"

"I dunno." As her eyes wandered the apartment, Tamra's heart raced. "She was always off investigating this or that. I kept telling her to be careful. I knew this would happen!"

"Think, Tam. If she knew you were coming back for her, she probably didn't go far."

"Right." Tamra tried to calm herself. "She talked about Camp Poverty, but that's quite a walk from here. And she talked about Easy Dolan. He seemed to know a lot about things."

"Like the Madness of Endurance?"

Tamra straightened. "Yeah." Then she said, "C'mon."

She picked her way through the cluttered apartment and led them to the Back Nine. They paused at Easy Dolan's door, looked at each other, and Tamra knocked.

Thumping sounded behind the door, and it opened.

Easy leaned on his cane, squinted at the pair, and then a smile burst across his face. "Why, you're Miss Annie's granddaughter."

"I am."

"And this must be..." Easy's eyes widened, and a slight grin creased his features.

Tamra said, "This is Zeph."

"Pleased to meet you, young man." Easy nodded toward him.

"Same to you, sir."

Tamra noticed a hint of reservation in Zeph's tone and, rather than look at him for explanation, trained her attention on Easy. "We're looking for my grandmother. Have you seen her?"

"Miss Annie? Pshh!" Easy swept his hand through the air. "Ya never know where to find her. Always snoopin' around. I keep tellin' her to be careful. But does she listen?"

"You're right about that," Tamra said.

"Come on in," Easy stepped aside. "I might be able ta help ya."

Tamra hesitated for a split second, and during that second, as she tilted slightly forward, Zeph snared her arm.

"I think we'll keep looking, sir." Zeph pulled Tamra toward his side.

She did not need to question Zeph's action. Tamra stared at Easy, studying his features, trying to identify the intangibles they had just discussed. And trying to identify what had spooked Zeph.

"I do believe I can help you out." Easy's smile seemed to grow even bigger. "C'mon in and warm your bones." He stepped back even further and gestured inside, as if he were rolling out a red carpet.

The apartment door nearby opened a crack, and a shadowy figure peered from behind it. A sickly sense of ambush overwhelmed Tamra. She turned to see a shadow moving across the wall behind Easy. Someone else was in the apartment with him. And she doubted it was Nams.

"No, thank you." Zeph turned and steered Tamra into the hallway. "We'll just keep looking."

"You sure?" Easy's voice rose.

"Yes, sir."

"Well, don't go gettin' yourselves in trouble, now." Easy issued a dry cackle.

Zeph and Tamra did not look behind them. They hurried down the Back Nine like speed walkers, turned the corner at the atrium, and stood with their backs to the wall, panting.

"He knows something," Tamra said. "Something's happened to my grandmother!"

Zeph nodded. "Do you remember what Weaver said about Fergus's father?"

"Yeah, but—"

"If his father was a part of this, if he knows something..."

"Laurel House. He's in the convalescent home." Tamra hurried down the opposite hallway. "C'mon."

She had been in Laurel House only once. Annie always curled her nose in disgust when the place was mentioned. The thought of shriveling away in such a facility was antithetical to everything the rambunctious woman stood for. She vowed she'd rather die running than live sitting still. Just the reminder of her grandmother's feistiness sent anxiety coursing through Tamra's limbs.

They followed the walkway over the bridge, through the bristlecone pines, and Laurel House came into view. Perhaps it was an unconscious act, but Tamra glanced at the sky as they approached. The cloud cover had remained thick all day, casting a melancholy mood. Soon nightfall would set in, and Tamra Lane did not want to be caught anywhere near that old mine when it got dark. She had to trust that Annie would use her intuition, investigative prowess, and maybe even her Swiss Army knife to keep herself safe.

Tamra greeted the first nurse they saw, a plump, pink girl pushing a cart of bedding.

"Excuse me," Tamra said. "We're looking for Mr. Coyne."

"Coyne. Right down that—" The nurse turned and, upon seeing Zeph's scar, stopped. She cleared her throat, looked away, and continued. "Right down that hallway." She pointed around the corner. "7, um, 8. 708."

Tamra thanked her, and they began to leave when the nurse asked, "You're not with that other fella, are you?"

Zeph and Tamra cast puzzled glances at each other. Had Little Weaver come by? Or had someone else beat them to the punch? Before they could query, the nurse said, "Tall guy, kinda sullen. Ross, or . . . no—Roth."

"Roth?" Zeph furrowed his brow.

"Been a frequent visitor lately. Said he was a close associate of Mr. Coyne. But, I dunno, if you ask me, he's kind of weird."

"In what way?" Tamra asked.

"Keeps odd hours, for one thing. Amy said she found him standing at Mr. Coyne's bed at two the other morning. Shows up at weird places too. I found him out back at the Dumpsters one day. Not sure what he was doing, but he scared the daylights outta me." Her cheeks turned even pinker on this admission.

Zeph looked at Tamra, who said, "Yeah, that is weird. We're not with him, but we'll be sure to keep an eye out. Thanks."

They turned the corner and began scanning the room numbers. The smells of the convalescent home set her stomach on edge, as did the apparent spiral of their situation.

Zeph spoke softly. "That was the guy Lacroix and his partner said I should watch out for."

"Roth?"

"They said he was with the government. He kicked them off my case."

"The government?" Tamra stopped in her tracks. "What is going on here? And if those detectives were off your case, what were they doing at your house?"

"I called them, remember? Whoever Roth is, he's tied in with all this. And I doubt he wants folks snooping around. Besides, if he's really with the government, then he probably has a lot of resources at his disposal."

Tamra refused to ponder the possibilities. She pointed across the hall to Room 708.

An old man lay with his mouth open inside, eyes twitching under buggy lids, as a television set cast garbled noise. Zeph led the way and surveyed the room before slowly walking in with Tamra behind him.

A window was open, but its curtains remained listless, showing only the sunless autumn sky. Someone lay huddled under a sheet in a nearby bed, their back turned to the room. As Zeph and Tamra approached the bed, the old man's eyes fluttered open, and he seemed to rouse from sleep. His mouth moved, but only spittle and garbled sounds emerged. By the looks of it, they would not be extracting information from this man.

"Mr. Coyne?" Zeph approached the bed, studying the man's face. "Mr. Coyne?"

As Zeph did this, something caught Tamra's eye. Fluid of some sort lay puddled under the other bed. She reminded herself that this was a convalescent home. Nevertheless, she stepped closer for inspection. A frail spine showed from under the blankets, the body unmoving. She leaned over the person. Whoever it was, he did not appear to be breathing.

Tamra turned to tell Zeph.

He was hunched over the old man. He had grasped Coyne's head in both hands and was studying the man's skull. Zeph looked up. "Something's been done to him. These scars—he's had some sort of...lobotomy."

When he said this, something rustled behind Tamra and she jumped. An arm slipped out from under the sheet and dangled limply.

Tamra gasped and Zeph rushed over and flung the sheet back.

"Oh my—" Tamra removed her hand from her mouth. "It's Fergus. The custodian."

The bloody pillow on which his bulbous head rested required no explanation.

Zeph looked to the door. "We need to get outta here."

"Shouldn't we tell someone?"

"Like who? Easy? The director? The guy on the walkie-talkie in the tram?"

Tamra's stomach dropped.

"He's been swapped," Zeph said. "Someone'll probably be by to dispose of his body. So I'm guessing there's another Fergus around here, one who's very much alive."

"But—we need help."

"C'mon." Zeph went to the door.

Tamra remained looking from the dead body to the old man. What had been going on here? All this time Nams had been warning her, and here they were in a convalescent room with a lobotomized physicist and his dead son. If only she'd listened to her grandmother when she had the chance.

They hurried into the hallway, but as they did, Tamra and Zeph hit the skids.

At the intersection of the hallway, the nurse was talking to two men. Even from behind, Lacroix and Chavez were unmistakable.

Zeph shoved her back into the room. "Don't know about you, but I'm not up for talking with these guys." Zeph pointed to the window. "You know how to hike, don't you?"

Coyne's eyes followed them across the room. Zeph wrestled the screen off the window, helped her out, and then followed. As he straddled the window, he looked back at the old man and said, "If anyone asks, we weren't here."

Coyne raised a trembling hand toward him, before letting it fall back to the bed.

Zeph climbed out, and they stood side by side, looking into the foothills.

"Weaver said something about Camp Poverty."

"It's an old ruin, or something," Tamra said. "A historical site of some sort. Up above Marvale. I've never been there."

"Can you get us there?"

Without answering, Tamra hurried down an embankment onto a thin trail that wound its way into the mist-shrouded mountains, aimed straight for the old miner's camp.

ams!"

A hellish star had risen inside Annie, a flaming chaos collapsed in upon itself and cresting the horizon of her imagination, draining away the feeble particles of hope from her being.

"Nams! Wake up!"

The words ripped Annie from that dark place. The shadow inside her fragmented at the familiar voice.

Annie woke to pain. She slouched with her back to a cool block. Her leg stretched unnaturally before her, and her shin oozed thick blood. Her temple throbbed, and she wondered if she'd been hit. However, the greatest of Annie's pain was the realization that she was still bound in the bowels of Camp Poverty, and that her granddaughter was now here.

Tamra hunched over her, wrestling the gag from Annie's mouth. She tossed it aside, and Annie coughed weakly.

Tamra hugged her with such force that Annie cried out. "My hands! Ow! Ow!"

Tamra gently released her.

"Is it..." Annie tried to focus her eyes. "Is it really you?"

"Of course it's me!" Anger lanced through her granddaughter's teary eyes. "I thought I told you—" Tamra straightened and looked aghast. "Who did this? And what's going on out here?"

"He's still alive!" someone shouted.

It was Zeph. With Tamra's help, Annie sat up enough to see him huddled over Little Weaver's body. The pile of corpses was smaller, but the fleshy, acidic odor remained. Easy's body had been rolled onto its side.

"My knife." Annie wrestled weakly against her restraints. "It's in Easy's pocket."

"Oh my—" Tamra grimaced at the bodies. "Then who is that back at his apartment?"

"It's an impostor." Zeph approached the corpses with his hand

270

over his nose. He fumbled at Easy's body, patted his pockets, and then removed the Swiss Army knife, gagging as he did so.

A knot the size of a duck egg crowned Little Weaver's forehead. He sat woozy. One lens of his goggles was shattered, and his hands were bound behind him like Annie's. Zeph used the knife to loose the Indian and then hustled over to free Annie. She gasped as the binding released and brought her hands around, wincing as she did so.

"It's a trap," Annie said, massaging her wrists. "They want you to go up there."

"Who?" Tamra asked. "Who's doing all this?"

"Roth." Little Weaver rose unsteadily. "NOVEM was a success."

"Then that's what this is all about." Zeph's gaze drifted about the dank subterranean compound.

"The journal," Little Weaver said. "It reveals everything. The military conceived of an army of interlopers. Legions of ubermen conjured for their bidding."

"An angelic army." Zeph stared off into space.

"They had no idea the forces they had unleashed," Little Weaver said. "Subject X was one of the first swapped—General Walther Roth."

"Subject X," Annie said. "The one in the dossier."

Little Weaver nodded. "Roth knew Fergus had the gift. And with the angelic tongue deciphered, the seraph sensed it was only a matter of time. All Fergus and his father wanted to do was contact the dead mother. Instead they punched a hole in the Third Column and released the damned."

"Then this..." Tamra stared at the basin and the vats of acid. "This is what happened to all those bodies."

"The government was summoning dark angels," Little Weaver said. "Experimenting on them and then liquefying the evidence. Who knows how much DNA fills the sewers here? When Roth was swapped, he told his superiors to terminate the project. They had no idea what they were dealing with. And those who did, Roth managed to silence."

Zeph said, "Like the old man down in Laurel House."

"A sad tale indeed." Little Weaver examined his shattered goggles. "For years they have operated in secret, blending into society. Roth made sure to facilitate Fergus's ghastly séances. This ancient place has continued to serve their purpose, as you can see." He touched the knot on his forehead and winced. "Fergus has finally been swapped. His angel has become mighty—a seer capable of summoning the black cherub. They go to the Rift now for their final consummation, to speak the incantation that bridges the worlds. We must hurry, or I fear this tale will have a sad ending."

"No," Annie protested. "We can't."

They looked at her.

"Fergus has changed, become something hideous." Annie closed her eyes and could see his bulbous head in her mind. "He's a monster now. Don't you see—they want you to go there. We're the only ones standing in their way now. If they can kill us, no one else will know about this. And no one will ever be able to stop them."

Tamra nodded enthusiastically. "I've been saying that all along—we should just go to the police."

"Well, if we wait long enough," Zeph said, "the police'll come here."

"If they are police." Little Weaver looked at the pile of carcasses, then engaged her with his eyes. "Annie Lane, there is no other way. Some stories require such risk. Fergus wields the rune of the dark angels. The language of hell is his. Indeed, if we fail, they may never be stopped. Nevertheless, we must trust. We must trust one another. We must trust the Branded One." He looked at Zeph. "And we must trust the Teller, the Author of this Great Tale. Ha!"

Little Weaver's words stirred Annie. He was right. She had been called to be a remnant, to stand in the gap, and could not allow the darkness to obscure it. Her leg might be broken, her hands aching into numbness, but she could still stand in the gap.

"You're right." Annie nodded. "We have to try."

Something sounded in the bowels of the tunnel, a sharp echo that reverberated in the dark.

"We must leave." Little Weaver signaled for Zeph to help Annie.

"Careful." Annie grit her teeth as Zeph and Tamra positioned themselves on each side of her. "My leg, it's—"

They lifted her. Pain tore along her leg, a blistering fire that caused her to yelp. They eased Annie back to the ground. The wound on her shin was now oozing dark blood, and bruises riddled her skin.

If it wasn't broken, it would be if she walked on it. The chances of Annie being able to get to Otta's Rift was about as likely as her being rescued by Miss Marple.

"What're we gonna do?" Tamra asked Little Weaver.

Then Annie looked up. "Zeph. Don't you remember?"

He glanced into the tunnel and then knelt down beside her. "Remember what, Annie?"

"When we first met?"

"Nams," Tamra scolded. "Not now."

"You were just a boy," Annie continued. "I went to one of your crusades."

"Nams, we gotta get outta here!"

"You prophesied to me." Annie reached out and took Zeph's hand. "You said, 'You will be a remnant.' That's what you said. 'You will stand in the gap.' That was the word you gave me. It saved me, Zeph. Did you know that? It saved me. And that's what I've tried to do—stand in the gap. Just like you said." She smiled weakly. "So, how did I do?"

Zeph stared at her. And something seemed to kindle in his eyes. He smiled, a charming boyish smile full of vulnerability and joy, a gesture so sincere no scar on earth could mar its innocence.

"You've done great, Annie." He squeezed her hand. "Now you've saved me."

Annie met his gaze. She nodded with satisfaction and settled back on the cold stone.

Tamra looked at them. "Okay, we gotta go. You have to try to stand up, Nams. Now, c'mon."

As they hoisted her up, she cried out again, and the sound echoed down the dark tunnel. Yet behind it rose a terrible scratching, clawing, as if something were being dragged along the stonework.

Little Weaver peered into the tunnel. "It is no wonder they left us here untended. We are not alone. The soul eaters awaken."

"Well, we're not waitin' to meet 'em. C'mon!" Tamra locked her arm around Annie's waist, while Zeph managed the other side. Annie gritted her teeth as they struggled up the stone steps toward the platform and the heavy metal door. Searing pain raced up her leg, threatening to send her plummeting into that black, unconscious abyss with every step.

A ghastly, inhuman wail pierced the air.

They stopped and stared into the tunnel behind them. Annie looked past the acid barrels and the bodies strewn on the block. A black object had attached itself to the wall some seventy-five feet down the tunnel. It skittered sideways on spindly limbs like a monstrous horsefly. A pale smudge hovered atop its frame as it crept into the light. That smudge was becoming a face.

"It's one of them!" Tamra yelled. "Go! Go!"

A covey of forms approached from behind it. In the mouth of the dark tunnel they wafted forward like fog on the subterranean air. Tittering and squealing, an insane gibbering of inhuman tongues. Wings arched in feral delight. And their faces took shape as they approached.

"Run!" Little Weaver had removed a long, narrow blade from under his coat. "To the mine. Hurry!"

Annie hobbled on one leg. But she knew she would never make it to Otta's Rift. And now she did not want to.

Insect-like chatter rose behind them, an inhuman prattle that froze her blood.

"Don't look!" Tamra pulled her forward.

They reached the entryway, and Little Weaver stood guard as Tamra helped Annie through the door. As Annie passed, she noticed a length of wood used to barricade the door from inside. Nearby was the padlock she had seen last night on the outside of the door. Annie did not want to reveal the location of the lock, so she quickly looked away. She limped out and leaned against the exterior wall in exhaustion. Little Weaver passed through, followed by Zeph, who pulled the door shut behind him. He fumbled at the latch and began scanning the ground. "There must be a lock."

"They have taken it," Little Weaver joined him. "Or hidden it. This was a camp for the miners. A house. It bolts from the inside."

"What're we gonna do?" Zeph said. "Those things'll be here any minute."

Little Weaver quickly slipped his long blade—the one she had seen in his laboratory—through the barrel of the latch and tested the door, but the blade prevented the latch from giving. "This will hold them shortly. They are still in transition, little more than foul vapors. Once they take shape, they will break free." Then he turned and scanned the mountains.

Little Weaver pointed to the foothills. "We must hurry. The remaining daylight will slow them. Look!"

They followed Little Weaver's gaze to the crimson twilight behind the shadowy foothills. The setting sun had turned the gloom into a canopy of roiling crimson.

"The red sky gives us hope!" Little Weaver declared, as if seeking to bolster their withering resolve. "It is the fire of the Almighty."

As they looked there, Annie saw her chance. She quietly pushed off from the wall, slipped Weaver's blade from the iron latch, and leaned her shoulder into the door. She clamped her jaw as the pain torched her leg, but she did not cry out. The door creaked open.

"Nams!"

Before Tamra realized what was happening and could reach her, Annie limped inside and slammed the door shut. It required all her effort to hoist the wooden brace and drop it into place across the door. The pain was so great, she sagged to the earth, tears springing into her eyes.

"No!" Tamra pounded on the door. "What're you doing? Nams! Open this door!"

Annie did not dare to see how close the dark angels were.

"*No!*" Her granddaughter shrieked, but Annie could not comply.

Little Weaver was right—they had to go to the Rift. If the dark angels overtook her companions, they would never have a chance. Annie had to trust them. She had to trust the Branded One. She would only hold them back. Besides, she had another assignment to complete.

"Go!" Annie yelled. "Hurry!"

"Grandma!" She could hear Tamra weeping. "Don't d–do this!"

"Annie!" It was Zeph. "Open the door."

She could feel the presence of that dark horde bearing down on her.

"Run!" Annie shouted. "I'll hold them off!"

"Grandma!"

Annie forced herself to ignore her granddaughter's pleas. This would be a better way. She had to believe that.

"Grandma-a-a!"

She prayed silently, then turned to watch as the fetch hobbled and scrambled toward her, a hideous menagerie of parts. Then she whispered to herself: "I am the remnant. I will stand in the gap."

Chapter 61

He did not attempt to console Tamra. Instead Zeph walked behind, nudging her forward with vain encouragement and an occasional shove. Annie's actions had shocked him, as they had everyone. Strangely enough Zeph sensed that her sacrifice had somehow propelled him toward the task ahead.

"Why?" Tamra asked between sobs. "Why would she do that?"

"It is the destiny of her choosing." Little Weaver trudged hastily along the mule trail, leading them to Otta's Rift. "Would that all were of such courage."

"Courage?" Tamra spat the words. "She's too stubborn! And now she's in there with all those things."

"Only the true of heart can withstand such darkness." Little Weaver looked over his shoulder. "Or one with an exceptionally skilled guardian angel."

"She did it to help us get up there," Zeph said. "So the least we can do is finish what we started and see how it plays out." Despite his attempt to bolster their resolve, Zeph's mind had already begun to recoil at the thought of the hellish mine that lay ahead of them.

Little Weaver led them forward into the tangled woods. The red sky had paled and turned misty, and the branches formed a skeletal canopy, dripping moisture.

"It is a different kind of battle here." Little Weaver kneaded his gloved hands together. "Not of force, but of will. Be strong, friends. There are more who are with us than are against us. Listen!" He stopped and put his hand to his ear. "Can you hear them?"

Tamra and Zeph skidded in the gravel. They exchanged puzzled glances and strained to listen.

"Of course not!" Little Weaver's laughter echoed through the gloomy foothills. "They are of the First Column."

Zeph scowled. "Is this really a time for jokes, Weaver?"

"Ha! There is always a time for laughter, Brother Walker. Perhaps more of it would do you good."

Zeph could not deny that, so he curled his lip and resumed their forward march.

Little Weaver turned off the fire trail into the thicket. He hummed a soft, sad tune as they walked through the mat of leaves and tinder. Finally they crested the ridge. Birch leaves gently clattered behind them as they stood at the barbed-wire fence. A faint phosphorescence seemed to sprinkle the ravine, a toxic sheen just above the range of seeing. Zeph stared down on the charred gash in the mountainside, sweating from the climb. Approaching that cursed ground for a second time left his insides churning, as did the memory of Pearl's ghostly presence.

"Big Weaver was there," the Indian said solemnly, staring into the canyon. "The gates of hell could not prevail."

Zeph squinted at the Indian. "What do you mean, he was there?"

"At the Madness, my friend."

Tamra seemed to share Zeph's perplexity. "That was, like, a hundred and forty years ago."

"Bah! Barely enough time to tell a good tale."

Tamra shook her head. "Yeah, but that would make your father... no way."

"My father?" Little Weaver turned and, with a wry smile, said, "Big Weaver was my brother."

Zeph and Tamra stood speechless.

Somewhere in the foggy woods ravens cawed out a discordant warning. The smell of mulch and mud thickened around them. They remained mute, studying Little Weaver as if he were an alien species. What manner of man was this, wielding crossbows, javelins, and an odd sense of humor?

"Then it *was* you at the cemetery." Zeph peered at the Indian.

"It was like yesterday, was it not?"

Tamra spoke as if skeptical of his story. "Then your brother, he witnessed the suicide?"

"It was not a suicide that cleansed the land, Warrior Soul."

"What do you mean?"

Little Weaver said matter-of-factly, "It was an extermination."

Zeph cleared his throat. "You're saying that those miners, that all those people, were..."

"Murdered?" Tamra said.

"No." Little Weaver straightened. "*People* were not murdered. They had been overshadowed long before, their souls leeched of life. Silverton—the entire city—had been swapped. Just as Endurance will be if we are unsuccessful. Yet before the dark angels could summon the black cherub, Big Weaver drew them to the Rift. No, the Madness was not a suicide. It was a genocide."

Weaver pushed down the barbed wire with his gloved hand and held it for them.

Zeph stared at the man, his mind staggering under the weight of this new information. He helped Tamra over and followed. Little Weaver took the lead, descending the switchback. Tendrils of mist had already begun to seep from the soil. A cool blanket seemed to envelop them. Finally they reached the base of the gorge and stood gazing at the Rift.

Facing shipwreck and starvation was bad, but Robinson Crusoe never faced anything quite like this.

Zeph said nervously, "I've never encountered a real, live gateway to hell."

"Be thankful, Brother Walker."

"So, uh, how am I supposed to close it?"

Little Weaver looked surprised. "You have the wild magic. I don't know how it works."

Zeph scratched his head. "Well, maybe that's why it's *wild*, because I'm not sure how it works, either."

Little Weaver peered at him. "You are a peculiar person, Brother Walker."

Strangely enough Little Weaver's assessment bolstered Zeph's heart.

Shadows loomed in the thickets, and rivulets of water traced the rock face. They stood in anxious anticipation of their descent into Otta's Rift. Although his mental faculties had been dulled by years of rationalization and poor judgment, Zeph forced himself to focus on the task ahead. Tamra stood behind him, and Zeph could tell her thoughts were pitching.

She said, "He's in there, isn't he?"

Little Weaver nodded and turned to them. "Such is the unfolding. The seraph is terrible to look upon, the deformation of all that was once good. Yet what lies inside this cavern—" He touched Zeph's chest. "—the cavern of the *heart*, is even more monstrous. Steel your minds." His eyes sparkled with a strange gaiety, as if preparing to plunge into the gates of hell was exhilarating. "And take heart. We are friends of the land. In that company there is much power."

Zeph was not sure if he should shout a rousing "Amen!" So he simply nodded in agreement.

They worked their way over several logs, and the walls of the ravine loomed overhead, black swaths disappearing into the misty gray. As they crunched over the blighted meadow to the mouth of the cavern, Zeph could make out splinters of bone and charcoal showing through the gravel.

Plink.

Smoke rising on the subterranean air.

Pa-pa-plink.

He froze at the sound. Pearl was in it, and the rotting remains of his strangled brother, and the moldy cellar, and—

"The werevane." Weaver pointed at more bone chimes dangling inside the tunnel. "Do not heed its charm. Bah!"

Zeph shook himself from the encroaching panic.

They reached the mouth of the mine. A claustrophobic dread jabbed at Zeph, and his breathing turned choppy. Tamra was behind him, and he wanted to turn and ask her if she was doing all right. But fearing he may startle her by his own paranoia, Zeph just swallowed hard and peered into the dark.

Little Weaver led the way, and they began their descent. The mysterious Indian had to duck to keep from scraping the ceiling. His hulking silhouette nearly blotted Zeph's entire field of vision. Crude symbols etched the walls, demented graffiti issuing crude epithets and bad tidings. It stunk of urine and mold. The light from the entrance dimmed, yet as it did, an orange glow became apparent below. Kerosene smoke wafted up the tunnel, turning Zeph's halted breathing even more erratic, and with the smell came a warble, a voice, dirge-like and doleful, echoing in the dank tunnel.

"There's someone down there," Tamra whispered.

Zeph did not answer. He knew it was another prophet. That's what this was—a showdown. Like Elijah and the prophets of Baal, or Moses and Pharaoh's magicians. Only this one involved a modified realist and a snaky something from the Third Column. However, if Zeph was the good guy in this story, they were in deep trouble.

The railroad track disappeared under loose gravel. Several shafts intersected the tunnel, but Little Weaver passed them and continued forward, tools clanking dully under his jacket. The only light now was the flickering glow from somewhere inside the mine. Musty roots fingered through the tunnel walls, and water seeped into muddy pools. Something round and glassy peered from one of those stagnant puddles, bringing Zeph to an abrupt stop. A lidless eye rolled back and forth in the murk, watching the intruders.

"Brother Walker!"

Zeph caught himself breathless and inhaled.

He snapped to attention. Little Weaver had turned around and was tapping his temple with his fingertip. *Think, Walker! Think!* Zeph looked back to the murky pool, but the eyeball was gone. He had been hallucinating.

The tunnel dipped and then opened into a larger chamber. The Indian came to a stop. The light was brighter here, and the voice that had sounded moments ago was silent. Little Weaver stood on the edge of what appeared to be a sunken shaft.

This was the end of the tunnel.

This is where it would all go down.

Zeph wiped sweat from his forehead. The mine reawakened memories of the old cellar. All those nights and days locked in that subterranean vault, just him and his dead brother. Waiting. Waiting for the Telling. Waiting for his mother's intervention. But Belle was gone, his father had disowned him, and the Telling had abandoned him. Now, just like then, Zeph felt *completely alone.*

Tamra stepped to his side. She seemed captivated by the cavern. What type of girl would follow a disfigured prophet, an avowed recluse, and virtual stranger into a haunted mine? Perhaps he would need to rethink that part about being completely alone.

Zeph approached, but it took him a moment to make out what he was seeing. The mine ended in a natural chamber. Symbols and splattered discolorations marred the flume, amidst images of winged creatures notched into the rock. Pallid fingers of light shown from overhead vents. Odd roots traced the wall here, like tentacles from some primeval entity choking the granite shaft. A lantern hung from a beam, swaying and sputtering, illuminating crude steps, which ended below at a massive stone monument.

It was a megalith, a dolmen, comprised of three large stones. Behind it, in the granite wall, rose a cleft or fissure. And Zeph knew this was the portal of summoning.

Bats squealed somewhere in another tunnel, yet Zeph was fixed on the figure perched near the megalith. Fergus, or whatever he had become, sat leisurely on a rock shelf before a pool of crystalline water. The lantern illuminated his livid, misshapen body. His head was tilted forward, swollen and bulbous, as if too heavy to be sustained by his torso. His face was sunken, and inside that bilious crater two beady eyes blazed. Behind him winged bat-like appendages slumped.

"Oh, my father." Fergus's jaw slung drool, his voice echoed in the chamber. "Beelzebub, Lord of the Flies. Receive these offerings." He motioned to Zeph's company. "Complete thy power. Thy kingdom come."

And as he spoke those words, Zeph could feel his windpipe constricting.

uard your minds!" Little Weaver yelled. "The tome of darkness seeks root!"

But Zeph was too busy grappling at his collar, struggling to breathe, to guard his mind.

"*Cheth, iod.*" Fergus turned his gaze upon Zeph, eyes radiating hatred. "*Grimel, nun ixle.*"

"Silence, devil!" Little Weaver descended the stone stairwell, eyes trained on the inhuman figure.

The dark angel sprung to its feet, reared back, and brayed like a goat.

Zeph's breathing returned, and he sunk to the ground, gasping for air.

The hideous sound of Fergus's cry echoed through the mine. So disconcerting was it to hear such a sound emerge from something this humanlike that Zeph fought to keep from fleeing and abandoning his mission on the spot.

Something moved beside him, and he lurched upright and strafed to avoid it. Tamra had fallen to her knees with her hands clasped over her ears to drown out the goatish cackle. Zeph bent and put his arm around her shoulder.

Little Weaver reached the base of the steps and slowly approached the dark angel. It stepped to the megalith and stood like some pagan priest, its wings arched in what appeared a defensive posture. The appendages were feeble, scabbed, and mottled, looking far more reptilian than angelic. Yet its eyes glowed like nuclear pinholes in infinite space.

"You are the damned!" Little Weaver's voice was almost a growl. "And to damnation you shall return."

"Shut your pie hole!" Fergus bellowed and stretched his hand toward Little Weaver.

The Indian stopped. His face grew taut, and the tendons in

his neck strained. He could not advance farther and seemed to be laboring against an invisible current.

"You're a coward!" Fergus bellowed at Little Weaver. "A traitor! And you'll pay for it, Weaver. You and the rest of your kind."

Zeph watched, dumbstruck by the standoff between these two beings.

"They ain't worth it!" Fergus's gaze rolled toward Zeph and Tamra, a hate-filled stare that would have surely vaporized them had he not returned it to Little Weaver. "It's their fault. All of it! The land. The heavens. Rent for their wrong!" Spittle flung from his rancid gray jaw.

As Fergus raged, Little Weaver managed to remove the flint-lock pistol from under his jacket. His hand trembled as he raised it toward Fergus.

The creature's wings arched, and its monstrous head rose in seeming glee. Until Little Weaver turned and aimed the gun at the dolmen and the dimensional rift.

"No-o-o!" Fergus clawed the air.

A wild yip sounded overhead, a cacophony of screams, and a flurry of motion followed. Zeph stumbled back, taking Tamra with him. They watched in horror as the walls and ceiling came to life with fetch—blazing yellow eyes, teeth drawn, wings unfolding in an orchestra of evil. The hideous cloud swooped on Little Weaver.

His gun discharged, followed by several inhuman shrieks and a further flurry of motion. But the dolmen remained untouched.

The horde of dark angels drove Little Weaver back, near the base of the granite steps, where they enveloped him in a writhing mass. Howls and honks filled the tunnel. Zeph squeezed Tamra to himself, fighting to cover their ears from the awful celebration. Yet he could not tear his eyes from the devilish unfolding.

"The lord'll relish dining on your remains," Fergus hissed, watching the fetch batter Little Weaver. "And when Helioth, the black cherub, subsumes your prophet, we'll have a feast in your honor!"

He laughed, a hideous belch of derision.

Zeph Walker had witnessed miracles. Once he had seen Father Fitzroy awaken a woman who had been in a coma for twelve years. Zeph didn't know why she was in a coma, but he could attest to the unbridled joy the event produced in her relatives. The woman went on to live a normal, productive life, while the priest shunned the ensuing publicity. No one could doubt the nature of the event. Yes. Zeph Walker had witnessed miracles. Nevertheless, he had never witnessed anything quite like this.

Tamra now sat on her haunches, staring at the fantastical event. Any confidence Zeph had entering the mine seemed as errant as the Indian's wooden bullet. If the dark angels had such power over Little Weaver, Zeph's chances of closing the gateway had just diminished exponentially. He struggled to his feet alongside Tamra, gawking as his friend fell limp upon the rock floor.

"S–s–stop it." Zeph's voice was feeble but aimed straight at the dark angels. "I s–said, stop it!" Zeph stepped to the edge of the rock balcony and stared down at them. "Let him go, man!"

The swirling mass of angels seemed to flinch and falter. Lifeless eyes glared at him through the churning spectral haze.

Zeph took a great breath and bellowed, "Let'm go!"

The fetch squealed and fled back into the nooks and crevices of the chamber, leaving Little Weaver lying torn and lifeless.

Fergus laughed, his glazed little eyes barely peeking at Zeph from within that dark sunken face. "You'll have to do better than that, Zipperface."

Suddenly the Indian's body convulsed, as if overtaken by a seizure.

Then Fergus opened his arms and swiped them through the air in Little Weaver's direction. The Indian slid across the granite, leaving a bloody streak, spun up and struck the rock wall with such force that the lantern overhead rocked with the impact. Tamra screamed and stumbled back.

Little Weaver flopped to the ground and lay motionless at the base of the hewn rock stairwell.

The dark angel swayed and then looked at Zeph, trailing foam and saliva. Its eyes burned savage and bestial.

Zeph tore his eyes away, knowing he could get lost in that terrible gaze. "Don't look at it!" Zeph cried to Tamra.

Fergus chuckled. "Guess it's just me and you, Zipperface."

Zeph stood dumbfounded, glancing at the loathsome being. Shadows scudded across the cavern from the rocking lantern like winged phantoms joining the *danse macabre*. If ever he needed the

Telling, it was now. A word, a prophecy to dispel this darkness. He'd toppled Blaise Duty with a few sentences. Perhaps God would reveal a string of words now so that he could fulfill his destiny.

But, as he expected, the Telling did not come.

And why should it? Zeph had forfeited his destiny.

"Look into the black mirror," the seraph gurgled, and motioned to the stone archway. "It is yours. You've opened the way. Come, see the reflection of your soul. Witness, your *darker self.*"

"Don't!" Tamra called from behind him. "Don't do it, Zeph!"

Zeph looked at Little Weaver's lifeless body and at the awful gateway.

"It's the wound of your making." The seraph hunched forward, wings wrapped about its frame like a black coat. Its breathing was labored. "The highway to your heart."

"Zeph!" Tamra's voice echoed in the mine. "Don't listen to it!"

"We are here to do your bidding." The dark angel bowed.

"Zeph-h-h!"

But Zeph knew the words were true. It *was* the wound of his making. All of this had happened because of him. Tamra would not be here, if not for him. Annie would not be locked inside Camp Poverty, if not for him. None of this would have happened if Zeph had not renounced his calling and ran like a coward. He should have listened to his mother. They were reaping the rotten fruit he'd sewn. How many souls had been harmed by his indecision? How much darkness had bled into the world through his regret and bitterness? It was the price of the gift. The land he'd been called to protect had been sundered by his own despair.

Which is why Zeph was drawn toward that dark portal.

He descended the steps, eyes fixed on the megalith and the swirling black mass inside it.

Tamra's pleas grew faint as he approached the Rift. The stench of the dark angel was nothing compared to the burning dark that now mesmerized him. The Fergus-thing lowered its wings as he approached, almost genuflecting before him. The ceiling was alive with wide, glowing eyes.

"Behold! You are the black cherub." The dark angel motioned to the abyss. "You are the bridge between worlds, the holy one. You are the one the world awaits. Your destiny—*it has found you.*"

Then it stepped aside, twitching and muttering.

Zeph stood before the black mirror.

It was a hole, not in the rock, but in the atmosphere. Much like the scar on his face, this gash should not have been here. A ripple in the atmosphere bleeding black, a dimensional vent, a turbine of darkness, and as he approached, it moved, a spasm that shifted, widened.

Zeph stopped. He stared, fixated upon the terror of its possibilities.

Otta's Rift. A wound in the epidermis of time. A gateway to worlds no living man should look upon. The genesis of a new order. Like the tree of the knowledge of good and evil, this too was loosed by human curiosity, its putrid fruit poisoning the world. Zeph felt he was witnessing both the beginning and the end of all things. A space, indistinct and rippling, that changed as he turned. A puncture in the fabric of creation. A doorway calling him to a world without pain, a world with only sorrow.

Behind him a shuffling of movement tugged at the periphery of his mind.

Tamra could not stop him. He wouldn't let her. Besides, he knew he could never love a woman. Freaks of nature were better suited for the circus, not normal relationships.

He stepped toward the dolmen.

Wraiths, gaunt and sallow, hovered inside it, pining for release. Ancient. Primal. Long before man they existed. They waited. Stewing on their own remorse. On their hatred for the Almighty. And Zeph knew, with a word, he could unleash them. He possessed that power.

That word was on the tip of his tongue.

He glanced overhead. The fetch huddled in their dark apertures, all eyes frozen upon him. Just like Shiloh.

Shards of light—dazzling—turned the chamber into a plume of brilliance.

The seraph squalled and flung a scaly arm over its face. It crumbled onto the floor, shielding its eyes from the vivid light.

Zeph stumbled back as if he'd been punched. His senses followed. He turned to see Little Weaver standing, removing his gloves. His flesh was torn. Bruised. Yet his hands—his hands glowed like the sun, radiant and blinding.

Zeph wanted to laugh. He wanted to shout at the splendor that burned in that defiled cavern. Nevertheless he remained frozen by the majesty of the unfolding.

"Sing!" Little Weaver shouted. "Sing, Brother Walker! Out of your brokenness! Sing!"

Little Weaver's hands were raised, leaving electric trails in the dark. Zeph had fallen to the ground, peeking from between his trembling fingers at the glory that was the angel hunter.

The dark angel now hunched forward, buckled in on itself, a recumbent mass.

"I am Little Weaver, heir of Big Weaver! Ha! Gatekeeper and Friend of the Land."

Zeph struggled upright, partially shielding his eyes, mesmerized at Little Weaver's triumph. As he did, the luminosity of the man's personage dimmed. The light in the mine paled. And he was Little Weaver again.

Zeph gaped at the Indian.

"Tell the tale, my friend. Tell the tale." Then Little Weaver laughed, a full, gracious laugh that bounded off the granite walls.

And with a mighty roar, Little Weaver lowered his shoulder like a middle linebacker and strode forward, driving the seraph back into the megalith. Their bodies hurtled into the fissure and disappeared.

"No-o-o!" Zeph staggered forward. "No!"

He fell to his knees, clawing the earth. As their screaming faded into the bowels of the Rift, a great rush of air sounded. Cries and moans and lamentations followed as the fetch were plucked off the walls, one by one, and sucked back into the dimensional rift.

Zeph watched, aghast, as the chamber was drained of the inhuman inhabitants. Except for the sputtering lantern and the dim shafts of the light, the cavern returned to darkness.

"Weaver!" Zeph hunched forward weeping. "Why? Why-y-y?"

He could have stayed there, bereft. Lost in his grief. But someone touched his shoulder.

"Zeph." It was Tamra.

He did not rise.

"Zeph. Look."

He brushed tears away and looked up.

A figure rose inside the Rift. Gauzy and pale, like smoke twining up a chimney. Zeph staggered to his feet. He approached the fissure and peered at the figure. As he did so, it reached out and pulled him through a cold sheet of blackness, into the dimensional doorway.

Chapter 63

First, it was an apparition, a specter that rose to the fore in the black crevice. As Zeph watched, its features crystalized.

As they did, time seemed to stand still.

For the figure was his. Identical in every way. Hair. Cheekbones. Eyebrows. It was all the same. Just like the doppelgänger at the morgue. Except for one feature.

The face staring back at Zeph Walker did not have a scar.

The image startled him. It evoked a longing he would have thought died long ago. Zeph stared at that perfect face, entranced by its fairness. How many times had he stood before the mirror, cursing his scarred visage, wishing he could be complete again?

He stared into that pristine image of himself. The infinite cold chilled him to the marrow. Was he floating? Perhaps he was dead, trapped in some infernal loop, never to be seen again. But whole nevertheless.

Zeph.

The word was distant, dreamy. He ignored it and stepped deeper into the Rift, the cool, cavernous air ebbing on his skin.

Zeph.

This was the culmination of his calling. It was his destiny to be whole. It had to be! By surrendering, he could become complete again. That's how it worked, wasn't it?

Zeph!

Someone was calling him, but...

Someone fumbled at his fingertips, and Zeph flinched. Tamra gently pulled him toward her, back through the haze, through the cold, back into the world. And stood beside him. Blood trailed her nose. She was holding his hand.

"Zeph, it's not you." Her eyes shone bright, almost as bright as Little Weaver's hands. Her words were unwavering. "It's not you!"

She was right. And there was something in her touch.

Something like... *symmetry.*

"I can't hear it." Zeph's voice quavered. "I can't hear the Telling.

290

He's left me, Tam! There's no words. There's nothing. He's left me, just like He shoulda a long time ago. I've lost everyone. I–I have nothing to say."

Zeph fell to his knees at the base of the altar. Beaten.

"Zeph." She knelt beside him with her arm around him. "Zeph, remember Daniel in the lions' den?"

Zeph nodded.

"God was there," Tamra said. "In the dark, He was there."

As far as Zeph knew, there were no lions in Otta's Rift. Which made her words all the more true.

"You don't need the Telling. You have something else. Something special. Just...*speak*."

Her words were like an adamantine spike, a revelation within his murky thoughts. He knew the wound that festered was his. The darker self that stood before him, that stood between his healing, was his own. He knew that *his* healing was the healing the Land awaited.

Zeph stared at that ghastly apparition inside the dolmen, that perfect, unscarred persona hovering before him.

He drew a deep breath. "I–I'm Zephaniah Walker. The guardian of this land." Zeph swallowed and glared at his perfect duplicate. "And you can g–go back to hell."

Time seemed to stop.

Then the face he stared at in the Rift changed. Its perfect, unscarred features melted together, became animalistic, morphing into that of a raven, then a serpent, then a wild feline.

The black cherub.

Zeph stumbled back, watching the transmutation.

There was no magic, even though Zeph Walker believed everyone was born with a certain magic. No angelic choirs or fire from heaven. Tamra gently pulled him away from the ancient dolmen.

Something groaned in the tunnel, a subterranean rumble.

Then, a single snap sounded.

A crack became visible on one of the columns. It fingered its way along the rock, scattering pebbles at its base.

"Zeph!" Tamra yanked him back, and they tumbled onto the floor together.

As they watched, the leg of the megalith cracked and collapsed on itself. The entire structure crumbled into a heap of thick stone. Dust filled the cavern.

Zeph and Tamra huddled together, choking on the airborne grit and peering at the smoking ruins. As the dust cleared, Zeph rose, mystified. He went to the pile, staring at the granite wall. It looked different.

The crevice was gone!

He ran his fingers across the smooth stone surface just to be sure. The fissure had disappeared. Had it ever even been there?

A shadow loomed on the ledge above them.

They both turned to see Chat Chavez staring down at them.

Zeph and Tamra looked at one another, and then Zeph's stomach dropped.

"I always hated this place," the cowboy growled.

Tamra joined Zeph, and, taking his hand, they watched the detective.

Chet pulled a stick of dynamite from a nearby ledge. "And now that I'm here, I hate it even more."

He held the dynamite to the lamp, its stout blue flame sparking on the wick. "Hurry up!"

Tamra and Zeph glanced at each other and then, without a word, hustled up the steps. As Zeph reached the top, he turned one more time to see the place where his friend Little Weaver had disappeared. The megalith lay in ruins, and behind it stood a smooth blank wall.

"Did ya not hear me?" Chat held the dynamite up, his features glowing in the lamp light.

"Yes, sir," Zeph said. "I sure did."

"All right, then. Git!"

They stumbled up the tunnel, past the graffiti and the mining debris, into the gloaming. The fresh air pelted Zeph, and he wondered if anything had ever smelled as good. Chat scrambled out with unusual agility for a man his size and hustled them away from the old mine.

The explosion rocked the canyon wall. Shale and mud tumbled down the granite face. They stood with detective Chat Chavez watching Otta's Rift collapse on itself.

As the dust cleared, Zeph turned and said to the detective, "I always knew you had a good heart."

Chat looked sideways at Zeph. "Wish I could say the same 'bout you."

Chapter 64

The ashen sky, which draped the day in its gloom, finally yielded to murky twilight. It mirrored Zeph's mood. Despite the elimination of the seraph and the closure of the Rift, Zeph's emotions remained gray. Little Weaver was gone. And Annie's fate remained grim.

As they descended the mule trail and hurried through the gate into the Marvale property, he mopped sweat from his eyes. Zeph had done his best to slow Tamra along the way. She had run the entire way from the Rift, falling several times and skinning herself badly, calling on God and making vows as she went. The pace she maintained worried him. More than once Zeph had been overcome with altitude sickness from exertion. Yet something other than adrenaline was driving Tamra Lane.

Down the trail, lights were visible in Camp Poverty. He could only imagine the scene that was unfolding. Chat had stopped on the road above them and was doubled over, fanning himself with his cowboy hat. His recollection of what went down at Camp Poverty had only fueled their fears. "I ain't seen nothin' like it," Chat said, before informing them that the entire Endurance police force was on the way.

Sprawling brush scraped at Zeph's clothing as he tried to keep up with Tamra. Now that she'd seen the lights, she was practically jogging down the trail.

Zeph's mind drifted back to Little Weaver. "Tell the story," Weaver had said before hurtling himself into the dimensional gateway. Would Zeph ever be able to accurately explain what he had seen, though? Or who the massive Indian really was?

Reaching Camp Poverty, Tamra stood on the trail, panting, staring into the stone amphitheater. The chill in the air turned her breath into spectral plumes. Zeph stumbled to her side, and they surveyed the scene before them.

A generator puttered near the far rock wall, feeding two floodlights on telescopic stands. The area was awash in their brilliance.

Several uniformed police stood scribbling on notepads while others knelt over the odd, tangled remains of bodies, many of which were very inhuman.

"Nams!" Tamra skidded down the gravel incline. Her eyes were fixed on Detective Lacroix and the body at his feet. "Nams!"

Several people turned at Tamra's cry, as did the white-haired detective.

Tamra hurried through the stone archway with Zeph right behind her. She pushed past Lacroix and fell before the charred body of her grandmother, sobbing.

A radio crackled, and several of the officers stopped what they were doing to watch Tamra hunched over the body, weeping.

A pungent, musky stench tainted the air. Zeph navigated through several moldering corpses, much like the one he'd encountered at the morgue. He approached the detective, staring at the remains. The woman's body appeared to have been blasted by intense heat. Annie's face sagged to one side, a hideous deformity. However, there was no mistaking the features were that of Annie Lane.

"Why?" Tamra knelt over the body, her chest heaving. "Why d– did you do that?"

"It was her destiny." Zeph uttered the words without thinking.

Yet as Zeph studied the corpse, his heart leapt. Annie's arms were just hollow skins.

Like those of a dark angel.

Lacroix cleared his throat. "I believe you are looking for her."

Tamra looked angrily at the detective. Her eyes glistened in the light.

Lacroix pointed toward the rock structure where Annie Lane sat wrapped in a blanket, her bloody leg resting on a log. She looked tired, beaten up, and very much alive.

"Nams!" Tamra scrambled to her feet, laughing and crying at the same time.

Seeing Tamra's wild approach, Annie waved her hands to fend off her granddaughter. She managed only to partly stifle the ensuing bear hug, wincing as Tamra embraced her neck.

From somewhere nearby Sultana emerged from the shadows carrying some gauze and ointment, and Jim, the electronics whiz from Meridian, was right behind her. Sultana stopped and smiled as Zeph approached.

"We knew you could do it," she said as she bent over Annie and began inspecting her wound.

"Yeah, well..." Zeph shrugged. "I didn't."

Sultana chuckled and shook her head.

Then Zeph looked at Annie. "So, what happened? How did you..."

Annie's gaze flitted about the encampment. "Weaver?" she asked, but as if she knew the answer.

Sultana rose and fixed her gaze on him.

Zeph glanced at Tamra and then said, "He didn't make it."

Annie sighed deeply. "I think he knew all along he wouldn't make it."

Zeph nodded ruefully. "I think he knew a *lot* more than he was saying."

An all-terrain vehicle arrived pulling a cart of miscellaneous items. Two men stepped off in hazmat gear, looking officially irritated.

"So, what happened?" Tamra said, brushing tears off her cheeks. "How did you get away?"

Lacroix approached, producing a notebook and pen from his coat pocket. "You can thank her." He motioned to the open stone doorway into Camp Poverty.

Zeph and Tamra simultaneously turned to see Janice Marshman emerging from the shadows, her face glowing with an eerie luminescence as she gazed into her digital device. She stopped and, seeing they were watching her, raised one eyebrow, then said, "I trust you will be taking Miss Lane to the hospital?"

"Uh, of course," Tamra said. She looked quizzically at Annie and then back at the director. "So, you knew all along?"

The director clicked off the electronic pad and closed its cover. "As I told your grandmother, I am well aware of the history surrounding this area and the uniqueness of the Marvale properties. I've had suspicions. However, it was the remnant that enlightened me to *other* possibilities."

Zeph straightened.

"Like I said," Annie winced as Sultana applied ointment to her bloody shin, "we were watching you."

Sultana looked up. "Earl's back down at the retirement place. He couldn't make the climb, as you can imagine. But according to the detective," she glanced at Lacroix, "Earl didn't miss out on much."

The director peered at the steaming corpses that littered the yard. "I can only imagine what state my facility is in."

Lacroix looked up from his tablet. "Apparently, a sizable number of individuals have simultaneously dropped dead, leaving your beautiful facility and its residents in quite the panic. But I can assure you, ma'am, we will have this situation under control as quickly as humanly possible."

"I should expect no less," the director said curtly. Then, turning to Zeph, she said, "I have long been aware of the tunnel complex that existed here. Fergus's behavior—and his frequent visits here—had piqued my suspicions. The remnant contacted me, connecting the history and the mythology and warning of a larger plot. Mind you, I am not one to embrace the mystical with abandon, and I was skeptical at first. But being an avid reader, my mind is sufficiently stretched to include the, shall we say, *weird*."

"An avid reader?" Zeph asked.

The director slipped a paperback novel from her sweater pocket. On its cover was an oval spaceship with three spidery legs.

She quickly returned the book, cleared her throat, and continued. "As I am commissioned to oversee Marvale's operations and the comfort of her residents, I must consider all angles, young man."

"Uh," Zeph cleared his throat. "Yes, ma'am."

"With this additional information, I realized something quite large may be occurring here, something possibly in the realm of...*weird*. I kept a close eye on Miss Lane. However, things only became more mysterious. Reports of people changing, outbursts, late-night excursions, missing bodies. It was the stuff of Hollywood. When the detectives arrived tonight, we found her apartment looted and learned of Fergus's death. I was prepared to make the journey here. It was fortuitous that we did."

"Indeed," Lacroix said. "Being yanked off the investigation by Roth seemed rather fishy to us. When we learned he'd flown the coop and was operating covertly, without his superior's license, we suspected someone did not want us seeking you out. Or snooping around your whereabouts. Luckily we did."

"So, what happened?" Tamra asked, staring at her grandmother. "When we left, those things were coming out of the tunnel. How did you, I mean, how did you not get...*eaten?*"

They all turned to Annie.

"It was like a dream." Annie stared into the growing dark, recalling her tale. "A nightmare. Full of monsters. They came at me, and you all were there. Zeph and Tamra. Miss Marshman. Ghastly dry things. Not all there. And then I saw..." She reached out for Tamra's hand as she spoke, and her granddaughter took it. "Myself. Something that looked like me. Its eyes glowed. And when I looked into them, it was awful. Everything I had ever lost, all of my grief and regrets, were in those eyes."

They listened, spellbound, to Annie's tale.

"All those dark things came around me, snickering and squealing. She hovered there—my other self—coaxing me in. Inviting me to surrender to the pain." Annie shivered, staring into the twilit sky. "And I prayed. I clung to that word, Zeph. The word you spoke. *You will be a remnant. You will stand in the gap.* And it was like a beacon, son. Like a beacon calling me home."

Finally Lacroix cleared his throat. "I would not have believed it had I not seen it with my own eyes. Whatever these things are, they scattered when we emerged from that god-awful tunnel. My partner managed to shoot several of them. Miss Lane fled out here, and they followed like some Pandora's box set free into the world. Only to drop dead on the spot. Shortly thereafter we heard an explosion in the hills. Whatever happened up there, it cut off their lifeline."

Lacroix cast a long, hard gaze at the courtyard and its commotion. Then he turned to Zeph. "Seems we are back where we started, young man."

Zeph looked at Tamra. "Not exactly, sir."

The director clapped her hands and ordered the remaining employees back to work. She turned to Annie. "The hospital?"

"Yes," Annie said, squeezing Tamra's hand. "We're leaving now."

The director nodded and then marched into the courtyard like a general surveying his wounded battlefield.

Lacroix straightened his blazer. "Quite a brave grandmother you have there, Ms. Lane."

"Pshh!" Tamra snorted. "Pretty reckless, if you ask me."

Chat ducked through the archway, glistening with sweat. Lacroix seemed relieved to see his partner.

"They're gonna cordon off this area," Lacroix announced. "So I suggest you all pack up and get this lady to the doctor. And don't go too far. We will definitely require statements and whatnot." He winked and then strode into the courtyard.

Annie was staring at Zeph. "I knew you could do it."

Zeph sighed. "I didn't really do anything, Annie. It was all of us."

"And the Telling?"

He looked at Tamra and smiled, but did not offer a response.

Chapter 65

The mud-splattered Crown Vic pulled up in front of his house. Zeph drove the final nail into the new sign and climbed down from the ladder. He laid the hammer near his toolbox and wiped sweat off his forehead. Then he met the detectives at the gate.

Lacroix walked around the car, surveying the new sign on Book Swap. "I thought you were givin' up on this place."

"I was."

"Change of heart?"

"You could say that." Zeph brushed sawdust off himself. "Besides, I need to get my books from somewhere. So why not here?"

Chat shut his door and leaned against the car with his arms folded, peering from under his cowboy hat at Mila's house. Several strands of crime scene tape still lay in the yard, and a path had been beaten along the side of the house where investigators had trod while exhuming her body.

Lacroix followed his partner's gaze. "I take it you will be moving?"

"Actually," Zeph said. "I'm thinking about buying the place and turning it into a cactus jelly factory."

Lacroix furrowed his brow. "Either you have a warped sense of humor or more money than you are letting on."

"Both," Zeph said. "So what's the official word?"

Chat looped his thumbs under his belt. "Cause of death was asphyxia. That's all they're sayin'."

"And except for finding her body buried in the backyard," Lacroix added, "there is no evidence of foul play."

"Uh, being buried in the backyard is quite a bit of evidence. So who's the suspect?"

Lacroix drew a long tired breath. "At the moment? Walther Roth."

"Roth?" Zeph exclaimed. "You know it wasn't him."

"I don't know what I know anymore, young man." There was affliction in Lacroix's voice. "Our only other option is to conclude that interdimensional doppelgängers were murdering their counterparts.

Which may work for a sci-fi sitcom, but'll hardly fly in a court of law."

"They weren't doppelgängers," Zeph said. "Not exactly, sir."

Lacroix brushed at the shoulders of his jacket. "Well, it's in the Army's hands now."

"The military has the case?"

"Moppin' up what they started," Chat groused.

"Whether Roth was human or not," Lacroix said, "whether he survived this event or was taken in it, he is our only link to the bizarre goings on. And an easy scapegoat. Whoever Walther Roth was, he sufficiently fooled the United States government, which, I admit, is not a difficult task. And whatever connection he once had with the military, they have not divulged. In fact, they have taken great care to obfuscate. Which leaves us to surmise that Robert Coyne and his son were the last vestige of Roth's pet project. But what that project entailed, we may never know."

The three stood pondering the enigmatic unfolding.

"This is the last remaining artifact from our adventure." Lacroix reached into his jacket pocket and removed the plastic bag with the wooden bullet. "I suppose you wouldn't want it as a keepsake?"

Zeph's eyes widened. "Very much so."

"Just don't say you got it from me."

"No, sir." Zeph took the bullet but didn't tell the detectives it was forged from the Sacred Tree.

Lacroix massaged the nape of his neck. "I would be remiss in not tellin' you this entire affair has expanded my conception of what kind of universe we inhabit."

"I share your conclusion, sir." Zeph glanced at Chat. "How 'bout your partner? Does he feel the same way?"

"I liked that big Indian," Chat said without emotion. "I only wish he hadn't died in that cave-in."

Zeph peered at them. "So that's what that was—a cave-in?"

Lacroix nodded. "That ol' mine was a death trap from the start. And whatever was goin' on in there deserves to be buried forever. Fact, maybe it was never meant to be opened." Lacroix steadied his gaze upon Zeph. "I am unsure as to what powers you possess, young man. But I cannot deny that you possess them. Things are fallin' to your advantage. Course, the authorities will manage appropriate consternation over why twenty-seven people throughout our city, randomly connected, all managed to drop dead at the same moment. They have already floated the possibility of chemical contamination and mutant viruses. Even radioactivity. It will, no doubt, lead to bureaucratic overkill—studies and surveys, all manner of punditry and conjecture. Before being buried. But there is no way that you, or your girlfriend's grandmother, can be indicted on some form of conspiracy, in case you were wonderin'. So whatever has gone on up there, and whatever type of phenomenon we were privileged to have witnessed, like everything else about this case, it will conveniently be swept under the rug."

"And that thing in the morgue?" Zeph asked. "The one that looked like me?"

"Probably quarantined along with some alien artifacts in a remote underground warehouse in Area 51. Like the rest of 'em—it is long gone."

Zeph let his eyes wander. He thought about Ginny and her mummified remains at Meridian. Maybe evidence of the dark angels had always been right under their noses.

"Is somethin' wrong?" Lacroix asked.

"Naw." Zeph shrugged. "It's nothing."

Jamie skittered from around Zeph's house and stormed the fence, yapping at the detectives. Zeph intercepted the dog and held the shivering animal in the crook of his arm as it growled at Lacroix.

The detective snarled at the dog, walked around the vehicle, and opened the door. "I'm sure they will have some questions for you. But I suggest you keep references to angels and extraterrestrials minimal. So whatever you do, do not leave the country. But please…do leave your house more often."

Zeph smiled at the ribbing. "I will." As Lacroix stepped inside the vehicle and prepared to leave, Zeph said, "Hey! Thanks for everything."

Chat touched the tip of his cowboy hat and slung his thick, tanned arm out the window. As Zeph watched them drive off, he noticed the marquee on the Vermont had changed. This morning the sign read: TODAY IS THE TOMORROW YOU WORRIED ABOUT YESTERDAY.

He wondered, among other things, who had changed the sign.

However, this day seemed a lot brighter than the one he'd worried about yesterday.

As he pondered the words, another car approached, a turquoise sedan that looked vaguely familiar. It slowed at the Vermont before proceeding, doing a U-turn in front of his house, and parking at the shoulder. Annie opened the passenger side door and swung her casted leg out.

"Nams," Tamra said, hurrying around the car. "Just stay there. I'll take care of it."

"What do you think I've got crutches for?" Annie shooed her granddaughter away.

Dieter came barreling out of the backseat, skidding in the dirt. "A library!" He pointed frantically at Book Swap. "Tam! Tam! Is that a library?"

Tamra glanced at the cottage. "I guess you *could* say that."

Her response sent the burly young man into a near jig.

Upon seeing Tamra, Jamie wriggled out of Zeph's arms, bolted to the gate, and nuzzled his way through. With a delighted little laugh Tamra picked the animal up and held it at arm's length as its tongue lapped the air.

"Where's the scooter?" he asked.

"At home. With my grandma disabled, we'll need something more practical. Anyway, I figured it was about time I dusted off Old Gloria."

"Gloria?"

"Old Glory for short."

"So, do you name all your vehicles?"

"Come to think of it, yes. Some appliances too." She nestled Jamie under her arm. "So, Nams wanted to get a book. She'll be immobile for a while and has lots of time on her hands."

"Not if I have anything to say about it." Annie got out of the car and steadied herself on the crutches. She clucked her tongue at Tamra's effort to assist.

"She's staying with me." Tamra glanced at her grandmother. "Like she should have been doing a long time ago."

"When I get better," Annie said, "I'll reevaluate."

"Oh, shush." Tamra's gaze drifted to Book Swap. "Hey, you painted a new sign."

"I figured it was time for a change. In fact, I'm getting serious about painting again. Just like Mila wanted." He motioned to the easel on his front porch and a watercolor he had started. "Weaver would want me to tell the story. And Mila would want me to paint. So I guess I'll have to find a way to do both."

"Well, if you're fixing things up, I'd like to help." Tamra motioned to Book Swap. "I noticed your front door needs to be rehung, and the plaster inside needs to be patched."

"Well..."

"My tool belt's in the trunk." Tamra set Jamie down. "I'm off today..."

"Your grandmother said you couldn't fix everything."

"She's right." Tamra smiled. "But I can fix some things."

Standing there gazing at Tamra Lane, Zeph was hard pressed to deny that.

Overall, it was an event that rivaled the Madness of Endurance and would propel the ninth gate of hell into official urban legend status. Twenty-seven people dropping dead without apparent cause and rumors about wispy humanoid carcasses appearing around town only fueled speculation. The government would come snooping around again, before quarantining parts of Marvale, permanently leveling Camp Poverty, and reconstructing a new fence and barrier at Otta's Rift. Admissions of their involvement were token and anything but incriminating. However, on this day, the world could not have seemed like a brighter place.

Little Weaver was right—the world was full of tales. And somehow, whether by fate or chance, Zeph Walker had found himself in one of them.

As Zeph drifted in thought, watching the constellation of freckles spreading under the full moons of Tamra's eyes, the world seemed to go mute. The clucking of the chickens and the distant morning traffic along 395 disappeared, replaced by a cosmic inhalation.

His breath grew short, and his skin bristled with expectancy.

It was the Telling.

"I have a word for you, Tam," he said. And without hesitation, Zeph spoke it.

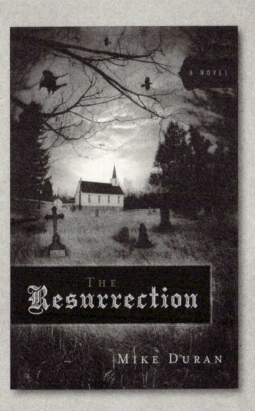

When Ruby Case raises a boy from the dead, she creates an uproar in the quiet coastal town of Stonetree. But this resurrection has awakened more than just a dead boy... the forces unleashed by Ruby threaten to destroy them all.